At Summer's End

At Summer's End

Courtney Ellis

BERKLEY
NEW YORK

BERKLEY
An imprint of Penguin Random House LLC
penguinrandomhouse.com

Library of Congress Cataloging-in-Publication Data

Names: Ellis, Courtney, 1992– author.
Title: At summer's end / Courtney Ellis.
Description: First edition. | New York: Berkley, 2021.
Identifiers: LCCN 2020050121 (print) | LCCN 2020050122 (ebook) |
ISBN 9780593201299 (trade paperback) | ISBN 9780593201305 (ebook)
Subjects: LCSH: World War, 1914–1918—Fiction. | GSAFD: Historical fiction. | Love stories.
Classification: LCC PS3605.L4646 A8 2021 (print) | LCC PS3605.L4646 (ebook) |
DDC 813/.6—dc23
LC record available at https://lccn.loc.gov/2020050121
LC ebook record available at https://lccn.loc.gov/2020050122

First Edition: August 2021

Printed in the United States of America
1st Printing

Title page art: floral background © smash338 / Shutterstock
Book design by Alison Cnockaert

For Pops, who always told the best stories

Art is restoration: the idea is to repair the damages that are inflicted in life, to make something that is fragmented—which is what fear and anxiety do to a person—into something whole.

At
Summer's
End

1

JUNE 1922

It didn't take much to excite the neighbors—only a little feature in the *Times* accompanying a photograph of my painting, the winner of an art contest put on by the Royal British Legion. Four years on, there were still plenty of funds needing to be raised for veterans of the Great War.

My painting had received first prize. I delighted in the opportunity to parade the crimson ribbon before my family, but the true victory was having my name in print. It was my name shortened, but no matter. Everyone who saw the feature would think Bertie Preston a man. Or so I hoped. For who would commission a painting from an unknown female artist?

Our neighbor Mrs. Lemm would, and after seeing the article, did. My very first.

On a Tuesday afternoon, I completed the portrait of her Yorkshire terrier, Duchess, and accepted annuity of four shillings, sixpence. The amount made no difference to me; I was only pleased to be paid for my work at last. It was only four shillings, sixpence, but it was four shillings, sixpence closer to a room in London and a life of my own.

Unmarried at twenty-eight, one might resolve to consider oneself a sad and lonely spinster. Only I wasn't sad, or lonely. I rather enjoyed an empty room with an easel in it.

After leaving Mrs. Lemm's house, I used my earnings to buy a bunch of peonies. It was while I was out that the earl's letter arrived.

Our maid Jane didn't come to the door, so I set down my easel, hung my cloche on the rack, and went through to the parlor, where I was accosted by the odor of wood glue. My father had lately taken the hobby of building model boats, which he then sailed on the local pond of an afternoon. Now he sat at a table once reserved for games of bridge, painting tiny strokes on his toy boat's hull. Painting! *My* father! Who, as a retired banker, was a man of numbers and not creativity. I never knew my parents to engage in the arts, which was why I'd been under their scorn since adolescence for lacking focus on anything apart from painting.

Mother came through from the kitchen, where she was surely bullying our cook about the state of dinner. Neither of them had noticed my arrival, so I announced, "Peonies!" and held the bunch in Mother's direction. "Won't they be lovely?"

Her mouth was permanently downturned, but the creases deepened at the sight of the flowers. "Oh, Bertie, you know your father's hay fever is the devil in June. Do put them outdoors."

Father peered over wire spectacles balanced on the end of his nose. "No, no bother to me, surely."

"I'll not have you bedridden over a few measly blooms. Please, Bertie?"

On cue, Father sneezed. I sent my eyes skyward and trudged back to the foyer, swung the door open, and tossed the flower bunch—which I'd spent a hard-earned penny on—to the front path. How remarkable the glue odor should have no effect whatsoever on Father's lungs.

Back in the parlor, Mother leaned over his shoulder, watching him tinker. "How does Mrs. Lemm do, Bertie?"

"Well," I answered. "Charming as always. I had a lovely time." I shrank to the window seat and pinched a piece of my newly chopped bob. A smudge of paint clung to my thumb, the rusty shade of a terrier's whiskers.

"So good of her to have you, wasn't it? She knows how much you enjoy doing your paintings." Here, Mother implied I wasn't an artist at all, but a hobbyist like my father. "Mrs. Flynn called by earlier; she'd seen the *Times* and wanted to have a look at the prize painting. You remember her boy John was killed on the Somme?—poor lamb burst into tears."

My painting, entitled *Something for the Pain*, had begun as a sketch I'd done whilst serving in the Voluntary Aid Detachment, stationed near the Western Front. It captured a nursing sister in her grey uniform and veil, lending her strength to a soldier patient outside a tented ward. They'd been chatting about lice—*Ever 'old a fag to one and 'eard them poppin', Sister?*—and hadn't known I was drawing them.

Drawing had been my way to cope with the horrors I saw in my wartime career. I tried to capture the lovely moments in between, the now blurred memories of friendship and warmth between nurse and soldier, between men and women stuck in the worst of what the world had seen. Perhaps I ought to have been documenting the worst of it—the pain and torn flesh and mud. But in the end, I couldn't decide which was more important to remember, so I chose what caught my eye. One day it was the look of utter exhaustion on the face of the walking wounded, another, the beaming smile of a freckled VAD serving weak tea and dog biscuits.

"I remember John," I said. "Living in London, was he not?"

Mother nodded solemnly. "Left behind a wife and baby girl, God rest him." She selected an envelope from her pile and handed it to Father. "One from Violet, dear."

Violet was one of my two elder sisters. Father took it eagerly, setting his paintbrush aside.

We were similar, Father and I. In retirement, he worked ardently on his boats to keep busy, as I had done with the Red Cross in war. When armistice came, I hardly wished to leave my post. In peacetime, I was redundant, merely a single woman with no purpose or use. When the men returned, all were quick to forget what worth their women had.

"For you, Bertie."

I looked up from my thoughts. Mother held out a letter, eyes elsewhere. I stood to collect the envelope, turning it over and over as I paced the airless room. All windows were to be shut in summer months. Hay fever, of course.

It was postmarked Braemore, Wiltshire. I didn't recognize the hand, though my heart quickened all the same. For the letter was addressed to Mr. Bertie Preston.

Mister.

I tore open the envelope and removed a single, crisp bit of stationery. At the top was an embossed golden crest, and the words EARL OF WAKEFORD, CASTLE BRAEMORE.

"Good Lord!" I blurted.

Mother sighed, lifted her weary face. "Honestly, dear, you know I dislike you speaking so harshly."

I ignored her, began to pace. There was absolutely no reason I should have had a letter from a nobleman. I'd never met a lord, much less an earl. Or maybe I'd nursed one? An officer, perhaps? No; I certainly would not have forgot that.

I took a deep breath and read.

Dear Mr. Preston,

I am seeking to commission an artist for several paintings of my Wiltshire estate, Castle Braemore. As an admirer of your work, I would be delighted if you would be my guest at Braemore for the summer months to gather the inspiration necessary for your process. If you should accept the undertaking, please enclose with your response a list of materials you shall require, which will be provided upon your arrival.

I eagerly await your reply.

Sincerely,
Wakeford

My cheeks set flame. The room spun. I was not a woman who swooned—I'd been elbow deep in blood during the war and hadn't batted an eyelash—but now I thought my knees might give out. I ran to the window and threw it open.

Mother scoffed. "Bertie, what on earth—?"

Father stood, scraping back his chair. "Fantastic news, everyone—Violet's expecting a third!"

I thrust my head out the window and took a gulp of summer evening air, the letter crumpled under my hand on the windowsill. Behind me, my parents embraced, delighted to be grandparents yet again. My sisters were really rather good at producing children, and with Heather widowed and me hopeless, Violet was their champion.

Old news. For I had a commission! A real one!

I plucked a petunia from the flower box and brought my head back indoors, shutting the window with force. When I turned, my parents had gone. I could hear Father chatting to the operator in the other room, telephoning Violet to congratulate her. The letter shook in my hands.

Someone—a bloody earl!—wanted me to paint for him. For *money*. This had been my goal when entering the contest. But how could I ever have expected such a commission? An earl might display my paintings where his titled friends could see. It wouldn't be long before more commissions came through and I had the income for a solo show, to submit a piece for entry in the Royal Academy Summer Exhibition, to rent a flat with a view of Hyde Park.

Now I certainly *was* going to faint. I sat down in a nearby chair to save myself the fall and put the petunia under my nose to breathe the warm sweetness.

I was finally on my way.

NOT WANTING TO follow up Violet's news too closely, I waited until dinner to give mine. As I settled in opposite Mother, I flapped the letter, beaming so hard my cheeks ached, waiting for someone to ask about it. Jane came forward with the tureen under her arm, offering me an odd glance as carrot and ginger soup was ladled into my bowl.

Father said to Mother, "We'll stop with Violet and Henry at the weekend. She'll be wanting you."

As ever, neither of them were paying me any attention at all. So I said, "I've had an exciting letter."

Eyes remained on soup. Mother sipped. "How nice. From whom?"

"Why, it came directly from the Earl of—" I had to read again; I'd forgot his name. "The Earl of Wakeford!"

Bless Jane, the only body to react, dropping the lid onto the tureen. Mother sent her a scowl before turning to me. "I do love you, but all this jesting can be so wearing."

"It isn't a jest!" I made to hand her the note, then changed my mind and gave it to Father. He set down his spoon and pushed his spectacles up his nose.

I watched his eyes dart back and forth as Mother waited impatiently, breathing more audibly than before, every exhale a sigh. Was there not more in life to be excited by than babies?

"'I am seeking to commission an artist for several paintings of my Wiltshire estate, Castle Braemore,'" Father read aloud. "A castle, Bertie?"

I could hardly sit still for how excited I was. "Indeed. And I to be the artist. I've already sent my reply, accepting."

Mother blinked rapidly and snatched the letter from Father's hand. She read it herself, mouthing the words, then tossed it down beside her soup. "His lordship writes to a *Mr.* Bertie Preston. It is all a mistake; you must write again immediately to set it right. A telegraph. Jane?"

"Naturally, it's a mistake," I said, shooting the maid a warning glance as she came forward. "A mistake I've been hoping someone might make. Nobody wishes to commission a painting from a woman, Mother, hence why I entered the contest as Bertie and not Alberta."

"And I suppose you mean to resemble a man as well?"

"Oh, for heaven's sake, it isn't *that* short." I self-consciously fluffed my bob. "Will you not be glad for me?"

Father played a tattoo on the table with his fingers. "You ought to have discussed this with us before responding."

I shrank in my chair. Father was my supporter. He had gifted me my first set of brushes. He'd given me permission to join the VAD in 1915, to accept a post abroad. Now I saw doubt in his eyes. He viewed my painting as my mother did—an *accomplishment* only. Something to show a young man to prove I was a woman of substance.

"This is a real opportunity," I said, "to prove myself, to make a name—"

"It isn't *your* name, Alberta!" Mother clapped her hand down on the table, rattling the china. "You cannot allow this man to carry on believing you're someone you are not."

"It was his mistake. He may turn me away if he likes, but I shan't forfeit the chance."

"At any rate, we cannot in good conscience allow you to stop at this strange man's home without a chaperone. Have you heard of this Wakeford, George?"

Father shook his head. "His lordship's note is rather brief . . ."

Mother gave an arrogant nod. "I've always been of the mind that a man of such few words has something to hide."

I sat up again to reach for the letter. "I'm more than sure he's an old, married chap."

"With unmarried sons, we may assume."

"Did I not stand over the beds of hundreds of men during the war, and return unscathed?"

Her face was unmoving. "I shall not allow it."

"I'm a grown woman; I don't require your permission."

"Yet you require our allowance." Mother was proud of her response, chin lifted. "Your father will not pay the train fare. Will you, George?"

Father shifted in his seat. His eyes drifted to the letter, now in my hands. I could tell he wished he'd held it longer, further dissected Wakeford's words to find a viable reason why I should be permitted to go. This time, however, he would not defend me. Whether it was my mother's glare, or some deeper belief that I was undeserving of the commission, I wasn't sure.

He lifted his spoon and said, "I'm sorry, Bertie."

The room hushed to scraping spoons and the sucking of soup. I stared at my plate, thinking of Violet and her swelling belly, sitting to dinner in Hertfordshire with her stodgy husband. Violet was the ideal daughter, everything I was meant to be but could not imagine emulating.

"With thanks to Mrs. Lemm, I've my own money now," I said, a calm threat. Surely, if they knew I was to go it alone, they would not withdraw their support.

It had worked on my father, at least. He set down his spoon again with a sigh, taking the moment to knead at his forehead. "Perhaps you will wait until I've written to the fellow . . ."

"How am I to be taken as a professional if my father writes ahead of me?"

Mother inserted, "You are *not* a professional."

"I may yet be!" I heard the pitch of my voice change and tried to steady myself. How could I explain to them that I felt my very life was at stake? "You know this is all I have ever worked towards. I've spent my years not looking for a husband, not building a family, but *painting.* I am nothing without it, and if I stay here, nothing I shall remain."

"If that's how you feel," said Mother, "then I have failed you."

My desperation boiled to the surface, reddening my vision. There was no use arguing, that was clear. "I shall take the train to Braemore soon as I have word from Lord Wakeford. I would prefer to go with my parents' blessing, but I see now it is too much to ask."

I pushed back to stand, making a show of dropping my napkin on the table and moving in my chair. In reality, I was stalling—waiting for one or both of them to see sense, to see that their youngest daughter was upset, and move to make amends.

But it was no good. Mother's eyes welled with tears, her face crumpled, and Father began to mumble words of reassurance as he set his hand over hers. My own resolve weakened as Mother took a shaking breath.

"If you leave this house against our word"—she blotted a tear with the back of her hand—"do not expect to have a place here when you return."

I drew in my lips to keep them from trembling. It no longer mattered how many years I'd spent dreaming of the day I would leave home—the notion, come so immediately and in anger, was terrifying. I was a girl again, watching timidly as the other children played, not as yet willing to abandon the comfort of Mother's hand in mine.

"Mummy, please don't say that—" At this, she turned her head as to avoid my eyes. "Surely you don't mean it?"

I looked to Father for help, but he had nothing to say. If he wouldn't defend me, then we were no longer allies.

It was difficult to speak through the lump in my throat, but I managed a curt "Very well."

As I left them, I tried to remember that their response did not diminish my success. I had done it. I had earned a commission on my skill alone. That still felt good—for the moment, good enough to distract from the idea that I was suddenly and permanently on my own.

But everything important and remarkable I had ever done, I'd done on my own.

2

My stop was a small village station distinguished only by a single sign that read BRAEMORE. With cases in hand, I smiled at the porter and trudged from the platform. Only a few passengers came off with me, striding determinedly up the road, one climbing onto a sprung cart to be drawn away by an anxious horse. I waited on edge, hoping I hadn't been forgotten. Walking to the house would be a challenge in heels and with two cases.

Then a motor came swiftly off the road, pulling into the station with such haste that it spat dust and gravel in its wake. The cream-colored Rolls-Royce tourer glistened in the sun, her top down, and her driver sat comfortably with one arm slung across the door. The car came to a halt and he stood, removing his straw boater to lean over the windscreen.

"I say, madam?" he shouted. "May I ask if you've seen the three fifteen call, please?"

For some reason, I looked behind me, but there was no one else to answer. "I've just come off it."

The man climbed out of the car. He wore a clean linen lounge suit and tinted spectacles, removing them as he drew near. Beneath, his cat-like eyes were young, dark, and undeniably handsome. This could not be Lord Wakeford's car. I expected he might be driven about by a uniformed chauffeur, in a limousine or landaulet.

"Was there anyone else?" the man asked.

"Yes, but they've gone."

He considered this for a moment, swinging his spectacles by the arms. "You wouldn't happen to be a Mr. Bertie Preston?"

I smiled. "Bertie Preston, yes. *Mister*, I fear not."

Sensitive brows tilted away from one another as his lips spread. At least he was entertained. "Well, well."

I set one of my cases down to offer my hand. He regarded it oddly for a moment, then shook. "Are you engaged by Lord Wakeford?" I asked.

"Good Lord, no. I'm his younger brother—the Honorable Roland Napier." This was said mockingly as he bowed, sweeping his hat behind his back. "Your servant, madam."

My laughter came breathless with nerves. Roland's polished accent made me clip my own words more sharply. "I beg your pardon, sir. I thought you too young to be the earl's brother."

"Conversely, I'm much too old to be his son."

"Oh—I suppose I assumed his lordship to be . . . getting on in years."

"I imagine Julian wasn't terribly detailed in his correspondence."

"Julian—?"

"My brother."

I felt my cheeks color. Just as well I'd given the rouge a miss that morning. "His lordship was quite short, in fact."

"That's Julian for you." Roland lifted one shoulder. "You mustn't take it personally; he's short with everyone. He gave *me* the impression you would be a man."

"It's the name," I said, taking up my case again. "Happens all the time."

I waited for him to tell me it was off. He was kind enough, perhaps, to send me directly home without humiliating me before his brother. I expected he might even pay for my return ticket.

Instead, he smiled. "*Miss* Preston; excellent. Shall I take those for you?"

My relief nearly felled me. Roland brought my cases to the car and, rather than fasten them on the rack, dropped my luggage into the back seat. Then he reached over the passenger door to open it and handed me in. "I hope you don't mind I've driven us. Fine day for motoring."

I settled happily into the tan leather seat. "Quite so, Mr. Napier."

"Call me Roland, won't you, Miss Preston?" He shut my door with a click. "If you agree we're to be friends."

He grinned wolfishly, and though the spectacles covered his eyes again, my stomach flurried under his sure gaze. I nearly told him to call me Bertie, but felt loath to put an end to the lovely way he pronounced *Mizz* Preston.

"Yes, of course. Friends."

"Smashing." Roland patted the top of the door, and went round to join me.

As he flipped switches and turned knobs, I indulged in a nourishing breath to calm my nerves. What was there to be concerned about? The chap didn't seem bothered with my gender. So why should the earl? I removed my hat to let some cool air blow across my brow.

The engine tumbled to life, surprisingly quiet. Roland tossed his boater at my feet, and ran a hand through his sable curls. "Right, then. Off we go."

And off we went, fast as the thing could move. This was like no other motor I'd ridden in before—built for sport rather than practicality. But after the initial jolt in my heart from the speed, I enjoyed the breeze blowing my hair, and the dusty, floral scent of country as we pulled onto a winding road.

"Where is it you're visiting us from, Miss Preston?" Roland asked.

"Surrey," I shouted over the rumble. "Though I hope to be in London soon."

"You must live in London, as an artist. Or Paris!" He revved the engine proudly. "I'm ashamed to admit, however, I've not seen your work."

"You wouldn't have." I pushed a blown piece of hair from my eye. "Which is why I was rather astounded to receive his lordship's invitation. I've yet to establish a name."

Roland tapped his thumbs on the steering wheel. "My brother knows everything—he *reads* everything, rather. Every last word on every last newspaper. Any chance he spotted you?"

"Actually, yes . . ." I silently vowed to donate a portion of my earnings to the Legion if all went well. "Is your brother a great lover of art?"

Up ahead, a herd of sheep wandered into the road. Roland slowed the motor to stall and watched a few pass before slinging his arm over the back of the seat.

"Julian was a bit of an amateur painter, when we were younger." Roland looked back to the sheep as one of them bleated at us.

I was suddenly aware of how close our legs were on the seat, how warm and solid his arm was behind my shoulders. Never mind Roland seemed to be much younger than me, I couldn't deny the healthy rush of a handsome man's attention.

"If his lordship is an artist himself, why hire one?" I asked.

Roland let his head fall to one side, fingers fidgeting behind me. "In honesty, I'm uncertain. Though I've no doubt you'll do a marvelous job, Miss Preston."

I wasn't sure whether the news made me more delighted or more terrified. Praise from another artist was always welcome. But it also meant his expectations would be high.

"What is he like, the earl?"

"He keeps to himself," Roland said. "I very much doubt you'll see him."

Before I could question him further, the sheep baaed once more, announcing he and his mates were quite finished clearing the road. Roland turned to face the wheel, and we went on, slowly at first, then back up to speed.

"Is there a Countess of Wakeford?" I asked.

Roland wet his lips, and paused for a bit longer than necessary to consider. "Our mother passed some years ago. You'll not have been to Braemore before?"

"No, never. I've never been to *any* lord's home before."

He laughed and turned us onto another, narrower road that dipped down a shallow hill. "I must admit, my sister and I, we've been awfully excited to host you. It's been some time since a guest room has been opened."

A twinge of excitement. I'd been uncertain as to where I would sit in the hierarchy of a grand house. Hired for a service, would I be considered of the belowstairs lot? Or somewhere in between servant and equal? Now it seemed I had risen directly to *guest.*

"Does his lordship not host house parties?" I asked.

"Heavens, no. There hasn't been a party at Braemore since before the war."

And perhaps that was why I was unfamiliar with this prominent family. By no means was I a religious reader of gossip columns, but I did enjoy a dash of fantasy now and again. If they were not throwing opulent parties, they mustn't have been worth writing about.

"Lord Wakeford is . . . reserved, then, is he?"

"I should say so."

"The way you speak of your brother—he does seem mysterious."

Roland chuckled. "Sure, if you like."

"But do you think that—" I paused, worrying over what I hoped to ask. "Begging your pardon, but do you expect he'll be cross that I'm *Miss*?"

We were climbing another hill, slightly higher than the last. At its peak, Roland touched the top of my hand so briefly I hardly felt it. "Keep your eyes forward. We're nearly there."

I reluctantly obeyed. The motor dived down the other side of the hill, creating a weightlessness in my belly. A limestone archway stood between low walls, reaching in either direction, well fitting of a castle, though I had yet to glimpse the castle itself. We were flanked on either side by hedgerows, hiding anything that might lie ahead. It was beautiful. I imagined mixing cadmium yellow and raw umber for just the right shade of golden brown, and making the gentle, even stroke of the arrow-straight road.

"Have we far to go?" I asked. Roland only smiled and nodded ahead.

The drive led us up from the side, and as the west facade of Castle Braemore came into view, I found myself tipping forward for a better look. I'd expected the castle to be grand, but my imagination had failed me. I couldn't have predicted how immense a single home could be—taking my entire field of vision—and tucked away so unassuming on a humble patch of country.

It was not a medieval castle with battlements and towers, but a baroque palace, stretched lazily across the immaculate emerald lawn. The center structure was crowned with an elegant dome and flanked by symmetrical wings, moody aged sandstone broken up by arched windows and carved pilasters, with urns and cherubs and a dozen chimneys adorning the roof.

To our right, a two-tiered fountain spewed a narrow surge high into the sky. At the center, a god draped in flowing fabric carried a marble globe upon his back—steady, but bent beneath the effort. Four angels lounged about him, holding high their ethereal trumpets as water rolled down bare chests and into the basins they guarded. Lilies floated in the wide charcoal pool, where the perfect mirror image of Castle Braemore was reflected back.

Further still was a steep hill, climbing up to a plateau. It was far off, but from where we approached, I could just see a platoon of statuary guarding a limestone folly with a dome to match the main house.

I was speechless. A real rarity for me.

My expression must've given me away, for Roland laughed and asked, "Do you reckon it will do?"

"I reckon the king mustn't be aware this is here. Otherwise he wouldn't be wasting his time at scrubby old Windsor."

Roland stopped the motor and hopped out, coming round to open my door. "So you won't have any trouble painting it, then?"

With all of my excitement over seeing Braemore, I'd yet to consider how so much detail would affect my work. I had a real challenge ahead of me. Though I wasn't going to admit as much to him.

I stepped down into the raked gravel. "No trouble at all. Though I must say, I'm a trifle disappointed there isn't a moat."

"Braemore isn't a real castle, I'm afraid." Roland removed his spectacles, eyes trailing up. "Only built near the site of one."

"Well, she's earned the title, I'd say."

Roland looked at me, and I noticed the sharp edge of his chin, shaved clean. "I like you, Miss Preston. Shall we go in?"

I replaced my hat. "I thought you'd never ask."

As we climbed the stairs, I relished the luxurious way my heels clicked on the sandstone, heightened by a warm breeze and the distant fizz of fountain mist. All I needed was a mink stole to look as fabulous as I felt.

A butler opened the front door, towering over both Roland and me with perfectly parted grey hair and the face of a basset hound. We stepped indoors, and as my eyes adjusted to the change of light, my jaw hinged open. The hall was tiled in black and white marble, lined with Roman columns and statuary and baroque portraits. Above was the dome—I craned my neck to see it better—which hosted a celestial scene suitable for Vatican City, vibrant pastels lit perfectly by a ring of arched windows. Beneath it, a gilded balcony with the promise of more wonder beyond.

"Huxley, this is *Mizz* Preston," Roland said. My attention was momentarily drawn away from the decor. "See her cases are brought upstairs."

"Certainly, sir." Huxley bowed at the neck as a footman took Roland's hat and then mine. "Shall I inform his lordship of Miss Preston's arrival, sir?"

"No need. Do you require refreshment, darling? Tea is served at half past five."

Roland was looking at me. I shook myself from a daze. "I can wait. Will you tell me who did the artwork in this room? It's exquisite."

Before he had the chance to answer, my eyes caught a flourish of muslin as a young woman looked down over the balcony. She darted and disappeared, the sound of her heels echoing from a marble stairwell flanking the hall, then materialized again. Her tubular dress was simple but for brightly colored embroidered wildflowers—daisies and poppies and marigolds—with a modern scalloped hem. Dark curls were bobbed slightly shorter than mine, with a light, wavy fringe. Presumably, this was his sister.

"Roland, you didn't say you were going yourself. Hello, there." She eyed me curiously, then looked again to her brother. The siblings resembled one another in brows and nose and full lips, though where Roland was sharp in jaw and chin, his sister was perfectly soft and cherubic. "Where's the artist? Did he miss his train?"

"The artist is here." Roland swept his hand in my direction. "May I introduce Miss Bertie Preston. Miss Preston, my sister, Lady Celia Napier."

The girl spoke before I could, a little choke in her voice. "*Miss!* I say!" She blinked rapidly at Roland. They seemed to converse silently then, Roland shaking his head ever so slightly.

I was nervous again. "This is a pleasure, my lady."

Celia's chin turned to me. "How sweet. She's incredibly sweet, Roland. Does Julian know?"

"That Miss Preston is incredibly sweet?"

"That Miss Preston is a *Miss*."

"I should think not."

All at once, Celia went dour. "That's probably best. What will Gwen say?"

"There's more of you?" I asked.

Roland nodded. "Gwen is the eldest. She doesn't live here anymore"—he looked pointedly at Celia—"so it need not concern her."

Some additional silent words passed between them, and I waited patiently for direction. It was Celia who spoke next. "I suppose you should show Miss Preston the Music Room."

"Oh, I'm not that sort of artist, my lady." Still, how lush! A room entirely for music.

"That's where we have your things." Roland offered his elbow and I took it, trying desperately to absorb all the portraits as we left the hall. There was simply too much to look at. "Cece—?"

She was just behind us, a slow click of heel and swish of skirt. "Yes?"

"Miss Preston will prefer the Princess Bedroom to the Duke Bedroom, do you not agree? It's far more suitable for a young woman, surely."

"Indeed. I shall have it opened."

She tried to whirl, but Roland made a humming sound of protest. "Not just yet. Come along to the Music Room with our guest."

Celia plodded after us again as we passed the stairs and turned into a long arcaded passageway. My feet would have stopped dead if it were not for Roland pulling my elbow. The Gothic vaulted ceilings were lit at the end by a window of stained glass. Everywhere was a finer piece of art—landscapes, brass sculptures, porcelain urns, and Grecian statues on pink marble pedestals. By the time we reached an end, my neck ached from the strain.

It was becoming clear to me that Wakeford and his family were collectors, which in turn made me wonder why the devil he'd hired *me* when he could so obviously afford someone with a dash more prestige. Or any prestige, for that matter.

We must have passed six doors before we arrived at the one Roland was after.

"This will be perfect for your studio," he said, turning the knob. "It has the best light, and is just off of the Long Gallery."

I started. "There's a *gallery*?"

"Where else did you imagine your work would be displayed?" Roland pushed the door open, and I followed him inside.

I had to squint at the sunlight pouring in through four high windows. Being the corner room, this had twice as many windows as the other rooms facing this direction; I'd have no trouble ventilating the space. Light reflected off yellow damask walls and the canvas tarpaulins laid down to protect the floors. I was certain there had once been furnishings and instruments, but everything had gone besides a single wooden chair, a long table, and my supplies.

There were three easels, and stretched canvases—dozens!—leaning against walls and stacked up in the corner. A pile of parcels sat just inside the door. I leaned over to peek in.

"Paints, pigments, and things in the boxes," Roland said. "We thought you might like to organize them yourself, so we asked the maids not to unpack. If there's anything else you might need, you may give a list to Huxley and he'll send for it."

I could hardly hear him over the sound of my own beating heart. After years of painting in my childhood bedroom, I would have settled for any separate place to do my work. This was more than I dared dream of.

"But won't you need this room for music?" I asked.

"Julian insisted this should be your studio," Roland said. "It's been closed for some time; nobody comes in here anymore."

"And why should they?" This was Celia, finally, glancing about the room as if it was terribly drab. "*His lordship* has taken the piano upstairs."

My stomach fisted at the thought of Lord Wakeford, for I had him to thank for all this. As I looked at Roland and Celia, I wondered why he'd sent them in his place. It should have been enough that his lordship admired my painting, and would pay me to do more. But the larger part of me was aching to lay eyes on him, to ask him why the painting had convinced him of my merit.

"Is Lord Wakeford at home this afternoon?" I asked. "I should like to thank him in person."

The question cleared the air from the room. Celia moved to the window, allowing her brother to take up the duty of answering.

Roland drew a breath and locked his hands behind his back. "You may send up a note, if you like, but I'm sure your gratitude is implied by your agreeing to come."

"I suppose it can wait until dinner." I smiled, but Roland's face fell yet further. "Will Lord Wakeford not be dining with us?"

"Celia and I are happy to host you during your stay," he said, "but his lordship has invited you here for this." He gestured to the room. "By all means, you should enjoy your time here, Miss Preston, but I'm afraid you will not see Lord Wakeford."

It seemed I was good enough for the Princess Bedroom and Braemore's gallery, though too common to shake the hand of the Earl of Wakeford. It was silly of me to expect otherwise.

"Will you at least thank him for me?" I asked.

"I'm sure I shall be glad to, if by chance I should see him."

How curious that Roland might only see his brother in their own home by *chance*. He was reserved, unmarried, hosted no parties, and received no callers. What, then, did he spend his time with, besides newspapers and an appreciation for amateur art?

"Now"—Roland clapped his hands together to end my musing—"should you like to see your room, or shall we leave you to get settled in here first of all?"

I could tell he was hoping I'd agree to the latter, and so I did, ensuring them I'd be all right for a time whilst my new room was prepared. Once they were gone and the door was shut behind me, an enormous smile spread over my face, and I laughed for my impossible luck.

My own studio. In a castle! All my Christmases had come at once.

By then I had clean forgot my mother's threat.

I'D LOST TRACK of time when Huxley knocked on the door to take me to my room. We went back through the passageway and up the side stairs. He pointed out the bathroom as we passed it, and my door was near the end of the east wing, where guests were stashed away apart from the family.

The Princess Bedroom was aptly named, with feminine, regal drapes, bed curtains, and quilts of pale blush. Sage wallpaper was striped with more pink between white cornices, and a gilded mirror hung over a marble mantelpiece. The enormous bed and divan looked rather welcoming, my feet aching from the journey.

"Mr. Napier expected you might like your tea brought up," Huxley said. "Dinner is served at eight o'clock in the East Dining Room. A maid has been assigned to attend you; do ring if there's anything you might need, miss."

I turned, my head taking its time to follow the rest of my body. It had been an awfully long day. "Thank you, Huxley. You've been very thorough."

"Unless there's anything else, miss?"

"Not a thing. Don't let me keep you."

The butler left without another word. It seemed the Napiers did not have a rapport with their servants as we did with Jane and our cook back home. That would take getting used to.

That and everything else.

After finding my belongings unpacked and folded away, I decided the washstand was no match for the dirt of the road, and set off for a bath. On my way, I gathered the east and west wings were separated by a third, shorter corridor, where rooms faced the garden on one side, and the front of the house on the opposite.

There, a voice came from around the corner. Something made me slow and tiptoe to peek through a fern. Huxley brought a silver tray to a set of double doors, set it on a neighboring table, and knocked. Another muffled voice from within, then the door opened. Huxley took up the tray again with perfect grace and went inside.

Before the door closed, I glimpsed the outline of a man facing away, broad shoulders and a head of dark, softly curling hair, much too long to be Roland's. He began to turn as Huxley greeted him, but before I could see his face, the door shut again.

I smiled. Here was his lordship.

I prickled to go to the door, to make myself known to him. One question, perhaps, would ease my regard: Why have you chosen *me*? But I couldn't risk going against Roland's instruction. It was enough, in the moment, just to know Lord Wakeford was more than myth.

I stayed hidden until Huxley emerged with his tray. The last thing I needed was for him to report me to Roland as a spy. When he was gone, I moved out from behind the plant to continue my quest for a bath, and heard a crash.

The jolt of it made me still. I went around the corner to see if Huxley had had an accident, but he had vanished. Closer to Lord Wakeford's door, I could hear the clinking of broken china, and frustrated male muttering on the other side.

It was like a past version of myself, living dormant since the war, had suddenly come alive. Had he spilled hot tea down his front? Could he have cut his hands on broken glass? On instinct, I took the few paces that brought me to his lordship's door, and lifted my fist.

No—I couldn't. Perhaps he'd already rung for Huxley, who would return any moment. And anyway, Roland had made it clear I was unwelcome. I dropped my arm. Oh, but what if his lordship was hurt? The least I could do was check to see if he needed help. Some situations were dire enough to push propriety to one side. What was the worst that could happen? Roland was lovely as could be; why should his brother be any different?

I could still hear Lord Wakeford on the other side of the door, growling and shuffling about on creaking wooden floors. One knock would do. Just in case.

I rapped three times.

Nothing.

I knocked again, thinking perhaps he hadn't heard. Then a voice, deep and cautious: "Is that Huxley?"

My hands flapped at my sides as I considered what to say. "It's Miss Preston, my lord. The artist you've commissioned? I was passing and heard a crash."

The floorboards creaked again and I held my breath, expecting the door to open. But it remained closed as his muted voice came again: "Preston?"

"*Miss* Bertie Preston, yes, my lord. Are you all right?"

Another long pause. The light under the door broke up as he shuffled behind it. Wakeford was just on the other side, close enough to touch if there were not three inches of solid wood between us.

"If you should need anything," he said, "you may speak to Roland."

I shook my head as though he could see. My curiosity had got the better of me. "There's nothing I need; I thought you might be hurt. Otherwise, I'll be on my way . . ."

I looked about me and shivered unexpectedly. Quiet lay more thickly in such an expansive house, where endless dark corners held ghostly potential for hidden eyes and ears . . .

I heard the key in the lock and turned. The door slowly moved away.

Wakeford didn't open enough for me to see inside—only his shoulder and half his face were visible. Here were the same feathered brows and round lips as his siblings', face soft as his sister's under a trimmed beard, umber eye stern as it bore down on me through round wire spectacles. I wasn't sure if I was more shocked by the idea he'd opened the door, or how striking he was to look at. He was certainly not the portly, grey man I'd imagined, but so young—perhaps early thirties—and beautiful.

My eye caught on a curl which hooked over his earlobe, and I stared at it thoroughly before realizing I hadn't spoken yet. "How do you do?" I said dumbly.

Wakeford swallowed hard, collar unbuttoned to reveal his tightening throat. "I do apologize, Miss Preston, but I am not receiving anyone now." Without the door between us, I noticed the hint of a speech impediment, the Ps not quite punching.

"I see." I noted his hand resting on the doorjamb, bleeding from a clean slice across his thumb. "You are cut, my lord?"

His eyes rounded in something I might have seen as fear, if he'd had anything to be afraid of. He dropped the hand out of sight. "It's nothing."

"Shall I send someone to clean it for you?"

He shook his head. "It was good of you to come, but I'm quite all right. Now I'm afraid I shall have to say good day."

The door shut. The bolt slid back into place.

I stepped away, enthralled by the great mystery of this man, the glint of his eye like wet oils, still perfectly formed in my memory.

On such a grand estate, there were endless things that might have inspired me, and dozens more within the castle walls that I had yet to discover. But in that moment, remembering all the glorious pigments and pristine canvases awaiting me downstairs, the only subject I wished to paint was the alluring man behind the door.

Homecoming

APRIL 1919

"See that?" Gwen nodded beyond the window. "They haven't burned the place down."

She longed for Julian to smile, even a bit. For a long while, Gwen told herself it was his scars that prevented him, but she knew better. Her brother had no physical trouble speaking, eating, or laughing—though he didn't do much of any of them anymore.

Now he coughed—she was concerned about that cough—and nodded. The stone facade of Castle Braemore dominated their view. It was home, even for her, though she had one of her own now. There existed no other place in the world that made her feel so warm as this.

Julian, however, saw it with fear. When the driver opened his door, he hesitated on the running board, the next step too far a leap.

"I'm just behind you," Gwen said.

Her words must have provided some comfort, for he put his boot out and bowed his head to climb down. Gwen hurried around the motor and took his elbow. "Shall we go in?"

Julian's response was to begin walking, straight backed, like a soldier. Sometimes it was hard to see her little brother in the body that had returned from war. This new man was thinner and harder, and lacked the color and innocence of youth. It was difficult to believe he'd been smiling on the day he told her he'd applied for his commission.

Roland was waiting inside with Huxley and the maids, come to welcome his lordship home. One of Braemore's footmen had been killed in the war, the second had lost his leg, and the third was still waiting to be demobbed. Julian kept his chin low. Gwen ought to have told Roland to greet them alone. It was too much at once.

A maid offered a proud "Welcome home, your lordship!" as Julian passed. He couldn't smile at her. The girl didn't seem put off, at least, which was a blessing.

But where was Celia?

Roland came forward, putting out his hand to Julian. "Long time, eh? Remember me?"

Julian shook with him firmly. Gwen had warned Roland he wasn't talking much. A treatment of electrical shocks had cured his mutism, but only just.

"Where's your sister?" Gwen asked Roland.

He lowered his voice. "I tried."

But Julian had heard. Gwen could tell because he began to cough into his fist.

She rubbed his arm tenderly. "Come. You'll want to get settled in."

The door to Julian's apartments had been left open. Curtains drawn. Everything spotless. Gwen was sure it was a welcome sight to a man who'd spent the better part of the year in a hospital and convalescent home. Yet there was no visible change in emotion as he sat on the settee and pulled his cigarette case from his chest pocket.

Gwen sat beside Julian in a huff. "How does everything look? Roland has been such a dear—he's had the entire estate in hand, and will look after things until you're quite ready to return. Your post is on the desk. The piano's here just as you've asked, and I've had it tuned . . ."

Julian blew smoke and stood, sitting again in an armchair to Gwen's left.

She slumped. It wasn't the first time she'd forgot his deaf ear. "A thousand apologies, dear. I said I've had the piano tuned—"

"Celia hasn't come round."

Gwen laid a hand over the rush in her chest. She hadn't heard his voice all morning, not on the steamer, or the train, or the motor. Topic aside, it was a relief to hear it now.

"Celia is sixteen," she said. "Sixteen-year-olds are impossible, always feeling hard done by. I'll have a word with her."

"She's right to be cross."

"How is she right?"

He looked away. Gwen hadn't expected an answer, still frustrated when one was not forthcoming. "You're after a sentence, is that it?" she said. "I am happy to oblige. Though in my opinion, you've suffered your penance."

To which Julian replied, "Her birthday is Tuesday week."

Gwen reached over for his hand, but he evaded to tap the ash from his cigarette. "The dust *will* settle. Now you're home, everything shall be as it was."

He knuckled at his eye, then dropped his hand to his leg with a clap. "I'm tired."

Gwen stood, brushing down her skirt. "I should just think you are. Why don't you go and lie down for an hour; I'll come and wake you for dinner. Shall I send a maid? Wouldn't you like a hot bath?"

"I don't want maids in here."

"One must come eventually."

Julian darkened, his eyes alarmingly cold. "No one is to enter this room."

Gwen took a deep breath. Julian had been kept at the hospital long after his physical hurts had healed. The doctor said it was neurasthenia muddling his mind, requiring special treatments. *An invisible wound*, said the nurse. But looking at him now, Gwen thought she could see it clearly, festering just beneath the surface of his pallid skin.

"Fine," she said. "Rest, now, my boy. It is all behind you."

THE MIRRORS HAD gone. Gwen's doing.

Their absence was more obvious than Julian expected. Though he'd become accustomed to washing his hands, cleaning his teeth, dressing, and combing his hair without ever seeing his reflection. They hadn't mirrors at the hospital either. They had special blue benches in front to warn passersby that the patients sitting upon them were disturbing to look at.

Julian got out of his uniform; he didn't want to wear it anymore. He didn't want to look at it again for as long as he lived. Removing the jacket and dropping the trousers felt like shedding a hard, battered skin. Underneath he was smaller than he used to be. Frail, even. Not a soldier. Not a lord either. A wisp of what his father had hoped for him to become. Julian rarely thought of his father anymore, but as he crawled over the vast bed, lay under the suffocating quilt, he wondered if his father could see him now, and what, if anything, he thought of his heir.

Julian tried to ignore the rapid pounding of his heart, wondering if Celia had not greeted him because she was still angry, or because she was frightened to see what had become of him. He hoped it was the latter. For he'd rather she be disgusted by his scars, something that was not his doing, than by his actions.

It was impossible to be still when his heart was bursting. The blanket was an anvil, the mattress too malleable, sinking him like mud. Men were buried alive in churned-up mire. They shouted and gasped until they died, their feet sticking up towards the sky. Feast for the rats, fat on the fallen.

Julian threw the blanket and stood. He paced, his mind slipping in and out of the present, back to an overcast morning on the front line—*Fix bayonets!*—then forward to that afternoon—*Where is Celia?*—then back further—*Mind the wire, mind the wire*—further again—*You lout! You brute!*

He clutched his head, willing it to stop. Back—*Stand to arms!* Again—*I wish you didn't have to go.*

It became impossible to breathe. Julian's hands shook at his sides as he stalked the bedroom like a caged animal. He swallowed hard. Ten seconds, that was all. Count and breathe.

The room was too close, too dark. He trembled before the window, throwing open the curtains, sun stinging his eyes. If he could just open it—let in the birdsong—the other noise might fade to the tenaciously cheerful call of a skylark.

When Julian turned, the walls were closing in.

Rats skittered across his feet, lice bit at his stomach, and the stench of rotting horses filled his senses.

It started as merely a groan. Closed mouth. Frustration. But it wasn't enough, never was. His mouth fell open and the ugly came out, rumbling his chest, burning his throat. Fire from the belly of a dragon. It was primal, whatever this was. Monstrous. It made him forget he was a man and fear he'd never be one again.

Then the need to defend, to destroy, unused muscles pulsing. Julian pushed the lamp from the bedside table. He hardly heard the crash, but was satisfied. He swept his hand over the top of the dresser, sending the clock and other meaningless, fragile things to the floor. It made him cross to see how easily they shattered. What the hell was the point?

He heaved another cry, leaning against the bedpost to steady himself.

Julian hadn't heard the door open, but Gwen was suddenly there. He blinked hard, over and over. They appeared now and again where they weren't meant to be. They wore white soaked in blood. Called his name where he could not answer.

He shouted again, wishing he could formulate the words to tell her to please go.

"It's all right, darling." Gwen raised her hands, the tamer to his lion. "There, now. You're all right."

As she neared, Julian crossed his arms to keep them from hurting her, digging his nails into his torso. There were lines of age around her eyes. They had deepened since she'd visited him in hospital. In his dreams, Gwen was always sixteen. This was real. She was real.

"Come away," she bade.

The next sound he made was quieter. Strength had left his throat, his lungs sore. Gwen's hands were warm and dry as they closed around his wrists, leading him from the bedpost. He melted to her side, sank into her motherly softness like bathwater, and then they were both sitting on the floor with their backs against the bedstead.

Julian cried because he was frightened and because his sister had seen what he'd become, and because he wished, more than anything else, he had breathed his last in the slime of No Man's Land. He wiped at the tears, alarmed by how odd it was to find them on only one side of his face.

"You could do with a brandy," Gwen said. "I'll be but a moment." She left and returned with a tumbler, wrapping Julian's hand around it. "Take that down, go on."

He did. It stung. Then it didn't.

With Gwen's hand running up and down Julian's back, it was easier to breathe. The room was his again, old and familiar. He'd been allowed to sleep in the earl's apartments since just after his father passed. Julian had been only twelve, not yet old enough to leave the nursery, but Gwen had already left and Roland was so small, soon to be sharing with baby Celia. This room felt more like home to him than the other parts of the house. It still smelled of his father in the deep corners, between the pages of his books, under the cushions.

"Are you all right?" Gwen asked, pulling him from his thoughts. "Physically?"

Julian nodded. His body felt like a stone. He could sleep for weeks. But otherwise he was well as could be. Gwen's face was flush, but calm. He had a distant, fond memory of that face leaning over him while he woke in his cradle. An imagined memory, surely, come of Gwen telling him how she always used to pet his hair and pinch his teardrop toes.

"You scared the life from me, you know," she said, holding her heart. "I cannot lose you, Julian. Not you, too, not after—"

Now Gwen cried, too. Julian wished he could speak to comfort her. Instead, he took her hand and held it as tightly as he could manage.

Shifting to face him, she wiped her cheeks. "I thought perhaps I'd fetch the children and we'd stop for a few days . . . if you'll have us?"

Julian nodded. He didn't have to think. He wouldn't have come this far without Gwen, and he wasn't ready to be without her. He'd never been.

She smiled at his answer and held him close.

3

I made a point of being the first down to breakfast. I couldn't have the Napiers thinking me lazy, nor that I'd forgotten my true purpose for being their guest. I nearly had the night before, when I had joined Roland and Celia for dinner. They had fidgeted opposite me at an enormous table laid for three; clearly it had been a while since their last formal dinner. I had decided not to mention my meeting with Wakeford, the formality of polished silver and liveried footmen begging simple and polite conversation. I managed to mostly listen as Roland told me about the house and their family—Gwen had two little ones and had lost her husband in the war.

Wakeford himself had been mentioned but once before Celia, who'd been quiet, quickly stole the conversation to ask me which medium I preferred. Oils, I'd told her, and pencil drawings, as plate after plate was brought from the kitchen. The amount of wine was truly staggering, and had caused me to do just that—all the way upstairs to flop onto my bed.

The hangover only lasted as long as it took me to wash and dress, for breakfast cured me in an instant, plate piled with poached eggs, bacon, smoked herring, and roasted tomatoes from the sideboard buffet. A small voice in the back of my head warned, *Slow down, Bertie, or you'll not fit your girdle for long!* I told her to pipe down, and had another slice of toast. The war had taught me not to take fresh butter for granted.

Celia and Roland came down at precisely the same time, leading me to wonder if they'd been having a chat about me beforehand. Perhaps I'd spoken too freely at dinner? Mother was always saying I was too bold. I could only hope I didn't offend.

Celia went directly to the tea urn, hardly meeting my eyes. Roland, however, plucked his plate from the table and smiled. "Good morning! I trust you slept well?"

I dabbed my lip with my napkin, nodding. "Rather. Better than I have in years. My old mattress isn't at all forgiving." That didn't take long.

"You mentioned you were thinking of moving to London," he said from the sideboard. "What is it that keeps you on a lousy mattress?"

"I'm afraid my parents don't agree that an unmarried woman is capable of living independently." I sugared my tea and lifted the saucer. "And since I don't yet make my own money . . ."

Celia faltered slightly at the last bit. Drat; I oughtn't to have spoken of money. I sipped my tea and hoped the comment would pass quickly.

In the interval, Roland assumed the head, kingly with his straight-shouldered posture. Huxley came forward with a silver salver to deliver the post, bowing his head to speak softly to Roland: "His lordship has taken his breakfast, sir."

Roland thanked him and returned his attention to me so instantly that the last few seconds might've been a trick of the eye. "You hope, then, to make a living selling paintings?"

"Hope, yes," I said. "I often think it's all I've got."

"Nonsense! Have a look around." Roland lifted both arms, indicating the walls. We ate in what the Napiers affectionately called the "small dining room," though it hardly earned the name. Hand-painted wallpaper depicted a scene of great palms and curly clouds, under which soldiers trudged with determination towards the sea, lapping up against the fireplace. "There are hundreds of great houses in England," Roland went on, "all with dozens of rooms and thousands of walls, sheltering wealthy men who wish nothing more than to pay for someone else to make them beautiful."

He was right. Everywhere I looked here—from the furniture to the arrangements to the ceiling—there was art. And soon, my canvases would be amongst them.

"And, you've caught the attention of one already," said Roland, plucking up his fork. "My brother has an eye for such things. I daresay you've more than hope, Miss Preston."

I pushed my food around dreamily, relishing in Roland's encouragement. Had anyone been so confident that I'd succeed? I began to imagine the hundreds of houses with their dozens of rooms. What I wouldn't have given to speak to Lord Wakeford just a moment longer, to ask what had moved him to give me such an opportunity.

Celia stirred her tea erratically so the sound of silver on china arrested the room's attention. "I think it's topping that you wish to live on your own, Miss Preston. How courageous and *modern*. I should really like to do the same. I cannot bear this house."

Roland chuckled. "You wouldn't survive a day on your own, sister mine."

"I believe I would," she said, raising her chin. "I've been on my own a sight more often than any of you."

Rather than have another go, Roland simply smiled at her and shook his head. "Well, considering your contempt for Braemore, I suppose I shall be the one to show Miss Preston about this afternoon. If she's agreeable."

I chewed hastily and swallowed. "Quite, though I had been hoping his lordship might give me an idea of what he'd like me to paint."

"I meant what I said yesterday. He won't see you."

But hadn't he opened the door for me the previous evening? Surely if he indulged me once, he might do it again. "He saw me yesterday, in fact," I said.

A fork fell against china, and Celia's eyes came up, wide with shock.

I looked from her to Roland. Golly, it hadn't taken long for me to do myself in.

"Forgive me for moving against you," I said. "Last evening, I was passing his door and I heard a crash. I thought he might be hurt . . ."

Roland's brows knitted. "He opened the door?"

"Yes . . . sort of."

Both of them looked confused. Either that, or I'd certainly overstepped, and would soon be out on my ear. "You didn't see him?" Roland said. "You didn't go inside?"

"I didn't—" I paused, seeing their distress. I had gone too far already. One more stumble would risk everything I'd sacrificed to be here. "I was concerned about the crash, that's all. I promise it won't happen again."

Celia wrinkled her chin and sent a scorn to Roland. He ignored it, his face softening in a way I couldn't have expected. "Julian was injured in the war—badly hurt by a blast. He keeps himself hidden away, has done for years now."

I winced. I'd seen such cases on active service. Shells exploded upwards from the ground, taking with them entire pieces of a man. Some had to learn to walk again; others wrenched in agony as we fed them egg flip through rubber tubes. I had only seen a glimpse of Lord Wakeford—there was an abundance of things that might have still been ailing him.

All along I'd been picturing the earl as a much older man, too old to have fought. But he was just like the rest of them, wasn't he? His eccentricities no longer required explanation. No man had returned from war the same as they were when they'd gone.

"You don't ever see him?" I asked carefully.

Roland shook his head. "He takes tea with Gwen once a week, but he won't see anyone else. Which is why we're astonished to hear he spoke to you."

All of a sudden, I felt responsible for Celia's distress. "I'm sorry; I didn't know."

"Never mind—no harm done." Roland turned to put his hand over his sister's, but she pulled free and stood to cross her arms. "Cece, please—"

"You must see it, Roland, surely?" Her tone was sharp. "The first chance he gets, and again—"

"Hush!" Roland's ears flushed, eyes daggers. "Not here."

Celia scoffed, arms falling to her sides. "If you'll excuse me." She marched from the room, and I stared curiously at her uneaten breakfast, wondering what had lit the flame.

"You must forgive her," Roland said. "She was but a child when it happened. Doesn't quite understand."

"Of course." I forced a tasteless bite of egg and chewed, thinking he was wrong. There *had* been harm done, perhaps not to Lord Wakeford, but certainly to his sister, and all because I'd failed to keep my nose from where it didn't belong. And I was so concerned with being taken as a professional! What true artist would dare to meddle in their employer's business? I was meant to be an observer only, like the butler who stood silently at the sideboard.

Roland's chair creaked under him. I expected he would quit the room, leave me to finish my breakfast alone. Probably, it would be for the best.

Instead he leaned forward, voice low: "Given he opened the door once, I wouldn't discourage you from knocking again."

I was so surprised I merely stared at him like a doe who'd caught the scent of danger. "I couldn't . . . I would hate for him to feel I was imposing."

"What if I told you my brother would never have the heart to turn you out?"

"I would say that unlike me, you've nothing at stake."

Roland broke into a smile. "Too right. Though I do wonder . . ."

I looked at the tiny tea leaves remaining in the bottom of my cup, as if to read them for answers. Naturally, I wanted to knock again. Apart from my curiosity, I truly did wish to speak with Lord Wakeford about my work. I was starving for affirmation, for someone to look me in the eye and tell me I had any worth as an artist.

"You expect he'll see me?" I asked.

Roland shrugged and returned his attention to his breakfast. "We all feign to understand Julian, but clearly he's more complicated than we imagined."

AFTER BEING SWEPT off of my feet by the romance of Castle Braemore and its inhabitants, I had to regain my footing. I certainly did not wish to disturb the family any further than I had already done, but would need their trust if I hoped to bring pathos to my paintings. If I could prove my integrity, both as an artist and a woman, perhaps I might gain entry to his lordship's apartments and speak with him properly. And to do that, I decided to offer him a sample.

I told Roland I preferred to wander the house alone for inspiration. He gave his blessing, and said nothing would be off-limits to me, besides of course the earl's dwellings. So I fetched my new sketchbook and pencil to begin my wander.

I strolled with no real direction, opening doors as I went. There seemed to be an endless number of reception rooms, some clearly decorated for entertaining women, others smelling of centuries' worth of smoking tobacco. Another was adorned with gilded wallpaper of Japanese cranes flying in endless circles, and furnished with antiques from the Far East. Further into the house I found the library, fuggy and dark with heavy curtains blocking the windows, and a lonely study. Even the passageways were meticulously furnished, serving some purpose to display either a collection of minerals or a stretch of aging tomes.

Through double doors beneath the balcony in the Great Hall, I found the saloon. This must've been where the Napiers had once held their balls. Simple, gilded furnishings dared not distract from the rococo ceiling—robin's-egg blue with intricate moldings of griffins, garlands, and fleurs-de-lis. Two enormous teardrop chandeliers hung low, magnificent crystals catching sunlight to send it blinking across damask walls. Floor-to-ceiling windows glimpsed vistas of the Italian garden and rugged hills beyond, with three sets of French doors leading out to the terrace.

It was a shame to see such an ornate room all but forgotten.

On the terrace, I belted my cardigan. The previous day's weather had been teasing—now the sun bobbed in and out from behind clouds, and the breeze carried a damp chill. Two substantial stone urns stood at either side of the stairs, housing scarlet geraniums, their sweet perfume enticing me down into the gardens.

Holding my hat, I turned to look at the house as I stepped away. It was breathtaking, entirely different to look at up close. Perhaps I'd have to do a larger, more detailed picture, and another with a vantage point farther away to include the landscape. I squinted in the grey light, gazing over the rolling green ahead. In the distance, a lake shimmered low on the parkland. That might do for a bit of movement.

My heels drilled into the plush lawn. I'd need to ask for boots next time if I had any hope for my shoes to survive the summer. Still, it was impossible not to enjoy the walk, feeling so delightfully far from home. Everything here was so immaculate, not a single hedge with a wayward sprig, nor weed disturbing a flower bed. Yet I could see no evidence of a being who might be caring for it all. If I didn't know better, I would have assumed its perfection organic.

In fact, the property was so vast and seemingly empty, I was relieved to stumble upon a family of deer. They would bring much-needed life to my drawing. I had always been keen to paint scenes with people in them, capturing moments that were otherwise lost to memory. But looking back at Braemore, it didn't seem the place would ever budge. How could one forget how it looked just now? Surely it would look just the same in a hundred years.

The notion gave me a newfound sense of purpose.

The bank of the lake was overgrown, an old dock sun-faded and missing boards. I walked the perimeter until I came to the other end, and by then I was warm enough to remove my cardigan. I laid it in the grass to sit on, smiling at my accomplishment.

Yes, this was just where I needed to be.

I began to sketch the lake in the foreground, skirted by trees. Then the parkland in the middle distance, neatly trimmed and dotted with deer. Beyond, hedges stretched over the gardens nearer Braemore itself. I drew rough lines where I wanted the house—to the right of the trees to create a satisfying balance—then the clouds in the background behind the dome, lined in silver light from the hidden sun.

My hand took over. I lost myself in the lines, in the sounds of rippling water and swans honking. As I drew, I thought of Wakeford. How might he see Castle Braemore? He loved it, of course, or else he'd never have written to me. I imagined the estate through his eyes. First, the small boy who was brought up playing on these grounds, knowing they'd someday be his. Then the man who'd gone to war with no notion of whether he'd return. Thoughts of Braemore, plush and warm, must've been a respite when remembered from a cold trench. Finally, I imagined how he must see it now, his family's unchanging home after so many years of uncertainty.

I saw it with pride.

A change in lighting brought me back to the surface. The sun had moved, casting shadows across the parkland where I didn't want them. I paused to wipe a bead of sweat from my brow, studying what I had. It was terribly rough, but it was all there, the plan for what was possible.

Returning to the house, I took the stairs in leaps before I could lose my nerve. All was quiet outside the earl's apartments. It was just before luncheon—I would need to make haste or risk crossing paths with Huxley. Carefully, I tore the drawing from my notebook, using my now dull pencil to sign the corner of the piece. After a moment of hesitation, I turned over the page and made a short note.

My lord,

I hope you can forgive my disturbing you yesterday. Your home has been the most extraordinary subject.

Yours,
Miss Bertie Preston

Then I bent and slipped the drawing under the door.

4

Over the next few days, I repeated the gesture, drawing Castle Braemore from different points of view, homing in on small details, learning its lines and curves as I would a living model's face. Before luncheon, I signed the best of the bunch and slipped it under Lord Wakeford's door. Owing to Roland's and Celia's tendencies to be absorbed into the house between meals, I spent much of the time in solitude, exploring and shopping for things to sketch. Celia had continued to keep her distance, showing late for breakfast, missing luncheon, and leaving dinner early. It bothered me that I didn't know what I'd done to offend her, but hoped with time as the summer passed, she'd come round. Perhaps she was only shy, like Wakeford.

On the third day, I returned to my original place on the far end of the lake, pleased to see I was already showing improvement. Before going to Wakeford's apartments, I changed my dress and rouged my cheeks. Part of me wanted to look presentable for luncheon. The other part of me wanted to look pretty in the hope that the earl might finally open his door.

People generally said, *But you're so pretty, Alberta.* Never stunning, never beautiful—nor ugly, mind. *Why haven't you settled down?* As though my looks were the only reason a man might find me worthy of marriage, or that I wanted marriage at all. Objectively, I can say that I'd a pair of underwhelming blue eyes, apple cheeks, an inquisitive nose, all aligned properly, apart from the brows, one of which could never keep up with the other.

The truth was, I had been with young men, finding they had use outside of love and marriage. Those were two things I couldn't imagine for myself. In twenty-eight years, I hadn't met anyone remarkable enough to show interest in me outside of hurried intimacy. But no matter—I'd been working to create a life of my own, and thus far it was moving forward well enough. There was no place in that life for a man.

It was easier to approach Wakeford's door, now much of the intrigue had evaporated. I pushed my drawing underneath, lingering as I always did for a few seconds. Accepting another defeat, I huffed and turned to go downstairs.

I had made it only a few steps before I heard the door open behind me.

Holding my breath, I paused for fear that Wakeford would be spooked to find me lingering in the corridor. The moment stretched, and then, timid yet clear, he spoke: "Thank you, Miss Preston," and the door was shut again.

There were moments when I had imagined my drawings crumpled, for the dustbin or the fire, or simply buried in a drawer. But Wakeford's careful words proved he possessed a tenderness, a sincerity behind his appreciation of my work. The notion gave me a new urgency, and I returned to Wakeford's door. I was too close now to be cautious.

Before I could rethink things, I lifted my fist and knocked.

The response came quickly: "Huxley?"

"I'm afraid it's Miss Preston, my lord," I said. "I was hoping we could—might I have a moment of your time?"

There was a lot of creaking, and I imagined him pacing back and forth. Was it really such a difficult decision? To open or not to open . . .

Then the key turned and the door swung away.

Again, I was offered only half a glimpse of the man's face. It looked just as nice as it had the day before, in a swirl of cigarette smoke. The thumb he'd cut with the broken china was bandaged, and in the same hand he still held my drawing.

"Miss Preston," he said. "I should have told you that you needn't come to me for approval. I'll be happy with whatever it is you choose to paint, and shall pay you fairly."

"I understand." I offered him a smile. "As I'm already here, however, I'd be obliged if you would offer your thoughts." I pointed to the drawing in his hand.

I might have been on fire for how Wakeford hesitated. Without meeting my gaze, he lifted the paper as if seeing it for the first time and stepped out of view.

I fluffed my bob, heart fluttering with nerves. "It's only a rough idea. I wasn't sure if you'd want the back of the house as opposed to the front. I believe—I feel that having your thoughts and memories of Braemore will only add to the work, and . . ." I couldn't force myself to stop rambling, filling the quiet. "Roland told me you were invalided out of the war, and you ought to know that I was a VAD—it's why I was so worried you were hurt the other day—and I've treated all manner of wounds. Whatever you've got can hardly be worse than what I've seen before."

Part of me expected the door might be closed again. There was comfort in the silence, for it meant Wakeford was considering my words, considering the picture.

He spoke again from his hiding place. "Where was your detachment stationed?"

"I began at an auxiliary hospital near home," I said, "then applied for foreign service and spent the duration at a stationary camp hospital outside Le Tréport."

I waited again, poised to answer any further questions he posed. But the knob jiggled and the door was pulled open.

My vision flooded with sunlight. I squinted to see Wakeford walking away from me, in grey trousers, and shirtsleeves rolled to his elbows.

He put a hand through his hair, stopping to scratch the base of his neck where the length of it ended.

"My lord?"

"You may come in if you like."

I stepped over the threshold, closing the door behind me with a rush of doing something forbidden. Strange man; no chaperone.

As I gazed around, I was careful not to look directly at him, not wishing to call attention to his wounds. There was plenty else to see. This was a sitting room, walls painted moss, brocade curtains drawn back from two large windows with gold tassels. Between them, a mahogany writing desk and chair. A baby grand piano dominated one corner, clearly taking up a space it was not intended for—a settee and armchair had been pushed too close to one another to make up for it. There was a round breakfast table and a well-used wingback facing a fireplace. Scattered trinkets from abroad looked to be simply left, rather than placed particularly.

None of Braemore's rooms intrigued me so completely as this one. For this one was truly lived in—cushions displaced, carpet unswept, open newspapers and abandoned teacups and full ashtrays. It smelled distinctly of a wealthy man, leather and tobacco.

"Is this where you sleep, my lord?" I asked. Perhaps too bold.

But he answered, "There is a bedchamber through there," and pointed to a door beside the fireplace.

My eyes lit on a painting hung over the mantelpiece. It had not been the original fixture—I could tell from the square of more vibrant paint behind it. Golly, was it spectacular—a landscape of a small corner of countryside, perfect in the moment the artist had captured it. A cool palette created an impossibly warm feeling; I could practically smell the lavender. I lifted my hand to mimic the motion of the quick, wispy brushstrokes that inspired my own work.

"Beautiful," I said. "It isn't—?"

I turned. Lord Wakeford stood unmoving. He dragged his cigarette from the exposed right corner of his mouth, and exhaled a plume of smoke. "Monet."

I wanted to reply, but words escaped me.

To say half his face had been damaged was entirely accurate. A prosthetic mask covered the left side from brow to chin, maneuvering around his nose, with gold wire spectacles holding it in place. It must have been made of metal, as it was calling card thin—painted with hard enamel perfectly matching the tone of his flesh, no inhuman shine. The false brow was real hair, and the eye—lighter creases of open lid and all!—had been painted in the same burnt umber as his own. Cheeks were rosy, pinkish-grey lips were full and eternally closed. There were no whiskers on the mask, however, a rather odd asymmetry.

He noticed me staring and looked away. "I apologize if it unsettles you."

"No, no—it's . . ." *Striking*, I might've said. Exquisite, even. Though I could understand how one without an artist's eye might find it eerie, like a doll staring listlessly from the window of a bric-a-brac shop.

I thought it best to move on. "I'm a great admirer of Monet. How splendid it must be to see this every day."

Wakeford nodded, stifled his cigarette at the desk. "I had it brought here from the gallery after the war."

That was why this room was overcrowded. It was filled with things from all over the house, things he'd otherwise go downstairs to appreciate—stacks of books, a telescope, a drinks tray fit for a party, and of course the piano, so conspicuous in the corner.

"I can't say I blame you." I took a courageous step closer, clasping my hands behind my back. "Roland said you're an artist yourself."

"Not any longer." He faltered when he realized how close I'd got. Nearer now, I could see the bluish hue on the jaw of the mask, mimicking cleanly shaven skin.

"What do you think of the angle?" I asked, returning to the drawing. "Might I try something nearer, or farther away, to capture the folly? It is a rather charming folly."

"No—don't paint the folly," he said with a sudden gravity that gave me pause. "This is my favorite place on the estate. Well done."

I was suddenly shy, thanking him as he put the sketch in my hand. "A piece of glass, was it?"

He looked down at his bandaged thumb on the drawing. "Er, a teacup. Clumsy moment . . ."

"Happens to us all." I smiled and he stepped away to light another cigarette. With space between us, I relaxed. "I hope you don't mind my asking, my lord, but I'd very much like to know what led you to choose me as your artist."

Wakeford exhaled smoke and shuffled through a slew of papers on his desk. I noticed his left ear, though not covered by prosthetic, was badly scarred, some shape lost from the cartilage. Just enough of the helix remained to support the arm of his spectacles.

He drew a newspaper from the pile, already folded to a familiar article. I smiled down at the photo of *Something for the Pain* with a rush of pride.

"You must forgive me for mistaking your gender," said Wakeford. "I assumed you were a soldier."

I handed the paper back to him. "You don't mind, then? That I'm a woman?"

"Why should I mind?"

I could hardly give him an answer, much less think of one. Instead, a challenge: "I suppose you might pay a female artist less for the same amount of work."

He bristled as his sister had at the mention of money, but remained poised. "I planned to ask you to name a price, Miss Preston, if this suits you."

I could have cheered. Instead, a curt, professional nod. I was improving already. "That suits me fine." We both looked back at the newspaper while the awkwardness faded. "Was it the soldier that drew you to the piece, my lord?"

"I was drawn to their bodies," he answered. "The way they're positioned. The posture is . . . natural. It isn't a portrait, but an instance. The way you place your strokes—no hard edges, no detail. Even their faces—"

"I didn't have time to sketch them fully. We were only on tea break."

Wakeford allowed the hint of a smirk. I wasn't sure if it was his injury or a simple quirk, but the corner of his mouth turned down rather than up. The imperfection made my heart flutter.

"I think it's remarkable."

His words were a drink of too-hot tea, warming every inch of my body as it descended. Nobody had ever said such a thing of my work. "Thank you, my lord."

"Have you sold it?"

"I don't mean to. I'm quite fond."

Wakeford's grin wavered. Disappointment? He scratched his beard and set the newspaper on the desk. "Where did you study?"

"My bedroom, mainly." Now it was Wakeford's turn to blush. "By that I mean I'm self-taught. I wanted to study at the Slade, but my parents wouldn't pay tuition, so Louise Jopling was my only teacher; my copy of her book is in shreds. I've developed much of my own style from her, and Laura Knight, Dorothea Sharp, Sir John Lavery. Monet, of course . . ."

He tapped his ash. "I see."

I tensed. Here was my greatest fear—that I merely mimicked and was nothing truly special. "You find my work derivative?"

Wakeford shook his head. "It's very special."

A compelling silence grew between us, neither sure what to say next. Then something illuminated Wakeford's eye, and he moved his attention to his watch.

"You'll want to be making tracks for luncheon, I suppose," he said.

I opened my mouth to stall. If I left now, there was no guaranteeing I would be allowed in again, and every moment spent with the earl was of value. "We've a few minutes still," I said, spotting the carriage clock on his desk. "Unless Huxley is bringing yours . . ."

Wakeford considered me again, assessing the potential dangers of hosting this strange woman in his sanctum. If only I'd still had a starched apron and a Red Cross to prove myself his ally. He seemed so unsure that I nearly gave in, not wishing to cause him any more distress. But then he squared his shoulders and spoke under his breath: "A few minutes."

I looked past him at the seating area, hoping to plant the idea in his head. Sure enough, he cleared his throat and indicated the settee. "Do sit, then, Miss Preston. Please."

I made it obvious I was pleased to, taking strides and brushing down the back of my skirt as I sat. Surely this was more than he'd offered anybody in some time, and I did not take the notion lightly. If I could manage a friendship, as it were, perhaps he'd even be willing to recommend me to his friends with their dozens of rooms.

Wakeford didn't sit straightaway, hovering on shifting feet. There was hardly anything left of his cigarette, but he kept it smoldering between two fingers. He looked so awfully lost.

"Is something the matter, my lord?" I asked.

"I wonder whether you wouldn't mind terribly sitting at the other end."

"Oh—" I shifted myself until I was flush with the opposite arm.

Finally, he lowered himself to a seat, tossing his spent cigarette in a tray. "I'm deaf in my left ear; I wouldn't have heard much if I sat on your right."

Another result of his injury, I imagined. "No bother. It's quite nice to meet someone who prefers to hear what I have to say."

In lieu of response, he leaned back to cross one leg over the other. I admired his profile, the way the tip of his nose dipped slightly over lips that lay outward past the hairs of his mustache. Handsome as his siblings.

I had to keep him talking. Clearly he was only too glad to sit in silence. "Did you study art yourself, my lord?"

"No, no," he said. "I read law at Oxford."

"That sounds miserable."

"Rather."

Our shared laughter blew off any remaining chill, and I pivoted myself towards him. "I've always thought it would be terribly exciting to be at Somerville. Though I would have no hope of passing the entrance exam without a proper tutor. I fear I'm really not so clever as I think I am."

His lordship did not reply promptly. Was this not the sort of thing to speak to an earl about? And what were the acceptable topics? Real estate, perhaps? Or weather? I faced forward again. "Forgive me—"

Wakeford ignored, or else didn't hear, the beginnings of my apology. "Perhaps your intelligence lies elsewhere," he cut in. "Not in maths or Latin, but in compassion and empathy. Both necessary to capture people as well as you have done in your painting, and not something that can be taught, as such."

It was the most I'd heard him speak at one time, and the music in his words, the compliment—I could hardly believe. There was so much soul in his gaze that I would have fallen over had I not been sitting. "You saw all that in my painting?"

"Amongst other things." His eye shifted over my shoulder, then back. "I've yet to ask if my brother and sister have made you welcome . . ."

"Oh, yes, they're lovely. Roland especially."

Then Wakeford really did surrender a smile—his timid, flopped-over version—so full he had to touch his mask when the movement caused it to shift. "Roland especially?"

"Don't feel left out; the two of you look quite alike. Though I think you more closely resemble Lady Celia."

Something in my reply made his face relax to somber rest. Not so different to how Celia had reacted at breakfast.

"Roland is far too young for me, of course," I went on. "But I'm an artist, and have a keen eye for pretty things to paint."

"You will paint Roland, then?" Wakeford asked.

"If he should agree to it. But I'd rather paint you."

Wakeford turned his face to the windows. At once, I knew I had overstepped. There was a reason why I had been asked here to paint his lordship's estate, and not his portrait. Why would a wounded man who hid himself away like to be reminded of his appearance?

"Of course you must have had your portrait done already," I tried.

With patience, Wakeford drew a breath and turned back to me. Immediately, I could sense something had changed in him. There was a palpable shift in the atmosphere, and I knew for certain I was in the wrong.

"Why did you knock on my door, Miss Preston?" he asked. "Was it truly to ask my opinion of your drawings, or did Roland tell you there's something to see?"

In a panic, I let my words fly without thinking. "He told me of your injuries, yes—"

Wakeford's mouth bent into a cold, wry smile.

"But they aren't why I've come. I didn't know the severity—"

"And now you would make a study of me?"

"No!"

He stood, putting space between us. "Then why not say the truth, if you're so bold? Why did you insist to see me?"

"I will tell you if you would only let me speak!" I rose, feeling stronger now we were eye to eye. My heart was pounding in my ears. I knew how easily a shell-shocked man could be driven to rage, so tried to keep my tone soft. "I knocked because I wished to know the man who saw me—out of all the artists in England—the man who spotted my work and saw potential. You might have changed my life, asking me here. I want to shake your bloody hand!"

Wakeford's expression softened. The blunt contrast of his emoting face against the stagnant serenity of the mask was astounding. Oddly, it had matched the mask better when he was stern. Now it seemed the feelings in his eye and brow were impossible to replicate.

His chin dropped to his chest, and he opened both hands to study them. As he fussed with the bandage on his thumb, I stifled the urge to tell him to stop. In another moment, whatever had lit within him was defused, and the tension cleared from the room.

Wakeford held out his hand and I shook it eagerly, feeling the gesture solidified our contract.

"I apologize that I've misjudged you," Wakeford said. His hand slipped from mine, landing in his pocket. "But, I think it's time you rejoined the others."

Disappointed as I was, I did not argue. I would need to do more than a handshake if I wanted to mend the fragile trust I had built between us, and he needed time. That was all right. I happened to have plenty of it.

An Afternoon Bathe

JULY 1907

It was the kind of hot which made one's clothing stick to one's body, even as one sits perfectly still. Julian had had enough of it, of sitting still in the study, of pretending to focus on the task at hand—shares. The broker had come to discuss his shares, something a schoolboy of sixteen couldn't comprehend and didn't wish to. But the task had come to him, for his mother never wished to dabble in estate business, and believed strongly it was Julian's duty, as the Earl of Wakeford, to handle such matters.

In any case, it was dull, and Julian was eager to be outdoors.

But he sat still until the broker said what he'd come to say, and they agreed to pull shares from one place and put them in another. The broker was happy with this, so Julian was, too. He shook the man's hand firmly, showed him to the door, and set out for the lake.

Miss Quinn had the children in the garden, sitting on a rug, Roland with his tin soldiers and Celia with a porcelain doll made to her likeness. They all looked up when he approached, the governess to say, "Good afternoon, my lord," Celia to say, "Julian! Julian!" and Roland to beg permission to come along to wherever his brother was headed.

Julian mussed the boy's curls and crouched to pluck up one of the soldiers. "You can't abandon your men in battle," he said, setting the toy in Roland's hand. "Stay here with Miss Quinn, and I'll return later on to play with you."

"Julian! Hullo, Julian!" said Celia impatiently, never allowing Roland to have more attention than she got. She propped herself on nubby knees and made the doll hop in his direction. "Did you see my baby? She's called Grace."

"Such a pretty name you've chosen," said Julian. "Well done, pal."

"Are you returning to school tomorrow?"

Roland groaned the way boys do when they think their little sisters have said something stupid. "It's summer, Cece. Of course he isn't."

"I didn't know!" Celia hugged her doll.

Julian couldn't help but smile as Roland rolled his eyes and sat again amongst his soldiers. The sun reddened his nose and cheeks, an appropriate color for a fuming boy. What reason did he have to be grumpy so often? Julian wondered.

He stood and wiped a bead of sweat from his brow with the back of his hand. Longing eyes turned to the lake, then back to his siblings. "Behave for Miss Quinn. I'll look in on you after luncheon."

Someone would have to. Their mother was not interested in children.

As Julian trudged from the garden, he thought of Mama, sitting inside fanning herself, drinking lemonade, and pretending she was the only person in the world. Sometimes he thought she was glad to be widowed, glad to have done her duty in producing an heir and spare, glad to have nothing at all left to do but simply be.

The sun reflected sharply off the lake's surface, making Julian squint as he reached the bank. This was what he missed most when at Eton— the freedom to escape here, to sink beneath the cool water where he could remain unseen; no sound, no questions. It was less than a minute before he'd undressed to his drawers and padded to the end of the dock, the wood burning the bottoms of his feet. He didn't mind. He didn't mind the heat of the sun beating on the back of his neck, not now that his respite was so close at hand. Water lapped gently against the dock, playing a hypnotic rhythm. Julian took a deep breath, filling his lungs with thick, musky air that smelled of baking mud and pollen. In this place, time meant nothing. For the lake had been here before Castle Braemore, before the first Earl of Wakeford, and if Julian stood looking this direction, over the water and not behind him where there was evidence of a peopled world, he could pretend he was not himself. That he was nobody and nothing.

In the midst of that lovely thought, he dived.

The water was warm at the surface, but cooled as he swam deeper. Trout brushed his bare knees, not bothered by his interruption. He might've been one of them for all the time he spent in the lake, swimming back and forth until his lungs burned. As he emerged, he took a great gulp of air and floated on his back, eyes closed against the sun. He forgot the heat, forgot the broker, forgot his mother and her fan, and Gwen gone on her outing with the man who'd been courting her. Heaven help him when she was married and away—Roland and Celia would be left with nobody to care for them.

Julian dropped again beneath the surface, blowing the air from his lungs and sinking, sinking, until his bottom touched the muddy depths of the lake. He stayed there until a fish bit his big toe, waking him. He swam for a while, taking laps, enjoying the strain on his muscles. Julian was never one for sport; there was too much aggression. Swimming was simple, solitary—at once both calming and exhilarating.

He tired and swam to the dock to lie out and let the sun dry him. His signet ring sparkled against the dull wood, slipping about now that his fingers were no longer swollen from the heat. As he gripped the edge to lift himself out of the water, he saw a girl.

It was Lily, the maid who looked after Gwen. She let down blond hair from her cap—it was longer than he'd imagined, and swayed down to her lower back. Julian watched as she reached behind herself to unbutton her grey dress. The frock fell to her feet in a heap, and she stepped out, drawing her hair over one shoulder.

Julian knew he should look away, but he was mesmerized by the way she moved, so unabashed by her bareness, out in the open as she was.

He peered as she removed her corset and set it neatly beside her uniform. Through her thin chemise he saw the shape of her hips, her narrow waist—did they not have enough to eat belowstairs?—and her broad shoulders, strong from work. He'd never looked at her so closely before, never noticed the color of her skin, like honeyed milk. It wasn't until she began to tug the chemise upwards, revealing the bareness of her calves, that Julian finally looked away.

He slapped two open hands against the water to make a splash so she'd know she was not alone.

Lily yelped. Words flew from her mouth as she gathered up her clothing: "Forgive me, forgive me! I had a moment and I thought—I know I oughtn't—oh please, forgive me!"

But she didn't know to whom she was speaking, and when Julian hauled himself up on the dock and she turned around to see him standing there in his drawers, her jaw hinged open.

"Milord!" She bowed her head. "Forgive me, please, milord—I only wanted a bathe. Please don't tell Mrs. Burns. I need this job."

Julian found himself smiling. It was wrong of him, perhaps, but he was amused by the notion this girl would think he'd be cross with her. Hadn't he come for the same purpose?

"I won't tell," he said.

Lily's chin raised tentatively, eyes stumbling on Julian's bare chest before meeting his. "Thank you, milord. I promise I'll return straight to work—"

"I'm happy for you to stay, if you like. Seeing as you're already . . ."

She blinked at him, cheeks flushing.

"Oh no . . . I didn't—" Julian turned his back to her, a sad effort at modesty. "I've finished here. You may stay—alone."

Lily was silent for a moment, then he heard her splash into the water. She swam around the dock until she was in front of him, treading water. "Your lordship is very kind. It was so bloomin' hot in the laundry, I nearly swooned."

Julian smiled again. He liked that she was unafraid to speak to him directly. He was young for his rank, but even as a boy the servants treated him the way they were meant to, avoiding eyes, only speaking when spoken to. He would have preferred getting to know them, getting to know Lily. She was lovely, Lily. Great blue eyes he longed to sketch.

"I'm pleased you didn't," Julian said.

Lily splashed a bit, then came forward to rest her arms on the dock. Julian sat on the hot wood, crossing his legs. He didn't know what either of them were doing, and because he was young, did not think of the consequences of someone finding out. It was only Lily's eyes he cared about in that moment, and the mole just under her hairline that moved up when she smiled.

"I've seen you here before, milord." Her accent was Welsh. Julian wondered how long it had been since she'd seen her family. "Keen swimmer, aren't you? Like a pike fish—that's what Mrs. Burns says."

"Does she?"

Lily nodded. She dipped her hand in the water, then brought it back up to make a perfect print on the dock boards. "She says you're good to work for, far better than your father was. Says you're shy." Lily tilted her head, squinting in the sun. "Are you?"

Julian shook his head. *Shy* was a word he hated—though everyone was always saying it. *You must forgive Julian, he's frightfully shy*. People thought him simple or rude, but he merely had little to say, and especially not to people who only knew him as Wakeford and nothing else. He saved his words for the people who mattered—Gwen, Celia, Roland.

Lily.

"I'm glad we've met today," he told her.

She made another handprint, just inches from Julian's knee. "It won't do, will it? The two of us talking? But I've always wanted to know your lordship, ever since I came here."

"Why?"

Lily let go of the dock, dropping back into the water. "Begging your pardon, but you've a lovely gentleness about you. I've never met a man of that sort."

"How do you mean?"

"I mean you're good." Lily smiled again and disappeared into the water.

A motor rumbled in the distance, and Julian's heart sank. It was time that both of them returned to the house. Gwen was home.

GWEN HANDED HER hat to Lily. "It's finished. I never wish to see the fellow again."

"I'm sorry, milady. Dreadful luck."

"No—no, it isn't dreadful. He was hardly worth the effort." Gwen removed the brooch from her high collar and unbuttoned her blouse. It had been stifling all afternoon, and she'd wanted nothing more than to be out of these clothes and into a cold bath.

It was good to be home, and rid of the exhausting young heir to an earldom she'd spent the afternoon with—such tiresome conversation! The man hadn't a single original thought, and looked appalled anytime she offered one of her own. No; she would not be seeing him again, would not be *seen* with him again. Sometimes she thought she might prefer to be an old maid, if it were possible to be single *and* a mother.

Lily poked about the wardrobe and returned with a tea gown of white lace. Yes—that was precisely what Gwen needed. Out of her stays and into something comfortable.

As Lily got to work on the laces, Gwen looked at herself in the standing mirror. "Have I got fat, Lily?"

"No, milady," Lily answered. Naturally. She'd hardly agree.

"Mama thinks so. She's told me I'm wanting a spot of calisthenics—can you imagine? And she a woman who hardly moves except to come down the stairs for meals. Of course she's impossibly thin, a trait passed to, and entirely wasted on, her sons."

Gwen caught Lily's smile in the mirror and was glad. They'd had plenty of conversations in the two years she'd been on as housemaid.

The girl was young, only Julian's age, and always lent an ear to Gwen's nonsense.

Lily pushed a wayward piece of her hair behind her cap, and Gwen noticed it was wet. "It didn't rain?" she asked.

"No, milady."

Then Gwen's corset came off and she slumped onto the divan. "I shall have tea, and then a bath. And might you fetch Celia here? I've not seen her today."

"Yes, milady." Lily curtsied.

As she was leaving, Julian caught the door. He smiled at Lily and said how do you do—odd—then stuck his head through. "How was he?"

"Can you not see that I'm indecent?" Gwen gestured to her underthings. He remained unflinching in the doorway. His hair was wet, too. "It didn't rain?"

Julian shook his head. He'd been swimming, then. He had the rumpled look about him: sleeves rolled, no tie. Gwen couldn't understand his aversion to a bathing costume. His fingers were smudged with the evidence of charcoal.

"How was the fellow?" he asked again.

Gwen groaned; her head was splitting. "It's finished."

"I sincerely hope you didn't scare off another one so you can stay at Braemore." Julian sat heavily on her bed.

"Are you so eager to have your sister married and away from you?"

He absently picked at the dress Lily had laid out. There was something odd about him, a dreaminess in his eyes. Julian wasn't one to look dreamy. Stern, perhaps. Or glum. Or bored. Never dreamy. *Dreamy* implied he was yearning, and she'd always known him to be quite content with his lot.

"If you stain that, I'll have your head." He ignored her. "What is the matter with you?"

Julian finally looked up. "Pardon?"

"You're languishing."

He cocked his head, oblivious to his own long face. Behind him, the door opened again and in came Lily with the tea things, Celia pulling on the poor girl's skirt. She was always doing that—Gwen really ought to tell her to stop.

"Careful then, little lady," Lily said to Celia as they struggled to fit through the door in a jumble. "We don't want to spill, do we?"

"I'm helping!" said Celia. She let go when she saw Gwen, running over to throw her arms around her neck. Gwen kissed her curled head and round, hot cheeks.

"My favorite sister," said Gwen, kissing her. "How do you do?"

"Roland shoved me, but I'm all right."

"Heavens! He didn't!" Gwen feigned surprise and pushed some of Cece's hair out of her face. Good God, she had a lot of it. "Shall we send Julian after him? Julian? Go and thrash Roland, there's a lad." She laughed; Julian didn't even smash spiders.

In any event, Julian was ignoring her again, because here was Lily, pouring tea, and she seemed to interest him suddenly. Well, that was it, wasn't it? This was why Gwen couldn't leave Braemore—things like this happened when she was not about to prevent them.

"That's fine, Lily; I'll pour," she said. "Ready the bath, please."

Lily curtsied, stealing a coquettish glance at Julian as she rose. After she had gone, he stared at the empty space she'd left behind.

"Julian?" Gwen finally had his attention. "Go and tell Roland he's not to push his sister."

"He pinched me, also!" Celia put in, hugging Gwen tighter. "And pulled my hair!"

"You're fibbing now, aren't you?"

Celia pouted. "No, I swear it."

"Don't swear. Julian—?"

Julian dragged his gangly sixteen-year-old body to the door like it was simply the most difficult thing in the world. He paused at the threshold, looking over his shoulder. "I'm not eager for you to leave."

"Good. Nor am I."

Celia bounced. "Nor me! Bye, Julian." She waved as he closed the door, then bounced again on Gwen's lap. "May I help Lily? She lets me pour the rose water."

Gwen smiled at her little sister. How could she say no? How could she explain to Celia that she was a lady, and not meant to follow the poor maid about all day, as though her work was something exciting and fun. It wasn't right—it wasn't *kind*, surely. But Gwen couldn't say no to Cece.

"Trot on, then. Mind Lily."

As Celia left, Gwen leaned back on the divan and held her head. She was finding she hadn't the energy to pour the tea, let alone drink it. There was too much to think about, too much to worry her. Julian and Lily, Roland and his temper, her own round hips and their mother who told her she wouldn't find a husband until she slimmed. And then, of course, the notion that she didn't in fact *want* a husband, not if it meant leaving home.

She closed her eyes and tried to picture him, this unknown future being with whom she would someday share a bed. To marry was her utmost duty, and she would abide, though it would be an end, she expected, to the life she'd come to adore.

5

Following our less-than-cordial adieu, I decided another drawing slipped under Wakeford's door would do no good. It was time to begin the job I had come to Braemore to do.

After all, it would be rude to allow those perfect metal tubes of oil to sit longer than they already had. I was itching to crack open the lids, breathe the familiar scent of turpentine, feel the texture of canvas under knife and brush.

But what to paint? I was hesitant to start with the exterior of the mansion itself—far too large an undertaking. Though I hardly knew where to begin. Anything but the folly, though I couldn't think why his lordship was so opposed. It was one of many mysteries that lay like dust in the forgotten corners of Castle Braemore, behind lock and key. Much as Wakeford was himself.

Later that day, I ambled about the house, searching for *something*. It had to be the perfect something, not only to display my skill, but to move Wakeford the way my prizewinner had done. I couldn't forget his notion about the intelligence of compassion and empathy. I was determined to prove to him, as much as myself, that I truly had it.

As I walked past the parlor, Celia was coming out with a book. I bid her a polite "Good afternoon!" but she was off before a reply was necessary. It seemed the girl was not overly fond of me. Perhaps her tolerance for boldness was not as strong as her brothers'.

I'd been too intimidated to enter the Long Gallery when I first arrived. Now I was ready to face the artists I'd be keeping company with. I found myself at one end of a narrow room that stretched the length of the wing. The outside wall was lined with bookshelves and tall windows dressed in scarlet curtains, the inner with framed artwork and gilded console tables, pottery, and embellished *dressoirs*. A few of the furnishings were under dust sheets. I lifted one to find a complexly carved chair with velvet cushions, upon which the Wakeford crest was embroidered in silver thread.

This space, like the Music Room, had reached its retirement.

I crept softly under crystal chandeliers and corniced archways. The quiet was impossibly thick, the air stale with dust and damp. My heels echoed, though seemed not to move me any closer to the opposite end, identical arches creating the illusion of an infinite hall.

The paintings were many and immense. I had to remind myself this was Wakeford's home and not the National Gallery. Though these were not like the tranquil fluidity of his Monet. They were of a masculine eye, grim and brutal, with scenes of ancient wars—women with gowns torn to expose white breasts, reared horses with wide eyes and flared nostrils, spears piercing ribs, and bloody anger.

I tried to understand how my work would fit into this collection; it wasn't remotely in keeping. Would something be brought down to accommodate the new?

On one end of the room, doors opened, hinges complaining over centuries of use. Roland sauntered through, paying no mind to the artistry about him.

"I saw you come in," he said. By the time he reached me, he was short of breath. "I thought I would come and ask how you are settling in."

"Well, thanks very much." When he didn't say more, I nodded overhead. "Interesting collection you've got."

"Needs a bit of freshening, doesn't it?" He regarded the carnage above us with a wince. "I don't believe the art was ever the real draw of the room. It was built so ladies had a place to *promenade* in winter."

I looked one way, then the other, feeling the room was swallowing us down an endless esophagus. "They must have been jolly fit."

Roland chuckled. "Yes, the peak of athleticism."

For a moment we both stared upwards, attempting to fill the emptiness between us with the apparent anguish pictured in the frame. Before long, I had to turn away. My eye caught on a frame, sitting on the ground and leaning inelegantly against a bench. I had to use both hands to gently lift it and flip it round.

Behind me, Roland scoffed. "I shouldn't wonder if he grew weary of her looking down on him all day."

The portrait was of a young woman, clothed in a wedding gown and veil that were perhaps forty-odd years out of fashion. Her gloved hands were daintily folded, and she stood at an angle to display her train and distending bustle. A pluming lace collar forced her to keep her chin lifted, her neck erect, as though she'd been trapped in a noose. The woman's oval mouth was serene, eyes detached beneath lowly arched brows. She was stunningly soft and ethereal, despite the structured nature of her gown.

"Who is she?" I asked, though I had an idea.

"Mama," Roland answered, pulling up his trouser legs to crouch beside me. "It originally hung in the earl's apartments."

The gilded frame, a striking contrast to the moody background, might have matched the phantom lines behind Wakeford's Monet. My eye was drawn to her ladyship's right first finger, where she wore a gold ring over her glove—thick enough to hint it was once a man's. There were no diamonds or embellishment, but the artist had used special care to ensure the tiny engraving of the Wakeford crest was visible.

"She was terribly pretty," I said.

Roland tilted his head, considering. "I suppose."

"Did you not get on with her?"

"She made life difficult for all of us." I felt his eyes on me as I stared at the painting, seeing it anew. "Julian hasn't had you back, has he?"

I had suspected this question to be the reason he'd been so eager to speak to me. I stood fully and Roland followed. "He has, in fact."

This was met with a look of genuine amazement.

"Never!" Roland folded his arms. "What did he speak of, I wonder?"

"We talked of art for a moment," I said wistfully. "But then all at once he seemed to want me gone."

Thoughts clouded Roland's face as he ran a hand through his hair. I couldn't help but feel guilty. I had done what Roland could not, and now he stood before me, worry heavy on his brow. Wakeford was shy, but there had been nothing unusual about speaking with him. One would not imagine he'd been stashed away for so long, avoiding his family.

I looked to his mother again, wishing there were more to devise from her expression than the humdrum nature of modeling. Suddenly, I knew just what to paint.

"I wonder if I might borrow you for a few hours tomorrow?"

Roland had been distant. It took him a moment to put a thought together. "What to do?"

"To sit. If I have your permission to paint you."

"Paint *me*? Surely Julian didn't put you to the task."

"I want to. Have you sat before?"

"No—well, yes. We sat once as children. An utter disaster, if I recall. Entirely my fault." He tugged at his collar, as if remembering the discomfort of being a child in a necktie.

"You won't fuss this time, will you?"

A handsome smile. "Some say I've matured since. You'd really like me to?"

I nodded with a rush of excitement. The last person I'd convinced to sit for me was Violet, and content as she was with her lot, there hadn't been anything interesting about her expression. Roland, however, had *something*.

"Shall we say ten o'clock tomorrow?" he asked.

Ten o'clock was perfect.

THE NEXT MORNING, we began precisely on time. I thought it rather early for a drink, but Roland stirred Pimm's into tall glasses with ice and lemonade. I'd told him to wear a dark suit, thinking the contrast would do nicely, and he had—double breasted in navy wool, with slit pockets for gold watch and chain.

Seeing him in that suit, it struck me suddenly how young he was. Not to say he hadn't dressed smartly before. Both Celia and Roland wore only the finest clothes, tailored to suit them perfectly. But each of them, while lounging about the house, adopted various states of dishevelment—shoeless feet, abandoned jackets and ties, Roland with his trouser legs rolled to reveal sock garters and pale knees.

It was the lack of a mother, I decided. There was no looming matriarch to ensure they behaved as lady and gentleman. There was only Wakeford, who did not see nor hear what went on outside his quarters.

In any case, Roland looked a gentleman now, and smiled as he handed me a drink. "Shall I do, do you think? I've another tie, if this one's wrong . . ."

"It's a lovely tie," I said, and sipped. I'd never had this drink, but with the botanical sweetness and bright mint, it was nice for a mid-morning refresher. I reached up to push one of Roland's curls away from his forehead. It was fine, really, I just wanted to touch his hair.

He chose a simple armchair, and together we moved it closer to the window for better lighting. Then Roland sat, and I readied the paint on my palette—titanium white, yellow ochre, burnt sienna, alizarin crimson, and ivory black—buzzing with content. Here I was, painting the Honorable Roland Napier at Castle Braemore, and I would be paid handsomely. After all, Lord Wakeford said I could paint what I liked. I liked Roland. I liked the way he mouthed the words to the tune in his head.

"Shall we have music?" he asked.

I didn't see why not.

While I used a knife to mix shades to match Roland's coloring, he cranked the gramophone. The space filled with the song he went on singing, louder now in a funny voice mimicking Eddie Cantor—"*My little Margie, I'm always thinkin' of you; Margie, I'll tell the world I love you!*"

Where on earth had Roland come from, when his brother was so reserved and unsure of himself? I wondered if once, before the war, Wakeford had been so animated. I chuckled, imagining him singing.

With a stiff brush, I began to roughly outline Roland's face, marveling at the handsome shape. The late earl and countess must have been dazzling to produce such a comely brood. We bobbed heads to the music while I got on. When the song ended, Roland stood to change the record and replace the needle.

"What is Julian like when you're with him?" he asked.

It was still strange to hear his Christian name so plainly. "He's *your* brother. You know him better than I, surely."

"*My* brother doesn't open his door for me." The music started up and Roland fell back down into his chair. "I've not seen him in a year, at least."

I set my paintbrush down to sip my drink. An entire year? I couldn't say I was terribly close with my sisters, but I had never gone so long without seeing them. "Don't you need to—I mean—aren't there things you must discuss now and again?"

"We exchange *notes*." Roland punctuated the word to emphasize its absurdity. "I used to knock, but . . . One can only be turned away so many times before one becomes a nuisance. So you see why I'm curious about this meeting you had yesterday."

"Rightfully so." I returned to painting, marking out Roland's eyes, almond shaped and deep set. "I can't think why he let me in. Though I did tell him I was a nurse."

That pricked Roland's ear. "Were you?"

"A VAD in the Red Cross—only for the duration."

"So you've seen like cases?"

I nodded. "How long did you say he's been in that room?"

"Two years . . . perhaps longer. At first he would come out during the day—to and from his study—but he wouldn't dine with us. We saw him less frequently, then not for several days. Then not at all."

I stroked in shadow beneath Roland's cheekbone with light pressure. "Turn your chin a bit, please? Towards the light."

Roland raised his eyebrows, having forgot what purpose we had for being there. "Better?"

"Yes, thanks. How was his lordship when he first came home?"

Roland rubbed his palms together. "Distant . . . he didn't speak—not a word. I followed him about, hoping to get something out of him. Maybe I drove him to it—"

Now I was intensely curious. "Have you seen his scars?"

"Only Gwen has."

"What about in hospital? Did you visit him there?"

"Only Gwen."

The light had shifted wrongly again. I leaned around the canvas. "Chin up, please."

Roland lifted his head and tried a smile. "Sorry—miles away."

Now his expression was completely different to the one he'd started with, the ever-present pensive line in his forehead replaced by gloom. It was my doing, so I'd have to work around it. As long as the paint was still wet, I could manage.

Roland took a deep breath. "There's something, I think . . . something about you that's different."

I chuckled. "Different how?"

"I don't know. Maybe it's enough that you aren't one of the family. Or maybe it's . . ." He scrubbed his hand in his hair, shifting the curls. I refrained from telling him off, though it was another thing I'd have to amend in the painting. "See, the thing is, Miss Preston—"

"Bertie."

"Bertie—the thing is, with Julian . . . well, you were there, weren't you?"

"Where?"

"The war."

"Not exactly—"

"But you know at least some of what he's seen. Better than we do, in any case. I'm sure it's why he's able to confide in you."

My color changed. "I would hardly say he confided in me—we've had one conversation, and only because I pushed in with questions."

"Yes, but can you not understand—or leastwise *imagine*—why after two years of the same, one small change should seem so significant?"

Roland looked at me so earnestly, I put down my brush and moved to sit opposite him under the window. My head was spinning. All I'd wanted when entering his lordship's rooms was to thank him, to ensure the work I was doing here would please. What had I let myself into?

"I shouldn't have gone to his door at all," I said.

In the light, Roland's jet eyes shifted to pewter. "Only you did. And it opened." He reached across to pinch the ends of my fingers. "It isn't fair of me to ask it of you, I'm well aware. But if you were a nurse, you understand perhaps better than any of us—"

"I can't mend him," I said. "I can bandage, I can give medicine, I can empty a bedpan, but shell shock? Even doctors have struggled for a treatment."

"It is that, then? Shell shock? Julian isn't mad?"

For all the time I spent worrying over coming to Braemore, I'd never imagined it would come to this. Maybe the earl wouldn't like what I'd painted for him, or I wouldn't get on with his siblings. But this? An unwell man and a brother desperate to help him? What authority had an artist to intervene?

"I can't tell you whether your brother is mad," I said.

"Please, Bertie. Just . . . see him again. Talk about the paintings. It would mean the world to me. Julian is in there—behind that bloody mask—I know it."

As Roland grasped my hand, I knew I'd say yes. But to what? I tried to assure myself that a friendship between Wakeford and me would only help my career along. The neighbors would faint to hear it—Mrs. Lemm would be beside herself. I could return again; I could talk to him, maybe inquire about future commissions.

"I'll bring him this painting when we're through, shall I?" I said. "And if he invites me to come again, I'll accept."

Roland's face cracked into a smile, and he looked himself again. "Thank you, Bertie. Truly. I must sound so completely desperate to you."

"He's your brother; of course you want him to be helped."

"As he's helped me." A distinct period ended the comment and kept me from asking for more. Roland rounded his shoulders, at ease for the first time since we'd begun. "We ought to keep this between the two of us. Celia, she . . . she and Julian had a falling-out long ago. They haven't seen each other since the war."

The information gave me a shameful thrill. I'd been anxious for an explanation for her odd behavior. "You don't think she'd like me speaking with him? Why?"

"I beg of you not to ask. It's an old story you mustn't worry over."

"You don't suppose it has anything to do with how he's changed?"

"Who can say?"

I stood to take up my palette again, wondering what had happened between brother and sister to set them at odds. I'd been recruited to help Wakeford's recovery, but what if the missing piece of the story made him unworthy? I would need to trust Roland, and assume Celia's problem was irrelevant and none of my business.

Only I wanted to make it my business so badly; the mystery of it coiled around my stomach and pinched ever tighter.

At least there was work to distract me. Once Roland fell silent, I cracked on with the portrait. We stopped for luncheon after another two hours, and were back to it until the sun was nearly gone. Without light, I'd done all I could do for the day, and told Roland to come have a look. He paused on the other side of the easel, face bleached.

Paintings aren't like photographs—they don't always tell the truth—

and they're not objective. An artist infuses herself into each portrait. I could understand his fear.

Though I was quite happy with how it turned out.

When he finally looked, Roland let out a long breath. "My, Bertie. You really are something."

The coil round my stomach loosened. "You think so?"

"Look at that. I'm even handsome."

"Were you expecting otherwise?"

"I was expecting that perhaps Julian had made a grave mistake, and I'd be required to do some acting, but this is . . . *brilliant*."

He squinted his eyes, taking everything in. I'd ignored the background, instead sweeping the area behind Roland with a spackling of light blue and beige, some brown shadowing around his face. I'd used short strokes and muted colors for the effect I wanted—a remembered moment, as Wakeford said. What one would recall was the emotion of the sitter, whether exactly or through a feeling, and so I held the focus on Roland's expression, lit by the sun. His lips (very pink, I found) were pressed together, his brows pulled towards center. In the eyes was that *something* I'd hoped to capture. The left was open wider than the right, and focused not on me, but far off. There was no doubting he was deep in worrying thought. His hands were clasped between his knees, shoulders bowed without losing the perfect straightness of his back.

All in all, I'd made my mark. Roland looked like a nobleman, but a young one. Confident more in himself than in his place in the world.

He turned to me. "You've made me look rather serious."

I smiled. "As it happens, you rather are."

6

Once I had completed the portrait of Roland, I slipped a note under Wakeford's door. I wanted to allow him advance notice of my arrival this time, hoping it might ease his nerves. I wrote that I had something to show him, and would come the next day. Whether or not he would open the door remained to be seen.

To my surprise and relief, when I knocked Wednesday afternoon, there was little pause before his voice sounded from within: "Miss Preston?"

"*Bertie,*" I answered. "How'd you know?"

The door came open. Wakeford was dressed for company in a grey saxony tweed lounge suit, half belted and tailored at the waist, hair carefully arranged as neatly as could be at a length. I allowed myself to gawk, astonished that he not only had read my note, but had anticipated my arrival with a touch of formality.

"I recognized your knock," he said.

"I've never been recognized by my knock before."

Wakeford minded the canvas warily, as though it might leap to bite him if he made sudden movements. "Is that—forgive me, how do you do?"

I found his bashfulness utterly charming. "I'm well, my lord. And yourself?"

"Yes, well." He pointed. "You've brought a painting?"

"Would you care to have a look?"

We bent in tandem to lift the canvas, nearly knocking heads. I forced a laugh at the blunder while he backed away, clenching and unclenching his fists.

"Mayn't I help you with it?"

"Yes—yes, do. Thanks." It wasn't heavy, but I could tell chivalry was embedded deeply in his person. How dare I refuse? "Oh, take care; it isn't quite dry."

Without another remark, he maneuvered the canvas carefully through the door, pausing in the center of the room. "That chair, there. If you would?"

I closed the door behind me and followed his gaze to a simple bergère near the window. I moved it out from the wall and faced it towards the light. Wakeford leaned the painting on the chair, hovering his hands to ensure it was steady, then came round to stand with me.

I don't think he was expecting to see Roland.

He touched the knot of his tie, which hardly needed adjusting. He smoothed his mustache with the pad of his thumb. He changed his stance three times.

We weren't familiar enough for me to deduce whether these were good omens or bad, but they made me anxious. "I did say I would paint him, didn't I? Of course, if you don't like it, there's no need to have it. I do think Roland was keen—"

"He looks old," said Wakeford.

I started. "That's funny. I thought he looked quite young."

Lord Wakeford twirled the longer whiskers under his chin. He adopted a rather similar expression to the one his brother wore in the portrait. "I suppose in my mind he'll always be a boy of thirteen."

I was reminded instantly of my father. *I'm not a little girl anymore*, I was wont to say to him, and he'd reply, *You'll always be a little girl to me*,

Bertie. The memory hit me like a fist in the gut, with the realization that I didn't know when I would see him again.

Wakeford breathed a laugh through his nose, bringing me back to the room. Though he seemed to be far off in the world of the painting.

"I know I was commissioned to paint Braemore," I said. "And I will. But I was inspired, and I think perhaps you'll agree that Roland is as much a part of Braemore as the fountain. He belongs in the gallery, don't you feel?"

Wakeford went into his chest pocket for his cigarette case, and held it to me. I accepted and he raised his lighter, hands smelling of bergamot and tobacco. We smoked. I waited for some sort of indication of whether what I'd done pleased him.

"I don't plan to hang your paintings in the gallery," he said.

My heart slipped to my feet. The rest of me wished to follow, down, down to the Persian rug, where I might curl into a ball and forget my wretched dreams.

But I was standing before the Earl of Wakeford, who did not find a touch of gravity in his statement, and so I merely nodded demurely and said, "It isn't any of my business."

Wakeford cleared his throat and pushed the bridge of his spectacles to adjust his mask. "I'll have it, of course. I hope Roland thanked you?"

I nodded again, disappointed he didn't explain where precisely my paintings *would* go. I dragged hard on my cigarette and looked about for an ashtray, finding one on the end table. Wakeford appeared behind me, indicating the settee. I willed myself to move past my ego, and remembered to sit on the far end so I had his lordship's ear.

Right. I was in and past the difficult bit. I couldn't forget what I'd promised Roland. But how to begin? I couldn't ask Wakeford why it was he locked himself away. I was reluctant to even mention the war—most men preferred not to discuss it. It'd been easier to talk the last time, when I was so very sure of myself. When I hadn't been given the mission to cure a shell-shocked man. When I'd been ignorant of his falling-out with Celia. All those turbulent years and not a word between them!

I looked at Wakeford and tried to see a cynical man, a man who could hurt his little sister so thoroughly. But all I saw was the brother Roland spoke of.

"If I may?" I said. "How long have you been the Earl of Wakeford?"

He finished his cigarette and stifled it in the tray. "My father passed just before Celia was born."

"I'm so sorry . . ."

"It was a long time ago." Wakeford tilted his head left and right. "For one who doesn't care for attention, the title has been more a bother than anything."

"I can't imagine. I love attention." He met my gaze suddenly, causing me to blush down to my toes. "I have to fight for it, you see. My sisters make the perfect daughters and I . . . make a fool of myself, mainly." Wakeford was staring still, with purpose it seemed. "What?"

"You've a bit of—paint, I think." He touched the flesh of his neck beneath his ear.

I mimicked the motion, feeling the patch of dried oil. What a ninny I must have looked! I dispensed of my cigarette and scrubbed with my fingers until I'd got most of it. When I sat back again, Wakeford was still looking, the hint of a smile.

"You have sisters, then?" he asked. Lovely of him, really.

I tucked my hair behind my ear to regain some composure. "Two. Married and mothers. Very accomplished indeed."

"No brothers?"

"A blessing, I've come to find." I could tell by his nod that he'd taken my meaning. So much for avoiding the war. "Roland didn't fight, did he?"

"He was too young, thank God."

"That didn't stop most boys."

Wakeford shifted in his seat, and opened his jacket for his cigarette case, turning it over and over in his hands. "I made him swear not to follow me."

"I'm glad," I said. "Though I find myself wondering why you were on the front lines. Might a nobleman have petitioned for his use elsewhere?"

Wakeford opened his case, shut it with a click. Opened, shut. "I don't believe I'd the right to be exempt."

"That's very admirable, your lordship."

He turned his chin towards me. I thought he'd spotted another smudge on my person. "You needn't go on with formalities . . . I do appreciate your respect, though—" His words stuck in his throat. A twitch of the jaw and he continued. "My captain in the army didn't care much for me. He would call me 'your lordship' facetiously, and now I think only of him when I hear it."

"Why did he dislike you?"

"He felt I was overly soft on my men."

I was oddly relieved. Between his sudden anger during our first meeting and the rift with his sister, I expected at every turn that he might prove himself unkind. "I do find it difficult to imagine you barking orders."

Wakeford nearly smiled, but it only reached the corner of his eye. "I was exacting when it was required of me."

I drew one leg under the other, settling in comfortably. Wakeford observed my movements as if I was practicing skilled gymnastics. "When you were wounded—if you don't mind my asking—where were you?"

He tapped the corner of his cigarette case against his knee. "Somme. Eighteen."

"Nearly through it." I sank, a familiar weight in my chest. "So many men came into our beds on the day of armistice. None of it was fair, of course, but those men . . . and those who died minutes before the end. We could hear the guns sometimes on the wind, muffled in the distance. I remember how instantly the firing stopped at eleven o'clock that day. God, I've never heard the like . . ."

I shivered despite the warmth of the room. Wakeford pressed his cigarette case between praying palms, touching fingertips to chin. His eye closed.

I'd taken things too far yet again.

"I'm sorry," I said softly. "You don't wish to talk about it, do you?"

Wakeford remained so still I thought my apology had gone unheard. Then he stood, set his cigarette case on the table in front of us, and removed his jacket, draping it over the back of the settee. He went to the piano, sat on the bench, and opened the lid.

I held my breath, thinking I'd done it—I'd offended the earl, and in one fell blow, ruined my chances of ever being anything at all in the world. He'd chuck me out tomorrow.

Wakeford turned over his shoulder. "Perhaps you'd like to—?"

I waited for him to finish the sentence. But there was only a drawn silence, lasting until his hand lay palm down on the bench, indicating a space for one to sit beside him.

I flushed. It was a narrow space. If I sat there, I risked brushing sleeves with an earl, and I thought that might break certain rules of propriety. Still, his hand remained as he waited, and so I took the chance and sat there.

Wakeford played a few notes strung together by the mere promise of a melody. "I've nervous hands," he said.

"Have I made you nervous?"

"Rather." A small smile. "Pleasantly, though."

It seemed that despite his restraint, his lordship was terribly charming. "Go on, then."

Wakeford rested his hands on the keys, poised to play a chord. He had hands I could stare at all day—impossibly smooth and so pale they were almost bright, the thumb with a natural backwards curve, the knuckles masculine, yet delicate.

There was no music on the rack. He played from memory, something I'd never heard before that instantly weighed on my chest—melancholic yet syrupy, for a tale of lost love.

"You play beautifully," I said over the music.

"I've had much time to practice."

His hands moved with laziness attained from playing a piece so frequently that every muscle knew the timing. They were strong, too, pressing heavy keys as though they were nothing. Music filled the space, so round and full it thickened the air. I was sure the sound of it reached all the bedrooms, even the hall below.

Wakeford's song slowed to a romantic swirl of lithe notes as his hands crept closer to my side of the keyboard. "You weren't wrong to speak of it," he said to the keys. "The truth is, it's been years since I've spoken to someone who'd seen it, and I—" He paused abruptly and so did the music. My ears buzzed in the sudden silence. "Do you ever feel you're in a dream?"

Wakeford's stare was strong enough to take my breath. "Yes."

"Speaking to you just then," he said, "I felt the floor solidify beneath me."

Then he turned to the piano and began to play again, from precisely where he'd left it.

I'd always been a distracted person; perhaps that was why I had a dozen unread books, why I never courted properly with men. I couldn't sit still long enough. But now—oddly—I was perfectly content to idle beside this man as he played. Comfortable without conversation. Without the sound of my own voice.

When the song finished, Wakeford began to play another, but it broke up into spare notes, and then he drew his hands from the keys to rest in his lap.

"You must think me mad," he said.

I shook my head. I was frightened of startling him, but I leaned in his direction, just enough that his shirtsleeve brushed my elbow. He didn't even flinch; no rule after all.

"Why don't you paint any longer?" I asked.

He bowed his head to study his hands, which were now trembling slightly, I guessed from a mix of nerves and the strain from playing. A symptom of shell shock I was all too familiar with.

Wakeford tilted his chin halfway, and then enough to meet my eyes. "When I was young, my mother believed an interest in art was affecting my temperament."

"So you gave it up?"

"It wasn't worth the argument."

I was preparing my rebuttal when a knock at the door made me jump. Julian, however, remained perfectly steady. I thought he hadn't heard it at first until he said, "That's tea."

"Oh, yes. I'll just . . ." I hid my disappointment by standing and starting towards the painting.

Wakeford stood as well. "Miss—" Another knock interrupted him. "I may send him away."

"No, no." I lifted the canvas, nearly forgetting it wasn't entirely dry. "You'll be wanting tea; I daren't keep you."

"Stay, then."

I idled dumbly in the center of the room with canvas in hand, edges cold and sticky on my fingertips. What use was there in scrambling off now? "I should like to."

Wakeford swallowed hard. "Do."

Three more brisk knocks.

Lord Wakeford admitted Huxley with his tray. The butler hardly blinked at me, and I wondered what he'd heard through the cracks in the door. He set the tea things on the table, and asked whether his lordship would like an extra place brought up. Wakeford answered this was not necessary, thanked him, and let the butler off, closing the door.

When he turned to me, I hadn't moved an inch.

"Good of you to invite me," I said.

Wakeford took the canvas from my hands and set it back in front of the window. He then ushered me to the table, and pulled out one of the chairs for me to sit. I did, and watched him pour.

"But there's only one cup," I said. "It ought to be yours, surely."

He lit a cigarette. "Please."

As if under a spell, I added sugar, milk, stirred, sipped.

Wakeford blew smoke. "It's been a long time since I've preferred company."

The comment lightened me, the way he'd surely meant it to. Perhaps Roland was not incorrect in his assumptions. I nibbled on the corner of an egg and cress sandwich while we drifted back into that same comfortable silence. I was finding I quite enjoyed it.

I didn't mind Wakeford's stare, and he didn't seem bothered that I peered back. He didn't eat or drink, only smoked. I reckoned he couldn't manage to with the mask on, as it covered half his mouth, leaving space enough for only a cigarette. It was easy to admire the mask when one sat opposite him. But the asymmetry of bearded face and clean-chinned prosthetic was beginning to niggle at me. I imagined the thin strokes it would take to mimic his whiskers, the colors I'd mix, the brush that would do the job.

The longer I looked, the less natural it appeared, the more I wanted it off and away. Roland was right—there was a piece of his brother hidden behind it, a piece I figured even Wakeford didn't know existed anymore.

In another minute, I lost my serenity and tapped my chin. "You wouldn't happen to have a clean sheet of paper and a pencil?"

Wakeford stifled his cigarette, a lift of intrigue in his brow. "Under the lid on my desk."

He began to stand, but I motioned for him to stay put, moving excitedly across the room. In his desk, I found the familiar stationery he'd used to write his letter to me, and two pencils that were unfortunately dull. Needs must.

I sat again at the table with a flourish. "Shall we draw one another?"

Wakeford's face bleached as if I'd raised a loaded gun. "No . . . ," he muttered. "No, thank you, but . . ."

I should have known he'd react similarly, though I wanted so badly to see his style as an artist. "Or, I could draw that vase behind you," I said, desperately cheery, "and you may draw the fern in the corner."

That eased him, but only just. "I've not sketched in years."

"In that case, you had better do me instead. I shouldn't like to insult the fern."

Oh, what a smile the man had. I could hardly believe his stern face was capable of such acrobatics. Wakeford watched my eyes for what felt like an eternity before finally reaching across the table for a piece of paper.

"You've done the impossible, Miss Preston," he said, curling his hand round the pencil and shaking out his wrist.

"Oh no, not quite yet."

He glared from under his dark lashes, shockingly waggish. "Be still."

I obeyed.

It ought to have been much as before. Me sitting uncomfortably straight, Wakeford studying my face. But there was no comparing this to any sort of polite discourse. This was a tryst, I realized too late, as my blood hummed under his eye. I was not accustomed to being the sitter, to being examined so closely. Many would assume a model was merely needed for an aesthetic, but I knew there was more—even for a simple sketch. He was reaching, and I could almost feel the sculptor's hands poring over every blemish, every hair, every stalled breath. It made me giddy to keep still, the room silent except for the scratching of pencil on paper.

When Wakeford looked up I nearly crumbled, as though I'd been holding up the ceiling. I waited for him to speak, to hand me the paper. Instead he gave a breathy laugh through his nose.

"It's rubbish."

I let myself giggle at the stark embarrassment on his face. "I don't believe it! May I see?"

He shook his head, looking down at his work. "You'll never speak to me again."

"I promise I shall." The words were out before I could think what they implied. "Please, may I?"

Grimacing, Wakeford sighed and pushed it to me facedown.

The hair on my arms raised as I turned it over. It was a rough sketch—mere lines and reckless shading, with no rubber to remove his mistakes. But it was me, certainly; it could not have been anyone else. And though he'd given my lips an almost comical tilt of amusement, there was an impossible amount of feeling in my eyes for what little detail the medium allowed. I was pretty—far prettier than the woman I saw in the mirror.

"Ought I to have done the fern?" he asked.

I realized I'd been smiling, achingly wide. "It's jolly good." He tried to wave me off. "Honestly! Why have you not taken it up again since your mother passed?"

Wakeford observed the pencil in his hand. "I returned from the war without the ability to see beauty where it once was."

The idea broke my heart.

I finished my tea and reluctantly told Lord Wakeford I really ought to be going. Despite the fun we'd had, he was still an earl and I his artist, and I needed to return to the job he was paying me for.

At the door, he offered a tired smile and told me I should keep the drawing. Neither of us remembered I was meant to have done one of my own.

"I *do* wish to speak to you again," I said. "If you'll have me."

He scratched his whiskers, a tic now familiar to me. "Perhaps you might bring another painting?"

I bit my lip to keep my smile from growing too obvious. He wished to see more of my work! And deep inside, I reveled at the thought that he might also wish to see more of me.

Starlings and Giants

MAY 1913

Celia sat on the rug with her doll, watching Miss Quinn doze on the window seat with a novel open in her lap. It was three whole minutes until the woman's dragging breaths rattled her throat and the first snore escaped her nose. Celia smiled. She stood and removed her shoes to tiptoe to the nursery door, turning the knob ever so slowly, and slipped through before closing it again.

In the corridor, all was still. Downstairs, Mama was hosting tea, and as Celia approached the balcony to peek through the balusters, she could hear dull voices competing to be heard over one another. Previously, when she'd heard Mama discuss a menu of trifle and simnel cake and cherry scones, she'd hoped to be older than her ten years so she might be invited. Now, it seemed rather a bore.

Though if she hurried, Lily might be able to snatch a scone from the kitchen for her before they were all gobbled up.

Celia went through the narrow door to the secret set of winding servants' stairs. She took the steps one at a time, clinging to the railing. It was a long way down, and her stockinged feet were slick on the treads, worn to a polish. Hushed echoes whispered up the walls. One had to be brave to take this way, and without an older brother beside her, Celia pretended she was. Wouldn't it be good fun to have a younger sibling? A baby brother or sister that Celia could teach things to and be brave for?

Belowstairs, things were busy enough that nobody noticed Celia running along the corridor. She always ran—it was too long and dark to linger. At the end, she nearly went straight into a footman who did a full spin to keep his tray of sandwiches balanced and called out, "Make way for the little lady!"

But nobody looked up from their work—not the hall boy covered in soot, nor the kitchen maid sweating over the stove, nor Cook, who stuck her pinkie into a bowl of something and tasted it. She shouted for more salt and it appeared in her hand like magic.

Celia found Lily in the servants' hall, sitting before a mountainous pile of clothing. As she approached the table, she saw they were *her* things—petticoats and pinafores and stockings that were torn or frayed. While humming to herself, Lily flicked the needle in and out of the silk with nimble fingers.

Celia crawled up on the neighboring chair. "May I help?"

Lily's eyes (the color of a robin's egg—how splendid not to be cursed with brown!) widened when she realized she was not alone. "You're not meant to be down here, are you, milady? Where to is Miss Quinn?"

"Snoring upstairs." Celia set her chin in her hand and picked at one of the dresses on the table. It was one she hated—the seams too itchy round her neck. She wished Lily would be rid of it rather than mending. "Are there any scones left?"

Lily set down her sewing. "You ought to be in the nursery, milady. I'll take the stairs with you, shall I?"

Celia bristled. The nursery was a dreadful place without Roland. It'd been months since she'd seen him, or any of her siblings. She had nearly lost Lily as well, when Gwen offered to engage her as lady's maid at her new home. But Lily had stayed at Braemore, not wishing to abandon her friends, not wishing to abandon Celia. So she surely wouldn't now.

"Or . . . ," began Celia, "we could go to the gardens."

Lily frowned. "I've work that needs doing, milady. Miss Quinn will take you out of doors."

Celia bent her mouth, folding her hands beneath her chin. "*Please,* Lily? Miss Quinn will only have me do arithmetic again. I can't bear it!"

Lily chewed on her bottom lip—something Gwen would scorn Celia for—and eyed her pile of sewing woefully. "I suppose there'll be laundry to hang."

Celia grinned.

The sewing was abandoned for a basket of wet linens. Lily plucked two cherry scones from the bench in the kitchen, and wrapped them in a gingham cloth, which Celia held as they plodded out into the courtyard. Celia sat on the setts, gorging herself with dense, buttery pastry, watching as Lily shook out each sheet and pinned it over the wire. A gentle breeze was on her side, pushing the linens forward and back.

When the task was done, Lily lowered herself slowly to a seat beside Celia, groaning as she stretched her arms. She was always doing that, sounding like the boys did after playing cricket. Celia offered the other scone and Lily took it gladly, giggling as the first delicious bite melted over her tongue.

"Good as sacked, I am, if we're found," Lily said with a full mouth.

"We're hid here."

The billowing sheets acted as a curtain between the servants' entrance and where they settled near the stone wall. It was a seemly fort, though Celia wished they'd thought to bring cushions to sit on.

Lily pushed a stray hair from her eye. "You've been lonesome, haven't you? Since Lady Stanfield married?"

Celia grumbled, "I hate being the baby." Miss Quinn would have scorned her for speaking with her mouth full. "I've no one to play with."

"His lordship won't be away much longer."

Celia shrugged and dusted the crumbs from her hands. A few curious starlings landed to hop on the wire, eager for a taste. "I wish Julian were here now."

Lily pulled her knees to her chest and hugged them, dancing her toes up and down so her boots tapped a rhythm. Her normally sallow cheeks suddenly brightened with a spill of pink. "Why not ask one of those starlings to fetch him home?"

Celia giggled. "Birds can't understand me."

"Course they can! They understood Branwen, didn't they?"

"Who?"

Lily folded her legs under her skirt, and gestured for Celia to sit in front of her. Celia went willingly—Lily was the only person who plaited without tugging her hair.

"Branwen was a heroine of Welsh folklore." Lily gently combed her fingers through Celia's curls. "She was married to a cruel king who lived far away from her family on an island. One day, Branwen was so sad and lonesome, she befriended a starling who'd nested beside her window. She asked the bird to fly to her home, and fetch her brother—Brân the Blessed—who was a giant, and the king of Britain."

Celia tried to turn and look at Lily, but was held in place by her hair. "Was he truly a giant? How tall?"

"Taller than Castle Braemore. So tall he didn't need a ship to cross to Branwen's island. He only had to walk across the ocean floor."

"He didn't drown?"

"Course not, you silly! The water only reached his shoulders."

"I've never heard this story before."

Lily laid the finished plait across Celia's shoulder, and wrapped her arms around her middle. Celia savored the rare feeling of an embrace, and leaned into Lily, who smelled delightfully of lavender and onions and beeswax.

"'Cause you're not Welsh, are you?" Lily pressed her cheek against Celia's. "Every Welsh boy and girl has heard of Brân the Blessed."

Celia knew from the way Lily spoke that she was not a local girl, but hadn't much thought about where the maid had come from. She'd been at Braemore since before Celia could remember. Now she wondered about Lily's home, about the talking starlings and the giants . . .

"Why did you leave Wales?" asked Celia.

Lily's embrace tightened. "'Cause me mam died."

"Don't you miss your father?"

"I've no father to speak of, milady."

Celia's eyes smarted with tears. She'd never met anyone else with a father they'd never met. "Nor have I," she said, and turned in her seat to toss her arms around Lily's neck. They stayed that way until the pattern of their breaths aligned.

"Let's you and me be each other's fathers, eh?" Lily said.

Celia pulled away, smiling again. "We can't be; we're girls!"

"Makes no matter. People have fathers to love and protect them, don't they? I reckon I can love and protect you just as well."

That seemed all right. In fact, it seemed lovely indeed. And most importantly, it meant that Celia would always have Lily's friendship, for family was the strongest bond.

"I shall love and protect you back," said Celia. "Always and forever."

"Always and forever!"

Lily laughed in a way that grown-ups do when they hear a child say something fantastic. But Celia didn't notice, for she was too glad to have a father's empty place in her heart filled at last.

They were not quite as well hid as they'd imagined, for moments later, the footman called Teddy came through the door and ducked his head under the linens. Celia and Lily both giggled at his cocked brow. Lucky it was Teddy, and not Mrs. Burns, for he looked upon Lily as the flower that was her namesake, and was all too pleased to keep her secret. Nevertheless, she was missed in the house, so Celia was left with only the birds for company.

Thinking of Lily's story, Celia stood under the wire with her fists on her hips, head craned to watch three starlings hop, hop, hop. They flicked their heads back and forth to gawk with grommet eyes, the sun catching on jewel-colored feathers.

"All right, you lot," said Celia. "I'm a lady, so you must obey me."

The birds hopped. Hopped, and tweeted. One of them lifted a wing to peck underneath.

"You're to fly to Oxfordshire—do you know where that is?"

The pecking bird stopped forthwith, head popping straight.

"Good," said Celia. "Lord Wakeford is there, and you must fetch him to me." She brought up her arms, flicking her hands into the sky. "Off now! Shoo!"

IT RAINED AND thundered that night as Celia lay in bed. She worried about her starlings, wondering if they could fly in such weather, and cowered at every flash of lightning. She stared at the other bed across the room, empty now, and wished Roland had not left for school. He always made her laugh when there was a storm, singing badly to distract from the sound of thunder, and making a tent of quilts to hide them from the lightning. Perhaps she ought to have sent one of the birds to Eton.

When she woke, Celia flew to the window, thinking her birds might have returned with news. But there wasn't a single starling in sight—only a few doves pecking the lawn for worms.

Mama wanted to see her, and so Miss Quinn fed her a breakfast of porridge and got her into one of her finest dresses. This was Celia's favorite part of time spent with her mother—she was permitted to wear her Sunday clothes without having to go to chapel. With a gloved hand on the railing, she skipped down the stairs, delighting in the sound her polished shoes made against the runners. Feeling so delightfully grown-up in her lace, she almost forgot about the starlings entirely, until she raced across the hall and straight into a lanky pair of legs.

"Where are you heading for in such a hurry, pal?"

Celia looked up and gasped. In an instant, she believed in magic again. "Julian! I can hardly believe it! The starling understood!"

"Starling?" Julian knelt before her, smiling crookedly. He looked a mess; Mama would not be happy to see him in naught but a wrinkled shirt and grass-stained trousers. His nose was red from the sun, and on his curls sat a crown of daisies.

"Lily said to ask a starling to fetch you home from Oxford," said Celia, "and so I did, and here you are!" She plucked the daisies from Julian's head.

She'd made a crown just like his only days ago with . . . "Were you with Lily?"

Julian touched his hair where the crown had been, and went pink round the ears. "No—why would I be with Lily? She's hard at work."

Celia shrugged. Lily was good at sneaking about, though Celia supposed it wouldn't be right to do it with Lord Wakeford himself. "She makes the best daisy chains. Who did this one?"

"I did."

"You didn't. You don't know how."

Julian plucked the chain from her hand and gave her stomach a pinch. "I'm learning."

"Did Lily teach you?"

He studied her eyes for what felt like a long time, and Celia held her breath. She thought she might be scorned, but wasn't sure what she'd done wrong. "Why aren't you with Miss Quinn?"

Oh, that was it.

"Last evening, I let all the wax dribble from my candle onto the floor and I burned my finger"—she held it up as evidence, and Julian took the hand to kiss the wound through her glove—"and this morning, Mama asked to see me, so I suppose I'll have a lashing. Did the starling talk?"

Julian's face melted the way it did when amused. "Who's been filling your head with nonsense?"

"It isn't nonsense. You're home, aren't you?"

"Yes, but I only came because—" Julian stopped with his lips still parted, then shook his head. "Why did you wish so badly for this starling to fetch me?"

"Because I missed you." She encircled him, breathing the musky male scent she'd been without, savoring the strength of her brother's arms.

"I missed you, too, pal," he replied. "Come on, then—tell me this story you've heard."

Celia nodded and took Julian's hand as he stood. With him by her side, she no longer feared entering the parlor where Mama was waiting to scorn her.

7

My first week at Braemore passed in an instant, and on Thursday Gwen was due. She came through the door short of breath, already talking at her brother and sister. I didn't catch the beginnings of it—because she was speaking quickly, and because I was completely taken by her.

With Celia's femininity, Wakeford's broad build, and Roland's confidence, Gwen had a bit of each of her siblings, though easily outshined them all. Pretty, though not in a way that was after attention, Gwen had high, ample cheeks, and eyes that crinkled with joy to see her family. Though her hair was done in marcel waves at the front, it was long and rolled in a sensible bun. Her hemline was a length her mother would be proud of, though her silk dress had a stylish dropped waistline and necktie.

She was stunning. In more ways than one.

Gwen commanded the household as if it was her own, entering with an exuberant child pulling either arm. Despite the genuine chaos that arrived with her, she had the utmost attention of butler and footman, not to mention my own, which was trained ardently. Gwen didn't look like the modern women I admired in magazines, but by God, she had every sensibility.

I took a step back as hugs and noises of greeting commenced, Gwen's voice ringing above them all: "Celia, are you eating? I know the fashion is for women to resemble boys, but it isn't healthy. And look at your brother—there's nothing of you, my boy! That color suits you well. But where's the blue tie I bought you for your birthday? Do wear it next time."

She released her grip on her children's hands and one of them whipped past my knees, heels slapping against marble as she ran for the stairs, a head of blond curls bouncing wildly.

"There goes Anna, off like a shot," Gwen said. "Someone catch her?"

Celia tugged Gwen's arm. "I need a word—"

"Please, be a love; she'll be banging on his door."

"I need a word about Julian."

That brought all of the whirling air to a cold still. Gwen fixed on her sister. "If he isn't on his deathbed, I'm certain it can wait."

Celia shrank, but didn't argue again. "I'll go after Anna."

"Good girl." Gwen handed her a red ribbon. "Perhaps you can coax her hair back into this. Look sharp about it, eh?"

Celia huffed and took the ribbon, setting off at a fair pace, voice echoing up the stairwell as she chased her niece.

Gwen touched Roland's arm. "What's this about Julian?"

"He's to blame for Cece's misery," he said. "Where is your governess?"

"That incompetent woman knew naught about raising a child. I dismissed her on Tuesday." Gwen waved her hand to shoo the notion like a midge.

Roland laughed. "That's the third this year."

"Yes, well, I'm uncertain why I bother. She'll be the last I bring on." Gwen brushed a fleck of lint from Roland's shoulder. "Handsomer each day. How is dear Freddie?"

They lowered their voices, and while Roland answered, I diverted my attention to her other child, a towheaded boy who had plopped himself down on the floor, making his worn teddy dance on the marble between his legs.

"Anna's gone to see the dragon," he said to the teddy. "Isn't there a dragon, Mama?" He looked up.

"Of course there's a dragon, love. He lives upstairs." Gwen waggled her brow at Roland, who shook his head. "Talking of which, I ought to be seeing about him."

"But you haven't met our artist." Roland waved me forward. I was so taken by this woman's massive presence I nearly forgot I was standing there, a stranger. "May I introduce Miss Bertie Preston. Miss Preston, our elder sister, the Dowager Viscountess Stanfield."

"Heavens, that makes me sound ancient," she said. "*Gwen* will do."

I wanted to say I was sorry to hear her husband was lost in the war, but knew the words would hardly bring her comfort. Instead I smiled and waited for a handshake which was not forthcoming.

Gwen passed her son's hand over to Roland's. "Keep a close eye on him. He's quite interested in throwing and making messes these days. Has tea been sent up?"

"As always."

"Fine. You may take the children outside, but if you return them with any tears, bruises, or stains, it will be your pretty head." She brushed her thumb against Roland's cheek, lovingly as a mother, and was off up the stairs.

The little boy looked up at Roland, his teddy now drooping from under his arm. "I want to see the dragon."

"Only your mama gets to see the dragon," Roland answered. "She's a dragon tamer, didn't you know?"

"But I *want* to."

I chuckled and knelt beside the child, righting his bear for him. "Hello, there. What's your name?"

He rubbed his nose and lowered his chin shyly.

"Go on, then." Roland gave his hand a tug. "Miss Preston doesn't bite. That I know of."

I elbowed him in the leg. "I'm called Bertie. What shall I call you?"

The boy sniffled and muttered, "Lord Stanfield."

Roland burst a laugh, mussing his nephew's hair. "She'll call you Richie, you cheeky thing."

The viscount swung his arms and stared at his toes. I could see I was getting no more out of him.

Then Celia came trudging down the stairs with niece in tow. Anna's pout was soon altered by the promise of cake, and we went out to the lawn to see where our own tea was laid on a table stacked high with bakes and sandwiches. Celia stood behind Anna's chair, running her fingers through the girl's flaxen curls to prepare them for the ribbon.

I sat beside her, and Anna's round eyes followed me as her head remained stationary.

"I like your hair," she said. "Mama won't allow me to have mine short."

I smiled, having found a kindred spirit. "Mine didn't, either, but I cut it anyway."

Anna's dark eyes sparkled and she covered her mouth to laugh.

Celia tied a bow in the red ribbon, making Anna skew her face. When her auntie sat down, she knitted her fingers into her hair and gave it a shake, loosening the tail. Then she brushed the crumbs from her hands onto her dress, and stood for the teapot, but Celia stepped in to help pour. Anna watched hungrily.

"I should like two lumps," she said.

Celia thinned her gaze on her niece, then smiled fondly and retrieved the tongs to plop another cube in the cup. "Don't tell your mother." It was lovely to see her cheerful.

Anna beamed and returned to her seat with her tea.

"Where's the dragon?" Richie asked from Roland's lap.

"There isn't any *dragon*," Anna replied. "It's only Uncle Earl."

I gave Roland a questioning look and he smirked. "'Julian' was too difficult for Anna to pronounce when she began talking."

"Will Mama have tea?" asked Richie.

"She's having her own with your uncle." Roland kissed his head and put a puff in his pudgy hands. "Now's the time to eat as much cake as you can before she returns."

Celia scowled. "*Roland.*"

"What? We're meant to spoil them, aren't we?" Roland jostled the child about on his knee, making Richie laugh with a mouth full of cream. "If there's sick, it's down to Gwen for trusting us with them."

As Anna sat with her tea, I noticed her eyes flicker to the windows above. I turned to follow them. There were four big windows in Wakeford's apartments, and Anna looked on fiercely, as though her mother's face might appear at any moment.

"Is that where you ran off to?" I asked her.

She nodded. "I'm not allowed in, but I wanted to ask Uncle to play piano."

Roland had overheard. "He always plays for you. You needn't ask."

Anna faced front and blew on her tea with pursed lips. She studied me over the brim, then twisted her mouth curiously. "Who *are* you?"

I chuckled, and offered my hand. "I'm Bertie. I'm doing some paintings for your uncle."

Anna's eyes widened, and she set her tea down, forgetting my handshake. She hopped from her chair and propped her hands on my armrest. "You're a *real* artist? Have you an easel? May I see your pictures?"

"Course you may."

"Oh no, dear." Celia sat forward. "You mustn't bother Miss Preston."

"It's no bother." I put down my plate. "They're in the Music Room."

Anna led the way, familiar enough with the house. She spoke nearly as quickly as her mother, telling me they lived not far from Bath on a much humbler estate (her words, truly). Her father had been a keen hunter, and they kept six English setters in the house. I was told each of their names and a detailed description of every spot and patch of fur.

"Do you want to know a secret?" Anna asked as we reached the Music Room.

I crouched in front of her. "I'd love to."

"I always save half my breakfast for the dogs. It's why they follow me about." She went pink all over, and then gave that wayward flop of a grin.

"That's very kind of you," I whispered.

"Now you must tell me a secret. Then we'll be friends."

I instantly warmed. In my years as an auntie, I hadn't grown tired of the small fancies and games that children played.

I tapped my chin. "Hmm . . . I've got something. When I was your age, I broke my mother's favorite vase, and blamed it on the maid."

Anna giggled. "I've done that."

"Friends, then?"

She nodded, curls bouncing. "Friends."

I hadn't much of a painting to show her, only Roland, who sat waiting to be framed, and a bit of lake that I'd been working on earlier. But Anna was taken by the sheer amount of kit. She sorted through my brushes, testing them all on the palm of her hand. I asked her if she'd like to mix a color of her own, and she nearly jumped out of her shoes. We sat with a clean palette, and she brought me her favorite color, French ultramarine, and we lightened it with white and added crimson and umber. In the end, it was a rather muddy shade of purple, but Anna was chuffed.

I wrapped her in my smock, and let her choose a brush and one of the smaller canvases. She hummed as she smacked a dollop of her paint down and swirled it round. She didn't seem to be going for any particular shape, but I recognized a spark of inspiration.

The door opened just as she set down the brush and was about to dip her fingers in.

"Anna, don't you dare!"

We both looked up to see Gwen in the doorway. Anna lowered her hand.

Gwen stepped carefully over the tarpaulin on the floor, glancing about the room as she entered. "I'm not imposing, am I? Roland said she'd be in here."

"No, come," I answered, though my pulse wouldn't settle. I helped Anna out of the smock as Gwen drew closer to study my work. "I'm terribly sorry—we got a bit out of hand. I did ensure it all stayed on the smock. Or me."

"Look, Mama. I made a color!" Anna rushed to her side to hold up her little masterpiece. "Bertie's a real artist! She has a hundred brushes!"

"That's beautiful, darling. How clever." She smiled and hugged the girl into her hip. "Uncle Earl's promised to play your song. Go on to the hall and have a listen."

Anna scurried off, forgetting the previous activity entirely. Left alone with Gwen's authority, I began to sweat.

"Is this what his lordship has commissioned?" Gwen gestured to the portrait of Roland. "Goodness, he looks proper, doesn't he? If only our mother could see—she would faint."

"That was just a bit of fun." I picked at some of the dried blue paint on my palm. "I'll be doing the house, next. I'm only . . . working up to it."

"He showed me your painting of the nurse. It's been some time since I've seen him so passionate."

I turned to replace the lid on the paint tube. "I'm incredibly fortunate he saw it. My own parents didn't notice the article until I circled it in red ink."

Gwen continued to observe the canvases that lay abandoned on the floor, as if they were more than vague shapes of brown and green. "Celia said you've been spending time with Julian."

I was struck still. Had Roland told Celia what we'd discussed? Or had she tumbled to it on her own? "He invited me in after I showed him that." I pointed at my sketch of Braemore, pinned to the easel.

"That, and *you*." Gwen folded her hands in front of her, looking me up and down. "Rather a pretty thing, aren't you? And charming. Anna's clearly besotted."

My defenses rose at once. I might not have been too bold for the other Napiers, but this one seemed to have taken offense to my very presence. "I'm only here to paint," I said.

Gwen's smile didn't waver. "That's right."

There was something oddly threatening in the kind look. I couldn't shake the feeling I was being interrogated. "Forgive me, have I done wrong?"

"Not at all, dear. No, nothing wrong." Gwen finally glanced away and I breathed easier. "As a matter of fact, I'd like to thank you. For accepting his invitation, for taking on the job so ardently. Our family have been through a great deal, but—you should know that despite his faults, Julian has a very soft heart."

My defense melted steadily away.

"We quite worry over Julian," Gwen went on. "He was always a quiet sort; even as he got older, it was difficult for him to be social. It's understandable why he reacted the way he did to his injury. I only wish there was something I could do to help him. He misses so much . . ."

"You seem to have a special bond with your siblings," I said.

"Certainly, but it was only I and Julian in the nursery for some time. I was completely obsessed with him when he was born." She beamed at the memory. "I was sure he'd been brought to the nursery for me to play with, that it was my responsibility to mother him. I suppose I haven't grown out of that."

"I'm sure he appreciates your visits."

She let out a quiet laugh. "Oh, I don't know. We've had a standing date on Thursdays since he was in hospital, but he didn't speak then, so he could hardly protest."

That quickened my curiosity. "Roland mentioned only you visited him."

"My, you know a lot." Gwen tossed her head as though giving in. "Well, in any event, my mother was confined to bed—she died shortly after he was wounded. Roland was frightened to see his brother ill, and Celia . . . too young, I should think."

As the afternoon sun slipped behind a cloud, the room darkened and I folded my arms across my chest. "Poor Julian."

"Yes, poor Julian. I sometimes think that's what he hopes we're all saying over tea."

Roland appeared suddenly in the doorway, setting my heart pacing again. He stumbled towards his sister over the abandoned canvases and palettes, all arms and legs. "Have you spoken with Celia?"

"I have," Gwen answered calmly. "The matter is in hand."

"Is it?"

"Yes, never mind." Gwen turned back to me. Roland took her elbow as if to beg her attention, but she didn't budge.

"It isn't how Celia says," he said.

Gwen put her hand over his. "I know, pet."

"He's improving."

"Yes, thank you. I'm quite caught up now." Then to me: "When will Julian be seeing you again, Miss Preston?"

I had taken a few small steps backwards, searching for an answer in Roland's eyes, but they were fixed on Gwen. Was I meant to deny that he'd asked me to be Wakeford's confidant? We had only discussed keeping it from Celia. Now it seemed Gwen would support our endeavor.

"I had hoped to finish another painting to bring to him," I said.

Gwen tilted her head, still smiling. "I should think he'd like your company."

Roland's eyebrows shot up. "Do you?"

"I do. He said as much." Gwen had the incredible ability to ignore odd glances, or else noticed and simply chose not to acknowledge them. "I'm thrilled you get on with Julian, Miss Preston. You have ever so much in common."

"She's *thrilled*!" echoed Roland, running a hand through his hair with a sarcastic puff of a laugh. Apparently this was not the reaction he was expecting.

Gwen gave him a gentle pat on the back. "There, there, darling."

Meantime, I was poppy red and trying to work out what she wanted me to say. We had so much in common, had we? Did she fancy her brother and I were fit for courting? She couldn't possibly wish to match the earl with a banker's daughter. Still, my mind drifted to the drawing Wakeford had done of me, which I'd stuck in the mirror on my dressing table. I didn't dare hope he felt the same tension as I had, though he had invited me back . . .

It was an intense relief when Gwen gave a resolved sigh. "It's been lovely meeting you, Miss Preston, but I'm afraid I shall have to be off. Roland, may you come and have the motor brought round?"

When they had gone, I turned back to cleaning up Anna's mess, glad for something simple to do with my hands. I'd expected Gwen would have something to say about my befriending Wakeford, but certainly hadn't expected—that. But why else would she have called me pretty and charming if not to weigh my potential as a sweetheart? And Roland was so adamant I knock on his brother's door again . . . I sensed there was a plot, and I one of the pieces which needed to move in a certain direction.

What was more, I felt an ebbing of my good sense, replaced with the image of Wakeford's lips pursed around a cigarette, of his sleeve brushing my bare arm. He had charmed me, with so few words and whilst remaining hidden behind his mask. There was no use denying that my desire for his attention was no longer bound to the fate of my paintings.

I left the mess to escape for a nourishing turn about the garden. But when I reached the Great Hall, I was arrested by a swirl of piano music from above. Anna and Richie stood hand in hand in the center of the room, giggling and dancing to their uncle's concert.

I smiled, but it faded fast. The family had adapted so well to living around Lord Wakeford's trauma. But how great a trauma it must have been for Wakeford to choose solitude over this: the Napiers' warmth and easy tenderness, which had already enchanted me entirely.

It was one thing to acknowledge my affection for Lord Wakeford. It was another to consider what sort of future one might have with such an extraordinary man.

8

On Sunday during breakfast, I decided it was time to write to my parents.

I hardly knew if they expected or even *wanted* a letter from me, but I couldn't help sending one with hope it would be opened. The previous night, I'd dreamt of the lavender hedges that grew in front of my childhood home, of resolving to paint them in my bedroom, only to find the stairs simply had no end. I woke heart heavy with homesickness.

When Huxley came to the table, I glanced up.

"His lordship has taken his breakfast, sir," he said only to Roland.

Roland nodded firmly and accepted the post from Huxley's salver. "Thank you."

These lines were performed each morning, quickly and concisely. Most days the scene ended before Celia came down. On this one, she'd risen early.

"Must he do that every day?" she asked, not looking up from her copy of British *Vogue*.

"Yes," answered Roland plainly, and took up the *Times*.

I returned to decorating my letter with a sketch of the hydrangeas on the table, mind drifting to Wakeford. Did he know how conversation spun around him so often down here? Had anybody bothered to express their worry to the man himself? I'd not stopped thinking about what his conversation with Gwen must have been like to spur such a reaction in her. Had he told her anything about me? Or had she only assumed?

When I was through drawing, Celia had gone and Roland was rubbing his temple, the newspaper concealing all but a squinting pair of eyes above the fold.

"Not bad news, I hope," I said, sealing my envelope.

He sighed and lowered the paper. "Not as yet." When he saw my sketch, he made a humming sound of fascination. "Julian used to do that."

I'd no idea what to say. Luckily, he stood, and I went with him politely. Here was where we would normally part ways—me for the studio, and Roland to vanish, only to be seen again at the next meal. I'd have to speak now. This was the first time I had him alone since meeting Gwen a few days before.

"Might I have a word?"

He hesitated, rocking on his heels. "I've arrangements to make for Freddie's arrival."

Being in my own head, I'd nearly forgot that Fredrick Neil, Roland's closest schoolfellow, was expected this afternoon. "It'll only take a moment."

With a quick nod, he led me out of the dining room to avoid being heard by the footmen who were clearing up. "All is well, I hope?"

"Yes, only I wanted to ask you about what happened with Gwen . . ."

"Ah, that." Roland skewed his face and studied mine for any tells of what I was feeling. "I rushed in because Celia's onto us, and I knew she would have told Gwen. I had hoped to prevent my older sister from discovering our agreement—she tends to make everything her business, you see, and I didn't think she'd approve. Turns out, she's in full support."

"In support of what, precisely?"

Now and again Roland looked entirely his young age of twenty-two, and this was one of those times. "Er, a friendship of sorts. Between you and Julian." I must have said all I needed to in the lift of an eyebrow, for he folded: "Or something else . . . if there's a chance it will help him."

This was my fear, why now it felt like an anvil had appeared on either shoulder. Though I certainly could not deny romantic longings toward Wakeford, I knew it was no remedy for what ailed him.

"I'm happy to be his lordship's friend," I said, "but I cannot mend a broken man with a few polite conversations about art. Why not see him yourself? Tell him how much you care. It may make a world of difference."

Considering this made Roland go slightly pale. His posture unbuttoned itself, and he looked all the more like a fussy child. He was afraid. Afraid to be turned away at Wakeford's door, or perhaps more likely, afraid to be admitted.

"That would do no good." Roland took my hand between his own, palms clammy. "But you've done more than any of us. No need to move mountains; we only want him to cheer a bit. Do you not wish to see him again?"

In fact, I was rather eager to. Wakeford was not the first of intangible men I'd fancied, but he was certainly the most consuming. I'd been completely undone by the idea he might be eager to see me, too. To what end, I couldn't yet say. But there it was.

"I do," I admitted. "But that is not the reason I'm here."

"Of course. You're here to paint, foremost, and we won't forget that."

Driven by either the boy's desperation or my own wretched heart, I conceded with a weak smile. But not before asking Roland why Huxley reported to him each morning in regards to Wakeford's eating habits.

"Because when he doesn't allow Huxley in with his breakfast, I know he's unwell," he answered. "In which case, I must send for Gwen."

I SPENT THE next hours in studio, painting lavender and sketching near the window, too intimidated by the task of much more. Roland had said my paintings were most important, and yet, with our agreement looming over my head, I could hardly concentrate on them. So after a quick bite of lunch, I took to the outdoors.

There was so much of it, from the kitchen gardens, to the parkland, to the lake, to the woodland trail, to the eccentric rock garden, to the infamous folly. The Georgian structure was taller than I expected from a distance, stood on a steep hill overlooking the heath beyond. Peeking through glass doors, I found it was only a single room of checkered marble floors. Odd that Julian was so adamant I not paint it. From the outside it was rather a triumph.

I tried the knob. Locked.

My wander led me back indoors, to the east wing. One felt exponentially more lonesome when idling in one of Braemore's many rooms on one's own. The quiet was too harsh, thick with age, and interrupted only every hour by the clang of a grandfather clock. It was better to move, to accompany oneself with one's own footfalls and the endless wonders of a castle.

As I drew near the end of the corridor, I thought of Wakeford, sitting upstairs alone as he did each day, and wondered again why anybody would choose such a life. For even though his estate was peopled by sister, brother, and servants, it was hardly a lively place. It would not have been impossible for him to go a full day without being seen, if that were his aim, without having to stay stashed away upstairs.

I thought of his face, the half I'd seen, in all its masculine beauty, the swell of the bottom lip, the curve of the nose, the reflection of light on midnight eyes—what an ideal muse for the artist tasked with creating his mask . . .

When my mind swam to the surface, I found myself in a place I'd never been. The room was just beside the Great Hall, carved out of the space beneath the stairs. A marble woman stood at the edge of a fountain pool of mosaic tiles, pouring endlessly from her vase. She was nude, proud breasts exposed. Wild hair fell over one shoulder, wrapping behind and drawn forward over hip and pelvis to hide her sex. Aphrodite, it must have been, with her lips parted, eyelids low, peering down at the pool as though it was her lover. The water rippled, reflecting blue waves across ivory marble and my own skin.

I sat to dip the tips of my fingers in the water and found it to be warm. Under the spell of the marble grotto I prayed silently to Aphrodite.

What is it worth? I asked her. *Is the comfort of love enough to appease mind and soul? Or can one be satisfied by the companionship of personal success alone?*

I looked up at her as though she might answer. Instead, her careful smirk only put me in mind of him.

So I went for my sketchbook, thinking if I didn't have another painting to show Wakeford as promised, I might draw him something to make up for it.

As I stepped up onto the landing, Celia was just coming down. She paused like a soldier spotting a commanding officer, wringing her hands. I could practically see her mind willing her to remember her manners.

"Good afternoon," she said.

"Hello," I answered. "Fine day, is it not?"

We may as well have been two strangers passing in Hyde Park.

She allowed a hollow smile. "Where are you off to?"

I began spinning a lie, until I remembered Celia knew everything. "I have some things to discuss with Lord Wakeford in regards to my next painting."

Celia's hands crept up her arms, gripping at the sleeves of her shawl. "Perhaps you oughtn't."

"Oh?" I was wicked for this, but too curious to know what she'd say. "Why ever not?"

"Well, he . . ." Celia blinked. I wondered for a moment if she could conjure a worthy excuse. "I think you'll find he isn't terribly good company."

If I hadn't known better, I would have thought she was looking for a chuckle. I went along. "Roland's rather busy preparing for his friend's visit, and I haven't got anyone else to talk to."

Celia's dark eyes trailed up the stairs and then down them, as though to ensure we were alone. Then, with caution, she unraveled herself and placed the tips of her delicate fingers on my arm. "Roland's suggested full evening dress tonight. Shall we get ready together? My maid will do your hair, if you like."

This was perhaps the most Celia had ever said to me. I was wrong about her being shy—her voice was clear and confident. And though I was anxious to see Wakeford again, I dared not refuse what could be my only invitation to convince Celia that I wasn't all that bad.

"Sounds like a laugh."

I fetched my dress and went to Celia's bedroom, more than a bit intrigued to enter her closed-off world. It looked like her—feminine with gold and lavender everywhere. Though I had not envisaged it to be so messy. There were magazines and books stacked on the writing desk and bedside tables, shoes kicked off and left without their mates, pots of rouge and lip varnish left open on the dressing table. I wondered if it was today's mess that would be sorted out while she was downstairs, or if this was the natural state in which she lived.

The maid Rebecca was setting out a selection of underthings on Celia's four-poster bed, adding to the mess. She had the anemic look of a domestic who worked indoors and hoped to blend in with her surroundings.

I was instructed to dress behind a folding screen. When I emerged, I felt no more glamorous than I had done before. Silly, really. I was a woman grown, and intimidated by Lady Celia and what she would think of my smartest frock—sleeveless raspberry silk crepe with a hip sash and handkerchief skirt.

Her own gown was surely hand tailored to suit the latest fashion; there was a higher level of couture than the women at home could replicate by adjusting last year's styles. The bodice was celadon taffeta perfectly fit to her figure, flaring out into a tulip skirt of gold lace, carefully adorned with beaded flowers that glittered as she moved.

She lightened as we did a full turn for one another in front of the standing mirror, and laughed at ourselves. It was lovely to see Celia so cheerful. She had a broad, openmouthed smile and an irresistible buoyancy that was infectious.

She approached me to study the dress more closely. "Lovely, isn't it? Perfect for a summer dinner party. I have the most adorable headband you must wear with it."

I couldn't refuse. I felt I was speaking to a new girl.

I sat at the dressing table for Rebecca and was reassured by her mistress that there was simply nobody so keen at doing hair. Rebecca styled my bob with curlers, sculpting tight marcel waves. Then my loaned headband was brought forward, gleaming as Rebecca's delicate hands held it up for me to see. The ribbon matched my gown perfectly, and when fastened in place, a cluster of pearls and diamonds rested just over my brow.

After Celia's hair was styled, the maid was sent off and returned with a carafe of sherry. "Mr. Neil has arrived, my lady."

"Thank you, Rebecca," Celia said. "That'll be all."

When we were alone, Celia plucked the carafe from the tray and sloshed some sherry into a glass, clearly unaccustomed to pouring. I watched, astonished by the sudden change in her. Could this be the girl she truly was? The girl I had not yet been allowed to see?

"Should we not go down and meet him?" I asked.

"Not yet." Celia swallowed some sherry. "The boys take ages to get dressed. They get to prattling and drinking and forget the clock entirely. They're worse than old hens."

I could hardly argue, feeling quite glamorous to be lounging beside Lady Celia on the chaise, the tray between us. We did look rather a pair with our bobs and our long gloves. I'd forgot entirely that I was nearly a decade her senior.

"He must be a special chap, your Freddie," I said. "All this fussing."

"He's our dearest friend," Celia said, toying with her knotted string of pearls. "He and Roland met at Eton, and Freddie has practically lived here since. Apparently his father is a brute."

"Bless him. And who would not prefer Braemore to home?"

Celia's face darkened and she finished her sherry. "When Freddie's here, it almost feels like it used to . . . before the war. I was too young, then, to be included, but I remember peering between the balusters, watching the couples enter in their finest. The band played so loudly that I could hear it in the nursery; I didn't sleep a wink. Gwen and Julian—" She looked away suddenly, then back with a smile. "They used to come to the nursery in the greyness of dawn to look in on me, smelling of cigars and French cologne."

Her sherry glass went down and then her eyes, and I saw the weight of the memory. The Napiers didn't often speak of what they'd lost, but the evidence was plain.

I hadn't yet touched my sherry, so went for a thirsty sip. "What's keeping you and Roland from having a party of your own?"

She chuckled and refilled her glass. "Nobody wants to come here."

"Then why not go to London for the season? Surely Lord Wakeford keeps a town house?"

"He sold it years ago."

"Really? What for?"

"Julian's quite content where he is."

That was true enough. I drank again, glad for the beginnings of a bright tingle behind my eyes. "All the same, if he'd known you and Roland would rather be there . . ."

"He doesn't appreciate we've got opinions on the matter."

I sat back, surrendering. Could it be I'd only been asked here so Celia could convince me of her brother's faults?

Something about all this did not add up. Castle Braemore was once alive with glamour and parties. The war could surely be responsible for robbing it of some things, but couldn't be blamed for all of it. And though I was coming to adore the Napiers, I wondered gravely if they'd be the only ones to see the paintings I hoped would be the catalyst to my career.

Despite Celia's misgivings, the boys were waiting in the drawing room by the time we entered, voices filling the plush space so it was hardly recognizable. A bottle of champagne was opened and standing proudly on the mantel, while the boys were draped over the furniture, two greased heads faced away from the door.

When Celia cleared her throat, they stood clumsily and buttoned their jackets.

Roland looked properly polished in his evening clothes, a white carnation on his lapel. He slapped his hand to his chest as if struck by a bullet, sloshing champagne from his glass. I had the feeling he'd had a few already.

"*Roland!*" Celia laughed. "What a mess!"

"But where is my little sister?" He came closer to take her hand and spin her.

"Grown. It is possible, you know."

"I daresay. Recognize this woman, Fred?"

Freddie had the room's attention then, and didn't seem to be unfamiliar with the spotlight. His suit was slightly loose—a loan from Roland, perhaps—but he wore it confidently, with a scarlet feather pushed through the buttonhole. Bronze hair was combed back in a wave, angled face shaved so close that barely a speck remained to suggest whiskers were possible. His lips were thin but flush, his smile was devious, and his hand was on Roland's shoulder.

"Grown indeed. I do hope you've got a maiden aunt to watch this one." Freddie winked at Celia, then his teal eyes moved to me. "And this must be Miss Preston."

The smile came easily to my lips. "Call me Bertie, Mr. Neil."

He took my outstretched hand. "You may call *me* whatever you like." With a small tug I was close enough for him to kiss each of my cheeks in the French way. "Champagne?"

Roland fetched the bottle, and two more glasses were filled. One of them was put in my hand, and three others were raised.

"To the Braemore artist," said Freddie.

Then Roland: "The Braemore artist!"

I hesitated, forcing a bashful smile. Champagne and I had never really got on. After one particular bubbly evening, my sister had called it *tart potion*: one sip, and all I could think of was finding a man's lap to sit on. I couldn't say she was wrong.

Three sets of eyelashes batted at me, waiting for me to drink first.

I lifted my glass. "Chin-chin, my darlings. Bottoms up."

When in Rome, after all.

A Friend from Eton

DECEMBER 1916

Julian's boots crunched into gravel. He wavered, grinding his heels deeper.

Home.

But there was something not right about it, something not whole. Sharp wind burned his ears and he raised the collar of his greatcoat. Before him, Castle Braemore sat at ease in its centuries-old place, prominent and ostentatious, heavy and weathered, swallowed by the landscape. It looked too tall now. Garish. The griffins bore down on him as a stranger. No little faces peered through the windows. No sound of falling water from the fountain. No birdsong, no motors, no braying horses or barking hounds. The lines around Julian's vision blurred, like a nightmare, like an ill memory, like something was hiding on the periphery.

The car door slammed behind him. Julian's heart stopped. His knees weakened, and momentarily, he could almost taste the gravel between his teeth.

But the gravel remained on the ground, and Julian remained on his feet.

Far away, the driver: "Milord?"

Julian had dropped his cap. The driver plucked it from the ground, swept a gloved hand over the top to scatter the dust. Julian accepted it with a nod.

Inside, the Great Hall was quiet and barren, footmen all gone to war, unused rooms closed. Julian had wanted to offer the house to the Red Cross for use as a convalescent hospital, but his mother had refused. She would not have the ill walking her corridors; she would not have strangers poking about her home. She would not get out of bed for the war.

Roland stood with his hands behind his back. How he'd grown! The last Julian saw him, he'd been the taller man. Now Roland had an inch on him. His brother smiled, his once soft, youthful cheeks carved and freshly shaved—shaving, too!

There was an odd, quiet moment as Roland took him in, the starched uniform, the combed hair, the shined boots. Julian knew there was little about the way he looked now that was reminiscent of who he'd been when he'd left.

"Lieutenant." Roland stamped his shoe and tried a salute. "Damn, you look old."

Julian chuckled and opened his arms. They embraced tightly, in competition to see who was the stronger. Thank God Roland was here, was clean, well-fed, safe.

"Mama?" Julian asked, stepping back.

"Taking a day in bed."

He'd hardly had to ask. "Is Celia hiding from me?"

Roland's face fell. "She's stopping with Auntie Margaret."

Julian handed his coat to the maid. "In Dorset? How long shall she remain?"

"She says until February."

Celia's letters had ceased nearly a year ago. Julian had hoped she wouldn't refuse to see him on his leave, when there was every chance it might be the last. A grim thought, to be sure, but a thought he had often enough, being responsible for a family, an earldom, and a sizable estate.

"I'll call there day after tomorrow," said Julian, tiring at the notion of more travel. "Come along, if you like."

"Is that wise?" Roland's face bent sympathetically. "You know how Celia is. She'll make a scene and Margaret won't spare Mama from the gossip."

The exhaustion of the journey washed over Julian, blurred lines drifting closer to the center of his vision. "Right you are . . ." He managed a twitch of the lip. "I might lie down for an hour. Then I shall have to see about Gwen." His elder sister surely was not faring well, having lost her husband only months ago on the Somme. "We'll speak tonight."

Roland nodded. "Oh—and I've asked a friend from Eton for a few days. Do you mind terribly?"

"No." Julian patted his brother on the shoulder. "This house could do with a livening up."

JULIAN WAS IN Braemore's kitchen gardens, where he'd frequently find her by chance. But it was all wrong. Where there were meant to be cabbages and celery stalks, there were shell holes, twisted wire, and burnt branches like skeletal fingers reaching up from the mud. He pulled one foot out of the slime, released with a sucking sound and a splash up his trousers. Then he lifted the other, only to find the first stuck again. It went on this way until he was so cross with his lack of progress that he cried out.

That's when she appeared, yellow hair blowing across her face, smiling as though all was well and the sun was shining.

The revetment and sandbags of a trench made themselves apparent. He was not in the kitchen gardens at all, and she was a long, long way from home. He threw himself forward to reach her, but remained stuck in the mud, sinking deeper with every breath. When the firing began, he called out to her to go, to leave, please run. Though no sound left his lips, only the feeble whisper of a man left without air. The firing kept on—*bap bap bap!*—and before he could think what to do, green gas engulfed her, and a bullet caught him in the belly.

Julian was shaken awake by the sound of his own voice, a weak, befuddled cry. On the other side of the door was knocking, the knuckle falls causing him to tremble.

He was on the floor; the bed had been too soft. But he'd only meant to shut his eyes for a moment. Sunlight stung Julian's eyes as he sat up to see the clock—nearly half eleven. How, when he'd arrived home late afternoon? His arm hairs raised as he realized the lost time. Julian had slept through the night.

On the other side of the door, Huxley stood straighter than most enlisted men. "Sorry to disturb, your lordship. The dowager countess requests to see you in her rooms."

Julian smoked a cigarette whilst he dressed. Part of the way through, he fell to a seat on the bed. The belt was giving him trouble, and the tie was suffocating, and buttons were great obstacles. He wriggled out of the jacket, leaving it abandoned on the mattress, and loosened his tie. It mattered little to Mama how he looked.

He took the short walk to her bedroom door and knocked.

"Come."

The room was stale and smelled too sweetly of potpourri. The dowager lay in bed, an invalid desk pushed aside. Her face had grown wan since he'd seen her last, her once thick, dark hair gone fine and brittle. She sat up against the headboard with a mountain of pillows behind her, quilt folded over her lap.

Roland stood beside the bed, head bowed. Kicked and scorned.

Julian didn't bother to say hello to his mother, didn't bother telling her he'd had a fine journey home. In return, she didn't bother saying she was glad he was alive.

"What's happened?" he asked.

The dowager looked to Roland and folded her hands. "Tell him, go on." Roland shifted on his feet, but refused to raise his eyes. "Tell your brother what you've done."

Julian's pulse throbbed against his tie. This felt all too familiar—Roland in trouble, and Julian called up to mend things. He thought

Roland had settled since returning to Eton, matured, stopped feeling so much like the world was against him.

But now he saw fear in Roland, cowed by his mother's scorn. So he went to the boy and put a supporting hand on his shoulder. "We'll go and have a word, shall we?"

"No." Mama pressed her hands against the mattress to sit taller. "I want him to tell you the truth, right here, so I know it's plain. Now, Roland. Tell him."

Roland chewed his lip and turned his head to Julian. His cheeks were colorless, eyes wet. "I'm sorry."

"Tell him!" The dowager's shrill voice set Julian's teeth on edge. "Tell him what you were caught doing at the folly with that boy."

"I was—" Roland's head fell again.

Julian gripped his shoulder. "It's all right."

Roland shuddered and wrapped his arms around himself. "I was k-kissing him."

From the bed, a sound of disgust, a glottal gasp that the dowager covered with a handkerchief over her mouth. "My own son—"

Julian hardly thought of the crime. For here was his little brother, terrified and humiliated before their mother. It mattered not what he'd done; Julian would not stand for it.

The dowager recovered from her moment of shock, and dropped the handkerchief from her mouth. "Well? What will you do with him?"

"We'll have a word—"

"You must telephone the doctor immediately—the boy is unwell. This isn't natural behavior, and an end must be put to it directly before anyone else hears of it."

Roland's back convulsed under Julian's hand. He felt the pressure of rage in his temples, in his jaw. "Roland does not require a doctor."

"The constable, then." Their mother's eyes were wild now, her cheeks ruddy with the surge of purpose. "That boy has never been right—how many times have I told you?"

"Enough."

"He's always been a wretched little beast."

"Enough!"

She closed her lips.

Julian hardly recognized his own voice at such a volume. There were times in battle, during drills, where he felt some other man was shouting through his open mouth. Even Roland demurred at the sound. But Julian had done what he'd intended. He'd scared his mother to silence.

"*I* will deal with this," he said.

Her mouth wrinkled, grey lips firm. "You're not fit to deal with this, Julian. You've always been too timid to discipline properly. You allowed him to run rampant as a child, and now look what shame he's brought us! This is your doing—all your doing—you spoil him!"

Julian held Roland closer, forgetting that his mother had ever been young, pretty, anything other than bitter. "If you do not find the way I run this house to your standards, I'm certain your sister Margaret has a spare room for you."

To this, his mother had no reply.

Roland dragged his feet to Julian's apartments. It had been clear since he was a child that something was awry. Roland never fit in his place as second son, never got on properly with other children. Always angry, always pinching his sister, always fighting every rule. Now it made sense. The boy might've been battling himself since he was small, uncomfortable in his skin, thinking himself ill.

Julian sat Roland on the sofa and went to pour himself a drink. He took the pause of a long sip to reorder his thoughts. Though the longer he lingered on the issue at hand, the less he was concerned with the actual *doing* of it, and the more he feared the consequences Roland would face if he was found out.

"Now," Julian began, hearing again the voice of an officer. He tried to be softer when he continued: "Knowing what you say will not affect how I feel about you as my brother, nor how I will regard you as a man—tell me again what has happened."

Roland took a shaking breath, wiping his eyes. "Freddie and I were up at the folly, sitting on the steps. I told him it was safe there." Julian nearly laughed. It had proven time and again to be a failed hiding place. "So I kissed him, and I suppose the groundskeeper saw us."

Julian tried to imagine Roland with another boy, both dressed finely in tailored suits, hot breaths mingling between swollen lips. It wasn't uncommon at a boys' school; Julian remembered the whispers and rumors and naming of names. It was not right, surely? Against the law and against nature, as his mother said. But Roland looked so very innocent.

Julian sat beside him. "Was it the first time you've done this?"

Roland shook his head. "Freddie kissed me at school. And I knew it was wrong, but—" He pivoted to face Julian. "I've never felt anything like it. I've never felt—whole. It was as if the world shifted to spin in the proper direction. Like I'd been wearing my shoes on the wrong feet."

Julian couldn't help but smile. He put his hand on Roland's back.

"Freddie's older, you see," Roland went on. "He's been called up, and he's leaving soon, and I think I might never see him again and I—damn it." His head fell to his hands with a sigh. "I love him."

Julian's first thought was to push the notion aside. In love? At Roland's age? No—he was young, this would pass. The boys would grow up and talk to girls and forget the game they'd played at Braemore when the world was ending.

Then Julian saw a flash of blond hair, a body beneath thin cotton, a wet handprint on the worn boards of the dock. He had been Roland's age when he met Lily—sixteen. He had been in love. Love that was impossible. And there was nothing he could have done to quell it.

When Julian stood to refill his glass, Roland's bloodshot eyes came up. "You won't really send for the doctor, will you?"

"No." Julian poured whisky and downed it in one. "There's nothing wrong with you." Roland's brows withdrew from one another and he sat back into a comfortable seat. Julian refilled the tumbler and put it in his brother's hand. "Take some of that, it'll help."

Roland did, grimacing at the burn. "Why are you so calm?"

Julian looked past him out the window, where the sun, a shock of yellow, pierced the cold greyness of a winter's day. It was warm inside, with the hearth burning. They sat comfortably on plush cushions, above where a hot meal was being prepared for them. What a contrast to war life, which Julian would return to in a week's time. So quiet here in the country.

Though, if he listened, he could still hear the spit of distant machine guns puttering in his ears like a wax cylinder recording that refused to end.

"I lost two thirds of my men on the Somme," Julian said, sitting beside Roland. "Many of them were boys your age—brave, no doubt, but having no place in a war. I watched them die—shredded and broken open in ways one could never imagine. I suppose seeing their lives lost so uselessly has given me perspective. I can hardly be cross with you for loving the wrong person, so long as you're alive and well."

Roland tipped his weight against Julian's shoulder. "Freddie wants me to go with him. He said I'm tall enough; I can lie about my age so we can go together."

Julian pinched Roland's neck hard enough to make the boy wince. Good—he wanted this to linger. "Hear me. You are not to go with him, do you understand?" Roland could hardly nod in his grasp. "I don't care what he or anybody else tells you—you're too young, and you must remain here for your sisters. Promise me."

"I promise—ow!"

"And you and this boy—you stay apart at school. If you want to be together, you'll come here to Braemore. I shall speak to Mama, I'll ensure it's safe for you, but it will not be safe outside these walls. Out there you are a criminal. Is that clear?"

Weaker now: "Yes."

One more long scorn and Julian released Roland's neck. Brought his brother's head roughly towards his face to kiss his curls.

Roland wiped his eyes on his sleeves, and sighed a rattling breath. Julian could see the boy's shock at how rough he'd been. It wasn't like him, truly, but it hadn't felt wrong until after he'd done it. Julian studied his hands, wondering if they'd ever be clean again.

"Thank you," Roland said. Julian looked up. "I shall not soon forget this."

GWEN NUZZLED HER nose against Anna's tummy. The baby shook with choking laughter. Gwen smiled and pulled Anna's dress the rest of the way down, then picked her up from the cradle to bounce on her hip.

"How pretty you are," she said, fluffing the hair at the nape of Anna's neck, long enough now to curl. "Pretty Anna—clever little girl. How are we?"

A quiet knock on the door. She called for the butler to enter, and he put his head in. "Lord Wakeford is downstairs for you, my lady."

A rush of warmth spread through Gwen's body. Julian was home. More importantly, he was safe. She could hardly wait to see him.

As she flew down the stairs, clinging to Anna, she already felt the pull of tears. Julian stood in the hall, accosted by a trio of Richard's setters, weaving in and out between his legs. Gwen couldn't help but think it was just how her husband would look, greeting his hounds.

Julian turned and smiled, hands still brushing over the wiggly dogs' fur. "I know, I'm frightfully late."

Gwen threw her free arm round his neck, with Anna sandwiched between them. One of the dogs barked his protest, and having lost Julian's attention, the three of them scattered.

"Thank God you're all right."

Julian seemed content to be held, said not a word. He smelled of harsh soap and winter air, the wool of his jacket still cold against her face. He was so solid now, so rigid—a man rather than a boy. Was he taller, or did she imagine it?

"I'm sorry," he whispered.

She kissed his cheek and stepped back to inspect him. My—he'd aged. Far older than his years, sunken and creased, the evidence of what he'd seen sketched darkly over what was once boyish charm. His chin was unshaven, the skin beneath his eyes swollen and purple, the rest stretched thinly over cheekbones she'd never known to be distinguished. The exhaustion of war had reduced her brother so severely that Gwen's eyes spilled.

She wiped her face, reminding herself Julian, too, was in mourning. More tears would not help either of them. "They don't feed you enough," she said.

He moved in what might've been a shrug if he'd had the energy. "I missed breakfast."

Gwen shook her head and smoothed Julian's lapel. His attention had caught on the child on her hip, and Anna was quite taken by him. Her gaze was wide, her mouth agape, in a twelve-month-old's stare that could go on all day if there was something pretty to look at.

Julian's eyes shimmered. "She's grown."

"More and more each day. Walking a bit, too."

"Good. That's good. Does she cry much?"

"No—never has. Sleeps like a dream."

"I say . . ."

Anna conjured a babble to make herself known. "Who is that?" Gwen asked her. "Why, is that your uncle Julian? Come to see you? How handsome he is in uniform, hm? Would he like to hold you?"

Julian shook his head, bracing hands into fists. He stepped back, boots clicking on marble. "I'm not, er—my hands are dirty."

"Don't be absurd," she said. "Go on, take her. She'll like your buttons."

Gwen moved the chubby lump of lace off her hip, holding Anna out so Julian had no choice but to scoop her up, cradle her against his chest. As predicted, Anna went for the bronze buttons, shiny and small enough for her to pinch with her newly nimble fingers.

Julian gaped at the boulder of a head like he'd never seen anything like it before. Then he dipped his nose, nuzzling the mess of silken hair. His brows tilted back, and Gwen's throat ached to see pain on her brother's face.

"There, see? Thick as thieves." She patted Julian's cheek, feeling the shift and flex of tense muscles. "She has a terribly good life; I don't mind saying so."

He surrendered a smile. "She's beautiful."

"Isn't she just?"

As they waited for the tea things to be brought, Gwen sat on the sofa with one of the dogs curled at her feet, and Julian paced the drawing room. Lulled by movement, Anna dozed with her head on his shoulder. Gwen watched, not hearing what he whispered to her child, knowing they were words of love.

"Do you know," she said, "you're beginning to resemble Papa."

Julian's eyes flicked to the ceiling cynically.

Gwen chuckled. "Honestly! You have his way of walking."

He shook his head, brushing his cheek against Anna's hair. To the ticking of the mantel clock, they considered the notion. Julian closed his eyes, looking keen to trade places with the slumbering baby. "Celia's in Dorset," he said.

Gwen's precious joy waned. So wrapped up in her grief, she had barely attempted to convince Cece to stay. "I know. I'm sorry."

"How is she?"

"Fickle as ever."

Julian moved for the window, then spun again. "Guinevere—?"

Gwen had not heard her full name used by anybody in years. To hear it from Julian's lips put her on edge. "What is it?"

Anna shifted and Julian began to sway, shushing softly, and cradled her neck with limp fingers. When she settled again, he said, "Roland."

Of course, just when he was beginning to show some promise as a gentleman. "What has he done now?"

"He'll need your help in the coming years."

"What with? Julian, please speak plainly."

"You must love him."

"I do, fiercely. Look; come sit. You're frightening me."

Julian sank beside her, keeping Anna close. "Roland is happy, as I was at an age. You must allow him to be happy. You must prevent him from repeating my mistakes."

Before Gwen could think of how to reply, the butler entered with the tea things. She waited patiently as he poured, wanting so badly to understand what Julian was on about. She saw a fear in him she recognized. She'd seen the look on Richard when last she saw him, as he looked at Anna and realized that his life was terribly fragile.

Alone again, Julian was the first to speak. "Richard said she has eyes like yours."

It was as though he'd seen her thoughts. At the mention of her husband's name, Gwen clean forgot all else they'd been discussing. "He didn't."

"He did. He said she had a mouth like a rosebud." Julian touched Anna's lip with his knuckle. She stirred, but didn't wake.

"You're just saying that to please me."

"I'm not."

Gwen propped her arm on the back of the sofa, attempting to hide her quivering lip with her hand. But the tears came anyway, and once they started, there was naught to be done. Julian produced a handkerchief from his chest pocket and put it in her hand.

Normally, Gwen kept her loss at bay. She distracted herself with the ritual of caring for Anna—washing, changing, naps, and playtime. She hated to think of what life might have been if she had lost Richard before finding her. With Roland at school and Celia growing up, Gwen was hardly needed by her family any longer. Anna's care was all that kept her going.

The house was empty without Richard. It was his, truly, not hers. She felt a stranger now that he was no longer there to warm his side of the bed. A sob shook her ribs.

"I loved him so dearly."

Julian put his free arm around her. "I know."

"He was only just here."

Anna woke, unsettled now her mother was upset. Julian brought her to his shoulder, bouncing her gently, and she calmed again.

"Did you really see him?" Gwen asked, dabbing at her eye. "Before?"

Julian nodded. "After they told us there'd be a push, we went into town for a drink. He'd only just returned from leave, and Anna was all he could speak of."

Gwen reached her arm around Julian's neck and pulled him close. She felt if she let go, if he moved an inch, she would shatter across the floor, irreparable. How had things gone so wrong so quickly? She was meant to have such a marvelous life, she and Richard and Anna. It had taken so long for her to find him and he had been perfect.

"I admired him," said Julian. "He was a better man than I."

Gwen brushed her hand down Anna's hair.

"He would have made a proper father."

They were silent for a moment, and Gwen's head started to spin, her face hot. She leaned away to sit straight, to close her eyes, and willed the sea of rough waves beneath her to calm. Julian touched her shoulder and she turned to smile at him.

"Are you well?" he asked.

"I am, my boy," she answered, and took his hand from her shoulder to set it on her tummy. "As it happens, Richard may have his heir after all."

9

We had an awful lot to drink.

And then we were on the dew-dropped lawn, sliding a skiff over the edge of the fountain to splash down amongst the lilies.

Before that was a blur—small plates of rich food, accompanied by wine, and then mille-feuille, accompanied by coffee and more champagne. In the intervals between food, I learned that Freddie Neil was excruciatingly polite, always in a cloud of smoke from hand-rolled cigarettes, always wearing a bright little something on his person to make him stand out—tonight it was that scarlet feather—the rest of him maintaining the absolutely clean-cut look of a gentleman.

Freddie was Roland's closest friend, easy to see by the way they spoke, bouncing from one topic to another seamlessly, filling in bits of each other's stories. It was clear Freddie had spent a number of school holidays at Castle Braemore. He leaned back in chairs like they belonged to him, stretched out on the rug before the fire like a child, spoke to Huxley as if he were the master of the house, and proposed group activities that always, *always* were accepted as the only thing to do at that very moment.

So after dinner, when he suggested sailing the skiff in the fountain because *If it has never been done in the history of this old place, we must be the first to do it!* nobody could argue.

Certainly not me, completely blotto and sweating in my finest gown. It was a spectacular sight to behold. The night was brilliant, cool but not chilly, with stars twinkling above, dressed in their best for us. We shouted rather than spoke to one another, our voices cutting through the thick summer evening, no concern at all for the lateness of the hour.

The fountain was so immense that the skiff had no trouble riding the ripples of its descent. Roland held it steady while Freddie hopped up on the stone edge, hands out to Celia. Then she was up and stepping onto the boat, falling so inelegantly to a seat that we all burst into hysterics. Next, Roland was helped in, and then it was my turn, though something kept me from taking Freddie's hand.

"I shall remain on dry land, I think," I said.

His eyes, glassy from the gratuitous wine, frowned. "Come, Bertie, you'll never have the chance again."

"I fancy seeing the view from here."

He was eager to get into the boat, so pushed no further. While Roland held on to the edge of the pool, Freddie raised both arms as if balancing on a wire and stepped into the skiff with hardly a wobble. He bowed to his audience of three, and we applauded his feat.

"And now, ladies and gentleman," he said, "we sail to the moon."

I went to sit on Castle Braemore's front steps so that I could see the entire scene play out with the full fountain in view, and the tall hedges aligned behind it.

Would that I had a pencil and paper, for this was surely a moment to be captured. Around they went, shrieking each time they approached the falling water, until the boat began to fill to the brim. There was splashing and flailing as the starboard dipped below the surface, and the bow followed. I couldn't have imagined the pool was so deep, but another few seconds and the skiff was entirely under, leaving Celia, Freddie, and Roland treading water up to their chins, laughing and twirling, not a single mind for the fate of their boat.

Celia was the first to climb out, with a boost from Roland. She collapsed to the flags, shaking her sodden hair. Then, under little more than pale moonlight, the bobbing heads of Freddie and Roland, still in the pool, drew closer. Roland said something I couldn't hear, causing Freddie to burst a laugh. He then placed a hand on either side of Roland's head—I thought to dunk him under the water. Instead he drew Roland's chin up, and kissed him.

I blinked and looked again.

Roland was kissing back, and when he took Freddie's face in his hands, neither could stay afloat, and they sank together, hitched by their mouths.

They came up giggling and coughing, and spilled themselves over the edge and onto the flags beside Celia.

"You're a terrible captain," she said to Freddie, and swatted his arm. "Aren't you meant to sink with the ship?"

But he couldn't answer, for Roland was kissing him again.

Odd, that it should seem so natural. But what I saw—the yearning, the glimmer in Roland's eye, the comfort between two bodies—was as natural, if not more so, than any look of tenderness I'd seen between my parents. It hurt in my heart, too. Because I saw between those two men what I could not imagine for myself.

I remembered my unanswered prayer to Aphrodite and offered another. *Have I given my life so completely to success that I've lost my chance at love?*

Watching them all under the blue moon and amber shifts of light from the house, I was incredibly lonely. Perhaps I didn't belong amongst them. Perhaps there was more to being known than just being introduced as Bertie Preston, the artist. Perhaps one required verve and gumption and no other ambition besides to live.

I stood and went indoors. With such noise, Lord Wakeford was surely not yet asleep.

I filched one of the champagne bottles from the dining room and found two clean glasses. After the stairs, walking in heels became impossible, so I abandoned them in the middle of the corridor. At Wakeford's door, I realized I hadn't a free hand with which to knock, so I used the base of the bottle. Suds erupted from the brim and I slurped them off.

"Good evening! Bertie calling! Are you in, my lord?" I laughed and knocked again. "Of course you're in. That's the thing about you—easy to find as you're forever in the same place."

No answer. But the floorboards creaked on the other side of the door, footfalls heavy and uneven, someone stumbling about the room.

I grew impatient and leaned my shoulder against the door. "Lord Wakeford? You aren't asleep, are you—"

The door opened and I tipped. He caught me, hands modestly placed, and pushed me back onto my feet. It was then he realized I was dressed for a dinner party, and realized it a few more times before finding my eyes.

"Why, hello," I said. "You were asleep, weren't you? Oh, dear." I could tell because he was in shirtsleeves, wrinkled and buttoned in a hurry. One had been missed altogether. I considered what was under the shirt, and how it looked against his satin sheets.

Damn champagne!

Wakeford blinked rapidly in the sudden light. "I wasn't asleep; I'm only deaf in one ear."

I giggled, leaning against the doorjamb. "You can be quite funny."

He stared, rubbing his chin. "Is there something I can help you with, Miss Preston?"

"Oh—yes." I lifted the bottle and the glasses. "I've all this champagne and need someone to share it with."

I began to enter, but he closed the door slightly, blocking me with his really quite striking torso. "You ought to be downstairs."

"Ought I to? I prefer it up here."

"It's very late."

"Or, it's very early. Art is about perspective, my lord. May I come in?"

This time, Wakeford stepped away. On wobbly legs, I bumbled into the room, setting the champagne on the sideboard, where he kept a drinks tray. My nostrils burned with the odor of peat. He'd abandoned a glass of whisky there, the foggy imprint of a lip left behind on cut crystal.

I poured our champagne, and turned to put a glass in Wakeford's hand. But he'd moved to the other side of the room to switch on a standing lamp. He wasn't wearing shoes. I became oddly distracted by the look of his perfectly tailored trouser hems over clean, bare toes. He stood with hand on hip, pushing the other through his tousled hair.

Apparently, he'd nothing to say, though I had plenty.

"Do you play jazz on piano?" I swayed my hips to a tune I hummed. He took the offered glass and set it immediately on his desk. "What's the matter?"

"I cannot drink it," he said.

"Can't or won't?"

"I can't." He pointed to his mask.

"Oh yes, I forgot. I'll turn around, shall I?" I went to the sideboard to pour more and drank—too quickly. It tickled my nose and throat, and I did an unattractive cross between a cough and a laugh.

A warm wall built behind me, and I looked up to find Wakeford, one of his hands on the small of my back. "All right?" he asked.

"Mm." His hand slipped away. Shame. I wanted desperately for it to stay there. So I reached down to take it, and the other. "What say you to a dance? We'll have our own party up here. Is there a gramophone?"

He watched his hands being lifted, eyelashes flickering. "Miss Preston—"

"If you don't go in for jazz, I can waltz. Not well, mind." I put his hand on my waist and set one of mine on his shoulder. Firm, it was, tensing beneath my hold.

Then we moved, mainly because I was stumbling and he had to keep up now we were hitched together. He tried not to smile, full lips drawn in and pressed firmly, but his eye gave him away. That eye! How dare Fritz take the other before I could see the two of them side by side.

"I'm having a much better time now," I said.

His smile deepened.

"Are you cross with me for pushing in?"

He shook his head.

"Are you certain?"

Wakeford's hand slipped up my back, making me shiver. We were suddenly closer, our chests meeting with every breath. My eyes were at the level of his lips, and I could almost taste the blaze of whisky on his breath.

"I'm not cross," he said.

I wasn't sure I'd be able to speak, so distracted by the heat from his body and that curl—the same one—caught over his earlobe. Using one finger, I withdrew the loop and brushed it back. Wakeford's chin fell forward, his exhale hot on my bare shoulder.

"Good," I said. "For I should like us to be friends, my lord."

He tilted his head so his nose touched my temple. "Julian."

"And Bertie."

His voice was low and gruff, but pronounced: "Bertie."

I fell in love with the way his teeth touched when he said my name, the crooked bottom row peeking out from behind his lip. His lip—my *God*, did I want to know what it tasted like. I thought perhaps it was time I stepped away to gain some composure, but Wakeford had a firm hold on me.

"Your siblings throw quite a do," I said. "You really ought to see."

"I see the bills."

The crinkle beside his eye smoothed. This was not another snide remark. That's the thing about quiet people, the thing that could never be said about me. Quiet people don't speak often, so when they do, it truly means something.

His hand fell from my back, and he went to the sideboard, where I'd left the champagne bottle. "I let them have what they like; it keeps them happy."

"A palace in the South of France would keep me happy, but I don't see why you ought to hand me the keys." It made him chuckle. "You spoil them. What for?"

Wakeford thought on his answer, refilling my glass to watch the bubbles deflate before handing it to me. "I don't wish for their lives to pass them by as mine did." A limp smile, and then he sat on the sofa.

I could feel myself wanting to say more, and had to instruct myself mentally, over and over, not to mention Roland. In fact, not to mention kissing at all. Not the kissing in the fountain, nor the kissing I very much wanted to be doing with Julian just now.

In want of distraction, I wandered the room, sipping my drink. "So, what is it you do up here all day? Hermits have odd hobbies, don't they? Have you a mummy collection? A bureau of hair jewelry? A chess set of carved chicken bones?"

Lord Wakeford, bless him, had a laugh. "My chess set is made of ivory, I assure you. Though we have got a mummy."

I turned so fast, champagne spilled over my hand. "You're teasing."

"My father made a hobby of purchasing useless things to impress."

"Where is it?"

Wakeford pushed his spectacles against the bridge of his nose. "Downstairs in the Egypt Room."

Of course there was an Egypt Room. I sat on the back of the settee so that over his shoulder, my legs were at Wakeford's eye level. With his elbow leaning nearby, he wouldn't have to reach far to touch my stocking. Instead, he looked at my face, rather ardently. Fine breeding, really.

"Will you show it to me?" I asked.

Wakeford dropped his chin, silent again. So I moved around to sit beside him. Too close, apparently, for he promptly stood. "It's late."

"Have you an obligation early tomorrow?"

"It isn't proper for you to be here—"

"Nobody knows where I am. They're too drunk to care."

He scratched his whiskers. I was taken by how chaotic he looked, the Earl of Wakeford, with his shirt wrinkled and untucked and buttoned wrong, with his bare toes and his dirty hair not quite lying where it was meant to. The mask was the only thing that looked as it should do—serious brow, stern eye, mouth both at rest and poised.

"You're very kind, Miss Preston," he said finally, "and you're beautiful—"

"Lord, there's a 'but' coming. Let me get my drink." I shot to my feet to pour the last of the fizz, trying not to be distracted by the fact he'd chosen to call me beautiful.

"However, you mustn't feel obliged to engage with me—"

"Obliged?"

Did he know what Roland and I spoke of? Had Gwen told him plain? I gulped champagne; my mouth was thickly coated in the stuff.

"I hired you, I did," he went on, "but you ought to be off painting and enjoying the place, not sitting up here in the dark."

I was relieved he was still ignorant of the scheme, but no less irked. Because the truth was, I'd come up here all on my own this time, in search of the comfort I'd felt the last day we were together.

"I was enjoying myself fine until you turned into stuffy Lord Wakeford." I mimicked his flat tone: "*You mustn't feel obliged to engage with me.* As if it's a chore!"

Leaning against the sideboard, I finished my drink. Lord, I'd had too much. There was nothing to be done about it. I was there and he was there.

We stayed silent for a moment. As he rubbed his chin roughly, I could hear his breath blowing hard against his knuckles. I thought I was about to be scorned, but it was difficult to imagine Wakeford raising his voice. I wouldn't have thought him capable of turning me out, either. Perhaps we'd stand like that all night, tense and breathing.

Then he said, "Sit."

So we did.

I faced Wakeford, though he gazed forward and smoked rather than offer me attention. He only managed half of the cigarette before stamping it out rapidly. "It's just that I don't—" Sighing, he kneaded the top of his leg with his fist. "I don't know what I'm meant to do with you. I'm bloody useless at this."

I smiled. I'd never heard him swear, minced or not. "'This' being?"

I hoped he might say *courting*. Instead: "Getting on with people."

"Oh, I'm not people, my lord," I said, "I'm an artist."

His lordship was a difficult man to read as it was. Having only half of the whole made it nearly impossible. I studied him, thinking by now it would not offend him if I looked closer. The faintest hairline of a white scar crawled out from behind the mask to his chin, parting the whiskers.

"May I paint in your beard?" I asked.

Wakeford's mouth opened as he turned to look at me. "Paint in my . . . beard?"

"You're rather lopsided. I feel it's my duty as an artist."

He wet his lips and ran his knuckles over his beard pensively. "I was clean-shaven when it was made. I hadn't thought of it before."

"Don't you ever look in a mirror?"

"I haven't got one."

I looked about us. Not a single reflective surface, decorative or otherwise. It was odd, in a house such as this one, not to see a single glass. No wonder he didn't want me to draw him—he mightn't have seen himself since before the injury.

"Well, if you're at all attached to the idea of facial hair," I said, "I highly suggest you accept my offer."

"Now?"

I nodded.

It was Wakeford's chance to study me. "Are you not . . . tired?"

"I do so love the way you choose your words." I laughed. "We're *drunk*. I'd never suggest this if I wasn't, and you'd never have told me I'm beautiful if you were dry."

"I haven't been—"

"You were drinking whisky when I came in. I smell it on you. Am I wrong?"

At last, he was amused. "I've never met a woman who talks like you."

"I talk honestly with everyone. Shall I fetch my kit?"

Wakeford thought. I tried to look prettier with a tilt of my head. He nodded.

It took no time at all to pop down to the studio and collect a few things. The gramophone was playing loudly in the drawing room, so I assumed nobody missed me.

When I returned, Wakeford opened quickly after my first knock. In the time I'd been out, he realized he'd missed that button and righted things, though his shirt was left untucked. Despite the balmy evening, he'd lit a fire for extra light. I supposed that at one point, he'd likely had to learn to do it himself.

A wave of secret elation lapped up my legs and over my body. I felt a child again, with permission from our cook to lick the cream-covered spoon, unbeknownst to my elder sisters. My special treat. And now I stood with the earl, in his apartments, and he'd asked me to return, all while everyone else was barred. I liked that he belonged to me in that fleeting moment.

We took all the lamps from the room and brought them round the fire, where we sat close on the rug. Wakeford's eye swept lazily over my palette as I mixed my oils. I fancied his mind was going full pelt. That was the difference between him and me; we had just as many thoughts, but my notions escaped whilst his were withheld.

"I've missed that scent," he said.

I was delighted he'd acknowledged his past without being prompted. "Right. Time to be off with it."

"I'll keep it on."

I glowered. I was hoping to finally get a glimpse at what lay beneath. "Some of these paints are toxic, you know."

"I promise not to eat them." His tone was light, but the look on his face showed a degree of severity I didn't wish to push. Instead, I'd have to lean in close to him, touch his face. We'd have to breathe the same small space of air. I must have gone slack, for he said, "Tired?"

"Not in the least."

Wakeford sat cross-legged, and I upright on my knees. When I gently pressed the pads of my fingers against his chin, he startled, looking up apologetically. Then he let me turn his face towards mine. We met eyes and I smiled. This was how kisses began.

But I released his chin and selected a pointed round brush. I was, after all, a professional. Looking between Wakeford's face and the palette balanced on my forearm, I began.

Though I hadn't painted a beard before, I *had* painted Mrs. Lemm's Yorkshire terrier, so I considered myself capable of capturing the unruly movement of hair and soft variation of color. My wrist trembled at first, until I found I could rest the heel of my hand on the mask without making Wakeford uncomfortable. Before long, I used his shoulder as support, and he didn't seem to mind. I became so lost in the piece that I nearly forgot there was a person attached to it until Wakeford wriggled and scratched his nose.

"How are you faring?" I asked.

Not a blink. He hadn't heard me.

"My lord?"

Brow went up. He turned his head to lend his good ear, so close now that his exhale blew against my hair. I was faced with a taut, slender neck and nearly forgot how to speak. "Will you be needing a break?"

"Thank you, no," he said, voice gritty from disuse. "I'm quite all right."

As I carried on, he closed his eye and planted his hands behind him to lean back. Surely it was impossible to sleep in such a position, but I swear he dozed, or else was completely at peace.

At some stage he stopped flinching when I touched him. At some stage I felt him lean into my hand, almost as though he could feel the light strokes on his own skin and savored them.

I'd finished the mustache and chin first to avoid smearing, then the sparser whiskers that climbed the cheek. Then the last bit, the jaw, where the hair thickened. I wiped my brush clean, and picked up a bit of grey from my palette.

Wakeford eyed it warily. "Surely not."

"You've got a few. We must be accurate." I chuckled and made the finishing strokes. "We ought to have done this in horsehair, you know, as they've done with the brow. Then it would really be something."

"It isn't horsehair," he said.

"Is it not? Yours, then? You certainly have plenty to spare."

Wakeford laughed—a delightfully deep and weathered sound I cherished for its rarity. Then I was through, and sat back on my heels to get the full look. I couldn't help but be proud. If I'd been standing across the room, I'd hardly know it was not real hair. Something about the painted beard lifted the mask to a new likeness, and my chest swelled. I'd always found him handsome, but now there was a truer picture of who he was.

He rather took my breath away.

"How does it look?" Wakeford's lid was heavy, his eye underlined with smudges of fatigue. I felt sorry for keeping him awake, but couldn't regret it.

"Exceptional. However, it's more to do with you than it does me."

Wakeford smiled so wide that the mask raised with the movement in his cheeks. I wanted so badly for him to take it off, to see what all of him looked like when he smiled this way, even if what was on the other side was twisted and ugly.

But it couldn't be ugly. This man was hurt, but he was lovely.

"I'll do, then?" he said.

I nodded, but had to look away from him for a moment. The room spun and my heart pounded—coming down from a night of champagne. Through a crack in the curtains, I spotted grey light. "The sun's come up."

I stood to shake the pins and needles from my feet. At the window I saw that Freddie and Roland had slept beneath the stars, wrapped together in a tartan blanket on the front lawn, two heads popping out and touching at the temple.

The floor creaked as Wakeford approached from behind. I turned to stop him, but he put a hand on my arm to guide me away. Cool dawn light caught on his eye as I waited for shock.

"They're safe here," he said. "I must ask you not to speak of it."

"Of course. But you knew?"

He nodded.

I looked again at Roland, feeling the same tug in my belly from earlier. They'd such affection, they two, such familiarity. The longer I stared, the more my skin began to itch with a dull ache to be closer to Wakeford. Though we'd behaved, mostly, and kept our distance, I felt closer to him than any of the men I'd been physical with.

It took every ounce of my willpower not to fall into Wakeford's arms, not knowing if he'd catch me.

"I'll let you sleep," I said. "The paint will take a day or two to dry."

Wakeford walked me to the door, and as he opened it, a sharp intake of breath made me pause. He cleared his throat and said, "Thank you."

"I should be thanking you, surely. For enduring me."

He reached out to my shoulder, plucking a white fluff that was caught on my dress, probably from Celia's ostrich feather fan. With it pinched between two fingers, he dropped his hand into his pocket. "I fear I might have frightened you off earlier."

"I don't scare easily," I replied.

He looked down and up, stirring my blood. "I'm glad."

Wakeford removed his hand from his pocket and stretched his fingers, skimming them over my knuckles as if testing the temperature of steaming bathwater. Then he scooped my hand into his, pressing his thumb against my palm.

When our hands fell apart, it was like they'd been severed.

"Good night, Bertie," he said.

"Good morning, Julian."

10

I woke late in the afternoon, still in my dinner clothes. As I lay in the warm light peeking through the curtains, pieces of my memory slid slowly into place.

The champagne. The skiff. The kiss. Dancing with Lord Wakeford.

I cringed at how I must have looked dripping through his door with an open bottle of champagne at an hour. But he had allowed me in. He had invited me back.

He had asked me to call him Julian.

I smiled as the memory grew clearer—Wakeford sat contentedly beside me, his warm cheek in the palm of my hand, his lips so near I could match the color. It was easy to wander further, past reality to what might have been. Strong hands on my waist, arms lowering me to the carpet beside the hearth, the bristle of whiskers on my chin . . .

In my mind, Wakeford's face flickered to mist, for I'd no notion how he looked behind the mask. Still, I enjoyed the fantasy, wishing either of us had had the courage. But could it be he wanted the same thing? I touched my shoulder, remembering how he plucked the wayward fluff from my dress, so carefully as not to make contact.

But then. Then he had held my hand—hadn't he? I lifted my palm to study it for a change. For surely it would never be the same.

Oh, but it was impossible! No matter what Gwen had in mind, Wakeford was a nobleman, I a commoner. My residency would last until the end of August, when I would leave, job well done. A job that I needed to make a name for myself, to take a room of my own in London. That was why I had come. That was what had been worth leaving my home behind.

I resolved to keep away from Lord Wakeford's apartments until I had some real work done. I'd been so easily enticed by the expansiveness of Castle Braemore and the electric people who called it home that I'd forgot my purpose.

NOTHING WAS LEFT standing in the way of my work apart from Freddie Neil and his wistful ideas. Over the next few days, I was invited on each of his schemes, including his suggestion of a bathe one morning—in the lake, this time. There was no turning him down.

I changed into one of Gwen's old bathing costumes (Celia's wouldn't have begun to fit), and tied a satin scarf over my hair before fetching my sketchbook. Now I could at least proceed to the lake with intentions of working.

Some of the overgrown brush had been cut away since I was here last, the muddy bank draped with rugs to sit on. Freddie lay out, bathing costume rolled down to his waist so his bare chest glistened in the sun. Roland sat beside him with a book, wearing his costume properly across his shoulders.

Freddie lowered tinted spectacles to watch me as I sat on the cool bank to sharpen my pencil. "What dedication you have, Bertie, bringing your work to playtime."

"I can draw you, if you like," I said, flipping open my book. "I *am* trying to improve my understanding of the human anatomy."

"I'll gladly pose nude, but I daresay our darling Cece would never recover."

Celia chimed from behind her novel: "I most certainly would not."

Since our time together in her room, she had vanished less frequently during the day, though was not yet completely at ease when I was near.

When everyone was settled again, I began my sketch. I believed in a keen eye, in seeing the world and being taken by it, in following the muse where she led. And today, despite the immaculate sky, the perfectly still water of the lake, and the castle towering on its hill, I knew what I must capture about this moment.

It was the way Roland and Freddie regarded one another with physical ease. When I'd been with men, it was always quickly and desperately, in an act that had more to do with needing than longing. That was how I knew what these men had was more than just a drunken kiss in a fountain. I knew because Freddie lay with his bare chest angled towards Roland, so subtly that one would easily miss it if not looking closely. One hairy knee bent and crossed over the other to form an arrow pointing to Roland as if to say, *This one is mine.* One arm was folded under his head whilst the other stretched behind Roland, not touching but only every few minutes, a tap-tap of his fingers on Roland's spine.

Roland, in turn, was less obvious about his affection. Each time he was tapped, he turned the page of his book and looked down at Freddie, smiling, and every so often gave him the slightest nudge with his hip, growing closer and closer until they were flush.

I noticed a long, uneven scar that ran down Freddie's leg, wondering if it was a war wound. As I began to sketch it in, Freddie hopped to his feet, pulling Roland's arm until he was up, book fallen to the ground. They raced to the water on skinny legs, pale bodies shimmering as they rose from the plunge.

I was so enthralled, I forgot I wasn't alone. When I noticed Celia's presence behind me, I closed my book.

"That's lovely," she said.

Seeing she had no negative reaction to the drawing, I opened the book again, and let her take a closer look. "I'm nosy; it's a terrible habit."

She smiled and moved closer beside me. "They do love one another.

I used to think—well, how is it possible? That isn't how it's meant to be. But it's there, isn't it?"

I nodded, taken by her modest wisdom. "How long have you known?"

Celia raised her hand over her eyes, and watched the boys. Freddie jumped up to press his hands on Roland's shoulders, dunking him under the water. Then he was under, too. Another second and they shot back up in a tangle of arms.

"He hid it until he was sixteen," Celia said. "They tried to hide it from me much longer, but by then I knew. I've spent the most time with Roland." My face must have appeared puzzled, for she tilted her head and asked, "Are we not what you expected?"

"If I'm honest, I couldn't think what to expect," I said. "I suppose I had a vision of grace and nobility."

Celia tossed her head back. "Grace isn't something we're known for. Oddity, more like. It's our oddity that killed my mother, or so says Gwen. Mama worshipped Queen Victoria; she had such an idea of how things were meant to be, and none of us managed to fulfill it."

"She knew about Roland?"

Celia nodded. "She thought he was ill."

Lady Wakeford was so seldom mentioned, I leapt at the opportunity. "Were you close with your mother?"

Celia plucked a fallen twig and turned it over in her hands. "Gwen says Mama hadn't wanted to be pregnant again, and so her confinement was miserable. She refused to see me when I was born. But my sister was there. She didn't like our governess."

It struck me how plainly Celia spoke of something that should have been heart-wrenching. It spoke volumes of the love her siblings gave her.

"Gwen seems to have mothered you all," I said.

"All she's ever hoped to be is a mother." She tossed the twig absently. "That's why she took Anna on."

Down in the lake Freddie let out a cackle while Roland stood on the edge of the dock, speaking with wide gestures though the wind carried his voice away. I looked back to Celia, wondering if the distraction led me to mishear. "Took her on, did you say?"

"I suppose you wouldn't have been told," Celia said distantly. "Anna was adopted."

The back of my neck bristled. How strange. I couldn't imagine noble families were in the habit of adopting—not when there were pure and ancient bloodlines to look after. Gwen must have been truly desperate for a child. I admired her all the more.

"And Richie?"

"Richie is hers. She'd abandoned hope of having children of her own when she adopted Anna, and a year later, she was pregnant. Funny thing."

Funny, indeed. Roland was not the only Napier with an oddity. They each had something the world would say made them different, and therefore wrong. Here was one of the most prominent families in Britain, finding Roland's behavior quite normal, for the other brother was a recluse, and the eldest had adopted an orphan girl into a noble family.

Poor Celia was still young but had, though by no fault of her own, an already spoiled reputation. Could this be why she was so sullen? Could she only hope for a future of isolation?

"Did you know Anna's parents?" I asked.

Celia pressed her hands together between knobby knees. "She came from a mother and baby home. Gwen said adopters aren't allowed to meet the mother. I reckon the father must have been a soldier, don't you?"

I nodded gravely. It was not an uncommon story. There were war babies all over England, born of desperate love and left fatherless.

Now Celia chuckled to herself. "Gwen's got her hands full now, so she's all but given up on the rest of us. Well, not Julian . . ."

My stomach tightened at the sound of his name, so rare from her lips. "Do you ever see him?"

Celia pushed her damp fringe off of her forehead. "I don't wish to see him. We don't get on."

Did I dare ask? How simple a question it would be: *What happened between you?* But I couldn't manage it. I felt I was teetering on the edge of something, one too many questions, and I'd plunge to the ground.

"So now you know why we don't have parties or go to London." Celia smiled. "We're good as dead to society."

I found little humor in that myself. "Because of Lord Wakeford?"

"He's certainly done his bit." Celia folded her legs and dusted off her hands. "But between the three of them, it's difficult to say which scandal tipped the scales. In any case, you won't see *Napier* on another guest list. We're finished."

When she stood, I went along, a bead of sweat trickling down my spine. "Truly?"

"Have you changed your mind about us, Bertie?"

"No . . ."

"Do let's join the boys, then. It's stifling."

She didn't wait for me, skipping to the water. The boys welcomed her with a lot of splashing and laughter. I remained paralyzed by the weight of Celia's words. *Dead to society.* Each of them. With Lord Wakeford in the lead.

No wonder he had hired an obscure young woman with a prize ribbon. Surely nobody else would dare risk their reputation by accepting his commission.

My opinion hadn't changed. Their blunders were hardly something at which to turn up a nose. If anything, I cherished them for their truths.

But something was still itching like a rash in a hard-to-reach place.

I had come to Braemore not to make friends, nor to get wrapped up in romance. I'd come to make a name. I wanted more commissions. I wanted my work to be hung in galleries. I wanted people to see my paintings long after I died, to be known to those who could afford fine art.

All along, I'd dreamt of the time after Braemore, of more commissions from Wakeford's friends, and money enough to move to London. Now I knew there would be no recommendation, not even if he revered my work. When I left at the end of August, I'd be richer, true, but I would be returning to the same obscurity I'd known all along.

With this new information, I felt a fire light under me, and stood to retreat to my studio. If I was to leave Braemore with no further prospects, I would have to make the best of my time whilst I was here.

MIMICKING THE COLORS of the lawn and trees would be easy with large windows as portals to the garden. But painting Castle Braemore itself could not be done from memory. My sketch from weeks ago was not as detailed as I'd need, and the photographs Roland had dug up for me didn't show the marvelous variations of color in limestone and gold.

In the end, I resolved to paint en plein air. I started for the outdoors, struggling with the folded easel under one arm and a canvas under the other, until Huxley spotted me and insisted he send footmen to do the rest. I argued best I could—*No, really, they've their own jobs to do!*—but Huxley insisted, and since I was in danger of dropping all of it down the stairs, I gave in.

I stood on the lawn as they brought my studio to me. In minutes, my easel was erected, the canvas was set gingerly in place, and I was brought the paint tubes I'd set aside, my brushes, my knives, my palette, as well as a chair and table. I was then asked if I'd like refreshment. I could've done with a cup of tea, but declined. I did not wish to delay.

It was beautiful weather: a cloudless sky, a slight breeze, warm, but not stifling. With a parasol on my shoulder to block the harshness of the light, I took my time mixing colors, approaching the house, then stepping away, looking at angles and details close up. All the while I felt I was being watched, perhaps by the earl himself from his window. It was a relief to know he could not see precisely what I was doing. Still, the awareness of his omniscient presence did put a wobble in my wrist as I lifted my brush.

The first strokes came easier than expected. I mapped the composition with major lines, deciding where to draw the eye—Castle Braemore, of course—with dome surrounded by wispy clouds. My first stroke of color came at the top, sky of ultramarine blue, cobalt teal, and white to achieve the right hue. I added a few strokes where the house would be, leaving the detail for later. I wasn't practiced in capturing the elements of elaborate architecture. Julian had seen my work—the somewhat shaky, blurred-lined style of a dream or faint memory. I could only hope that the style translated to this piece in a way he liked.

Adding burnt sienna to saturate my colors, I created depth between parkland and hill, sweeping down towards the lake in the foreground. In the midst, someone else took over, a ghostly figure leading my brush where it was meant to go. My head became light, drunk with the scent of oil and solvent, still in the summer heat. I mixed colors directly on the canvas, thick with pigment for impasto effect. I was covered in paint from knuckles to elbow by the time I'd finished blocking in the foreground, at which point Huxley brought me a tray of lemonade.

I wiped my brow, slick with perspiration. The cold drink gave me pause to view my work, and I saw what I hadn't realized before: I had what I needed. It was a vague, muddled starting point, but there would be more detail work once the paint had a chance to seize. I'd done what I could here, and if I had any hope of presenting something to Wakeford, I would have to put the brush down and be satisfied.

Whilst giving the paint two days to dry, I returned to my place on the lawn for a pencil study. With my original drawing to reference, I worked more slowly this time, using graphites of varying grades to reinforce detail I hadn't managed before, more than an hour of work, which I knew would be worth it.

I waited out a day of fog and rain, and was pleasantly granted the perfect clear sky the following afternoon. Setting up my easel on the lawn, I was giddy with nerves, dropping brushes and forgetting the tube of burnt umber altogether. When I had my head on straight, it was time for the precise, careful work that would complete the project.

I began brightening the intensity of the sky. Using an angled brush, I flicked in shadows to communicate texture in trees and lawn, then redefined the edges of the house itself, standing out with colors unique to the background or foreground. There was an impossible amount of texture on the house's facade—the aged stones, the Roman pilasters, arched windows, and exuberant carvings. I translated what I could of the decoration, enough to do justice to its splendor.

I let the painting dry again overnight, returning for the final time, eager to add more saturated color and the final details. I mixed my own greens to bring the lawn to life, then switched to a fan brush to add highlight in the grass. I took cadmium yellow on a soft pointed brush for sunlight on the trees, thin sketches of light blue across the lake to show movement. I returned to darker colors to redefine the edges and texture I'd lost. And finally, with a shaking, exhausted breath, I added the pinpricks of white across the heath in the foreground. I'd seen daisies there, growing as far as the eye could see.

I'd lost days inside the small world of the painting, an eternity if I considered the first, anxious strokes, mere jagged lines on canvas. My back and neck strained; my wrist trembled. Good pain, I noted proudly, for it meant that I'd given myself entirely to the work.

I stepped away, kneading the ache in my palm. Finished, at last.

It was not perfect—it wasn't a photograph. But that was the beauty. I'd captured Castle Braemore not as it was, but how I would remember it.

A tear streamed down my cheek, and I pushed it away. This was the finest thing I'd yet to create and I was proud. I hadn't been aware I was capable of such a feat until I'd put myself to the challenge. Seeing it on the lawn of Castle Braemore with the house behind it, the birds chirping above, the sun streaking through trees like twinkling diamonds, I felt a serene sense of accomplishment, and the feeling that here was where it would all begin.

I deserved to be here. I deserved to be seen.

I'D EXPECTED TO fall asleep quickly that night, the coil of anxiety around my heart having been released by finishing the painting. But as I lay in my bed—it was too easy to call it *mine* now—I couldn't forget my conversation with Celia only days ago.

We're finished . . .

My painting of Castle Braemore should have been the beginning of my career, but it very well could be an end. The way Celia spoke of them, her peers were petty—they'd shunned Gwen for taking in an orphaned child, they'd scoffed at Wakeford for war wounds. I didn't want to think of what they said about Roland. And what would they think of me if word got out that I'd accepted payment from the ill-reputed Lord Wakeford?

I could keep it a secret, of course, though that would land me right where I'd started, with no recognition at all. And did I want to pretend I'd never come here? Deny these people who had accepted me so instantly, had been my greatest allies? Roland had encouraged me, allowed me to paint him, told me his secrets. Begged for me to help his poor brother. Wakeford saw my talent, I knew he did, even if his decision to hire me was influenced by circumstance.

Compassion and empathy. Perhaps I didn't have them at all.

Nothing could be done about it now. I would start again, this time with the funds I needed for supplies and independence. More people would see my talents, once I had the chance to show them. It wasn't a leap forward, perhaps, but a half step, and in the right direction. I still had weeks ahead of me at Castle Braemore, to drink champagne, to dance, to paint, and to see Lord Wakeford . . .

No, *Julian*. With his dusky eye and strong hands and lopsided grin. A man I could see myself falling for.

Then why did I feel such a burdensome grip of dread? I rolled over in bed and pinched my eyes shut, remembering my mother's face as I marched from the dining room. I'd never admit to myself that she was right, but a small part of me flirted with regret.

From the hall, an anguished cry made me sit straight up.

With every muscle painfully stiff, I held my breath and listened for voices, for a struggle. I had never been afraid at Braemore before. Then it came again—a man shouting, followed by the thunderous crash of broken pottery.

Wakeford . . .

It wasn't a cry of fear after all. There was no startle in it. Instead, it sounded as if he was trying to clear something from himself with the release of sound. Over and over, until his voice went raw.

I threw the quilt off and stood, pausing at the door as the shouting continued. I had the instinct to dash out, to see what the problem was, to offer help. But after a moment, I came to my senses. What could I do? His door would be locked, and if opened, how would he react to me when in such a state? I was reminded of an evening on night duty when I'd taken a hit from a patient whilst trying to subdue him during a terror. I could still feel the sting of his knuckles on my cheek. It was better to stay in my room.

The shouting went on, three, four more growls before another, much quieter. Quieter again, and then all faded to silence.

Still shaken, I slowly opened the door to look out. Nobody was coming or moving about—neither Celia nor Roland—if either had heard.

I went to my dressing table, plucking Julian's drawing of me from the mirror, and retreated to my bed. I rested it against the lamp and wrapped myself in the quilt, willing myself to remember the quiet, subdued nature he'd displayed that day. My temples throbbed as I tried to forget the hideous sound, imagining how Lord Wakeford looked as the fit consumed him.

Little Birdie

AUGUST 1909

Mama had charged Gwen with finding Julian. As earl, he was meant to give a speech. Papa had done it every year during their annual garden party for the staff, to thank them for their work, to kick off the sack races and cricket and eating of cake. Julian had managed to avoid this duty for the six years he'd had the title. Now that he was old enough, he ought to start acting more like his father. That was what Mama said, anyhow. Gwen thought their father had been too arrogant when he was alive, too loud, too brash towards Julian. Though she'd never say as much to Mama.

So Gwen tramped down from the house to the lake, where she guessed he'd be. Julian was always somewhere odd. He was introverted with a wandering mind. She supposed whatever was going on within him was more exciting than what was going on about him. Though he was rarely frank, so she was unsure of what precisely drove his character inwards.

By the time she reached the bank, Gwen was sweating, and annoyed to be in the sun. But she'd found Julian, bareheaded beneath his favorite wych elm. He pushed Celia gently in the swing as she kicked new shoes over the lake, belly laughing as she willed Julian to push higher. One slip and she'd be in, lace dress ruined, face tearstained.

"I'm not sure that's a good idea, little lady," Gwen said.

Julian caught the swing's ropes, one of his long hands over each of Celia's small ones. She came to a gentle pause, whining as he lifted her from the seat and set her gently on the ground.

He didn't say a thing, of course, so Gwen spoke again. "Mama says it's time for your speech. All are wondering where you've gone to."

"Nobody's noticed I'm gone," he said.

"Julian's been hiding." Celia always betrayed him in the end, too addicted to the rush of telling a secret. When he dangled his head, she skewed her face. "Sorry, pal."

Julian patted her shoulder. "That's all right, pal."

The two of them had the same round, porcelain face, Julian's still full from youth, and Celia's not yet chiseled into a woman's. She was much attached to him and he doted on her. Where Julian went, Celia was surely underfoot, knowing their precious time together would eventually be interrupted by his first term at Oxford. She didn't like that idea one bit, and neither was Gwen overly fond. She thought boys ought to be taught at home, where they had someone to look after them properly.

"Where is your jacket?" Gwen asked Julian, pulling him closer to unroll his sleeves. Wouldn't do to have him stand before his staff so rumpled. "Please say it isn't lying on a mound of dirt."

"Hung from a tree branch."

"Oh, delightful." She rolled her eyes, making him chuckle. "Yes, I suppose it's funny, isn't it? *You* are meant to be Lord Wakeford, not I. Yet somehow I'm the one relied upon to ensure this event is a success."

"You'd make the better earl," said Julian.

"Without a doubt." She straightened his cravat. "There. Presentable enough, I reckon. They won't have too much of a go at you over their dinner tonight."

"I've given them beer and an afternoon off. They don't give a fig what I have to say about it."

Gwen sighed. He was entirely right, of course. She'd seen the glazed faces of the maids and footmen and upper servants as their father made his speeches. They'd heard it all before. But she couldn't allow Julian to know she agreed. Some duties must be done, no matter how unpleasant.

"It's only a few words," she said. "It will hardly be the death of you."

Julian's mouth rounded. His sun-kissed face lost all color in an instant. There was nothing, not a single thing in the world he feared more than speaking. Gwen thought it absurd. He was the *Earl of Wakeford*. She'd heard the blessed butler say more words than Julian.

She gave his shoulder a rub. "Shall we go up? Get it done with?"

He silently gave in, snatching his jacket from the tree branch. With Celia holding their hands between them, they returned to the party, where nobody noticed Julian had been absent.

Of course. Right again.

Mama called the attention of those present. Julian climbed the front steps to make himself seen, as Papa used to do. A hush blew over the small crowd, and Gwen lifted Celia onto her hip so she could see her brother. He looked a man up there, broad shoulders back and straight. A stone clogged her throat.

"Is Julian breathing?" Celia whispered.

He had gone rather pink, poor thing. It churned Gwen's stomach to see him so frightened. "Give him a wave," she told Celia. "Go on, do."

Celia jostled her little hand in the air. Julian spotted her and smiled, all else forgot. It was then he mustered some courage and returned his attention to the staff.

"Thank you all for—for joining us today." His voice projected quite naturally; a fine start. "I cannot begin to express my gratitude . . . for each of you and what you do for us—er, our family. Some of you have raised us; some of you have—have grown with us. Castle Braemore cannot run without its staff. Each of you. And, in turn, it—erm . . ."

Julian's neck convulsed and he rolled his shoulders uncomfortably. Gwen held her breath. His pause, which lasted only seconds, felt an hour.

"Braemore is not a home without you," Julian pushed out weakly. "All of you, who have become members of our family."

This time when he lulled, applause began from the crowd. Lily clapped loudly, hands raised, and it got the rest of them going. Julian forced a smile and nodded his head.

"We welcome you to enjoy as much beer and cake as you can stomach," he said. "After all, you were the ones who spent all week preparing them."

A rumble of laughter, and more applause. When the crowd began to disperse, Gwen saw Julian's shoulders rest, the burden lifted. He'd only have to do it every summer until he was dead, and most Christmases.

Celia wriggled in Gwen's arms. "Mayn't I have cake now?"

Gwen let her down and straightened her hat. "Off you go. And find Roland?" She'd not seen him since the cricket began—the little troublemaker. Their governess was a hopeless woman.

Gwen expected Julian to meet her following his speech, but instead he lingered near the steps until Lily approached. She looked pretty in her Sunday best, yellow hair pinned into a bun, straw hat embellished with a blue ribbon. Julian removed his hands from his pockets and clasped them behind his back, a confident rise in his chest.

Oh, dear.

But he had promised Gwen there was nothing there! And she asked him frequently enough if anything had come about, if she ought to have Mrs. Burns give the girl a dressing-down to remind her of her place. Julian had insisted there was no need.

They walked for a few paces together, making towards the gate of the kitchen gardens. Gwen had every impulse to follow them, but wasn't sure she could stay hidden. She tried to reassure herself: Julian was just being polite. Lily was thanking him for his kind words. She was calling him *milord* as was proper. And he was not flirting. Not Julian. Julian was certainly too shy to flirt.

Too shy, Gwen thought, to flirt with daughters of nobility. With Lily, however . . . ?

Gwen strode to the tea tent and found Celia stood at the table, pawing cake into her mouth with her fingers. Goodness, who had taught her such barbarous behavior? Her brothers, certainly. She snatched Celia's wrist to avoid getting sugar on her own hands, and pulled her aside.

"Would you like to play a game, Cece?"

Celia nodded, mouth full.

"Splendid. It's called little birdie."

While Gwen wiped Celia's fingers with a napkin, she explained to her the rules, which involved following Julian and Lily into the kitchen gardens. If she was spotted, she'd lose the game. If she returned without being seen, she'd get a brand-new box of sweets all her own. Celia agreed without second thoughts.

Watching her run off, Gwen felt a twinge of guilt. But she knew certainly that Julian had begun to rise earlier to wait in the drawing room for Lily to sweep the carpet and clear the hearth. She knew certainly that they chatted on Sundays after chapel, walking rather too close to one another for the whole parish to see. She knew certainly that Julian was intimidated by the girls of his set, and that Lily was kind and knew just how to get a conversation under way.

It was perhaps ten minutes before Julian and Lily returned from the gardens, abruptly parting ways. Then Celia skipped out, holding her hat. She found Gwen waiting on a bench, and sat down, panting from the run.

"All right, then," Gwen said. "What did you see, little birdie?"

Celia wiped her ruddy cheeks and took a deep breath. "Julian and Lily walked about the garden, but they were talking softly, so I didn't hear. There was a bee, and Julian shooed it off. Lily dropped her hat . . ."

"What else?"

"That's all."

"That's all?"

"This game is boring."

"They didn't, er . . ." Here was the trouble of asking a six-year-old to spy on a potential entanglement. Celia had been born after their father's death, never having seen her parents kiss. "Did they embrace? Or take hands?"

Celia shook her head. "I thought Julian ought to have offered his elbow. That's what gentlemen are meant to do, isn't it?"

"Yes." Gwen relaxed into her seat. She was strangely disappointed, guilty for suspecting Julian might have been so imprudent. Perhaps it *was* just talking, and Lily was one of the few people he felt comfortable with.

"Shall I have my sweets tomorrow?" asked Celia.

"Only if you promise not to tell Julian about our game."

"I promise." But she would, in time. Celia was not talented at keeping a secret.

"Then you shall have your sweets." Gwen smiled and set her free.

Gwen rose with intent to ensure Huxley and Mrs. Burns were enjoying themselves, when her mother came sweeping over the lawn. The dowager floated like a specter, her face entirely hidden by a wide-brimmed hat, chosen to shield her from the sun and from the company. She stopped short, pursing her lips at Gwen.

"You've dirt on your dress," she said.

Gwen looked down. It wasn't dirt; it was cake. She tried to brush it away, but only made the smudge worse.

Mama opened her fan with a flick, and waved it at her neck. "I must retire; it's far too hot for me in the sun."

"Have you seen the children today?" Gwen asked.

Music began near the tea tent, arresting Mama's attention. "Must there be a fiddle?"

"They'd like to see you."

Mama turned so her disinterest was visible under the hat's brim. "I'm not sure we'll do this again."

"The picnic? We have always done it."

"It was your father's ritual. Julian would rather not."

Gwen began to sweat again, dampening her lace gloves. "That isn't true. He just isn't keen to make speeches."

"They shall never respect him the way he behaves." She adjusted Gwen's necklace with long, ivory fingers. "It would be best to keep everybody in their proper place."

"The way he behaves—?"

"Julian is not suited for this; he's much too timid."

"He's young. Very young—"

"Oh, it's *hot*."

Mama began to move away, but Gwen lifted her skirt and caught her up. "Julian is doing his best, Mama. He's doing, I think, rather well."

The dowager came to a halt with a ballerina's delicacy, and closed her fan against her palm. "Why have you yet to marry, Guinevere? Hm?" She waited just long enough that Gwen thought she might expect an answer. "You would do well to worry less about your brother when you have pressing concerns of your own."

Gwen stood defeated as her mother drifted off, not bothering to acknowledge the servants who stepped out of her way with a polite *your ladyship*. She found the stain again and it seemed to have grown, sullying her white gown, making her feel as pitiful as she looked. When she righted herself, Julian was emerging from the marquee with the children, and Mama passed them without a single glance.

Gwen's own concerns could be damned. If she didn't worry about Julian, no one would.

She wiped a wayward tear as he spotted her and smiled. He said something to Celia and released her hand, sending her running in Gwen's direction, Roland close at her heels. She crashed straight into Gwen's legs, nearly toppling them both.

"Julian said I may have as much cake as I like!" Celia licked her sweet thumb, the other arm wrapped round Gwen's waist.

"Did he?" She found her handkerchief and shook it out. "What a fine brother you've got."

"I've got two." Celia pointed to Roland, who gave her a pinch on the arm as Gwen wiped her cheeks. By then, she'd learned to giggle instead of cry.

Gwen yanked on Roland's ear, and he shoved her off with a smile of missing teeth.

"Bully," he said.

She winked. "Pot calling the kettle black."

Julian arrived, handing one of his plates to Gwen. She accepted, though she wasn't eating cake any longer; she was tired of asking Lily to let out her gowns. Julian must have been able to tell she was out of sorts, for he bumped his shoulder against hers.

"What's this? Gwen is down in the mouth?" he said. "Chin up, pal."

She did as she was bid, hugging Celia to her, and attempted to move past Mama's words. It occurred to her then that Castle Braemore would never be what it was when Papa was alive. Mama would make a puppet of Julian until the house no longer ran in his quiet, liberal way. Gwen would have to ensure everyone remembered who they were.

Perhaps it was fine that no man would take her. For what disasters would befall her family if she married and left them all to their own?

11

Lord Wakeford and I found ourselves in a familiar position, though this painting was far too large to be leaned on a chair. Instead it was set on the floor by the piano, covered in a sheet. We hadn't long. It was Thursday, and nearing the hour of Gwen's arrival for tea.

We stood side by side, equally excited; equally nervous.

"Ready?" I said.

Wakeford looked at me as though to relay the question. Was *I* ready? Well, hardly. I'd spent the morning making up excuses not to go upstairs, not quite yet. Especially not when there was the cleaning of brushes to be done, and the reorganizing of my supplies. Then there was luncheon to be had, and I was starving, having been too nervous to eat breakfast.

And, not least of all, I couldn't forget the sounds of his shouting from down the corridor. What if whatever rage had set Wakeford off in the night had lingered into day?

But the time had come and Wakeford had opened his door. I was in his apartments, at his elbow, close enough to notice he'd been on cigarettes and whisky and had used cologne in an attempt to hide it.

"Shall you do the honors?" I said.

Wakeford appeared to be just as nervous, opening and closing his fists at his sides. Was he as fearful as I was that what I'd done would be a sheer travesty? I had my pride to think of, but he had his money. Whatever was under the sheet, he'd have to pay for. Presumably. Unless he retracted his offer. I could hardly blame him if he did.

"Please—" Wakeford's throat was raspy today, crackling sorely. "It's yours to reveal."

So I had a deep breath, took a corner of the sheet, and drew it away.

There it was. Castle Braemore in the distance, the lake in the foreground and the lovely deer dotting the lawn, breathing life. It still gave me a rush of pride to see it finished, perfectly lit in the sun coming through the window.

I dared not look at Wakeford. I was scared stiff, wringing the sheet in my hands.

For what felt like an age, he didn't move. Nor speak. I wasn't entirely certain he was breathing, either, but there was a rustle of clothing, so I had to believe his lungs were filling.

Then he stepped back. Brought his desk chair forward. Sat. Facing the painting, he leaned his elbows on his knees, chin in hand.

I waited some more. I was bursting to say, *Well?* but contained myself. After all, that isn't how people observe paintings in galleries. They don't go wailing at the brilliance of the colors, calling out to those around them, *Come look at this! It's genius!*

My heart pounded. Where was that whisky, eh? I could've used some.

Finally, Wakeford released a long breath, and with eyes on the painting said, "Thank you, Bertie."

I wasn't sure what that meant. It sounded like the sort of thing that came before *but*.

"Not at all," I said, trying to sound unguarded.

Wakeford unclasped his hands and wiped them on his trousers. Sitting up, he stretched the blades of his shoulders back. The chair creaked under him, the only sound in the room.

I had to say something. I was improving, but I had not been cured of my need to fill a painful silence. There were insects of all sizes buzzing about in my stomach.

"The thing is," I began, "this was always just a practice go. There are so many other angles by which to see the house. Why, I suppose not all of them will be ideal. It's all a matter of trial and error, is art. A piece is never truly complete—"

I stopped when Wakeford stood, resting his hand on the back of his chair. "I like it very much. It's precisely what I was hoping for, and that is why I've found myself without words."

I might have said that wasn't out of the ordinary for him. "So it'll do, then?"

"It'll do."

His smile was sad. But for what reason? If he was happy with the painting, why was he so somber?

Something in his silence set my teeth on edge. Why, *why* did he not speak? What understanding might come between us if he would only open to me, if I didn't have to grasp for every single word . . . ?

With my knuckles whitening, I pushed on. "If you're unhappy with it, my lord, there's certainly time to start again . . ." I trailed off, hearing how sterile my words sounded.

Unexpectedly, Wakeford's cheek washed with color. "Julian. Please."

"Julian. Is something not right with the . . . ?" Words escaped me. His face and posture had fallen so completely; it couldn't possibly have been my doing. "Are you quite well?"

Wakeford turned his chin to the window, light flickering on the lenses of his spectacles. Then he trudged to the divan below it and sat. I took the look he gave me as invitation, and joined him at a comfortable distance, letting the sheet drop at our feet.

"I didn't sleep last evening," he said. "You must have heard."

I nodded. "What caused it?"

He glanced at the window again. "Rage, I would have thought, at my own absurdity. Or perhaps fear. I had the idea to go downstairs—to my study—while no one was about, but I . . . I was arrested."

I felt myself thawing. His plight was more than wishing to be alone, more than self-consciousness over his mask. It was simple fear. Agoraphobia, perhaps, if diagnosed. Though I doubted he was wont to see a doctor.

Wakeford faced me again. "I'm under a great deal of stress, you see, and it's—it's to do with the reason I've asked you here."

I must have started—for he moved away to give me space. This was it; he was going to confirm my suspicion that he'd hired me in desperation. I braced myself for the truth.

"I haven't told my family," he said. "Only Gwen knows. I hardly know why I'm telling you now, apart from my eagerness to . . ." I lost him again to his thoughts. His gaze went beyond my shoulder, then returned. "My eagerness to prove to you that I'm a man—of flesh, and feeling."

I couldn't be certain where he was leading, but his tone and closeness made my eyes sting. I put my hand over his. To my astonishment, he neither started nor recoiled.

"War robbed me of something, Miss Preston. I feel strongly that a piece of myself was torn out and left behind, buried in the muck, and I'm uncertain who I was before. There are days I question whether I even started here at Braemore, that I belong in my own body and my face—not my own." His hand tightened around my fingers. "The missing piece, the empty place—there was nothing to fill it with when I returned, save the title. Lord Wakeford. That's all I've left of myself now, or so I thought. Until I met you."

Intent, I moved closer, stacking my hands over his. I ached for him, my heart breaking apart like the seeds of a dandelion, taking wing on my breath. It was an immense lightness, something I'd only wondered about but never felt. It was not my imagination. Lord Wakeford cared for me.

When I didn't speak, his mouth turned down in his odd little smile. "That was terribly forward of me."

"I like it when you're forward."

His eye creased handsomely. "What I began to tell you is that I'm under much stress at the moment, for I must sell the estate."

The floor fell from under me. "Oh no . . . you can't!"

"I must. I cannot afford to run this house any longer."

"But . . . the champagne," I said dumbly. "The footmen, the motors, Celia's wardrobe—"

"Have rather put me in debt. However, I would have my brother and sister enjoy their final summer at home, and I . . . would have a memory. That is why you're here."

I had so many questions—how he'd let it come to this, where he would go once he'd sold it, what would come of the gallery and the statuary. But one question stood out amongst the many, and I was selfish just for thinking it: How would Lord Wakeford pay his artist? If I left here empty-handed, I'd have nowhere to turn.

Wakeford's hand moved to work itself from mine, but I kept hold. Seeing now his anguish, relishing his words, I forgot the money nearly as instantly as I'd thought of it.

"Some of my tenants have opted to purchase their land," he said, "but if a buyer cannot be found for the house, we'll have no choice but to demolish."

The idea was horrifying. Braemore in and of itself was a work of art. Losing it would be like watching a Monet be trapped in a burning house.

"I'm sorry," I said. "This place; it's part of you, isn't it?"

"My ancestral seat, as it were." He gave a careworn smile, and I saw for the first time how the war had aged him beyond his years. "But I don't feel worthy of it anymore."

I was suddenly desperate to close the chasm between us, to break down the last of his defenses. I shifted until our legs touched. "Now I'll be quite forward, if you don't mind. But I should very much like to see the man you speak of."

Wakeford took my meaning. He touched the bridge of his spectacles as a flush curled over his ear and down his neck. My oil paint was flaking from the mask. I rubbed some of it away, brown flecks falling like snow onto his shirt.

I traced my fingers up the mask to his hairline. Wakeford shivered as I tucked my fingers behind his ear, where only thickened scar tissue remained. I felt the other side of his face to compare. Despite the perfect artistry of his mask, there was no contest. A metal sculpture could not mimic the uneven texture of skin, the warmth and pull of a cheek's dampness, the rigid top of his ear that bent and flicked back into place.

With his face surrendering to my hold, I tipped his head to my left and pressed my lips against the mask. It was surprisingly warm, stealing heat from his body, but solid, metallic, too severe. No give and, more importantly, no take. It didn't move with him, breathe with him. It didn't rise to my touch.

When I let go, he caught my wrists, setting my hands back on his face. Our eyes had never been pinned so firmly, our pulses never so quick.

"Ask," he said.

It was all I could do not to glance at his lips. "Please, will you show me?"

In a tangle of fingers, our hands moved together, pulling wire arms from over his ears. The mask stayed in place at first, so carefully molded to his features. As one again, we lifted it away, and with the peeling sound of clammy skin and metal, it was off.

His eye closed.

At first glance, it seemed things were not so bad after all. Having served at a military hospital on the Western Front, I'd treated new wounds, and rarely saw those that were fully healed. I was accustomed to gaps in faces—gaping holes through which tongues and broken teeth could be seen, jaws entirely gone missing, noses torn away. This was not that.

But there was something to hide.

One could trace the path that the shard of hot metal had taken as it cut him, starting at the corner of his mouth. The left half of his lip was shinier, dense with scar tissue, lacking the natural color of the other side. Slightly misshapen, a gap remained between top and bottom when at rest. From there, a deeper scar continued upwards, where flesh had been regrown, sewn back together. Whiskers grew in patches, here and there, in some places spare as fallen eyelashes that could be swept away.

The larger scar went up and spidered to what was the worst of it. His eye was gone. Remaining was a shallow, round bit of tissue with the slightest inward curve, a mere allusion to what it replaced. The eyebrow lacked an arch to match the other, feathery hairs at the front, but no tail. New flesh had grown in and taken over, like lines of clay added to a sculpture. Harder, denser, and perhaps unfeeling if I were to touch him.

I understood why Lord Wakeford decided to put it all behind his lovely mask. To keep the world from being discomforted by the ghastly remnants of war. I understood why, too, he hid them from himself. For though the hurt side of his face still held the structure and shape that other men lost entirely, it was wiped clean of what made the other half remarkable. What made the other half Julian Napier.

His eye remained shut as I felt around his cheek. He flinched away, making a small, compulsive sound of fear.

"Does it hurt?" I asked.

Wakeford shook his head, drawing his lips inwards. Then he leaned in, lifting his chin. Inviting me to try again.

As the pads of my fingers registered warmth, a part of me melted. It was not the same as the other side—it was firm to the touch, rough in places, and too smooth in others—but it was flesh, not metal. Living, pulsing flesh that twitched beneath my touch.

I kissed his face again, this time on his scarred cheek. My lips pulsed with urgency, wanting more than I could give them just yet. Wakeford sighed deeply, breath dusting my jaw and neck. I leaned into him. His hands moved blindly to my waist. My fingers threaded into his hair. We were suddenly flush, naught but our tangled knees between us.

I touched my nose to his, filling my lungs with his air, longing for his eye to open. When it did, the sheer intensity rendered me boneless and I fell against him.

He was beautiful, all of him. No longer the Earl of Wakeford, but Julian. The man.

My lips were humming, my legs on fire, my heart beating unbearably fast.

"Bertie . . ."

A knock.

We separated so instantly that I nearly fell backwards off the bench, but Julian caught me. He looked at the door, and then at his watch. "Damn."

Another knock.

"It's teatime."

12

Julian's mask had fallen to the floor. We neither of us had noticed, being otherwise engaged. With a short search, it was found at our feet. He replaced it while I patted at my skirt and hair, wishing there was a single mirror in the room to peek at.

Julian allowed Huxley in with the tea things. I planned to make my escape before Gwen arrived, but her voice swept in from the corridor: "I'm so sorry; I'm terribly late! Anna's been impossible."

I backed into the room, heart thumping against my ribs. Julian held his gaze straight ahead, looking like nothing at all was amiss.

"Did you not think your sister enough occasion to smarten for?" Gwen strode in and pushed a wrapped parcel into Julian's hands. "You look a mess. I cannot think how you manage to wrinkle so . . . What have we here?"

Her eyes trailed up from Julian's rolled sleeves to his mask, where more of his painted beard had flaked away. With a creased brow, she swiped the paint with her thumb as if it was a bit of leftover gravy from luncheon. "Well?"

Julian's lips remained pressed together. If I didn't step in, we could all be waiting an awfully long time. "That was my doing, I'm afraid," I said.

Gwen hadn't noticed I was there. She turned her head, blinking as everything settled in her mind. "Why, Miss Preston. Hello. How terribly rude of me to ignore you."

"Not at all, my lady. I was just going . . ."

Julian came alive then, removing his sister's hands from his arms. "Miss Preston has brought me a painting."

Gwen cocked her head, and her eyes lit on the canvas, set conspicuously by the window. "Heavens, you've been busy, haven't you? May I have a look?" Without waiting for an answer, she went to the window. Her expression was complex, somewhere between nonplus and the mournful look Julian had on when he'd seen it. "My . . . how magnificent."

I forced a smile. "Thank you."

Julian moved stiffly to stand beside me, drumming his fingers on the parcel he'd been given. I thought his silence read suspicious, though Gwen mustn't have thought much of it, or else knew precisely what had gone on and was glad.

"You must stay and have tea with us, Miss Preston," she said.

"Oh—you're terribly good, but I mustn't push in."

"I insist; I've been so eager to talk with you at greater length." Gwen arched a brow at Julian. "So long as his lordship has no opposition?" The pair of them had the family knack for silent conversation.

Julian raised his head. "Please, do join us."

There was no refusing now, though the thought of sitting at table between Gwen and Julian, whose skin I could still taste on my lips, was rather unsettling. I waited about awkwardly while Huxley laid our tea. Gwen sent him for an extra setting, even as Julian protested. Gwen's word was final, so we waited until a third cup was brought from downstairs. I decided, if the world were a fairer place, Castle Braemore would be run by the firstborn Napier, rather than the first son, and that son would be happier for it.

Once Huxley was dismissed, Gwen had a sharp breath and smiled at me. "All sorted, then? Lovely. I'll pour. How do you take it, Miss Preston?"

"Milk, please."

I felt Julian's eyes on me as I accepted the tea, the sharp sound of cup sliding on saucer thunderous in the silence. I could feel the warmth of his body at my elbow, creeping up my arm. His scent threaded my nostrils—sweet and heady.

If he regarded me similarly, I couldn't tell. He sat perfectly tall and still as Gwen finished pouring. "Now that I know you're an incredibly accomplished artist," she said, "I don't mind asking you what on earth you've done to my brother's face."

I was relieved by the humor in her tone. "It was a silly idea, I suppose. Not at all the right sort of paint for the job."

"Well, I must say, upon further inspection it does look rather convincing." She put her hand on Julian's so he would look at her. "Perhaps we can have Miss Preston do something about the rest of you. Do you cut hair, my dear?"

I smiled when Julian did. "No, my lady."

"More's the pity. Each time I see him, he more closely resembles a buccaneer. Shall we get a parrot for you, my boy?"

Julian responded by opening his cigarette case, and placing one in the corner of his mouth. The space filled with intoxicating smoke.

Gwen cut a slice of Victoria sponge and offered it to me. "Have you told Miss Preston about the last woman to paint your face?" Julian shook his head, waving out his match. "Her name was Anna Coleman Ladd, an American sculptor. Julian and I went to see her at her studio in Paris after the war. A fine thing, is it not?"

"A work of art, truly." I located a cube of sugar and dropped it in my cup. "If only I'd thought to use my passion so similarly to help our boys."

"She was an inspiring woman." Gwen regarded Julian with a mother's affection. "Worth the journey, wouldn't you say? And the ghastly process? Please stop that—such an unseemly habit."

Julian had been picking at his whiskers. He let his hand fall, leaning forward to ash his cigarette.

"What was it like?" I asked. "The process? If you don't mind my asking."

I looked from Gwen to Julian, who sat back in his chair. It was the quietest he'd been in my company, and I had to wonder if he'd be speaking more easily with his sister if we had not shared an amorous encounter only moments ago.

Gwen was hardly bothered, only waiting as long as it took to swallow her cake before answering. "It took a bit of doing; nearly a month's worth. Mrs. Ladd started by making a plaster cast of Julian's face—Lord, I thought he would suffocate beneath it, only a rubber tube through which to breathe whilst it dried." She swatted his wrist. "Do you remember how red your knuckles were when it finished? I spent the time squeezing his hand to ensure he was still with us. I think it was only half an hour before she removed it, but it felt like an age."

Julian stirred his tea, his response only the rhythmic, tinny clang of spoon on china. I wondered if he'd drifted into the memory, or it made him uncomfortable to hear it given aloud.

"We returned once she'd finished making the mask—out of copper, was it?—so incredibly thin. And we sat together whilst she showed him how it was to be worn, and did her marvelous work with the paint."

Both of us were suddenly caught staring at Julian—well, his likeness—and he finally glanced up, feeling our attention. His mouth twitched, not quite a smile, and he stamped out his cigarette to begin another.

"I'm afraid I bullied Julian into it," Gwen said, refreshing her cup. "There was a man doing a similar sort of work in London, but I'd read about Mrs. Ladd and thought her the superior artist. Julian was an awfully good sport. I don't expect he regrets it. Will he say as much?" She raised her brows.

Julian let a stream of smoke through the corner of his mouth. "I'm glad we went."

"We tend not to look backwards in this family," said Gwen to me. "But I live with the belief that if I forget my past entirely, I also lose the opportunity to learn from it, to grow in perhaps a different, even better direction."

"I think that wise," I said.

Julian shifted in his seat, attention surrendered again to his full cup of tea. I was struck by the notion that Gwen had sent for that third cup, had poured hot tea into it, added the lemon wedge, and set it in front of him with the full knowledge he wouldn't drink it, not in front of me, not with his mask on. That was what she did for all of them. She looked after her siblings with nothing but a fragile thread of hope they might accept her care.

"Well," she said then, "perhaps you can share your chocolates with Miss Preston now she's here. It's high time someone enjoyed them."

Julian smiled, though his face went fully flush.

Gwen tilted her head towards me. "I've given Julian a box of chocolates every Thursday since he was in hospital, and he's never once eaten a single one. Have you?"

"You needn't bring them," Julian said.

"But they cheer you! At least, that's what I've been telling myself all these years. It's fine chocolate, you know. I order them special from Belgium."

"How thoughtful," I said. "The only thing my sisters have ever done to cheer me is say that although I'm unmarried, at least I've not put on weight since my youth."

Gwen's eyes widened at my boldness. Then her mouth stretched into a pretty smile. "Since your youth, darling? Why, has it passed you already? You look a young thing to me."

"I suppose war has made me feel older than my years," I said. "So much lost time."

It was then I realized why Gwen had chosen to tell me the particular tale of Paris and Mrs. Ladd, and the plaster and the waiting. Julian had pain in his past. He'd been mended. He was put back together into a lord. One fit for love.

Roland had asked me to befriend Julian. Gwen, it seemed, was hoping for a bit more.

"Years are lost so easily, aren't they?" she said, "so take my advice: you shall never find true happiness until you learn to allow yourself a second slice of cake."

Gwen and I chatted for a bit longer. All the while she sat forward, listening keenly. I had more respect for her than ever.

When she stood and set her napkin on the table, I hadn't yet finished my second cup, but Julian and I rose with her.

"If I leave the children with Roland any longer, there will be bruised knees or some other catastrophe." She took Julian's hands and pressed her cheek against his for a kiss. "Goodbye, darling. See to it that someone cuts that hair before next week, or I swear I shall take to your head with my sewing scissors."

"Yes, your ladyship," he said.

"Don't cheek your elders." Gwen's voice softened, and I moved my gaze away, feeling I was intruding. "You know, Anna would very much like to see that painting Miss Preston has done for you. I could fetch her upstairs for a moment—"

"I shall play her song," Julian said, with the tone of finality.

Gwen stepped away. "Until next time, then. It was lovely getting to know you, Miss Preston."

"And you."

I began to leave with her, but she rounded on me. "Do stay, dear. You haven't finished, and there's plenty more cake to be eaten—and those chocolates."

Gwen's eyes widened. I saw something I wouldn't have thought her capable of—desperation. It seemed I was right. She'd tried everything else. She'd come each Thursday, brought the chocolates, encouraged Julian to see the children. Love, perhaps, was her final hope.

"Thanks," I said. "I will."

She smiled, gave me a pat on the arm, and left.

Julian and I stood silently by the open door, unsure of one another. Part of me thought he'd say nothing more. Gesture for me to leave. Our discussion had unsettled him, perhaps even crossed a boundary he'd set between us that Gwen had taken down without his permission.

But I was wrong. For he reached out to touch my arm, a firm yet tender gesture, and said, "Please excuse me for a moment."

He went to the piano to play Anna's song, and I sat beside him. It was a cheerful tune, but it weighed on my heart. When the song ended, Julian folded his hands in his lap and looked sideways at me. "I daresay my sister has been plotting. Were you aware?"

I shifted in my seat, struck by the truth given so plainly. "Gwen has naught to do with my . . . unyielding resolve to kiss you."

God, but his smile was lovely. I couldn't help but reach up to remove the mask again, to see Julian's swollen cheeks, where kindly creases appeared when he laughed. He closed his eye, still timid of intimacy.

"When may I return?" I asked.

Julian held my free hand between his. I could see his learned restraint in posture, in brow. A nobleman before an unmarried, common woman. What could be expected of him now? This was not like courting at all; this was not how things were done.

"Tomorrow?" he asked.

"Evening?"

This, of course, required more contemplation. I could see Julian fighting himself until at last, he nodded. "Tomorrow evening."

In Want of a Wife

JUNE 1910

Here were gathered the finest selection of England's most prominent debutantes fresh from court, dressed in gowns designed a year in advance for such an occasion—and Julian stood admiring a painting. Gwen wasn't sure she'd ever convince either of her brothers that, to marry, one must court, and to court, one must first and foremost speak with girls.

She tapped Julian on his left shoulder and ducked to her right, making him look in the wrong direction. His chin went down, embarrassed by the blunder. "Must you?"

"You were looking far too serious."

Gwen took his arm and led him away from the artwork to show him what other beauties the ballroom held. The room itself was a sight to behold—glowing under brilliant electroliers and skirted by great palms and fresh flowers. Not to mention the eager young women who were seeing their very first season as marriageable persons.

A couple passed, and Julian pivoted his chest towards Gwen to avoid them. She nearly stumbled but he caught her by the arms, cheeks flushed from the inconvenience of a crowd.

In their close quarters Gwen said, "Have you asked a single woman to dance?"

Julian stepped backwards, finding he had the space again. Onlookers may have thought they were doing their own clumsy waltz. "Cards are full, I'm afraid."

"Bosh!" If they were at home, Gwen would have thumped him. She had been a girl herself not so long ago. Julian might be withdrawn, but he was tall enough, handsome, and had a title already at nineteen. Girls were saving lines on their dance cards for *Lord Wakeford*, if only he would ask. "Why don't we go and speak to someone together? Lady Catherine is present, she's quite pretty . . ."

"Engaged since March."

Gwen sighed. "Yes; well remembered. Perhaps Lord Hereford's eldest? Evie, is it?"

"Are you not the one of us in pursuit of a spouse?"

Another couple squeezed by, and then there were pairs materializing from everywhere, hurrying to the center of the room as music swelled. Gwen stopped to watch, standing on tiptoe to eye the men. "What will this be?" She glanced at her card. "Oh, the quadrille! I quite like the quadrille. Why haven't I been asked?"

Julian bumped his shoulder to hers. "You've frightened off half the country's noblemen."

"Frightened them—I?" She feigned offense with the flick of her head.

Julian chuckled and Gwen joined. She was not blind to her own shortcomings.

"If only you'd been born a woman, Julian. Having naught at all to say, the men would simply flock to your elbow."

Julian, as usual, had no response. His eyes drifted away and Gwen followed them, hoping they might land on Lady Evie. But they fell instead on the windows reflecting the room and its swirling dancers back to them. There would be no dancing for Julian. Because his timidities made bowing to a young woman a terror, waltzing a nightmare.

And because there was only one woman that occupied the serene space of his mind.

"You may not keep her forever," said Gwen. Julian looked at her with brow pleated, but she knew he understood. "You're young—you needn't marry for seven or eight more years—but you may not have a housemaid for a wife."

Julian whipped his head, checking for eavesdroppers, of which there were none. Gwen was a keen conversationalist, and knew when she was and was not heard. All focus was on the dance. She gave Julian's arm a pinch to beg his attention.

"The longer it goes on, the harder it will be to part. What will you do when I marry and engage her as my lady's maid, hm?"

Julian tensed, looking at his shoes. "I've not given you permission."

"Oh no?" Gwen tightened her grip on his arm. Julian was nothing but goodness, but he could never see past his nose. "She belongs only to you, does she? Is that the sort of man you wish to be, Julian? Is that how you'll choose to use your privilege?"

"No!" Julian fidgeted, trying to slip from Gwen's grip, but she held tight. He looked a boy, agitated by the tedious notion of bath time. "She doesn't belong to anyone, and I don't—I don't wish to talk of her any further."

Sometimes Gwen had to remind herself of Julian's youth. Most often he was mature and stoic enough to be a grandfather in dim light, and played father to Roland and Celia often enough, but he was still so quick to act thoughtlessly.

"You don't wish to *talk*," she said. "Ever. What if you explained to me how you feel? Perhaps I may understand. Start by saying what the two of you get up to when you sneak away."

He tightened his jaw, moved his gaze.

Gwen prodded him. "I'm not naive."

The music came to a thundering end, and Gwen let go of Julian's arm to applaud the dancers. He stood with clenched fists dangling at his sides.

"Don't turn inwards," she said. He said nothing.

Then the other part of Gwen awoke—not the protecting part of her, but the doting part—the part that had leaned over Julian's bassinet when he was an infant, and fussed over scraped knees when he was a boy. The part that loved him terribly and smarted to see him upset.

She took his limp elbow and led him back towards the painting he'd admired. He went willingly, either because it was less crowded there, or because she was his big sister and she wanted him to. With a jot more air between them, Gwen dropped his arms.

"I'm envious," she blurted. "There. How does it feel? I'm dead jealous that you've found love and I remain a hopeless old maid entirely unlearned in romance."

Gwen expected Julian might laugh—in fact, she was hoping he might. That would ease some of the tension between them. But he only smiled, a close-lipped and kind, brotherly smile, and she was glad.

"You're not an old maid," he said. "A young maid, perhaps."

Gwen sighed a laugh and watched over her shoulder as the younger women matched up with the men so simply, as if it was all written to be staged. "Forgive me," she said. "My only hope is for you to find happiness in this life of yours. Goodness knows it shan't be easy for you."

Another song began, and Gwen decided it was time to find a kindly gentleman who might lead her to the dance floor. She began to excuse herself when Julian offered his elbow.

"There's someone here I would introduce you to," he said.

An introduction? From Julian? Gwen nearly tossed her head to make a quip, but bit her tongue. There was no use discouraging such behavior by teasing him for it. Perhaps there was hope for the boy after all.

"Someone?" she said, as he led her through to the next room. "A male someone?"

"A Lord Someone."

Gwen's heart sped. She was sure she'd met every eligible heir south of Glasgow and found none of them to be of any more value than an afternoon's worth of her time. And here was a titled man apparently approved by Julian, who was an even harsher judge of character, preferring books and dogs to most people.

"You would really like to be rid of me, wouldn't you?" she teased.

Julian shrugged jestingly and led on.

In the refreshment room, small groups were assembled for chatter, holding tea and bonbons and silver cups of fruit ices, pausing only to swallow and check their dance cards. Gwen had completely forgot about her own, dangling uselessly from her wrist.

"Earl?" she asked.

"Viscount," said Julian.

That would do. After all, her father was no longer alive to insist on her marrying a man of equal rank, and she could hardly complain. "Is he a town or country man?"

"Country. A keen hunter. He's been on the continent this year doing just that."

Gwen could already imagine a likely man in tweeds, and the fine shooting parties she would host with him, and the children running about on the moor with red hounds at their heels . . .

"Do tell me he isn't German."

"Haven't the foggiest."

"Oxford or Cambridge?"

"Oxford, of course."

"And he's called . . . ?"

"Stanfield."

A strong name, and nothing that called attention to itself. Lady Stanfield. Lady *Guinevere* Stanfield . . . she liked that. "Why have I not met this Lord Stanfield before?"

"You must have done." Julian plucked a glass of lemonade from a tray and handed it to Gwen. "His estate is just northwest of us. I play cricket with him every season."

"You hate cricket."

"As does he. Hence the reason we get on. There . . ." Julian tipped his head, and Gwen followed to the corner of the room, where a man, much taller than her brother but fair, spoke to a couple who were rather entertained by whatever he was saying. He was broad, but lean, his pale hair grown long enough to reveal the slightest wave above a high forehead. Lips were surprisingly ample, nose a bit crooked, and as they drew closer, she saw he had a scar just beside it on his cheek, white with age.

She sipped her lemonade, only just realizing she was parched. "Where have you been hiding this fellow?"

"As I said, you've met. Shall I introduce you again?"

"Please. Oh . . . no, wait—"

Julian allowed himself to be yanked round so his shoulders masked Gwen's expression. She could hardly allow this Lord Stanfield to see her reeling over the idea of him.

"He won't disappoint me, will he?"

Julian smiled. "Only if you forget he's human."

Gwen let out a long breath, reveling in the sudden space between her flesh and the boning of her corset. She gave Julian her glass of lemonade; she hardly needed the sugar.

They arrived before Lord Stanfield, in time for his companions to depart, and when he raised his chin to smile at Julian, Gwen was struck still by the paleness of his blue eyes.

"Wakeford," he said, and thrust out a hand. She'd never seen Julian shake so grippingly. "How good it is to see a friendly face. I fear everyone's waiting for my father to arrive, and greatly disappointed to see me in his place. Hello." The eyes found Gwen.

Under any other circumstances, she might have been impressed that Julian was about to raise his voice so confidently, but in this moment, she was too distracted by the eyes. "Allow me to introduce my sister, Lady Guinevere Napier. Gwen, Lord Richard Stanfield. I don't doubt you've met . . ."

As Stanfield was familiar enough with Julian, Gwen saw it appropriate to offer her hand. He took it delicately, but when he didn't let go, she went hot.

"I thought your sister still in a cradle," Stanfield said to Julian.

And with that, Gwen swam instantly to the surface.

"Our little sister, Lady Celia, is seven years old this past April," she said, and felt Julian stiffen beside her. "I hardly think my brother would confuse the particulars of her age—you must have misheard, my lord. Or forgot?"

Stanfield, still holding her fingers, deepened his smirk and wrapped his knuckles against his temple. "Thick as stone, this, and twice as heavy. Can you forgive my mistake, my lady?"

She did.

Gwen allowed Lord Stanfield to fetch her lemonade, which she drank, too distracted by his eyes to think of the sugar. She allowed him to tuck her hand under his arm and lead her away from Julian, left treading dangerously in a crowd on his own. She allowed him to open the glass door to the terrace and usher her through, then show her a place for them to stand against the balustrade.

There they stood quietly at first, both reveling in the cool summer breeze and sudden shelter from the noises of the party. Now there were only the muted sounds of London on the other side of the courtyard—motors and hooves and church bells.

"I do recall meeting you," said Stanfield. He leaned his elbows on the balustrade. Like her brothers, this man seemed to find the optimal idling places for slouching. "It was quite quick—you'd hardly remember."

"Where, please?"

"Oh, Ascot, perhaps. Or polo."

Gwen turned herself so they were side by side. "If you can't place the particular occasion on which we met, the moment could not have been much more significant to you than it was to me, my lord."

"Call me Richard, if you like." For a rugged man, his voice was blithe. It captivated her to hear it coming from his mouth.

"Very well, Richard," said Gwen. "How long has it been since your father passed?"

Richard bowed his head and smiled. It was easy to see the grief on his posture, and she hadn't forgot the comment he'd made in the refreshment room. His discomfort with the way she addressed him led her to believe that his title was inherited recently.

"Two months," he answered.

That was why she couldn't place him. The Lord Stanfield of her memory was an older gentleman—she'd guess a friend of her father's. It was during her pause that Richard straightened again, facing her.

"I'm dreadfully sorry," she said.

"As am I." Another grim smile. "Wakeford did say you're clever."

Gwen felt her chest blush and was glad they were in moonlight. She leaned her hip against the railing and pretended to admire the stars, feeling the young man's eyes like rays of sun on her skin. What little there was between them. Night air, and a few layers of silk.

"What do you wish for, Lady Guinevere Napier?"

She tilted her head to look at Richard, admiring the sparkle of starlight on his eyes and thick yellow lashes. "Do you really want to know?"

He nodded.

There were a dozen silly things Gwen might have answered. For what girl hadn't asked a wishing star for her utmost desires? But because she liked Richard, and she wanted to see if he scared easily, she gave him the truth. "I wish to be a mother."

He laughed—but of course he did. Gwen could see he'd taken the statement as a young man would, as something hinting at indecency. She might have been embarrassed had he not been so willing to play with her earlier.

"Is it so absurd?" she asked.

"No, no—" He regained his posture by fiddling with his jacket. "Only . . . I suspected you of having more modern sensibilities."

Gwen scoffed. "Modern? Is that what's said of me?"

"It's said you're *clever*. Most clever women I know balk at the notion they're destined only for motherhood."

"Only—?"

That puzzled him. He righted himself and lifted a hand to gesture, though it fell before he thought of what to say. "Is there nothing more you wish to put your mind to?"

Because he was handsome, and because he'd called her clever twice,

Gwen gave him the benefit of the doubt. "I am intelligent," she said. "I see the world my own way, I read broadly, and I have opinions. I am destined for whatever it is I choose to spend my life doing. I've chosen to be a mother. I'm sorry if that disappoints you."

Richard scratched his scar and gave a wry grin. "You ought to be married to a man who's only after an heir."

"Perhaps. Or perhaps I ought to be married to one who values the strength and courage required of his wife to carry and deliver a child into this world."

In her wildest, Gwen could not imagine such a conversation happening between her and a single gentleman at a debutante ball, though she found the whole thing exhilarating. For Richard was *listening* to her. He paused to consider her notions, he challenged her but did not silence her. That was more than any other man had done.

Now he rested one hand on the balustrade, furrowing his brow. He did not speak. Gwen realized he was waiting for her to go on. How staggering!

"So you see," she obliged, "choosing motherhood above all else is not the ignorant choice, nor the easy one by any means. But it is *mine*, and I believe wholeheartedly that I shall be very good at it. And very happy. And very capable, I might add, of being both mother and anything else I may fancy being in future. You're a hunter, are you not, my lord?"

Richard was wide awake. "I am."

"And when you inevitably become Father, shall you cease to be?"

"Not on your life."

Gwen grinned proudly. "So you understand?"

Richard, whose face had, until this moment, been crumpled at its center in an expression generally found in a lecture hall, eased his stance. His new expression was filled with wonder, looking as if he was hearing a musical instrument that until that moment had yet to be invented. He chuckled again, though this time not at Gwen, and settled his cerulean eyes on her.

"I'd also like children, you know."

Gwen could not help the flutter in her stomach. "Oh? How many?"

"A whole litter," he answered, waving his hand in between them. "So many we shall have to bunk them, like sailors in hammocks. So many I forget the names!"

Gwen was laughing so hard, she hardly heard him say *we*. She couldn't remember the last time she'd laughed herself to tears, but here they were, clouding her eyes, and when she wiped them away, Richard was still there, tall and handsome and listening.

"You'll have to remember them for me," he said.

He opened his palm—a question. Gwen lifted her hand, retracting it only long enough to remove her evening glove. Then, lighter than a butterfly, she set the tips of her fingers on his palm. He did not try to close his hand, to capture her there. He kept it open, allowing her to explore the warm roughness of his flesh, the lines and scars borne by a man with a passion for the outdoors. But what she felt for—what she hoped to find—was a silly notion she'd conjured as a little girl reading fairy stories. She felt for a spark.

And here it was, like electricity between their skins, a magnetic pull that moved her closer to Richard involuntarily.

Seeing her blush, he smirked. "Shall we dance?"

They did.

In the motor on the journey home, Julian had shut his eyes and let his head fall back, a tactic often used to escape any further conversation. But Gwen knew him too well to think him asleep. She laid her head on his shoulder, and sure enough, he answered by leaning his temple to rest on her hair.

"Thank you," she said.

Julian, of course, did not reply.

13

I felt wicked, slipping away just after dinner the next day, making excuses that I was tired and wanted to turn in early. I went to my room to freshen up, dabbing scent behind my ears and patting rouge on my lips to tint them. They didn't need much, already bright pink from the mere thought of joining Julian for after-dinner drinks in his apartments.

It still thrilled me to think of him this way. *Julian.*

There's no lying here—I was not what one might call a virtuous woman. At seventeen, I'd discovered early the allure of sex after sneaking from a local dance with a boy my age. In the cover of darkness, we explored each other's bodies, and though his methods left much to be desired, I rather enjoyed the act, and sought to make it happen again, and again. Just simple dalliances. But if my parents knew the sort of girl I was, they would both drop dead.

In any case, I had thin faith that the Earl of Wakeford would be so untoward. Though if he were, I would be prepared.

I removed my shoes to quiet my footfalls, and padded down the corridor to Julian's door. He opened after the first knock.

The sitting room was fuggy, still smelling of his dinner, savory rosemary and seared meat trapped in the unmoving air. He'd already started with a digestif, a tumbler of whisky he'd left on a side table, near where the imprint of his body was carved in his wingback. We stood together just inside, both with a half smile, both unsure of what precisely we were doing.

To my surprise, Julian spoke first. "May I offer you a drink?"

"Please do."

He walked backwards to the sideboard. "I've had Huxley bring a fine thirty-year Scotch whisky."

"Sounds divine. I can't say I've ever had a drink older than I am."

While he poured, I went to see how my painting looked in the orange light of evening. It took on a sinister air—the sky in flames, clouds with the greyish hue of smoke.

"I was just considering how best to frame it," Julian said, coming up behind me with a glass.

"I think that depends on where it's to be hung." I breathed in the whisky. It was certainly the finest I'd had, rich, smooth, and tasting of all thirty years it had waited for us to drink it. "Where will you go after Braemore?"

I wasn't sure Julian had heard until he eventually answered, "Somewhere people pass without noticing."

Lamplight cast a glare over Julian's spectacles, making it difficult to read his eye, which for a man of such few words could be the only way to understand what he was thinking.

"Will you take it off?" I asked. "As much as I appreciate Mrs. Ladd's artwork, I'd much prefer to spend the evening looking at you."

Julian unhooked the arms from his ears and dropped his chin, letting the mask fall into his open palm. He set it gingerly on his desk and returned, pushing his hands through his hair.

"Much better," I said, and drank again, wandering away from the painting to collect Julian's abandoned tumbler to return to him. Now the mask was off, I hoped he might find himself at ease enough to drink with me. "It mustn't've been easy, traveling to Paris so soon after you'd mended. And France itself, in recovery." He looked down at his shoes, and I knew I'd overstepped. "We needn't talk about it any further."

I moved to the settee. Julian sat close and lifted his glass tentatively before draining it. As he set it on the table, he produced a handkerchief from his breast pocket and wiped his lip.

"People would stare," he said. "They stared at the scars; they stared at the mask—it didn't make much difference. It helped to be in uniform, but even so, women went pale . . ." He replaced the handkerchief and leaned back, stretching his arm behind me. "There isn't much to be done, is there?"

I was guilty for pushing, thinking perhaps I'd ruined any chance this evening might bring us yet again closer. I wanted us to be closer—to test how my heart might respond.

I took his glass to refill it. He lit a cigarette. When I sat again, he offered one to me, but I waved him off. "I'm sorry, truly. My mother always says I flog the dead horse . . ."

His hand went to my knee, heavy and warm. I had not thought him so bold, but was glad of it. I ran the tips of my fingers over his knuckles as a fire was lit inside me.

"You can tell me to stop talking," I said. "I won't be offended." The whisky had crumbled my defenses. "It's just that—you really listen, don't you? You don't just grin for etiquette's sake. Do you know how rare that is in a person?"

Julian waited to speak, demonstrating the simple beauty in a long pause. Outside the cracked window, sheep bleated in the distance, an owl *hoo*ed, wind hissed through trees.

"I like hearing you talk," he said finally. "And I don't mind telling you about myself. But I do mind that I know precious little of you."

"There is little to know."

"I don't believe that."

Julian's thumb brushed back and forth on my knee. It took my every ounce of will to stay still. I wanted to be closer, to move his hand to other places which were reaching out to him.

"Let's see . . . ," I began. "I'm nosy. Though I suspect you've deduced that already."

Julian smiled. "Go on."

I settled into my seat, letting my memory spread out before me. "When I was a girl, I wanted to marry the screever who chalked the pavement in Hyde Park. I would put by every farthing for his cap, surrendering it on day trips to London."

Julian listened with keen attention, pulling on his cigarette with curved lips.

"I have two elder sisters who are perfect—perfectly proper and perfectly boring. My parents haven't an ounce of creativity between them, but my father makes model ships now. He's very proud of them . . ."

My throat tightened. I missed him. I missed all of them—and I couldn't go home.

Julian leaned forward to tap his ash in a crystal tray, then resumed rubbing my knee. It was a welcome distraction from my heartache.

"I took some of my paintings to London once, and set them on a bench along Victoria Embankment to peddle them for a few pence. But I didn't sell a single one. It was humiliating."

Julian furrowed his brow and moved his hand behind me, elbow resting on the top of the settee. I shivered as his fingers traced the back of my neck, tickling as the short hairs moved to and fro.

"I slipped out to attend suffragette rallies before the war—perhaps I was too young, but I couldn't resist. My mother called me mad, unladylike. My sisters told me to leave politics to men. But I went because I believe in women. Though when I hear my mother's voice in my head, I wonder if I truly am mad for having such nerve, for cutting my hair."

Julian pinched a bit of it, twisting and releasing the strand. My neck burned.

"I'm afraid I'll die before I've done anything of worth. I'm afraid my mother is right, that the greatest thing a woman can contribute to the world is children, and I've spent so long chasing after some silly dream that I've run out of time for all that—for love."

I had never admitted that to anyone. Rarely enough to myself.

Julian pushed my hair behind my ear, angling my face to look at him. He said nothing, though his expression spoke words of comfort. I didn't want to stop. I wanted to carve my heart out of my chest and place it in his hands.

"When I was a VAD, I drew portraits of soldiers to send to their families. Sometimes I drew them without bandages, without sunken cheeks and black eyes. Sometimes I drew them smiling when they weren't; I drew them looking well when I knew they would be dead by week's end. I've never forgiven myself."

Julian dropped his cigarette in the tray and brought his other hand to my face, smelling strongly of tobacco. I nearly said it—I nearly told him all my fears of getting involved with a broken man. My fear that Celia's opinion of him was worth cautioning. Then a tear slipped from my eye. He caught it on my cheek with his lips, tracing upwards, clearing it away. When he kissed me, I could taste the salt, satiating and moreish, not nearly enough.

"Then I met an earl," I said. "I imagined he was a kindly old man with a potbelly, but as it happens he's rather young and quite lovely." I traced my fingers from his sunken left brow, following the track of his scar. "And I like him terribly."

Julian kissed me again, ever so briefly, and it felt like an answer. If he preferred to speak in kisses for the duration of our friendship, I would comply. Apparently it was a language in which I was fluent; I could understand precisely what he was telling me.

He pulled away with intention, and took my hand. "There's something I would like to show you."

Wordlessly, Julian led me to his bedroom. The lights were on already, a standing lamp glowing over one corner, another beside the bed. It was a colossal tester bed of regal mahogany, something belonging in a genuine Tudor castle, with maroon brocade curtains and an intricately carved headboard.

"Have a seat, if you like," Julian said, and went through another door.

I sat on the bed, feeling I must because of how breathtaking it was.

The room was thick with the peopled scent of a lived-in space, the lasting sharpness of bergamot soap and sheets steeped in the mellow tang of a summer-warmed body. I wanted to fall back to let the plush quilt catch me but feared I'd never get up.

Julian returned with a plain wooden box and sat beside me, not the least bit bothered by the idea we were on his bed. I watched curiously as he arranged the box on his lap and unlocked it with a key before lifting the lid.

"Oh!"

On the top was a tray lined with velvet, designed for jewelry. This one had military medals—many of them—colored ribbons in brilliant contrast to the black they were set on, bronze, silver, copper shining proudly. I thought this was what Julian wanted me to see until he lifted the tray out as if it mattered little and handed it to me to hold.

I touched the cold, rigid metal lion on a Victoria Cross, mind racing. To think what he must have done to receive it, to shake the king's hand . . .

"You ought to have these on display," I said.

He ignored that, pulling out the next-largest item from the box—a revolver—though not the make I had seen often in a British officer's kit. I must have reacted, for Julian set it aside gently and said, "Seized from an unlucky Hun."

I decided not to ask if the German man had been alive.

Then he rifled through what was left in the box—papers and letters, documents and scattered photographs. He handed me a leather-bound journal, which I opened to find his drawings. Most were silly cartoons with captions: a plump, mustached general titled *Passed Inspection*; a gap-toothed Tommy boxing with a rat of equal size, *Recreation on Dover Street*. Smiling, I turned the page and found less happy reflections—line drawings of a camp in pouring rain, a blackened battlefield, and an eerie makeshift gravestone that looked to have been made from a biscuit tin lid. *Remember Him*, Julian had written beneath it.

Then there was a drawing of a girl, her sudden softness and beauty a striking contrast to the previous images. Julian, who'd been looking over my shoulder, cleared his throat.

I couldn't say why, but I didn't wish to point her out. "These are very clever."

Before I could continue, a pressed flower fell from between the pages into my lap. Returning to the journal, I found more—poppies, bluebells, chicory, cornflowers.

"I collected those for Celia," Julian said. A shadow passed over his face.

"You must miss her."

He nodded.

"Why did the two of you fall out?"

Julian bowed his head, scratched his nose, stalling the inevitable. But I was patient. I'd waited this long to hear the story—another few breaths were of no matter.

"I've disappointed her," he said weakly. "She's every right to be upset."

Vague, as ever. I'd come to expect it. "How have you disappointed her?"

Julian leaned his shoulder against mine for support. I feared his answer, but was willing to have it, no matter how bitter the pill. I was through with secrets.

"I did things during the war that I'm not proud of. I've changed, and I—I suppose that's the reason I wanted to show this to you." He pulled a postcard from the bottom of the box.

It was a photograph of him, one of the postcards men sat for once they had their uniforms, and sent home for their parents to place proudly on the mantel. I had one of my own, dressed in apron and veil, just as honored to wear the Red Cross as the boys were to be in khaki.

Julian was young. Whole. He sat with his shoulders back, his peaked cap on his knee, hair short and combed neatly to one side. I wished he was smiling, but of course he was stern, eyes dark and deep, revealing only perhaps fear, or the agony of knowing what he must do.

His cheeks were rounder with youth, clean-shaven and pale. He looked the same and somehow completely different. I couldn't take my eyes from it.

Julian, however, kept his down and away.

"How young you look," I said.

"I was. Four and twenty."

"Were you a good officer?"

He thought, clenching his jaw. "Not at first. I've never been one for violence or confrontation. So when I began my training, I decided I'd have to be someone else if I was going to survive at the front. I had to"—a line formed on his forehead—"force myself in half. To cut away what I was until only a sort of primal skeleton remained. I cut away anything which was not fear or rage or hate. I lived that way for years, and when I returned, I couldn't find where I'd left the other part of myself, the larger part. And when I found it, they were two separate halves that wouldn't bind. This part"—he pointed to the postcard, then to his scars—"and this."

"You think Celia is upset by the change in you?"

"I know she is."

I lifted the postcard. "Why have you shown me this?"

Julian plucked it from between my fingers and set it back in the box. We replaced the book with the flowers, and the revolver, and then the tray of medals. It was all locked up again so neatly.

"I wanted you to see that I was just another of them," Julian said. "I could sense you were beginning to believe this bloody mythos my family have fashioned about me. I don't want you to think of me that way. I'm merely a man." His throat caught.

I took the box from his lap, setting it gently on the floor, and kissed him. Lightly, on the scarred side of his mouth. He pulled me closer, lips parting. My tongue slipped easily through the gap to taste whisky on his teeth. He drew away, tilting his face so that my next attempt landed on his unhurt side. That was something. For he deepened the kiss and hummed into my mouth. I echoed him, discovering that despite my best effort to move him past his insecurities, his strength did lie on this end.

He gripped my leg to keep me close, and I pushed his hand down and up again, under my skirt, the sensation causing my mouth to fall open. As he kissed my neck, I dipped my head, leading him to more until I was flat on the mattress, Julian beside me. I worked the knot from his tie, unfastened one button at a time. He rucked up my dress, opening my garters with two snaps. I pushed his braces off, tugged at his undershirt. My fingers splayed over his bare breast, stopping when the texture shifted. Scars like roots over his shoulder where he'd taken shrapnel.

I willed myself not to linger. Instead, let my legs fall apart to make room for his hips. He was not like I expected—flushed chest hard and carved like the Grecian statues in his garden, not usual for a man who hadn't known a day of physical labor. Unblemished skin rolled over prominent ribs. Julian sighed as I drew him down. We were wild. It came from somewhere deep within us; mine understood his.

And then he stopped.

Stopped moving, stopped kissing, stopped breathing, perhaps. He turned his face from me, eye closed firmly as if he couldn't bear the sight of me.

I waited. It didn't feel right to speak.

He rose and moved away from me to sit on the end of the mattress with head in hands. The sudden lack of heat made me shiver. I counted the notches on his spine, prominent under porcelain skin, gilded in the dim light.

I propped myself on my elbows and waited some more. When nothing came, I pulled my skirt down and sat up. "It's all right. We don't have to . . ."

I had a few guesses at what the problem was, only hoping it wasn't the idea that I was loose legged, or not attractive enough, or perhaps only too common. I took a chance and stroked Julian's broad back. He tensed, then relaxed, breaths slowing under my palm.

"I'm sorry," he said into his hands. "I warned you I'm no good at this."

"On the contrary, I thought you were doing quite well. Is something the matter?"

No answer. The well had run dry. That seemed to be what happened to him. After a time, he lost words as one loses breath on a long run.

"Hadn't I better be gone, anyhow?" I said. "You look spent."

"I should like you to stay."

That was good, for I was loath to return to my room, which would be too quiet and empty without him. So I fetched our drinks and his cigarettes. He accepted his whisky and had a tentative sip, then wiped what had drained down his chin with the back of his hand.

"If I'm staying, shall you mind if I get comfortable?" I asked. Julian looked up at me from under low brows, shook his head.

I rolled down my stockings to slip them off, then went to the other side of the bed, careful not to spill my drink as I climbed over the mattress. The quilt sank under my weight as air escaped, smelling of Julian. I leaned against the carved headboard, feeling at home.

"Fit for Henry the Eighth, isn't it?" I patted the space beside me. "Come; tell me more about the boy in the postcard."

Julian observed me over his shoulder, eye creasing with the beginnings of contentment. He moved himself back, settling close beside me. "He's always hated this bed."

I smiled. "Why not replace it?"

With a shrug: "Too much bother."

We paused to drink and it loosened any misgivings I'd been harboring. Julian appeared to be relaxing as well, crossing ankles and sinking into the pillows. He peered at his glass for a moment, then half smiled. "I've not shared it before."

"The whisky?"

"The bed."

There was no preventing my blush. "You've never come close to marrying?"

"I was too young, and then the war . . ." Julian sighed a stream of blue smoke.

"Had you never been in love?"

He leaned away to stifle his cigarette. "There was one girl, but she—I lost her."

The girl in his drawings? "I'm sorry. That must pain you terribly."

Julian regarded me as though I'd said something he didn't quite understand. He finished his drink, and set our empty glasses on the bedside table. I pivoted to face him for ease of conversation. His hand found my empty one. With that bit of touch, things were more comfortable.

"I've never been in love myself," I said, lacing my fingers through his. "I've been lonely, however, and I think perhaps it hurts in a similar way."

Julian watched our hands move around each other, in an amorous tumble of their own. "Making art is a lonesome business."

I nodded. "One is inspired by someplace, or some*one*. Then, inevitably, one must return to one's room alone and put it to canvas. But I crave more than a room. I wish to see things and meet people and taste and dance and find reason to be alive. Don't you?"

"I don't know."

"You're lonesome, though?"

He spread my hand flat on his and covered it with the other. "I've always coveted solitude. I used to believe that meant I wouldn't long for other people, but—I do . . . get lonely. I am, I suppose."

"Now?"

"Not now."

I unlocked our fingers and slid my hand over his wrist, following violet roots to a rigid arm that changed shape as the muscle contracted beneath my touch. I stretched to search further. Julian bent, threading his arm until my palm crested the sphered peak of his shoulder. Our noses met. He exhaled heavily against my lips.

I nipped at his mouth but he hesitated yet again. Bowed his head.

I stared at him, aghast. Most men I had met would not pause at this stage, their minds completely fogged by exposed skin and freedom of touch. Yet here was Julian, still holding me but refusing to move closer.

For the first time, I worried, truly, that what was not right about Julian was deeper than I was prepared to deal with. But he softened into me, and the way his arms weaved behind my back, I knew whatever was keeping him from me was not cynical.

"Are you frightened of me?" I asked him.

He blushed, but smiled, and met my eyes again. "Not any longer."

"But you are frightened of something?"

Julian lifted my hand to his mouth and kissed my palm, then cradled it against his chest. "Despite my failures at propriety, my utmost intention is merely to protect you."

A flutter in my stomach led me to smile again. I pushed the hair from his face and held it there, admiring him from inky black eye to plush, swollen lips. "I am a grown woman, Lord Wakeford, entirely capable of protecting herself."

And though the notion broke the tension between us, it also put an end to the reaching. I was moving much too quickly for him, and perhaps he was right to give me pause.

So I crawled beneath his heavy quilt and we lay side by side, where the heat of our bodies mixed and swirled. I knew I should return to my room if this was going to be an end, but I could not bring myself to leave Julian. This sort of closeness—the closeness that did not require carnality—was what I had wondered about.

As Julian's breaths evened beside me, I thought perhaps it was better.

14

I woke from a faint dream. White light trickled through a slit between the curtains, cutting the room in half. Julian's room.

A jolt rang through me as my mind swam to the surface, realizing Julian's arm slung over my hip, his feet between mine. I wriggled, and his breath shifted irregularly as he came to. He unraveled himself from me, disturbing the slick of sweat pooled between our skins, then jerked suddenly. I rolled onto my back to see what was the matter, and he pinned me down by my shoulders. Not playfully.

His face was clouded, eye blank and unseeing. Glistening chest pumped fiercely as an old bellows. I remained still, remembering my training. Never wake a sleeping soldier.

"Julian?" The eyelash fluttered. Nostrils flared as heavy breaths forced their way out. "It's all right . . ."

My voice shook him. Julian blinked and blinked, the gloss of sleep fading as he woke fully. He noticed his own hands gripping me, and withdrew to a seat.

"Forgive me—" His voice was thick from sleep. "I'd forgot you were there."

"I'm flattered."

Julian could not be amused. He rubbed his face, patiently awaiting his breaths to even. When I sat up, he recoiled, as if afraid we might touch. "Did I hurt you?"

"No."

He relaxed against the headboard. "You frightened me."

"I know." I gave him a smile. "I'm all right, see? In you come." I slid under the quilt, and after another pause of contemplation, he lay so we were face-to-face.

"I'm sorry," he said.

"Don't be."

His lashes floated downward, then up. "Did you sleep well?"

"Oh, yes." Truthfully, I'd tossed all evening. Though it was the fault of my anxieties, not Julian's bed. "You're a satisfactory bed partner. No snoring or kicking to report."

Julian painted his fingers down my arm. He looked different in the morning, movements slow and imprecise, tongue thick and lazy. I wondered how I appeared to him with hair pressed to one side of my face. Regardless, he stretched his neck to kiss me. There was a floral bitterness to his mouth that was not at all unpleasant.

He rested his hand heavily on my cheek. I touched his chest, flushed and heated from sleep, feeling down the line dividing his torso. Muscles tensed under my fingers.

"You look like a laborer," I said. "Solid, I mean. Were you—are you an athlete?"

Julian propped his head in his hand. I longed to sketch the bicep's coils and ridges. "I do calisthenics of a morning . . . part of a routine of things Gwen has me do each day. Is it ghastly?"

"Just the opposite. You resemble Michelangelo's David." Julian considered himself pensively. I chuckled. "What else is in your routine?"

He lay back, strong hands pulling me over him. I was thrilled. This was Lord Wakeford freed from decorum. Not so terribly shy after all. With my head on his shoulder, I was frightfully snug.

"I wake at half past eight," he said. "I make up the bed, drill, wash. Then dress and eat breakfast and read the newspapers—"

"That's how you found me?"

"That's how I found you." He smiled. "A doctor first recommended exercise for easing nerves. Swimming once helped to clear my mind."

"You had nerves before the war?"

A sore nod. "My father would say"—he scrunched his face mockingly—"'Be a man, Julian; nerves are a woman's debility.' He wasn't keen to leave his legacy to a lamb."

I brushed my hand through Julian's hair, thinking its length made him look vulnerable in a way I was rather fond of. "It's a dreadful shame that masculinity must mean hardness."

Julian studied my lips before kissing them delicately. Leaving his mouth resting on mine, he turned so our hips were flush. I was still dressed, but his hand found my hem, slipping under, slipping up—

Three knocks at the door.

Julian's head fell against mine. As one, we breathed plaints of frustration. I tried to sit up but he held me there. "Let it be. He'll go."

Heart racing and lips itching painfully, I wanted badly to concur. Perhaps our night together, tame as it was, had helped him pluck up the courage for more. But I hadn't forgot the lines read each morning at breakfast. I couldn't worry Roland by keeping Julian from his.

"Answer. I've already upset your routine enough as it is." This time he let me sit up. "May I wash up in your bathroom?"

Julian rose with a grunt. "Second door."

While he went to the sitting room, I tiptoed through the door to a dressing room. The walls were lined with cedar wardrobes and drawers, which I peeked inside to find shoes and hats and suits of every cut and color, hung pressed and ready to be worn. Even Julian's officer uniform was kept here, beside his evening clothes—immaculate white tie, and tails. What a shame that I'd never see him wear them.

Another door led to the bathroom. It was unlike any I'd seen, like a parlor in its own right, with a bathtub and lavatory. I padded across cold marble on bare feet, then onto a plush oval rug to the basin. There was no mirror, of course, and as I ran water over my hands, I marveled at the immensity of the rectangular outline where one had been.

I splashed my face, rinsed my mouth, and smoothed my hair. In search of a towel, I found a rack stand with one draped over its arm. Dry now. To the left of it, a chest of drawers was crowned with fine pots of lotion, brilliantine, cologne, and other things that smelled undoubtedly male. I read the labels of a few medicine bottles—cough suppressant, aspirin. Veronal. He must have been given it for nerves. He'd have to be careful there.

Back in the bedroom, Julian was just coming in carrying a silver tray. He set it on the bed and looked up at me, now wearing his mask, hair still wild from the night. "Help yourself."

I'd every intention of popping out to dress for the day, but was entirely too fond of how he looked topless in his trousers. So I climbed on the bed and sat cross-legged before the spread. Huxley brought a full breakfast—poached egg, sausage and bacon, oatcakes, rack of toast, and a bowl of fresh fruit. The coffee smelled strong, and I poured it to hand to Julian.

He accepted, and perched himself on the edge of the bed to remove his mask.

I brushed raspberry jam on a corner of toast and ate quietly while Julian lit a cigarette. I watched him lustfully as he blew smoke that curled in the ever-brightening light from the window, swirling like paint in a cup of water.

"You said you used to swim," I said. "Do you miss it?"

He nodded.

"Never thought to have another go? Likely day for it."

Julian answered in a tumble of smoke: "It isn't for me any longer."

I finished my toast and thought on this, wondering how else I might approach his leaving. Roland and Gwen remained in the back of my mind. Now I knew the truth about the debts, I saw the urgency of the matter. And so far, I had only given Julian more reason to stay in this room.

The notion gave me an ill feeling. I'd allowed my affections to overtake my sense. I had to decide what I wanted, and soon, before the flame grew to a fire I could not so easily put out.

AFTER CHANGING CLOTHES, I tossed my own bedclothes to appear slept in. A shame, really—the maid might have had a break. She also would have had rumors of how the artist hadn't slept in her room last night, and I wasn't interested in being thought of as that sort of woman.

Though I was. My God! I entirely was.

I hurried to make it to breakfast by my usual time. The others were having a rabid conversation over *The Tatler*, about upcoming nuptials between Edwina Ashley and Lord Mountbatten, the society wedding of the year, to which the Napiers were not invited because (as Celia put it plainly) a positive word had not been uttered about their family in years.

I pretended interest, anxiously awaiting the post. I was hoping for something from my parents. Perhaps if Mother had written back, it meant she was willing to negotiate, and the uncertainty of my future would stop keeping me awake.

"You bloody nobles are so tiresome," Freddie said, cigarette bouncing on his lips. He pinched it between two fingers and tapped the ash onto the open journal. "I can tell you—and Bertie will agree—that there is far more to life than blood and connections."

I was handed the attention of the table. "I really wouldn't know . . ."

Freddie went on gladly. "Well, I know for certain that in an hour's time, I can find you a far more glamorous party in London, with not a single highborn person in attendance. And nobody would care what your name is. They'd simply say . . ." He pointed his cigarette at Roland. "'Here, you are called *beauty*.'" Then at Celia. "'You are called *brightness*.'" Then at me. "'You are called *bravery*.'"

"And what will they call you, Freddie?" Celia asked.

He grinned, teeth gleaming. "*Blandishment*."

It was then that Huxley appeared with his salver. I held my breath. "His lordship has taken his breakfast, sir."

Roland nodded. "Very good."

The butler retreated, showing no obvious signs he'd been aware of my presence in Julian's bed. But his salver held something for me after all. As he handed me the letter, I heard my heart in my ears. It was not Mother's, nor Father's hand. Though the writing was familiar enough. It was from my neighbor, Mrs. Lemm.

Dear Bertie,

I hope this letter finds you well, and enjoying your holiday in Wiltshire. How splendid it was to call on your mother and learn that you are off painting for the Earl of Wakeford! All of us here in Brickyard Lane are so proud of you, and look forward to hearing about your stay at . . .

I folded and stuffed the letter back in the envelope. Not entirely worth the read, at least at the moment. I tried to hide my despair, beginning to take down food without tasting. I would have to speak to Julian about payment, to ensure that his debts would not affect this job. My heart aside, I needed to leave here with something to show for my time. With no home to return to, I was betting it all on receiving that check.

Freddie leaned forward for another piece of toast and tapped it on his plate. "How *is* our fair Wakeford, old boy? Well fed, it would seem."

Roland looked at me. Freddie noticed, and then I had the two of them gaping in my direction. When I didn't speak, Celia offered, "Julian is endlessly the same."

Freddie bit his toast and chewed while watching Celia opposite him. "I've never seen such a pretty face turn so swiftly sour."

Celia scoffed and poked her egg until the yolk bled out across her plate. But Freddie wasn't finished. "If he came through that door today, he'd not be the same, would he? Then would you have something kind to say of him?"

Roland's chair creaked under him. "Steady on, Fred."

"Don't look so dismal, my love; your face will wrinkle."

I should have thought the conversation grave if Celia hadn't plucked a grape from her plate and sent it across the table into Freddie's lap.

His face remained neutral. "That is not very ladylike."

She was giggling, and even Roland allowed a smile.

Freddie rolled his wrist, flourishing smoke. "I sometimes think I'm the only one of us with any manners."

Roland glanced down at his post, tossing a few things aside before declaring, "Gwen's throwing a birthday party for her nephew at the house, and she's invited us all. Must be desperate not to be left alone with Richard's sisters."

"See that, Cece?" Freddie said. "You shall dance after all."

For that, he was pelted with another grape.

Unable to shake my dampened spirit, I finished my tea and made my excuses.

My studio was in a beautiful state of artful disarray. I had not begun to clear up after I'd finished the last painting, and everywhere at my feet were the remnants of its color palette, still sticking to brushes and swiped across any surface with the space. I figured cleaning brushes would do to busy my hands for a while.

I needed to sort my thoughts. About Julian. About home. About my career. And how, if at all, they might someday fit in the same sentence.

I set Mrs. Lemm's letter on the windowsill to read later, and sat on a stool beside it, dunking each brush into a glass jar of turpentine. There was something cathartic about watching the color melt away and sink, joining what was congealed into a mud-grey putty at the bottom. Colors I had painstakingly mixed to perfectly match my intentions disintegrated into swill.

We were like butchers, we artists—or bakers, or servants—with all the mess done behind closed doors so that only the finished product could be appreciated. Would that the Napiers could glance at one of dozens of paintings around their great house and remember how it had started, as a spark and a shade of pigment, as a blank canvas and the ache in the artist's hand . . .

Julian could.

Why was I so anxious? My confidence was once the single thing about myself I could love unconditionally. I had been so confident when I'd left home, that I would impress Lord Wakeford, that my art would be seen by his peers, that more commissions would come flooding in and there would be no time to miss home. This was all before I knew there would be no recommendation, and possibly no payment. This was all before I'd come to adore them as people, come to know Lord Wakeford beyond that first, keen handshake.

He was lovely, I could not deny that to myself. But I had not come for romance. I had come to prove myself first and foremost as an artist. Where did a man fit in that life? To marry would mean abandoning everything—the chance to live on my own and travel and shake the restraints of my privileged upbringing. And though I called him Julian, he was still the Earl of Wakeford, which meant that whatever blossomed between us would be cut short come August.

One night. It was only one night, and one night it would remain. I could not lose sight of what I most wanted in the world for the warmth of a man's body beside me.

THAT NIGHT I put on my nightgown and sat on the bed, but I knew I would not rest. I was beginning to miss my parents, my old bed, and the certainty of home. The easy monotony of what I'd left behind. I had not had the foresight to imagine how stressful it would be to lose the comfort of sameness.

In the end, even sitting still was too difficult. So I took my candle down the stairs, leaving it just inside the door before stepping onto the terrace.

I was not alone. In the light of the moon, Freddie's cigarette glowed bright red against the night. I approached slowly, slippers dragging against the flags. He wore only a pair of drawers and a dressing gown, sat astride the balustrade, one leg dangling over the rosebush below.

"Come; join me," he said, with a wave.

I did, wrapping my dressing gown more tightly around myself. Freddie pinched tobacco from a box in front of him, and carefully sprinkled it onto a paper with narrow fingers.

"Can you forgive my dishevelment?" he asked, wiggling bare toes.

"Only if you forgive mine. Could you not sleep?"

"Roland falls asleep so easily—like a puppy in a basket. I'm not so lucky."

I shivered as a breeze blew back my hair, wondering perhaps wickedly if Roland and Freddie made love in their own way, a tangle of hard, masculine limbs and large hands brushing stubbled cheeks. Afterward, did they hold one another so tenderly? Did they whisper in the dark?

"Did you fight in the war, Freddie?"

His face fell to the stony, distant expression of men who came home. He tossed his spent cigarette into the roses. "How dare I refuse the call?"

"You seem . . ." How to word it? "You seem to have come through it well."

"I've spent my life pretending to be someone I'm not. There is nothing a little flourish can't hide."

Bringing the cigarette paper to his lips, he licked the edge, then rolled it between his thumb and forefinger. He held it up between us and I accepted willingly. After a fight with the breeze, it was lit. The sweet taste of good tobacco put me at ease.

"You're all right, then?" I asked.

"Apart from a small memento"—his scarred leg came up in display—"I'm fantastic. Young, beautiful, in love. What more could I hope for?"

I smiled, jealous of his confidence. "What will you do now Roland's through in Oxford?"

"Eat together. Drink together. Sleep together. Get old and fat together." Freddie patted his stomach, slim as can be, and we both laughed. "Mercifully, there's nobody to press Roland into the military or the cloth. So we'll live here, I assume." His eyes went up, flaring in what light came from the sleeping house. "Paradise, is it not? I would love Roland if he was a prince or a pauper, but Castle Braemore is my favorite place in the world. I'm ever so glad it's his."

I was grateful for the darkness concealing my expression. I knew what he did not—that this was the last summer he would spend here. I blew smoke and watched the night carry my ash away. "I suppose Roland wishes he'd been born first."

"Oh no. War scared the life from him. Roland was certain he'd have to replace his brother. That's the last thing he's ever wanted."

"You were quick to defend Julian this morning."

"Julian gave me shelter when my life at home became unbearable. He stopped Roland's mother sending him away. He's the reason we have a place to be together at all."

I'd known as much, truly, but Freddie's words rang through me. "What do you make of Celia's anger?"

Freddie sighed, and drew one leg up on the balustrade and held it to his chest, resting his chin on his knee. "Roland will give you a thousand excuses: she's young, she's naive. He's not spoken the truth to me."

That came as a shock. "Really?"

"There's something there they'd rather keep hidden. I'd wager they have good reason."

I almost disagreed, though it was certainly true. Roland and Freddie's secret was well worth keeping. It assured their safety. Their future together.

"I'll take your word," I said.

We were quiet while I finished my cigarette. Then Freddie asked, "What is it that keeps you up this night, Bertie Preston?"

I stared into his unguarded eyes. He trusted me with his secrets, even now admitting to me his love for Roland. He'd been honest so I would feel safe to speak plainly.

"I came here thinking that my career had begun," I said. "That a commission from the Earl of Wakeford meant I'd be painting for British nobility until I had fame and more money than I would know what to do with. But I didn't know this place would be empty. I didn't know the Napiers were so ruined . . ." A tremble of nerves. It was odd to be saying all this aloud. "If I spread word that I've been here, I'm guilty by association, but if I don't, I'm no one."

Freddie scratched the back of his neck, brow pinched. He wasn't at all fond of aristocracy, despite his devotion to Roland. Perhaps I'd salted the wound. Though when he looked at me again, he was almost smiling. "Why do you care so much about painting for nobility?"

I brushed fallen ashes to the ground. "I suppose after Julian's letter, I assumed I *could*. That I deserved to . . ." Admitting this made me feel childish.

"There are artists," Freddie began, "plenty of which are friends of mine, who make a living from their work without ever having shaken the hand of a lord. You need not aim so high, my darling. You need not waste your time making a name amongst people who think themselves better than you. They will only hurt you, because they fear what they don't understand. They fear things you know are lovely."

I had to look away from him to quell a rise of emotion.

"There are others out there . . . people who favor feeling over propriety. Those are your people, Bertie. Not the ones you'll find on the pages of *Burke's*. And as for the Napiers . . . you will never meet a family with more love in their hearts. If you turn your back on them for a check, you're just as cruel as those who would shame them."

I swept away a tear, but Freddie must have seen it, for he took my hand. "You have the talent to paint for the king, I've no doubt. But I imagine if His Majesty never pays a call, you'll keep on doing it, won't you? Because you're a painter. Art is your flame."

I thought of who I was in the weeks before Julian's letter, in the months and years before, mixing and painting in my bedroom, finding inspiration in every wander down the road, in each person who sat opposite me in the train. She would be disappointed to see me now.

Freddie was right. I'd developed a mad craving for recognition that now seemed so juvenile. How humiliating it was to have it reflected at me so plainly! I'd forgot what made my art important.

Julian had been moved by a colorless photograph of my painting. He'd seen more in it than even I knew was there. He'd risked the assurance of his seclusion to invite me to Castle Braemore. That was powerful. More powerful than fame and fortune.

Still, that ever-present knot tightened around my stomach. This would all come to an end once summer was over. "Are you ever frightened of the future, Freddie?"

"Fear is a notion, Bertie. The action that follows is far more important."

I left him there on the terrace to smoke another cigarette, and went upstairs on weary legs. I turned and kept on until I was standing before the door to Julian's apartments. As I'd hoped, there was yellow light beneath. I raised my fist and, as firmly as I dared, gave a knock.

I couldn't think what caused him to open with such little pause. But within seconds he was standing before me, bare chested, hair dripping from a bath.

"I can't sleep," I whispered.

Julian took my hand and shut the door behind us.

WE WERE NEARLY undressed when we fell into his bed. The linens were already in disarray, as though welcoming us back to where we belonged. Julian did not slow this time—not for a breath. We kissed as two people who were ravenous for something buried deeply within each other, a drop of sweet, cold water for parched tongues. He tasted so good that I wanted to take a bite, to savor, to let him melt in my mouth.

I knelt with one knee on either side of his hips and slipped out of my dressing gown. He rubbed the tops of my legs and watched as I tugged my nightdress up, up and over. His hands trailed slowly up my waist, gliding over my ribs. I rose and his lips brushed over my nipple. I arched my back, weaving my hands in his hair, holding him to me.

More, more, ever more—to break apart would surely stop our hearts.

I tugged his hair gently to incline his head, to kiss his mouth. His heart pounded against my chest, his breaths and mine the same sweet, hot cloud.

His defenses fell before my eyes. He pulled my hands down to his chest and I kissed him. We moved, floating on the wave of our breaths. I whispered his name. He kissed me back.

There was still hesitation, but it was smaller, a twinge in his brow, a lasting question in his eye. I put his hand between my legs so he could feel I wanted him, that I wanted *this*, that with him I felt safer than I had with any other man. It was in that moment of sheer vulnerability that he hardened and the last ounce of resistance melted away. I smiled into his mouth.

We both shook when we finally came together. We held on to the freezing bow of a ship that threatened to capsize. We locked arms around each other, clung to life. Breathing our last breaths. Gasping for time. Then the water rushed in, the ship went over, the ocean meeting us as we fell. He pulled me deeper and I drowned.

When I bit his shoulder, it was slippery with salt water.

"What was that for?" he asked with a breathless laugh.

"I'd like to eat you up."

We slipped under the quilt, slick skin sticking to clean sheets. I touched the rounded part of my inner thigh where the tepid evidence of Julian remained.

He lay beside me like a man on his deathbed, dosed with morphia. Not a line on his face. Not a muscle tensed. Not a visible thought.

I wished desperately for a pencil and paper.

His head tilted towards me as I wrapped one of his curls around my finger. I imagined sketching his features onto the blank right side of his face with sharp graphite, crosshatching for dimension on cheekbone, feathery lines to perfect the creases of his eye, shading over the bow of his lip, which I'd smooth out with the pad of my thumb.

I mimicked the action, and Julian reached behind me, making chills as he traced the bottom of my spine to the top, counting the vertebrae. His head inched forward, as though he meant to kiss me, but didn't make the full journey.

"Are you warm enough?" he asked.

I nodded. Julian closed his eye, and I swept my lips over the thick hairs of his brow. As his breaths slowed I whispered, "Very warm indeed."

French Postcards

SEPTEMBER 1915

France isn't far at all," Celia said to Julian, spreading jam on her toast. "Uncle Richard said you can even see it from Dover Promenade Pier. Is that true?"

"If Richard says so," he answered.

Celia nodded, proud to be correct. "When do you think you'll be back again?"

"I'm not entirely sure, pal. That all depends on what goes on."

It was only two of them in the Breakfast Room. With Roland at Eton and their mother abed, Julian allowed Celia to sit at table. Their mother would be aghast, as Cece was only twelve, too young to be out of the nursery. But Julian liked the company. He needed it this morning especially, as he sat feeling stiff in his freshly starched uniform. In a few hours, he'd be gone to the front.

"What about the picnic?" Celia asked. "Who will give the speech if you're not there? And Christmas? You must be home for Christmas. Mama will be ever so cross if you miss chapel."

Julian smiled and pushed his uneaten eggs with his fork. "I shall try to be home for Christmas." But he knew that he would not.

"If not Christmas, then my birthday. If you do come then, might you bring French perfume for my present?"

Julian sipped his coffee, hardly tasting it. This was all rather exciting for his little sister—the war, the men in uniform, the trip they were taking this afternoon to meet Gwen and Richard in London, where they would say their farewells.

But Julian was terrified. He'd been sick that morning, hands shaking so terribly he'd had to ring for a footman to help him to dress. The boy had taken great pride in fastening Julian's bronze buttons and Sam Browne belt, and talked of how excited he was to receive his own orders. Braemore would be void of men in time.

"Might you send postcards, too?" Celia said. "I'd like one of the Notre-Dame."

"Notre-Dame—of course." Julian wasn't sure he'd see Paris at all, but if it made her smile, he'd promise and do what he could. "In return I'll expect letters from you every week."

She slid her eyes to the ceiling in a very adult look of annoyance. Celia was so grown-up now—he would miss the last precious months of her childhood.

"I may as well send one every *day*. There will be heaps to tell you about all the trouble Roland gets into, and it won't all fit in one envelope."

This made Julian chuckle. Better that Roland was wreaking havoc safely at home than learning drills in uniform. "One per day, then. I shall never be homesick."

Celia's face fell. Something snapped inside her; something began to make sense. She knew not to make a fuss, not at table, where she'd promised Julian she'd behave, and so she sipped her milk quietly. Though she acted like a lady, she was still so small to him, so naive. She'd be alone at Braemore with Roland at school, ignored day after day by their mother, only Miss Quinn to keep company with until he returned.

If.

"I thought perhaps you may like to stop with Gwen for a while," he said, twisting his ring round his little finger. "She'll be lonely with her husband away. The pair of you can look after one another."

Celia's chin came up. There was nothing in the world she liked more than shadowing her big sister. "May I? Really, Julian?"

He nodded, glad to have cheered her. "She'll take you home this afternoon, and the two of you will discuss it."

Celia smiled and munched more toast.

Julian checked the clock on the mantel. The motor would be brought round in an hour, and then they'd be off. He'd likely not see Castle Braemore again for months.

"Cece, I must go and check my things have been packed properly. If you've finished, go on upstairs and ready yourself for the journey."

Celia hopped off of her chair, ever the obedient one of his younger siblings. "I've got a new hat for London," she said, and left him alone.

THEY HAD COME home on their final leave in crisp uniforms, their shoulders broader, their faces tanned, their hair cut modestly. Richard with a mustache.

Gwen watched him sleep. He'd said he had missed their bed, but mainly her being in it, and so she couldn't bear to get up before he was awake. This was their final morning together for perhaps—perhaps a long time.

He looked different to her, practically a stranger. Months of training had rid him of the softness she'd fallen in love with, below his ribs, under his arms. He was hard now, and perhaps too thin. The mustache was something to grow accustomed to, shaggy and reddish compared to his flaxen hair. Funny, that. Gwen smiled, running her knuckle down his cheek. After being married four years, there was still something to surprise her about him.

At her touch, Richard let out an audible breath, and turned his head. "Is that a fly?" She tapped her fingertips against his nose, his forehead, his lips. "Pesky beast. Bugger off." He swatted and caught her hand, then opened his eyes and smiled. "That's not a fly."

"Nor an insect of any kind." Gwen kissed him, his mustache tickling oddly.

"Thank heaven."

"I wish I were a fly," she said. "Then I would follow you to France and buzz in your ear when you're being mean to your men."

"Chosen their side already, have you?" Under the linens, his hands gripped her bottom. "Mother bear, always on the lookout for more blessed cubs."

Gwen shivered at his touch. "You're just a bully, you know. Always have been."

She laughed as he turned over, and welcomed the comfort of his weight on top of her. "I bullied you right into marrying me, didn't I?"

"Mm-hmm."

He dipped for a kiss. "Didn't have a single say in the matter, did you?"

"None."

He kissed her again. "And now you must bend to my every will."

"Every. One." Gwen fastened her legs around his hips. "What is your will just now, my lord? So I know."

Richard cupped her bare breast in his rough hand, kneading and drawing his thumb over her nipple. "My will is to ensure you think of nothing but me whilst I'm away. I want to make such perfect love to you that the lasting memory of it will keep you warm at night, alone in this bed. Perhaps put a baby in you."

Gwen's smile faded. He noticed the falter and quickly pressed his lips to her cheek. His breath burned her ear as he whispered, "We must hope."

"I do hope." Her breath caught. "I hope very much. Every instant. My God, I hope, Richard. I hope . . ."

He buried his face in her shoulder before her first tear fell. Gwen had forgot a baby entirely. She was crying for him. This wasn't like the last time they'd parted, when she'd had nothing but pride in him, thinking it would all end before he was called to the front. Now she held nothing but the fear and dread of losing him.

As she breathed back tears, Richard kissed her neck, her shoulder, her breast, her stomach, working to move her mind away from the future, bring it back to bed. Gwen rose to meet him, desperate to be one, desperate to hold him inside her, where he was only hers.

Gwen didn't cry again until he'd left the bed to bathe. She had the idea that she might get it all out of the way so she could be strong on the platform. There was only so much one could cry before one emptied. So she thought then.

They met her family at the Savoy. There was Julian in his uniform, silent and stoic as ever. Being in the same battalion, he and Richard would be off together on the train from Charing Cross. They'd both joined up directly after reading the headlines on 5 August 1914. Gwen remembered not knowing what precisely to do with herself that day. There was a lot of pacing, and wringing of the hands, and checking mantels for dust.

At the time, she hadn't been worried about Richard. She'd believed the talk that the war would end quickly, that he'd return to her before she had the chance to miss him. Besides that, Richard had been in the OTC at Oxford, he was tall and brawn, a hunter and a sportsman. One would be pressed to find a man better suited for the military.

Instead, Gwen worried for Julian. Despite his eagerness to follow his peers, he wasn't suited for it. Not feeble by any means, but too gentle. Their father had scorned him for it, she remembered vividly. He was meant to be what Papa called "a man," but Julian couldn't be anything but his lovely self. He didn't belong in a war, with a gun aimed at another living soul. My God, he refused to shoot pheasant!

But she knew he must go like his father before him. He was young and able-bodied and closer to the king than most men, so of course he must fight for him.

So as Gwen approached Julian now, she smiled, touched his perfectly polished buttons, pretended to brush a flake of dust from his shoulder, and kissed his cheek. She congratulated him, though inside she was bursting, screaming—*Don't do this! Be my baby brother again.*

Julian's hands were bare and icy in hers. "You ought to be wearing your gloves," she said, turning them over to see pink knuckles. "Where is your ring?"

He patted his chest pocket. She supposed only married men were allowed jewelry.

Gwen found a smile again and turned to her husband. "Don't we have the finest pair of officers England has ever commissioned?"

Richard put his arm around her. "What a shame Roland isn't of age; he'd round out the group."

"Not a shame," she corrected, seeing the similar dread in Julian's eyes. "Rules are made for a reason. Where's—? Celia, hello? Would you care to greet your sister?"

Celia was uncharacteristically quiet, dressed finely in navy wool coat and ribboned beret, which ought to have made her beam. Instead her face was long. Gwen had expected Cece might be holding Julian's hand or his elbow, but she stood at a noticeable distance, staring at her shoes.

Poor lamb. She must have been breaking inside to see her older brother leaving again. Gwen hurried forward and wrapped an arm around her.

Through tea, Julian said nothing, and ate nothing, only stirring his cup endlessly until it went cold. Gwen kept on smiling. At Richard, at Celia. Luckily, Richard was in high spirits and kept the conversation going. Richard was an optimist, a bloody insufferable one. He winked at Gwen and held her hand under the table, though all she wanted to do was burst into tears and take him home.

Celia was mute, not eating a bite.

Then they were on the platform, in what seemed like an instant. Where had the time gone? And why hadn't Gwen said more to Richard? Why hadn't she said *I love you* every minute? Now the train was coming, steam filling any space left between groups of bodies clustered on the platform.

One could almost feel the collective sigh as families embraced their men. Mothers cried, lovers kissed. Celia clung to Gwen's side, leaning into her hip rather than stand beside Julian, who was stiff with fear, both for the chaos and for their goodbyes.

"Kiss *me* first," Richard said, taking hold of Gwen's lapel. "I'm the husband."

She removed his peaked cap and rested her arms on his shoulders. His hands slid down her hips, no thought of what people might think. Gwen traced his face with her eyes, remembering every detail, every fleck of gold in his blue eyes, every slanted tooth, and the white scar that ran beside his nose from a childhood fall.

"I love you, my darling," she said. It sounded so sterile. But what else was there to say? There wasn't enough time. "I want you to think of me every time a fly pesters you."

He chuckled and held her closer. "I'll think of you every instant. My precious dove."

They kissed, and it didn't feel right, because Julian and Celia were audience. She knew their true goodbye had come that morning, and this was only for show. Before she could get too good a grip on him, Richard turned her bodily towards Julian and took his cap back. He pressed his mouth to her ear: "I'll look after him for you." Then he released her, fit his cap back on his head, and said for everyone to hear: "Make haste; we must be off."

How perfectly Richard. So tender in her ear. So steely on the exterior, where others could see him.

Gwen put her hand on Celia's back. "Give your brother a kiss for luck." She looked up at Gwen, eyes glassy. Shook her head. "You must. Now, Cece. The train is going."

But Celia shook her head again, and hid behind Gwen. She couldn't think what had got into the girl, who was usually generous with affection. Meantime, Julian stood with arms dangling at his sides, looking close to tears himself. He shrugged.

What had possibly gone on between them?

More steam flooded the platform, and Gwen forgot Celia for the moment. Julian was waiting for inspection. She wasn't sure why, or when she'd started, but she did it with all her siblings—checked their faces, made sure their hair was in place, looked for stains on their shirts. Julian was nearly immaculate for perhaps the first time.

Gwen pinched his cheek to make him smile.

He rubbed the spot with his palm. "What did I ever do to you?"

"You were born, of course. I was quite content in the nursery before you came along. I had all the toys to myself, and the evenings were so quiet."

His smile deepened, and he wrapped his arms around her. Here again, there was much left unsaid. Her only hope was that they'd see each other again.

When she let go, her cheeks were wet, but she refused his handkerchief. "Just don't die, for heaven's sake. Roland isn't fit for an earl."

Celia must have heard, for she lurched forward to knock Gwen out of the way. She latched herself to Julian's waist, leaking eyes pressed to khaki wool. He held her shaking shoulders, eyes pleading for Gwen to help.

"It's all right, dear," she said. "You shall see him again soon." She managed to pull Celia off, having to grip her as she fought to get back to Julian. "Please, Cece, do not fuss."

Richard's height appeared behind Gwen for support, but she was already crying herself as Celia wailed and pulled, ignoring her sister's pleas. "Cece, come away—"

The train was filling. The men had to go. But Julian knelt patiently before Celia, taking her hands in his. "It's all right, pal."

"I don't care about the folly," she whimpered.

Gwen was shaken. "Folly?" But neither heard.

Celia sniffed, breaths shaking. "I want you to stay."

"I cannot." Julian reached up to straighten her hat. "I have to be off with Uncle Richard. We all have to be off."

"Why?" Celia gasped. "Why must you go?"

Julian shook his head. He didn't have an answer. If Celia had asked Gwen, she wouldn't have either. She might have asked every last person on the platform and come up empty.

"I go to protect you, Cece," Julian said finally. "Like I've always done."

Their men were carried away on the current of khaki uniforms. Celia leaned into Gwen, clutching fistfuls of her coat. Gwen felt the sudden shock of desperate fear as she lost sight of them, and began to tremble. What if she never saw them again? How could she let them go?

Then she spotted Julian, pale face cut up by the hats of those passing in the opposite direction. He touched shoulders to move by them, searching the crowd fervently until he saw Celia. The train whistled behind him, threatening its departure.

A smile spread slowly over Julian's face as he waved his cap. "Send a starling!" he shouted, cupping his mouth. "Fetch me home, Cece!"

As Celia howled into Gwen's arm, the crush drowned him once more.

15

Once Julian and I had shattered pretenses and surrendered ourselves to the intimacies of body and soul, I no longer lacked inspiration. I felt as though the electric lights of Castle Braemore had switched on for the first time. I noticed things I'd been missing. I woke with an idea of precisely the emotion I hoped to capture with paint.

Perishing alongside discretion was my regard for order. The Music Room was unrecognizable; it was now, undoubtedly, an art studio. Upon entering, the lungs infused with the sharp, acrid scent of turpentine, a perfume I wore proudly. The tarpaulins were dotted and splattered with spills and prints from my studio shoes (a pair of old slippers), along with bare footprints, made once I'd abandoned shoes altogether. My table was so thick with spilled and intentionally decanted paint and fallen pigment, both dried and claggy, that there was no level surface left on which to rest a cup of tea.

I stopped bothering with a smock. The old dresses I wore in studio were stained beyond hope, and the oils had somehow reached my good clothes, leaving stains on elbows and hems. It seemed the job completely consumed me, physically and mentally, for I thought and wondered and dreamt of little else save the Napiers and Castle Braemore.

In this flurry of inspiration and obsession, I grew careless and the inevitable happened: Paint got through to the herringbone floor. It smeared across windowsills and doorknobs. When I'd confessed as much to Julian, he'd laughed. "Worry not," he'd said. "I'll bring someone in to mend things at summer's end."

His words had cooled me entirely. There would be a time after my residence at Braemore when all evidence of my projects would be scrubbed away. I tried not to dwell.

When I wasn't in studio, I was in and out of Julian's apartments. My visits came when I needed to awaken the muse, for Julian knew more about the estate than anybody, and spoke with great love, as if he'd planted every flower, trimmed every hedge, raised every deer in the park.

One day as he tried hopelessly to teach me chess, he'd told me of a castle ruin that sat a mile and a quarter beyond the lake on a low hill.

"The castle that gave Braemore its name?" I had asked, and he'd nodded.

"I used to take Celia there on horseback. The meadow is covered in wildflowers. Celia always made daisy chains to bring back for Gwen."

"You have horses?" I'd asked, enchanted.

Julian had gone instantly grave. "No; they've all gone to the war."

So the following morning, dressed in a pair of Roland's tweed breeches, I'd trekked on foot to the ruin with a map Julian drew himself, and found it was little more than a pile of old lichened stones. But it was beautiful, too stubborn to be forgot, carpeted by daisies and surrounded by an endless quilt of countryside. I'd stayed all afternoon.

Another day, Julian and I had stood at the window as he spoke of a particular section of garden that was his favorite. An egg-shaped hedge was trimmed with an alcove for a bench. But the branches grew widely, and if one was small enough, one could wriggle between them and end up within what Julian described as the chamber of a great, green heart.

"The first time I gave my governess the slip, I hid there with a book," he'd said with a laugh. "She would never have found me had I not become desperate for the necessary."

So I painted the hedge, too, posing Roland on the bench with a book, his face a mere suggestion by imprecise brushstrokes. I thought Julian might hang it in his new bedroom in his new home. I wondered often where he planned to go, and *how* he planned to go. Though he laughed off my light attempts to coax him from his room, I hoped one day he might accept. One day he'd have to, surely.

We kissed and made love. We shared his lunches and suppers and teas. We ate Gwen's chocolates and drank whisky, and smoked and talked endlessly. I became familiar with his routine and his drills, watching lazily from the bed as he exercised, grunting while muscles tensed under gleaming skin. Now and again I could convince him to sketch with me, though he imparted minimal effort, saying he preferred my work to his. A likely excuse.

We wasted long hours as though the summer would never end. I hadn't thought of how he'd pay me, and after a while I forgot why I had worried. Surely this was how a real artist lived: half-naked, drenched in paint and kisses and wine. Real artists lived on passion. The idea that I'd ever longed for London began to puzzle me. Why opt for noise and grey when one could have languid rural afternoons, and endless new pockets of space to discover in the country? I ignored small voices reminding me that our togetherness was temporary. I ignored my heart feeling things it shouldn't. I abandoned fear for a fortnight, until one evening when Julian fell asleep early.

I wandered his rooms absently, flicking through books he'd left scattered about. I reviewed a still life I'd started of the unmade bed, deciding I would draw the focus to the two tumblers on the bedside. I admired framed photographs on top of Julian's writing desk: he and Gwen as children, Roland and Celia arm in arm, an older one of a couple—his parents, perhaps?

Papers stuck out from the drop lid. I lifted it cautiously to find documents, letters, and bills crumpled in a heap. I looked over my shoulder. In the bedroom, Julian lay sprawled on his front, shoulders rising and falling in the even pattern of sleep.

I took up the first letter. *We must meet to discuss retrenching*, it read.

I chose another: *I urge you to remember the deadline.*

Another: *With all due respect, my lord, there are urgent matters which need to be seen to.*

With yesterday's date: *Did you receive my last note? I shall ring you at Braemore tomorrow.*

Rotten luck for this chap. The earl's apartments did not have a telephone.

I'd seen Julian hunched over the desk reading, rubbing his temple, lighting another cigarette. It was not my place to question whom he corresponded with or what he was scribbling on his stationery. In fact, I hadn't wondered until now. Braemore ran so splendidly well without him—whatever he was doing from this desk must have been enough.

Except there were debts needing to be paid, and the estate to be done away with. But Julian seemed to be putting it off. How many of these letters had he ignored? And what would befall him when his debts caught up and nothing had been done about them?

I wondered how much he had left.

Suddenly chilled, I crawled back into bed with Julian. In my mind, the things about us began to vanish. The settee, the piano, the crystal decanters. The lamps, the suits, the enormous Tudor bed. With all of it gone, Julian looked small. A nervous boy who needed his hair cut.

I settled in beside him, close enough that I could feel his breath on my face. In that moment, I could not doubt what my heart felt for him.

If either of us hoped for a future worth living, something would need to be done.

THE NEXT MORNING was the last of July, and Anna arrived in Gwen's motor. The little Viscount of Stanfield had been taken ill with a chest cold, and Anna was sent to Braemore to avoid catching it.

I thought Anna might be frightened to be apart from her mother, but when Celia and I met her at the door, she waved happily to the driver as he rolled away. Releasing her curls from beneath a straw hat, she skipped indoors and handed it off to a footman like a lady.

"Where shall I sleep?" she said. "May I choose my room? I'd like to be next door to Bertie."

Celia put her hands on her hips. "You shall sleep in the nursery, where little girls belong."

"I'm not a little girl today. I'm your guest. I should like a guest room, please."

"You're our guest who is also a little girl." Celia pressed her hand on the girl's back and led her towards the stairs. "Let's go and see you settled."

My relief was palpable. Flattered as I was that Anna wanted to be close to me, having her near would make sneaking to Julian's apartments a far more difficult task.

Anna looked back at me longingly while Celia drove her away. I stuck my tongue out, making her giggle into her stuffed dog's fur.

Freddie decided Anna ought to be spoiled, and otherwise entertained, and the perfect way to do so was to paint. And because it was Freddie's suggestion, it was so.

I was asked for a list of supplies and winced when handing it off, thinking of the letters on Julian's desk. But supplies were sent for nevertheless, and brought outdoors. It was an enchanting setup: the lawn its own studio, spread with old linens to protect the grass; easels, canvas, and an enticing buffet of paints and brushes. We even had a table with nibbles and lemonade—never a gathering at Braemore without refreshment. The boys brought several bottles of beer. Apparently this was to free their artistic sensibilities. I couldn't argue.

While they stood at easels, I sat beside Anna, each of us with a small canvas to start with. She mixed her colors, insisting on doing this as we had done before. She balanced her palette loftily on her wrist like an artist in a moving picture, and tapped the end of her brush against her mouth.

"What shall I paint?" she asked.

"What should you like to paint?"

"I'm not sure." Anna wrinkled her snub nose and regarded her blank canvas as a death-defying leap. I knew the feeling all too well.

"Start with your eyes," I said. "Look about the lawn and see what's taking your attention."

Anna sat up on her knees, chin high. She craned her head from one side to the other until stopping abruptly. I tried to follow her eyes, but couldn't tell what she was looking at.

"I want to paint a dog," she said.

I put my hand over my eyes to shield the sun. Surely there wasn't a dog anywhere near? The Napiers hadn't had hounds since Julian was small. Anna sat down again, and dipped her brush. Well, far be it from me to snuff the muse.

"There you are, then," I said. "What's made you think of a dog?"

"I think Uncle Earl would like a dog."

Even as I peered over the lawn to be sure, I knew it was silly. If Julian couldn't leave his room, the outdoors was surely too deep a plunge.

Anna tapped my shoulder. "He's watching. See?"

I followed her finger up to his bedroom window. Sure enough, there was a shadow, moving just enough to prove it wasn't a lamp.

Anna's tongue stuck out from the corner of her mouth as she slopped her brush onto the canvas. The grey-brown mess of a color she'd made happened to be perfect for an Irish wolfhound. "I want to paint something for him like you are," she said.

I put on a smile, but the notion made me sad. Julian watched all alone as we had our fun with what was left of his money.

While Anna was painting her dog, I painted Celia. She had grown weary of our activities early on, and thrown it in. Now she sat in a wicker chair, wearing a draped turban to protect her bob from the wind, holding her sweating glass and watching the boys.

It was her expression that drew me to her in the moment. She was the portrait of boredom, like the idea that all this lavishness—the fine crystal, the ribbon sandwiches and the petits fours, the stately home behind us—could not thrill her. What, instead, was on her mind? What was missing that might fill the void in her eyes?

By the time I'd finished the portrait, the boys were ready for a nap, Anna for a bath. While Celia brought Anna upstairs, Roland suggested that their niece join us in the dining room for dinner, for there was nobody to enforce silly rules as there were when he was a child. Then Freddie proposed an alternative idea—that we grown-ups eat with Anna in the nursery. No sense in forcing her into adulthood when there was opportunity for us old things to remember what it was like to be a child.

And so it was.

The gong was hit hilariously early, readying us to knock on the nursery door at six o'clock—mindful of Anna's bedtime. She promptly answered, giggling at the boys in their tails, a rarity for most nights at Braemore. She complimented Celia and me on our sparkling gowns as we kissed her on both cheeks. Freddie knelt and offered her his elbow, walking on his knees to be her size.

Huxley and a footman laid each course as we sat surrounded by teddies and dolls and puppets. It was a marvel to know each Napier had slept in this room, where they'd done all their pretending and dreaming. To think young Julian played with tin soldiers on the windowsill where they were still queued, no notion he'd someday be one of them. No doubt that was how all our lost boys were brought up, with wistful ideas of the glory of war.

Dessert was the main event, a towering croquembouche, covered in sugared almonds and drizzled chocolate. Anna's eyes were saucers as it was set at the center of the table, and we gave an applause Cook would never hear. Anna stood on her seat to reach the one on top, Roland holding her waist to ensure she didn't fall.

By the end of the meal, she drooped against his shoulder, the corners of her mouth stuck with chocolate and cream.

"I think this is the quietest I've seen her," I said.

"Adorable, is she not?" Roland tickled her ear. "Like a French poodle."

"I'm not a poodle." Anna nuzzled her forehead against his arm. "I'm a wolf."

"A wolf pup, then. Now, little wolf, what do you say to your mama when she's asked what you've been up to with Uncle Roland and Auntie Cece?"

Anna's eyes shut. "I ate my carrots and went to bed early."

Roland bent to kiss her head. "Clever girl."

Later, I helped Celia dress a barely conscious Anna for bed. She bent over the dozing child to sweep a tender hand over her hair. I wondered where Anna might have been this night if Gwen had not had the goodwill to adopt her as her own. When Celia straightened, we met eyes and I smiled.

"What a charmed world she's fallen into," I said. "She must feel so loved."

Celia nodded soberly. "I pray she does."

AFTER DINNER I went to Julian to find he had been drinking. Stripped away were all the extras that elevated a simple man into a *gentleman*—jacket, waistcoat, tie. I wanted to push his braces off as well. He handed me a drink and shut the door behind me, removed his mask, and set it aside.

We'd run out of words, it seemed. So we went to bed.

When we were through, Julian grabbed the quilt and threw it over us, blowing air thick with the scent of lavender and sex. I hitched him to me with a bent leg over his lap and fiddled with his hair—it was thrilling, truly, to know a man with a length of hair one could tousle and twist—while his fingers played invisible piano keys on my thigh.

"Where did you learn to do that?" I asked of a particular act which had never been done to me before but was wildly enjoyable. "From a French girl?" Julian smiled but closed his eye against the question. "Come, say. You don't suppose I'm unaware of those places with the blue lights? I've treated enough venereal disease . . ."

Julian wriggled. "Delicately put, as usual."

"I find the barriers of polite conversation quite smash when one is lying nakedly beside another."

He laughed, and I rolled a lock of his hair over my finger. Before I could kiss him, a noise made me pause. Julian hadn't heard it, not even blinking at the sound. I sat up. Again, tapping or . . . a light knock on the sitting room door.

"What's the matter?" Julian asked.

"Someone's in the corridor."

With a groan, he leaned to retrieve his watch from the bedside. "It's the middle of the night." More knocking, light but erratic, perhaps a palm rather than a fist. Julian ran a hand over his face, voice muffled: "That's Anna."

I flushed with panic. Had he not locked us in, we'd have been caught.

While Julian pulled on his trousers, I slipped my dress over my head. We met at the bedroom door, hovering in the threshold. With it open, we could hear Anna's voice, small and anxious.

Julian's face was frosted in the darkness. "What is she doing out of bed?"

I folded my arms against a chill. "You must return her to the nursery."

"I can't."

"You must." I took his hand, feeling a tremor. "She's all alone. It's a strange house."

His panic widened, shortening breaths, tightening the muscles of his stomach. "Might you?"

"I'm not supposed to be in here."

Anna called for her Uncle Earl, voice shaking between hoarse wails. My heart ached for her; I couldn't understand why Julian didn't act. He leaned his shoulder against the doorjamb, head hanging.

"You must go," I said. "It'll be all right."

He shook his head. "She doesn't know me."

"She speaks of you often."

"I'll frighten her."

"Julian, she's frightened already!"

As the banging continued, I watched Julian crumble beside me, holding his head as though it would burst. I gave in. There was no time to be cross, not now. Shoving past him, I went to the sitting room and turned the key to fling the door open.

Anna stood red-faced on the other side in her nightdress. Her howl was cut short, and she sighed as I knelt and took hold of her narrow arms. "What's the matter, love?"

"I had a nightmare," Anna whimpered. "I wanted to find Auntie Cece but I got lost. There are too many doors." She swiped the back of her hand over her wet eyes. It must have been the relief of seeing me that distracted her from asking why I was there at all. "I'm frightened of the dark. May I come in there?"

"I'm afraid not, darling," I said, chafing her arms. "Shall I see you back to the nursery?"

Anna shook her curls. "Please, it's too dark. Where's my uncle?"

I wiped a tear from her chin with my knuckle. "He's just fallen asleep, and what a shame it would be to wake him. Come, let's get you tucked up in bed—"

Anna wriggled and fought, pushing away my hands. As she let out a shrill protest, her eyes went up. I felt Julian's presence behind me and stood to find him dressed, mask on, hair pushed behind his ears.

Anna ran straight into his knees, and sobbed with a hiccup. Without a blink of hesitation, Julian swept her into his arms. She clasped her wrist behind his head, nuzzling her face into his neck, finally silent. I softened at the sight.

"You're all right, pal. I'm here." Julian stroked her back, but she was not yet fit to speak. "May I put you to bed?"

After a muffled cough and a sniff, Anna's face appeared. "Will you stay with me?"

"I will." Julian looked at me. "May Bertie come?"

I shook my head, but Anna nodded her answer. I was frightened of being seen with him at an hour, hair and clothing so conspicuously rumpled. But Julian could not do it alone, I knew after seeing his fear so plainly minutes ago. So we went.

My candle was a pitiful flicker in the soot of the corridor. Little wonder why Anna was so afraid; night was blacker here in the belly of the house. In the turbid silence, I could hear Julian doing battle with his lungs. I wanted to give him the comfort of touch, but worried the candle would go out if I didn't shield the flame.

Another few paces and Julian slowed. Then he stopped completely, sharp exhales blowing Anna's hair. I held up the candle to find his eye closed tight. "Julian?"

Anna might have been asleep until then, lifting her head to look about. Julian tightened his arms around her.

"Do you need to go back?" I asked.

In lieu of a response, he stepped forward.

We hurried our pace to the nursery. Once inside, Julian eased, though he remained clammy and peaked. I hovered near the threshold while he lowered Anna onto one of the beds. He drew the quilt to her chin, then rose the wick on the lamp, filling the room more fully with light. At his feet was Anna's fallen stuffed dog, which he retrieved and nestled beside her.

"There we are," he said, and sat on the edge of the bed.

Anna blinked up at him with heavy lids. "You look different."

Julian pressed the bridge of his spectacles. She sat up, reaching for his beard, causing him to flinch. Then he leaned so she could feel the whiskers. She tugged on a lock of his hair, then flopped back down. They smiled. I couldn't tell which was more in awe of the other.

"This was my bed, you know," Julian said.

"I know. That's why I chose it. Mama slept over there. I like this one better, though." Anna touched her uncle's knuckles absently. "Why don't you ever come out?"

Julian turned his hand so she could lay her palm over his. "I share your fear of the darkness."

"It isn't always dark," she countered. "Only at night."

Julian gazed about his old room. "For me, it is always dark."

Rather than puzzle, Anna, in her childhood wisdom, said, "Perhaps you ought to carry a candle, Uncle."

Julian smiled and straightened the dog's bow, telling him sternly, "*Smarten yourself up, soldier,*" which made Anna giggle.

"I painted a picture for you today," she said.

"Did you? Thank you, pal." Julian brought the blanket up further over her shoulders and smoothed it carefully. "You remind me of my little sister."

"Auntie Cece?"

"I remember when she was small as you."

Anna sniffed, rubbing her raw nose with her sleeve. "Did you know my papa? I never met him."

"You've met him. He held you when you were tiny."

Anna's brows knitted. "I wish he didn't go. But Mama said he was very brave."

"The bravest man I've known. He looked after me in the army."

With the dialogue at a pause, Anna's head bobbed until it settled deep into her pillow. Julian used his thumb and knuckle to wipe her running nose. Her eyelids flicked closed, open, closed again, until she drifted to a place between waking and dreaming, as children do so instantly. Julian moved off the bed to sit beside it, and reached up to lower the wick.

We were left in shadow. I felt as though I'd disappeared.

Anna stirred. Whispered, "Uncle Earl?"

Julian took her dangling hand and pressed it to the exposed corner of his mouth. "I'll not leave you."

Rustling as she turned, then all was quiet again. I sagged into a chair in the corner to wait, warm and drowsy. Julian stayed at attention, a sentry keeping watch for frightening thoughts and wardrobe monsters. Feeling safe and enchanted, I was lulled to sleep by the rhythm of their two breaths.

I woke when Julian touched my cheek. He offered his hand, and with what remained of the candle, we left a sleeping Anna to return to his rooms. In the doorway, I stood on my toes to kiss him, noticing dampness in his whiskers. "All right?"

Julian nodded.

"I should turn in, then."

Julian looked down, taking my hands in his. In his hesitation and the tightening of his mouth, I could see the fear he'd been stifling was fit to burst from him. And just as he was unable to refuse helping his frightened niece, I was unable to refuse helping him.

"Come," I said, "let's go to bed."

16

The next day, I walked the Long Gallery whilst Anna took the opportunity to sprint off all the cake she'd had at tea. Then she skipped. Then she twirled, plaits bouncing over her shoulders. I was enjoying her company a sight more than the artwork on the walls.

All at once, she came skidding up to me, panting, and pushed a loose curl from her face with a sweaty palm. "Which is your favorite, Bertie?"

None of them, truly. Then I remembered Lady Wakeford, leaning listlessly against the wall. I pointed. "I like this one."

"She looks like a princess," Anna said without a hint of irony. I realized, with a tickle of humor, that the dowager much resembled her eldest daughter. "My favorite picture is downstairs. Want to see?"

What would Anna have been doing belowstairs? None of us had any business down there. Though I was curious. There was more to Braemore—an entire living, breathing engine—that I had hardly considered and was crucial to its memory. That meant it was up to me to capture it. Having seen footmen and maids step aside for me in corridors, I had an idea of what they might think if I moved beyond my place, through the baize door and into their carefully functioning world. But if Julian was going to sell Braemore, and leave behind a centuries-old legacy, I was going to remind him who kept that legacy clean, fed, and clothed. I was glad Anna had given me the idea.

We procured a key from Uncle Roland, who'd led such an expedition in the past. With sketchbook under my arm, I held Anna's sweaty hand as we made our way to the door that led down from the dining room. It was then that Anna's name was called, and she tried to hurry me, yanking my arm painfully until Auntie Cece caught us up.

"*There* you are." Celia came cantering through from the Morning Room, rubbing her arms. "You were meant to stay with Uncle Roland."

Anna clearly did not feel as scolded as I did. "We're only going downstairs."

Celia lifted a skeptical brow. "What gave you that idea?"

"Bertie wants to see the pictures!"

Not liking the blame on me, I made a vague, breathy sound of protest. "Anna mentioned there are some paintings downstairs. I certainly don't need to see them—"

Anna looked up at me. "Yes, you *do*!" Then to Celia: "She does!"

Celia swept her glance to me, and I found myself patting my hair to ensure it lay flat. "Apologies," she said. "I'll stop her pestering you."

I waved her off. "She was keeping me company. It's no bother."

Celia's smile tightened. Her expression might have fooled anyone else into thinking she was aloof. But I studied faces frequently enough to know it was put on.

Anna stepped forward, taking Celia's hand. "Come *with* us. It'll be fun. Won't it, Bertie?"

I smiled at Celia. In truth, I very much wanted to see the hidden paintings, and thought this likely to be my only chance. "Only if it's all right with your auntie."

"The staff won't like it," Celia said, gripping Anna's hand. "I had better go with you."

Descending into the echoing depths of Braemore was rather like plunging underwater. Below, the temperature was cooler, the stone walls icy and rigid under my fingertips. The white, utilitarian corridors were lit by bare electric bulbs, the wires exposed. The air was haunted with moisture and smelled of roots, harsh soap, and decades of diced onion.

Celia clearly knew where she was going, ushering us along when we heard the clamor of voices from the kitchen. When we reached the storage room door, she used the key to open the lock. Together we pushed the heavy oak and squinted into the darkness. Lit by two windows six feet above the floor were various items of furniture, some pristine, others with fabric torn or legs broken. There were candlesticks and fineries, rugs that had been rolled up and leaned on each other in corners, oxidized mirrors and ones that were shattered, only jagged pieces holding on, all collecting dust and cobwebs.

Anna began to slip her way through the small spaces between items. Celia and I had a more difficult time, lifting our skirts to step over a fallen lamp. I fancied this place was a mausoleum for all the family's unwanted items. They'd never be stored so carelessly if they were precious.

Something foul in the air made me wrinkle my nose. "A tad whiffy, eh?"

Celia remained indifferent. "A dead mouse, I shouldn't wonder."

"You are curiously unperturbed by that notion."

She bent to pluck a broken piece of ceramic from the floor, and set it beside a sad-looking jug missing its handle. "I spent time down here when I was a girl. After Gwen married, and the boys were both at school, I hadn't much else to do when I was bored of my governess."

"She allowed you to leave the nursery on your own?"

Celia bit an impish smile from her lip. "No." I was impressed. I'd never have expected her to be so brazen. She went on: "The house always felt so empty, but down here there were plenty of people to talk to. Cats, as well, sometimes . . . The cats were for the mice, you see."

"Naturally."

I must have looked perplexed, and I was. Who would have expected that Lady Celia had spent her childhood playing with animals belowstairs?

We found Anna kneeling on the floor near where a few canvases were leaned against a wall. She'd already removed the dust sheets, though they hadn't done much to preserve the art's integrity. It pained me to see the works in such ill condition. The style was obviously different to the artwork in the gallery: impressionistic, vibrant. Clumsy, some of them. My stomach turned over. Could they be—?

"These are Julian's old paintings," Celia answered for me. "That one's of me."

I followed her finger. It was of the lake behind the house. A little girl in white bent in the foreground to pluck what might have been a crocus. Added later, perhaps. The work was naive, certainly done by someone untutored, not yet familiar with the intricacies of perspective. However, the colors were spectacular, and though Celia's face was a mere brushstroke, he'd managed to capture her character undeniably.

There was something off about the texture, though, and when I looked closer at the movement of the water near the bank of the lake, a slight variation in tone hinted at what might have once been the outline of another person.

"Look at this one, Bertie," Anna said, drawing me from my thoughts. The painting she'd found was smaller—hands on the keys of a piano. "Is it Uncle Earl?"

"Could be," I said, though I was sure. I'd spent enough time sketching those hands. How he managed to do a self-portrait of the very tools he needed to paint it, I wasn't sure. But I was jealous of his ingenuity. "I've seen this ring before."

I looked up for Celia, who had moved on to sweeping the dust from an old rocking horse, clearly unwilling to focus her attention on her brother. Anna caught sight of it and dashed away, easily distracted by the prospect of a child's toy.

"Did your mother have the same one?" I asked. "With the signet?"

Celia offered me half a glance. "Oh—yes, it's an heirloom. Passed between wives and heirs since . . . the seventeenth century? I don't remember."

"Why does he not wear it any longer?"

But no one had heard me, for Anna had begun shouting at Celia, asking could she please take the horse with them, and Celia was trying to convince her it was too old and dirty for the effort. In the end, Celia promised to ask Huxley to have it washed up and brought to the nursery later on. I had just enough time for a few quick sketches of the room before she declared we ought to be on our way back upstairs.

Emerging from the hidden corridor into the light of the Morning Room was staggering. I was pleased to return to the multicolored world we knew, though I wished I'd had a spare moment to draw some of what was going on in the kitchens. Perhaps another day.

Meantime, Anna spotted Roland and Freddie through the windows, descending to the lawn with tennis kit, and sprinted off to join them. I was left idling beside Celia, wondering if she'd suggest we follow. But her smile had gone, and the arms of her cardigan were stretched and wrinkled where she'd been worrying at the cashmere.

"Anna's rather taken with you," she said. I pressed on a smile, feeling self-conscious. "She isn't your responsibility, however; you're a guest here."

"I really don't mind entertaining her. She's a sweet thing."

Celia's brows straightened into a frown. "She's getting in the way of your work."

I sobered instantly. She'd never before been bothered about my work. Something else was vexing her. "Are you all right, Cece?"

She tucked a curl behind her ear, eyes ambling to the window, where Anna bounced down the steps to the lawn. "I'm not certain it's right for the two of you to be spending time together. Anna gets so attached to people, and . . ." Celia looked at me again, on the brim of tears. "You must leave at the end of the summer, and she'll never see you again. It isn't . . . it isn't fair to her."

My heart fell to the floor. I'd been thinking often enough of saying goodbye to Julian, to Roland, to Celia . . . but never once had I thought of what goodbye would mean to Anna. She *had* got rather attached—shadowing me all hours. Still, there was something deeper here. There was only one subject that ever turned Celia's mood so completely.

"Forgive me," I said heartily. "You're absolutely right."

Finally, a genuine smile. For once, Celia looked her age, not yet the worldly woman she pretended to be. "Thank you, Bertie. I know I probably sound like a shrew—"

"Don't be daft. I'll keep my distance from now on."

And then she nodded her goodbye, abandoning me for tennis I was not asked to join.

ALONE AGAIN, I brought an easel to the front lawn. Clouds were sliding in from the west, wind pushing the fountain's eruption to spray across the pool. But I'd been meaning to make a start on painting it, and my time was dwindling. I mixed blue and crimson, adding yellow to lighten and match it to the moody grey sky. The fountain's gilt statues contrasted brilliantly against the gradient, and I built them up thickly to stand out from the canvas.

I heard a distant rumble, assuming thunder, until a car came motoring up the long drive. The front door opened before it was parked, Huxley hurrying out to greet Lady Stanfield.

Gwen stayed for perhaps an hour. When her motor was brought round again, I still stood before my painting, a few steps back to work out what was missing. Gwen came down the front steps with a child on either side. Anna broke free, running to me for a hug. Her mother watched with her hand over her eyes.

"Bye, Bertie," said Anna. "I'll come back soon."

I squashed her lovingly, thinking that if she did return, I wouldn't see much of her. Though I would miss her, and that funny grin. "See you then."

She ran back to Gwen, who herded both of the little ones into the car. Then she came slowly in my direction, no rush to be gone. The wind took her skirt, and she held her cloche to watch the clouds. Before speaking, she paused to regard my painting.

"I wanted to thank you for being so sweet to Anna," said Gwen. "She can be imposing."

"It's no trouble." I expected to hear Celia's fears echoed, but nothing came.

Gwen peered over her shoulder at the car, ensuring her children were still inside and not running amok. She faced me again with a tight smile. "Anna said she had a nightmare and found you in her uncle's room."

A feather could have knocked me over. I took up a rag and wrung it uselessly to busy my hands. What excuse could I possibly make?

"Not to worry," Gwen put in. "She thought nothing of it."

I shook my hair to hide my blush. "What would you have me say? That I'm a woman of low morals?"

Gwen chuckled and folded her hands. "Dear, I cannot begin to cast judgment when it was I who urged you towards my brother from the first."

I glanced briefly at Julian's window. "Then why humiliate me?"

Her dimples deepened, a lofty look that made me feel a child. "That was not my intention."

"What is?"

"To speak with you, as adults. As *women*." Gwen let out a short breath and stretched her neck. "I know Julian is—he's difficult to get to. Others would have quit by now. But you haven't. And you've got through. He is enamored."

My armor fell in craggy pieces at my feet. Words of affection from Julian were few and far between. Hearing them put so plainly swelled my courage.

"You got him out of his room," Gwen added.

I shook my head. "It was Anna."

Gwen, too, was painfully surrendering her steel facade. "She knocks all the time. He only opened that door because you were there with him. You pushed him, did you not? You must have done."

I spared her the truth, that I had been the one to open the door, Julian coming in late. "He went to the nursery and back, that is all."

"Further than he has gone in longer than a year."

I couldn't stifle my dismay. Those steps—few as they were—had drained

Julian. When we'd returned to bed, he'd shaken before falling asleep. In the morning, I had waited for him to wake long after Huxley had come and gone. There was no mistaking those steps had been arduous. What would leaving Braemore do to him?

Gwen touched my arm, drawing me to the present. "Do you love him?"

The question hit me like a bullet. "I—don't know—"

"Because if you do, you must push him, even if it leads to a row."

"I'm not certain I agree with that."

"Sometimes you have got to be a bully," she said, suddenly stern. "Even if you love them—especially if you do. It's the only way to get through. Love is not always delicate and tender; sometimes it must be fierce, rigid—I can't explain." Gwen looked far away.

How easily I'd been seduced by the Napiers, by their lavish life and their twisted past. How gratifying it had been to nurture again, to be Julian's protector. But I couldn't offer them what they wanted. This wasn't a job for a nurse, and it certainly wasn't a job for an artist.

"I care about Julian," I said. "I really do. And I'm glad if our time together can help him. But I've come here to paint." Gwen turned to me, eyes frowning. "To paint is all I've ever wished for. And as for love—I want it, I do—but it does not fit in the life I'm after. Especially with a man whose entire world is a single room."

Gwen checked her children again. Two pale faces bobbed in the back window—Anna and Richie giggling. She smiled, though with far less brilliance than I'd seen before.

"I'm terribly sorry, Miss Preston. I've been trying for years and I can't—" Gwen pressed the pads of her fingers against her lips, pausing to digest a wave of emotion. "Our mother was a miserable woman. And one day, she lay down in her bed and she did not get up for a year. She lay there and she let herself die, bitter and alone . . . I cannot allow that to happen to Julian. Does he not deserve more after all he's come through?"

I nodded, unable to speak. Little wonder why Gwen had assumed mothering duties so ardently as a young woman, why she returned every Thursday, why she forced Julian out of bed each morning to eat and wash and dress. How easy it would be for him to lie down and give in, as his mother had. He was nearly there already.

There was a visible change in Gwen, a fragility I thought her incapable of, thinly veiled behind a weak smile. "I must make my apologies; it was wrong of us to put this on you, but I'm just, I'm—I cannot think what to do. He must leave this place to sell it."

Tears threatened as I imagined all that was behind me vanishing with the people in it. The more I thought about it, the more I wanted to run to Julian's rooms, to lock myself inside with him and never face the world again.

But lords married daughters of other lords. They strove to keep their family's blood noble, to produce an heir that would carry their legacy. I could love Julian; I could be with Julian, but only for so long. Eventually, he must fulfill his duties as Lord Wakeford.

"What will happen to me when he must marry?" I asked.

Gwen brightened. "*Do* you love him, Bertie?"

I sighed. Batted my rag against my palm. Goodness, I was in trouble. "Yes," I said. "I do."

Gwen's forehead smoothed as her arms slipped to her sides. She shed something—a thick skin she'd worn for a long time. Underneath she was younger, lighter. "My brother cares little, if at all, about rank—believe me, I've failed to convince him of its import. If you tell him you love him, he will be entirely yours. And he will, God willing, follow you when you leave here."

My heart swelled. But I was not yet convinced.

For I saw clearly the danger Julian presented to himself and could not, no matter how hard I wished it were possible, envisage a life with him if he remained the same. In the end, it was not a life. No amount of affection for the man would convince me to lock myself away with him forever.

Mothers of All Sorts

JANUARY 1916

It was a dreadful place. That Gwen expected anything more revealed her ignorance.

A maternity home was not a retreat, but a consequence. Here, young girls bared their shame alone, meditated on their sins alone, suffered alone, all while arms and legs filled their bellies. Painfully. Perhaps sweetly. Gwen had only ever dreamt of the sensation.

The putty-colored walls were thin. Gwen could hear distant cries of a woman in her labors echoing from somewhere above. Births were meant to be a joyous occasion, a celebration, if all went well. Here, Gwen was sure, they brought nothing but grief. For there was no comparing the pain to a lifetime of love for a child. Most of the girls could not keep them. Once strong enough, they were torn from their mother's breast and given away to well-off women like Gwen—married, desperate for children, and jealous of how easily they were conceived by feckless girls. The less fortunate ones would be raised as orphans, then sent to work.

How desperate war had made so many young people, driving them to love as fully as they could manage before their time ran out. The men died, or else returned with no wish to be fathers, the women left alone with no choice but to give their children away. What had happened to their passion? And why was it so easy for the men to abandon it, while the women were stripped of theirs by force?

Gwen shifted in her seat, worn leather cracking beneath her. She held Richard's letter in her lap, tattered and tearing at the folds from being handled. In it, he'd written his final permission to adopt an infant girl. Not a boy—he would not risk disputing his younger brother's inheritance. But a little girl, yes. He'd said *yes*. He'd risk their reputations. Because they'd been married five years, made love for five years, to no result. The doctor said perhaps never. Gwen wanted nothing more than to be a mother, and Richard loved her. So he let it be so.

Above her head, gas lamps flickered. It was cold and damp, not at all a welcoming place to enter the world. Gwen wondered how many of these girls would have a home to return to when all was finished. Her own mother would have sent her away before the bump, allowing her home only after she was well again so nobody would suspect.

Gwen placed Richard's letter against her heart, kneading it roughly. This was meant to be a happy day, was it not? A baby girl, at last! And still, she felt a sickening sort of dread deep within her. Maybe it was this place, with its cushionless chairs and fraying rugs, and crucifixes—she'd never liked those.

She wished Richard were with her. Gwen tried to imagine him where he was, in a tent or billet or a trench. She apologized to God for disliking the crucifix, and prayed he would watch over Richard. A godly man. Much godlier than she could ever hope to be. For he had said *yes*.

Gwen noticed the shouting had stopped, and held her breath. She had done the same when Julian was born, then Roland, then Celia, waiting for the cry that meant all was well. How blessed she was to have three of them, healthy and kind and lovely. Another half minute and the silence was finally filled by the screeching wails of a newborn.

Gwen wiped a tear.

She was glad when the matron finally came through from her office, a smile wrinkling fleshy cheeks. "Welcome, Lady Stanfield," she said, bowing at the neck. "So sorry to keep you waiting. I'm Matron Gilbert. It's a pleasure to finally meet you in person."

They had been exchanging letters for some time. Gwen made donations to the home to keep the girls comfortable—sweets, knitting wool, books, blankets, and items for their toilet bags. It was Matron Gilbert whom she'd first told of her hope to adopt a child, and Matron Gilbert who'd informed her of the birth of the baby who was to be Gwen's daughter.

"The pleasure is mine, Matron," said Gwen. "How is she?"

"Well, indeed. She's rather a good sleeper."

Gwen smiled. Celia and Roland had shouted, always—night and morning. Julian had been the quiet one, so quiet the doctor had been sent for often in his infancy to ensure nothing was wrong with him. Hard of hearing, perhaps? Or dumb? But no. Julian had simply been content with his inner world.

"May I offer you a cup of tea, my lady?" Matron asked.

"No. No, thank you." Gwen didn't think she could stomach anything. "What of the mother?"

Matron lowered her voice. "No family to speak of, I'm afraid."

Gwen felt her throat catch and cleared it. She held her handbag tightly against her stomach, willing the emotion down, down to her feet. "So the child—?"

"As there's no one to claim her, she's considered a foundling, and may be adopted."

Gwen let out a breath she'd been holding. It was a relief, though she wondered where the poor mother's body had been laid to rest.

"Most of Mother's effects weren't worth keeping," said Matron, reaching into the pocket of her apron. "But there are a few precious items that might go home with baby, if you'd like them."

She held out a small drawstring sack, weighted with what might have been coins. It didn't feel right to take a dead woman's things, though Gwen thought they might be discarded carelessly otherwise. So she tucked it into her handbag beside Richard's letter.

"May I meet her?" Gwen asked.

"By all means, my lady. Baby is quite ready to be home."

The prospect of seeing the child—*her* child—made Gwen forget all else.

They made their way down a long corridor towards the day nursery. Though it was drab, the place was clean at least—Gwen took note by gliding her finger on the back of a bench, checking for dust. Though the air was damp, there was the faint scent of laundry, and that gave her ease of mind.

Various sounds leaked from the rooms lining the passageway—coos and giggles, sobs and retching. Singing, from one. A softhearted lullaby.

A girl, of perhaps twenty years, swept the floor, arms stretched past a sizable tummy. Gwen couldn't help but smile at her, her glowing cheeks, her swelling breasts. How pleasant it must be to grow a child! Though as they passed, the girl only sulked. Another dusted a bookshelf, a third scrubbed the window at the end of the corridor.

"Chores before tea," said Matron. "Keeps everybody's mind at ease, a little work. And there's time enough for recreation and church."

Gwen nodded along. It was good to know the girls were properly looked after.

"We don't normally bring adopters to the nursery," said Matron, "but given you're one of our most generous benefactors, I expected you might like to have a look." They stopped at a windowed door, and entered to the lively sound of babies.

The nursery was well lit, mostly open but for the cots against one wall, and a few scattered chairs to one corner. There was a nurse sitting on the tiled floors, minding two infants as they lay on a rug on their tummies. Another walked between cots, hushing a crier and adjusting a blanket. A third sat in one of the chairs, feeding a bundled baby with a bottle. Beside her was clearly one of the mothers, an astonishingly young woman feeding from her breast.

"Where are the other girls?" Gwen asked.

"After three weeks, the babies are bottle fed," Matron answered. "We discourage holding and cuddling—makes it all a bit easier when it comes time to say goodbye. Apart from practical care, it's our nurses who look after the babies."

Matron was clearly most proud. Though Gwen could only taste the bitterness of horror on the back of her tongue. Being unable to have a child of her own was her greatest sadness. She could hardly imagine the trauma of coming through the pain of labors only to have the baby taken.

"Now," Matron said, "your little darling should be just over here, my lady . . ."

With a rush of suspense, Gwen followed her a few paces to the row of cots. Here they all were, in varying states of infancy. One was so red and wrinkled—he must have just come to the light mere days ago. Another was already filling out, blue eyes wide as Gwen peeked in and smiled. As she moved along, though, she felt a sinking dread once more, for she noticed the cots were labeled not with names, but dates of birth alone.

"Here we are, my lady." Matron stopped in front of one of the cots, tucking her hands behind her back. "Sleeping soundly."

Gwen approached slowly, the cries of another infant fading into the background as she was completely taken by the child.

Baby slept with one tiny fist up by her ear, the other buried within the blanket. The head was large and square with a mess of light, silken hair—so much hair! Her nose was snub and unfamiliar, the mouth round and pressed in a pout. Her feet had escaped the swaddle—kicking in woolen socks as she dreamt.

Altogether, she was the most beautiful thing Gwen had ever seen.

Tears fell freely, dripping down Gwen's chin. She didn't bother wiping them until one fell into the cot. Matron dipped carefully past the bars to scoop one hand under baby's head and the other under her bottom. Instinctively, Gwen opened her arms, eager to feel the perfect, warm weight of the wee body.

"She's put on a half kilo since birth," said Matron. "Just what we like to see."

She set the baby in Gwen's practiced cradle. Baby was waking, opening and closing her lips, gurgling as was hoped for at six weeks. She blinked and there were the eyes, dark, round, and curious. Gwen's head spun, overtaken with a peculiar sensation she'd done this all before.

"You're welcome to sit, my lady," said Matron, indicating a chair.

Gwen did, noticing the lack of softness, and made a mental note to donate new chairs next. She raised baby up in her arms, brushing closed lips over the warm, dry forehead, the hairs almost too fine to feel, and took a deep breath. There was nothing that could match the scent of an infant—the powdered, floral sweetness of new, doughy skin.

"Hello, my darling," Gwen said as baby's eyes locked onto hers. "Hello, hello. Do you know that I love you so very much? I love you already, my darling little one." She pressed her thumb into the tiny hand. "I've waited ever so long to meet you."

Baby smiled. Though she was not looking at Gwen, but the young mother who sat beside her, pulling silly faces for the child as she buttoned her blouse. Her own bundle, now fed, had been swept away by the hands of a nurse. She made a popping sound with her mouth, and baby wriggled with joy.

"Well done, you," Gwen said.

The girl shrugged meekly. "She's beautiful. What will you call her?"

"My husband likes Anna."

"Anna. Yes, that will do." She leaned over to tickle under Anna's chin.

Gwen was speechless, feeling the wretched ache of loss in her chest. How much longer did this woman have with her own child? Weeks? Days?

Matron *tsk*ed, setting fists on hips. "You are speaking to a *viscountess*, Sarah."

"Oh!" The girl stood to perform a clumsy curtsy. "Pardon me, your ladyship."

"Heavens!" Gwen balked, bouncing the baby in her arms. "I'm not that important. Please do sit."

Sarah did, close enough to brush Gwen's shoulder. "How splendid! What a fine home baby will have. And her father, a lord!"

Gwen laughed. Yes, how very novel.

Matron had taken a step forward, casting a shadow over the three of them. "I believe you have chores that need doing, girl."

Sarah's eyes widened, and Gwen could tell it was fear. She wanted to feel sorry for Sarah, who hastened out of the nursery without even saying goodbye. But little Anna kicked in her arms, and suddenly she could think of nothing else. Gwen pinched Anna's fist between two fingers, bringing it to her lips, so full of love she thought she might burst.

17

If I ever managed to have a show of my own, I could display an entire collection of my time in Julian's apartments. One might assume that a single string of rooms provided little inspiration, but in my time with him, I found there were countless angles, countless objects to shift, countless variations in light as the sun moved from one end of the house to the other.

Through plenty of objections, I'd finally won him round to sitting as my subject. "You'll love modeling," I'd told him. "It involves your two favorite activities: sitting quietly and smoking." Though I'd begun a few studies of him in the privacy of my studio, I hadn't had the honor of painting him from life, in the dwellings which had defined his post-war years.

I danced into his room excitedly that morning, and he made me suffer, knowing it was agony for me to wait while he smoked two cigarettes and wandered the room. I allowed him to choose the composition so he would feel comfortable.

In the end, he arranged my easel well behind the piano bench and sat facing the keys.

Of course.

I didn't bother to argue. At least I was getting some piece of Julian on canvas. He played on and off as I mixed my colors, delighting in matching his hair and flesh.

As assumed, Julian was the perfect sitter. He did not complain once, even as an hour passed by without my noticing. It wasn't until it had begun raining that he stood to close a window, and lingered in front of my easel. I allowed myself the pleasure of looking him up and down—his pressed trousers, his shirtsleeves, the angle of muscle that ran from his shoulder to his clavicle.

"You don't suppose I'm going to allow you to see it before it's finished?"

"I'd like to see your process," he said. "If I may."

I gave in, standing for him to sit in my chair. Once he was settled, I perched on his knee and waited. There was not much to see yet—no great detail—only the vague shapes of piano and a cabinet beside, topped with a vase of peonies I'd brought from downstairs, the curtains dragging over the floor, and the beginnings of what light had come through on Julian's left side before the sun went in.

"I was thinking of Lavery's interiors," I said. "*Lord Wakeford occupies himself in his immediate surroundings.* What d'you reckon?"

Julian's arms circled my waist, pulling me in so he could nestle his head beneath mine. "I reckon you've got my hair wrong." I tweaked his ear and he laughed. "No; the way you've played with the light here is brilliant. It's very fine, Bertie."

I would never tire of hearing that. "But do go on. Show me what you would do."

Julian's hand drifted to take up a flat brush. I held my breath. It was the first time he'd even dared. But it seemed he only wanted to hold it, to feel the worn wood between his fingers, to savor the weight of it before setting it down again.

He placed a kiss on the inside of my wrist, where he knew I got sore. "I'll leave you to it."

"Why? It may all come flooding back to you in a single stroke."

Julian tilted his head away, and I ran my fingers through his hair, away from his temple, and kissed the scar there. "I shouldn't like to devalue your work," he said.

"Oh, bosh! I saw some of your paintings downstairs; they were charming."

He said nothing for a moment, then lifted his eye. "You were downstairs?"

"I went with Anna and Cece," I said, hoping it would act as my defense. "And I think it's high time we got you painting again."

Julian shook his head. "I have enjoyed watching you work, but I'm too riddled with images I don't wish to make permanent."

I remembered what he'd said to little Anna, that he remained always in the dark. In my mind, it could help to take to canvas, to rid himself of the ugly, turn it into something physical that could be torn, or burned, or painted over. Otherwise the nightmares might become a sanctuary of sorts, a familiar place to hide whilst the rest of the world changed outside.

Gwen had said their mother stayed in her bed until the end. I couldn't help but agree with her that Julian was in immediate danger of the same fate.

"Julian?"

He spun the chiffon sash of my dress round his finger. "Hmm."

"I thought . . . perhaps another evening we might give it a go."

"What's that?"

I tightened my arms around his neck and leaned my chin against his hair. "The other night—with Anna? You made it far as the nursery. Do you think you might like to go again? A few steps, even. I'll go with you."

"It isn't your concern, Bertie."

I sat up so he could look at me, but his head remained bowed. "It is, actually. It matters to me what happens to you." Julian tried to shift, but I made it clear I was not removing myself. "Don't you see that I care about you? That I want you to be well?"

"I am capable," he said.

"I know. So why not make a start?"

"I will go when I must."

"You haven't much time."

"Bertie—"

"Why not try whilst I am still here to help you?"

Julian closed his eye, face soured as though he were in pain. The look frightened me so that I let go and stood from his knee.

"I don't wish to upset you," I said. "But you do realize neither of us can stay here?"

A long pause. Julian put his hands on his face, a shushing sound as they smoothed over whiskers. His body had gone tense, and I feared for a moment that I'd pushed him too far. When he moved from the chair, I knew I had, for he went to the sideboard and swallowed a pour of whisky.

I turned to face the window, feeling a fracture through my heart. How easily a good morning could turn to a bad night. Julian would have many more at this rate.

Then I felt him approach, wrap his arms around me from behind until we were flush. A hot tear rolled off my chin.

"I'm sorry," he whispered.

I twisted to face him, placing my hand on his cheek.

I love you.

The words sounded so simple in my head. Just three words; how easy it had been to toss them around lightly, costing me nothing. But now, looking into Julian's face, I felt a digging ache of fear. For I'd never spoken those three words before and truly meant them. What if now, I gave them away and they were not returned?

So instead, I smiled, kissing Julian. "I had better be off. The gong will go any minute."

"NO, NO, NO, don't go!" I shouted uselessly through the window at the sun. After spending so much of our lovely summer shining, it had reached August deciding enough was enough and now it was trying to rain. Though I suppose it matched my mood after leaving Julian last evening.

Even with my easel angled to catch every drip of natural light, I couldn't get a handle on my colors with an overcast sky. The chandelier in the Music Room had electric lights, too yellow and of little use. So I stood and shut the window, misty wind blowing back my hair, resolving to give in for the morning.

There was no excuse to avoid tidying up. I crossed the room with a jar of dirty brushes dangling from two fingers, stopping when a knock came to the door.

"Yes, come in."

In came Roland, clothed in collared shirt and sleeveless jumper. It seemed the weather had affected us both.

"Morning, Bertie." He rubbed his palms together and observed my mess. "I wanted to look in, seeing as you missed breakfast. You weren't, er . . ."

Idling, I jostled the brushes in my jar. Fibs were becoming rather tiresome, and I couldn't think why Roland would take issue with the truth. "With Julian? No."

Roland went so suddenly pale, I nearly offered him my shoulder to lean against. "He didn't answer when Huxley brought his tray."

His dismay was catching. I'd left Julian just after our row, abandoning him and the painting. Clearly, the turnabout was my doing, an apology overdue.

"Thanks all the same," Roland said. He gave a weak smile and ventured deeper into the room, stepping gingerly over paint stains he couldn't tell were weeks old. Something caught his eye and he bent over, snatching a bit of paper from the floor. "You will have dropped this."

I set down the jar and sighed. "Bloody wind. The weather has done nothing for me today."

Roland handed me the sodden paper and I turned it over. An envelope—the letter Mrs. Lemm had sent weeks ago that I'd failed to reply to. Or read. Leaving viridian fingerprints, I opened it absently, pulling out wrinkled stationery.

Dear Bertie,

I skimmed quickly:

I hope this letter finds you well, and enjoying your holiday in Wiltshire. How splendid it was to call on your mother and learn that you are off painting for the Earl of Wakeford! All of us here in Brickyard Lane are so proud of you, and look forward to hearing about your stay at Castle Braemore.

I wondered if you could find the time to step away from your work for an afternoon. My niece will be visiting from London come August with her new husband. He is a most prominent art dealer, apparently . . .

I looked up at Roland with wide eyes as if he had any idea what I was reading.

"It isn't bad news, I hope?" he said.

I shook my head. I couldn't speak just yet.

. . . and keen to represent young artists with (what he calls) 'a modern style.' Naturally, I thought of you straightaway and wrote to them in your regard, sparing no detail about where you have been painting these past months. He was fairly impressed, and has agreed to see more of your work. They are stopping the second week of August, remaining from the seventh to the thirteenth. I wondered if you would like to join us for tea . . .

"Crikey," I said.

"What?"

Oh, yes—Roland was still here. "What day is this?"

"Saturday. The Glorious Twelfth."

I beamed so fully it pained my cheeks. "The Glorious Twelfth indeed!"

I shook the letter and turned to look at the chaos of my studio. There were a few smaller canvases I could manage to carry on my own. Were they the best of the bunch? Hardly. But hey ho. I'd need to dispatch a telegram or phone Mrs. Lemm before getting on a train. I could hardly call by unannounced . . .

Roland appeared at my shoulder. "What have I missed?"

"There's an art dealer who wants to see my work. But I must go *today.*" I gave him the letter. "I have to put some things together; I must dress—" Lord, I was covered in paint from chest to toes.

Roland kneaded his forehead and let the letter fall to his side. "This doesn't mean you're leaving—?"

"I am."

Without a recommendation from Julian, I needed some promise of more work at summer's end. This art dealer could find collectors or even galleries who might be interested. I would start making the wages I needed for a room. It hardly mattered if Mother never allowed me home—I'd be a working artist. How perfect that it should have been Mrs. Lemm to rescue my career!

"It's Gwen's party today." I looked up at Roland. He was taller than his brother, but for a moment their similarities were so staggering I nearly thought the other man had appeared in his place. "And Julian . . ."

Yes, Julian. After last night, it was clear he was not able to discuss his future, let alone imagine me as part of it. It was as though time stopped when I entered the room, and there was no need to discuss my leaving, for the day would never come if we stayed tucked away inside his apartments. But with autumn quickly approaching, I had little choice but to assume we'd part ways indefinitely when I left Braemore.

Roland's eyes rounded as he waited for an answer.

"I'm sorry to miss the party," I said. "But I really need this chance."

Roland nodded, folding the letter. "Yes—of course. I'll drive you to the station myself and send a footman here to help you get sorted in the meantime. Ought one of us to escort you?"

The boy looked so earnest, and it was lovely to know he was willing. No matter what might happen with Julian, I knew I had friends to count on.

But if I ever hoped for a career of my own, I would need to start going it alone.

IT WAS PROPERLY tipping down by the time Roland and I left the house, huddled under a single umbrella. A footman had been sent ahead of us with a sampling of my smaller canvases, stowing them safely in the passenger row before the rain. We were taking the family landaulet, as they wouldn't have fit in Roland's boot, though he insisted on driving me to the station himself.

Roland held the umbrella over me while I got into the passenger side, then went round and fell into his seat, spraying me with droplets as he fought to shove the closed umbrella under our feet.

"Nice weather for ducks," I said.

He started the engine with a huff. "And a fine day for a garden do."

"It wasn't meant to be outdoors?"

The choice between attending a child's birthday party or a meeting with an art dealer had been a simple one. Though I had to admit I felt a bit guilty now.

"Oh yes—quoits and coconut shy and all sorts." Roland wiped a raindrop from his chin. "Now it's to be bored children confined to a stuffy reception room and no way to escape Richard's family."

"Are they that awful?"

He licked his bottom lip, considering. "Richard was one of a kind—a perfect match for Gwen. But his mother and sisters have never forgiven her for bringing a foundling into the family, and his brother resents Richie, I think, for arriving just in time to snatch the inheritance."

"My! What fun." I'd yet to consider other aristocratic families might possess as much controversy as the Napiers.

"A real knees-up bunch, that lot. Not to worry, though, we'll look after her." Roland squinted through the windscreen at the deluge. "Though I daresay Gwen was planning on using your work as a talking point. Anything to move the conversation from Julian . . ."

As the car rolled forward, I felt suddenly hot and removed my hat. Only simple nerves. This might be my second chance at a real break. And what if this art dealer did not like my paintings? Did it mean I showed no promise? That I was hopeless to find other commissions, or be admitted to display a piece at the Royal Academy? That Julian was truly the only person who saw potential in me?

I fanned myself with my hat, looking back at the house through my window, as if I could see Lord Wakeford there, see he was out of bed, see he was well. What had gone wrong that morning? What had prevented him from rising at his usual time, dressing, and answering the door for his breakfast? Roland minded Julian's eating habits so closely, sending for Gwen if need be. He couldn't do that today; she was busy with the party. Julian would be alone in the house.

"Damn." Roland thumped the heel of his hand against the steering wheel. I turned around to see we had stopped just in front of the great iron gates, which remained closed. "Looks like I'm going swimming."

Roland opened his door, his sleeve immediately darkening as the rain drenched it. He took a deep breath as if he were about to plunge into the ocean, and I grabbed his elbow.

"Wait!"

"What's the matter?" He closed the door again. "I must be quick or you'll miss your train."

I didn't know how to explain what was going on inside of me, the sudden fear that leaving Julian today would be a mistake. A few months ago, I should have given anything for such an opportunity. I'd gone against my parents to accept the Braemore commission. Now I felt leaded to my seat, desperate to return to the dry warmth of Castle Braemore. What if our quarrel last evening had upset him more than I imagined? What if something happened to him and it was all my bloody fault?

It was more than love. He might have been the only person I'd throw away such a chance for.

"I've changed my mind," I said to Roland.

Roland leaned towards me. "Bertie, you must be mad. It's only a children's party."

Maybe I was mad.

I opened my door, returning my hat to my head, and held it as I ran blindly through the rain.

18

By the time I reached the front door, I was soaked through, muck splashed across my stockings and the hem of my skirt. There was no one to take my coat, so I went straight to Julian's room. When he answered the door, fully clothed and awake, I couldn't think why I ever wished to leave.

I fell into his arms, and he remained silent. That was something lovely about Julian—he knew when and when not to speak. I buried my cold nose in his shirt, breathing him in, the tobacco, the bergamot. He held me and rubbed my back, sodden as it was, and I wondered how one could possibly think him anything but kind and gentle.

"Bertie?"

I looked up. He hadn't been wearing his mask, and I could see in his eye he'd been drinking. Though there were few days he lacked that glimmer. "Are you all right?" I asked.

"I'm fine." Julian pawed through my mess of wet hair to find my face. "What's happened? You ought to get out of these clothes; you're shivering."

I was. Though it wasn't the cold; it was a cocktail of all the emotions I'd felt since waking—uncertainty, excitement, fear, love. What a morning it'd been.

"Tell me the truth?"

Julian brushed his knuckles over my cheek. "It's been a difficult day."

I stood on my toes to kiss him, so glad I'd turned round. As brooding as Julian was typically, I could tell something was not right. "Would it help if I drew you a bath?" I asked.

Bless his decency; my boldness still made him start. "Are you not going with the others to the party?"

"Someone's got to keep you company, haven't they?"

I went away to tell Roland, who looked noticeably eased by the notion his brother would not be on his own. When I returned, Julian allowed me to lead him by the hand to the bathroom. I turned on the faucet whilst he rummaged through the cupboard for something to fragrance the water. When he returned the bottle, he took up another, the Veronal, and spilled out a cachet, taking it dry. I brought him a folded towel and we sat together on the edge of the tub.

His head fell to his hands. All was silent but for the running bath behind us.

I hadn't often noticed him take the medicine. Adding that he'd not got out of bed that morning, it was worrisome. "Are you unwell, Julian?"

"I'm fine, fine, it's—" He sighed. "It doesn't matter."

"Say what's wrong."

His head inclined, hands folding in his lap. "I've got this . . . heap of correspondence, and every time I mean to reply, the walls begin to close around me."

This was the first time I'd heard him acknowledge it. "Can I help?"

"No, it's nothing." Julian turned to test the temperature of the water. "Before you came in I was just . . . working to keep it at bay."

"The shouting?"

A weary nod. I leaned my head on his shoulder, worrying I might upset him further with more questions. I would have done anything to keep him from shouting again.

When the tub was filled and steaming around us, I turned off the faucet. He kissed me on the head, pulling my arm as I stood. "Stay? I need you to keep me awake."

I smiled, marveling at how much of his reserve had gone. "I shan't let you drown."

I got in first, sinking until the cold ran from my hair, and my skin prickled back to life. When I came up, I watched Julian methodically remove his shirt and cross the room to hang it on the rack. Unlike his sister and brother, who regularly left things lying about for maids to clear up, Julian folded his clothes and set them neatly aside. That was army training, I assumed, or perhaps the last few years he'd lived without someone to pick up after him.

He stepped in carefully and leaned back, arms stretching over the lip of the tub. I crawled into his lap and took the sponge from the rack, soaking it to squeeze over Julian's shoulder. The water trickled and parted through the Van Gogh swirls of his scars, through the sparse hairs on his chest. Whilst I distracted myself with the task, he stared at my face, forehead pleated.

"Why were you out in the rain?" he asked.

I wet the sponge and set it against the taut roots of his neck. "I had a letter this morning from a neighbor. She'd set up a meeting for me with an art dealer from London."

"Today?"

I nodded.

"And yet you are here with me."

When I wilted, Julian sat up to encircle me. I pressed my chest to his and ran the sponge down his back.

"I was too frightened to go, in the end," I replied. It was not entirely a lie.

Julian's cold nose touched my cheek. "I've never known you to be cautious."

"I just thought . . ." The truth became stuck at the back of my throat. "Perhaps I'm no good. Too traditional. Not avant-garde enough for—"

"You're a marvel, Bertie. Anyone with eyes will see that."

Pushing his hair away, I smiled into his neck. "It was foolish, I suppose. An art dealer might have helped my career . . . after I've left here. I need to earn money, enough for a room somewhere. If I don't . . ."

Beneath me, the muscles in Julian's legs flexed and he unwound himself to look at me. With his hair pushed back and wet lashes stuck in star points over his eye, I saw better the young man he'd been in the postcard. That man was still there, hidden below the rugged surface. The lost half, as he called it.

I cannot say why I was suddenly compelled to confess, but it came easily. "If I don't, I'll be without a home."

Julian's grip tightened, his thumbs pressing into my hips to make me quiver. "Your parents?"

"They won't have me. I went against them to come here."

"Why have you not told me that?"

"I don't know—it's hardly your concern."

"It is my concern." He brought his hands up to cup my neck, hot water drizzling down my breasts. My head jostled as he spoke passionately. "You'll not be without a home; I'll ensure you have what you need."

I was unable to be comforted by his words. It wasn't difficult to see how this man had fallen on hard times. At a young age, he'd learned to mend problems with banknotes.

"You shall pay me what I've earned for my work," I said. "Nothing more."

"You will have earned what I give you."

"Julian—" I removed his hands, sinking them under the water. "I'm not your responsibility. You've a family to be concerned with, and selling this estate . . ."

Julian moved away from me to lean against the edge of the tub. With one elbow propped on the lip, he twirled his whiskers and sent his gaze to the far wall.

"*Can* you pay me fairly, Julian? Even with your debts? Because if not—"

"I have money put by. I would never ask you here under false pretenses."

His words were sharp and sure. I believed him. But I couldn't ignore the absence of another option. If he was without a home, I would offer mine to him. Why, then, did it seem he would not do the same for me?

I fished for his hand and ran the sponge over his knuckles, between his fingers, up the arm. He turned his head to watch, and I was reminded of the very first blanket bath I'd given to a wounded soldier, the shocking weight of his fatigued limbs, the grateful expression in his tired eyes. Now, in Julian, I could see a similar glaze of chemically induced calm.

"Why do you not wear your ring any longer?" I asked.

Julian cleared his throat. "What ring?"

"The signet," I said, as though it was obvious. "I saw it in one of your paintings."

The crease in Julian's brow darkened, though his face caught the light beautifully. I imagined mixing a flick of cadmium yellow with white on an angled brush, sweeping it underneath to sharpen the opposing highlight.

"I lost it in the war," he answered.

"What a shame . . ." To that he said nothing, so I moved on. "Regardless of my fears earlier, I do think I've done some of my best work here. I'm quite proud, actually. I like picturing them hung on your new walls, reminding you of home."

"The paintings are not for me."

I shifted abruptly, water lapping up the edge of the tub. "Oh?"

"They're for my family. To help them remember Braemore fondly."

With this new knowledge, I felt I was looking at a stranger. "That's lovely. But won't you keep any of them for yourself?"

Julian's hands closed around the sponge, and he took his turn to run it down my back, bringing my skin to life. He tilted his head, tenderly nipping my cheek, and I forgot all else. Water rippled between us, our bodies disappearing into the warmth of the bath, skins with no beginning and no end, not together or separate, but floating seamlessly in the heat and slick. I felt drunk from heady rose water and the alcohol on Julian's breath.

"Your work is worth more than galleries and art dealers," he whispered. "Do you see that now? Do you understand how much it will mean to them?"

I nodded.

Julian kissed me slowly, mouth open and lethargic but not lacking purpose. Cold drops fell from his hair, dripping down onto my brow, over my lashes to my chin. I lay more flatly over him and we slipped down until the water touched his chin. We broke when he sighed, and he rested his forehead against mine. Then he sank, far as he could so that his head went under. I tugged him by the hair until he rose again, pinching drops from between his lids.

A bead dribbled from the slope of his nose. "That was unkind."

I laughed and sucked the sweet soapy water from his lips. "I promised I wouldn't let you drown."

We stepped out soon after. Wrapping myself in a towel, I spotted a seam through the wallpaper and coving on the other side of the room. I must have seen it a dozen times, and never thought to ask. "Is that a door there?"

Julian, whilst scrubbing his head with a towel, answered, "That's the Countess Suite."

"Oh." I would have imagined the earl and countess shared the rooms Julian lived in, though they were furnished rather like a place frequented only by men. "May I see?"

"If you like." He went to the basin and started fiddling with a toothbrush.

"Coming along?"

"I don't go in there."

Well, if he wasn't willing to look at a portrait of his mother over his mantel, I suppose it made sense to avoid the place in which she died.

Opening the door was rather like discovering a secret passage. On the other side, all was dark. As my eyes adjusted, I detected the thick, sickening scent of mothballs, and deduced this was a dressing room, the exact mirror of Julian's. Its shelves were empty—not a single lost glove by which to remember the dowager countess.

In her bedroom, ghostly furniture was covered in dust sheets. I pushed open musty curtains to let in the late-afternoon light. Dust coated the air, swirling as my body cut through it. The walls were done in delicate floral, the cushions stitched with vines. The bed was curtained from ceiling to floor, with a divan at its foot, and two large chests of drawers on either side.

I found myself unable to look away from it, sitting in the fog of unbreathed air. For there was where Julian's mother had—as Gwen put it—lain down, and not got up. The room, though stale, was drenched in an undeniable chill. My arms burned with gooseflesh.

The bedroom was a carcass left with its bones picked dry. Was this what was to become of the woman who married Julian? Locked up in an opulent palace only to fade to dust?

But there was presence. The dowager had left her mark, even in a space where all her fine things were swept away. I felt her ghostly hands pressing down on my shoulders, and as my pulse quickened, I had the sense I was being watched.

When I turned, Julian stood in the doorway, towel tied round his waist.

My hand went to my heart. "Damn you. I nearly died of fright."

He chuckled—my absolute favorite sound. "Grim, is it not?"

"Horribly bleak." I joined him in the doorway and leaned into his chest, still warm from the bath. "Where have her things gone?"

"We had everything cleared out when she died."

"I saw her portrait," I said, watching for Julian's reaction, though he remained as stone. "She looked unhappy. Was she always?"

Julian nodded, combing a heavy hand through my hair. "My grandfather married her to an older man whom she hardly knew. She was forced to live in his house, which she hated, and to have children, whom she despised for being his."

How strange it must've been to be brought up in such a time, when money was God, titles were saints, and connection was gospel. To think of how much suffering might have trickled down over centuries from the first man who gave his daughter away for a shilling.

How could I resent my own parents for worrying I'd never find love? Never have children of my own? Never settle because I was so focused on my bloody art? My mother and father loved me. They wanted happiness for me. I couldn't say as much about Julian's parents.

"Gwen said she was confined to this room for a long while," I said.

"During the war, her doctor gave her medication to help her sleep. It drained the life from her, but at least she kept out of our business."

I moved out of Julian's arms. It wasn't like him to be so cold. The Napiers had always been forthcoming about their feelings for their mother. But there was one thing I didn't fully understand, which had niggled at the back of my mind since I'd seen her portrait discarded.

"How did she die?" I asked Julian.

He rubbed his breast, just over his heart. "The doctor believed she overdosed by mistake. It isn't something we speak of."

Of course not. No need for more rumors. "Must have been an odd funeral."

I was intentionally vague, hoping to read what I could from Julian's response.

"I wouldn't know," he said, peeling himself from the doorjamb. "I didn't attend."

Julian left me alone with my unease. I shut the door to the Countess Suite quietly, as if not to disturb her ghost.

In an effort to return to the more pleasant beginnings to our day, I dropped my towel and climbed in next to Julian in his absurd Tudor bed—which I'd become quite fond of—and buried myself beneath the quilt. There was something indulgent about being in bed at this hour, though it wouldn't have been the first time we'd found ourselves here before dark. Julian closed his eye, and I laid my hand on his stomach.

"I need a cigarette," he muttered.

"Have one."

He groaned humorously. "Too tired."

I slipped out of bed into the cold dampness of the afternoon, and returned with his cigarette case. By that time, he was truly asleep in the soft golden glow of the lamp opposite the bed. He'd turned onto his front, one leg under the linens, all else bared proudly to the room. It was an image that begged to be captured, and I would oblige.

I wrapped myself in his shirt and fetched my sketchbook from the next room. Settling on a nearby chair, I began to draw. This was a rare opportunity to capture Julian as naturally as one could find oneself—naked, asleep, and completely at peace. We'd slept together enough times that I'd become familiar with the pattern of his breathing. Neither a snore nor a wheeze, air passed audibly through his nose, the sound reflecting that of his waking sighs. I could've easily recognized his gentle breaths in a ward of sleeping Tommies.

I'd had many nights on duty, keeping the stove alive to a symphony of dreaming sounds. Rarely did they remain so quiet. Nights were difficult on the men, when the darkness of the trench found them again, and the smallest noise triggered an influx of terror. I saw it in Julian, the catch in his throat, the faint murmurs of fear trickling from his nightmares into the room.

Julian slept always with his scars on the pillow. Not to hide them, but to keep his good ear to the room, pricked for danger. He harbored an irrational fear of invaders. I noticed it every time I touched him in the mornings; I'd found the trench knife in his bedside drawer.

Now he was serene, his arms stretched up and bent under his pillow so that I could see every stretch and flex as his lungs filled and emptied. I drew him slowly, careful of the details—the one curl that looped itself under his earlobe, the kite-shaped muscles on his back from his daily drills, the birthmark on his bottom.

As I was shading his brow, he shifted. "Bertie?"

"Just a moment. Don't move."

He obeyed. It was not the first time he'd caught me sketching him unawares. When I was through with his perfect ovate mouth, he brought his head up.

"Are you drawing my arse?"

I broke into a laugh and, holding the book under my arm, returned to bed. Julian rolled over like a dog daft with content, and I pinned him where he lay. With eye half-open, he observed my exposed flesh with undisguised favor.

"Show me, then," he said, words thick from sleep. I turned the book round. He reviewed it briefly, face unflinching. "Filth."

I stifled a yelp as his hands gripped the crease above my thigh. He shoved me onto my back and kissed with a playful roughness that made the room fall away. When I urged his hips towards me, he paused, lowering his weight so we sank together. I moved my legs to be flush with his. I wanted every inch of our skin to meet, to adhere; I wanted to be one.

Julian brushed his lips across the tip of my nose. "Stay with me." For a moment, I thought he meant forever. Then: "I'll send for dinner in a while."

When he rolled over, my disappointment made me move away to face the window.

No man had returned from the war the same. They'd lost pieces of themselves, physical and mental; they'd been changed, unable to see the world as it was before. Unable to hope, to dream. To find purpose.

Julian was a broken man. It was clearer to me now than ever before. I was strong, but was I strong enough to go up against whatever he was battling within himself?

I did want to stay. I wanted to remain in this room where it was only Julian and me. Julian, who adored my paintings, who believed in me, who allowed me to ramble and challenge him. Julian, who made me feel things I'd never dreamt of. What use had I for the outside world, or the people in it? They only disappointed me. They only told me, *You can't.* It was better with Julian.

Nearly the instant the thought came to me, I pushed it aside. Such thoughts were what kept Julian in his rooms, comfortably stowed away from life's difficulties. If I let myself join him, would I lose a piece of myself? I had missed a meeting with an art dealer today, but what of tomorrow? How many more opportunities would I need to sacrifice to remain here? To set my needs aside to soothe his hurts?

I loved Julian. I could even see a future as his wife, as part of his charming family. But I had dreams and ambitions, a profession I adored, a career that had only just begun. A marriage meant a joining of our lives, not a sacrifice of mine. And I wasn't even sure he would ever propose a marriage. I wasn't even sure he loved me.

The thought made me slip out of bed before I could change my mind. I had not seen the art dealer, but more opportunities would come; I was not one for giving in. If Julian truly cared about me, he needed to say so plainly, to speak of the future, to promise not to sink any further into the darkness. Otherwise, there was no reason for me to remain at Castle Braemore.

I returned to the bathroom to dress quietly. If Julian had any protests, he didn't voice them. By the time I returned to put out the lights, he was asleep again, and I leaned over to place a soft kiss on his brow.

It was good night, and perhaps goodbye.

19

The following morning, I went down the main stairs to find Roland and Freddie playing football in the Great Hall. I couldn't have been sure if they'd woken early or been up all night. They were dressed in undershirts and drawers, their hair dripping wet, bare feet slipping on the marble. They'd been swimming.

As I neared, Freddie charged Roland, grabbing him low around the waist and hoisting him up over his shoulder. When Freddie turned to see me, he was so startled that both of them nearly went tumbling to the floor. "Why, Bertie! Look at you—how radiant! My love, you look positively fucked. Do I know the man?"

They'd been drinking as well, then. A rather impressive feat at half past ten in the morning.

"There's no man," I answered. He'd asked on the rare occasion I'd woken alone.

The dangling Roland gave Freddie's arse a smack, and Freddie tossed him forward to land on his feet with a grunt. Roland then pushed Freddie to fall to a seat on his bottom.

"Stay," said Roland, mussing Freddie's bronze hair. "Good boy."

Freddie *woof*ed and attached himself to Roland's leg.

"Were you able to get word to your neighbor about canceling?" Roland scratched Freddie behind the ear. Freddie's leg wiggled, his heel *thump, thump, thump*ing against the marble.

I folded my arms. "I wrote to her this morning. I hope she isn't too disappointed."

"The dealer certainly will be."

I shrugged. "I'm sure it was no loss to him."

Freddie's mouth gaped open in drunken wonder. "No loss to you, darling! The sodding bastard. Who is this fellow we're on about?"

"Never mind, love," Roland said. "Does this mean you're staying, Bertie?"

In that moment, I was sure he meant indefinitely. But Castle Braemore would be neither of our homes for long.

"Bertie cannot stay here. She must spread her wings." Freddie looked up at Roland and frowned. "Unfortunately, it's too late for me. I've a life sentence."

Freddie gave Roland's leg a tug until his knee buckled. He went over, landing on Freddie. I quailed at the sound of knees and elbows meeting marble, but they were too merry to notice any pain.

When the scuffle ended, Roland wrapped his arms around Freddie's neck. "You may stay as long as you like, Bertie. If only to put the Music Room to use."

My affection kindled. "That's kind. But I had better be moving on at the end of summer. I'm becoming *far* too comfortable living like a countess."

Roland stood, hauled his friend to his feet. "We're sampling some wine at the folly following luncheon. Join us. A glass of something will set you right."

I raised a brow. "Sampling?"

"Yes . . . apparently we've an entire room belowstairs full of wine? It's remarkable, all those bottles in a row. They're dusty, you know. Unloved."

Freddie nodded. "We've decided it's high time they've had a good seeing to."

I accepted without second thoughts. I could certainly use a drink, and was eager to see the folly from the inside. I'd been dying to know what the fuss was about.

With sketchbook in hand, I made the long trudge up the hill ahead of the others. I sat on the stairs to wait, roughly drawing the folly with a light hand. It looked lonely, seemingly the only place on the estate that was not kept pristine. Perhaps it was a place used more often in the days of old when there was formality at Castle Braemore. Now it was a place to escape to. To be away from ears and eyes. Where it was quiet, besides the sheep and the breeze rattling panes of glass in aging wooden muntins.

Each of the four walls had French doors, with Roman pillars standing proudly outside them. On two ends were wistful statues of women in draping gowns, eyes far off. One in particular enthralled me, her hands open to the skies, lips parted in plea, lichen spots like teardrops.

My work was interrupted when Freddie's and Roland's voices echoed up the hill. Celia trudged behind them, along with two footmen to carry the crate of wine and hamper, and a third with a rug rolled under each arm. It was clear how Julian managed to bury himself so deeply in debt: having three footmen was expensive, and hardly necessary these days. I had an inkling why Julian kept them on. They'd have fought in the war, survived. Needed jobs.

Celia stopped before the stairs, shielding the sun with her forearm. "I hate this place. What about the lake instead?"

"No." Roland went straight up the stairs to unlock the door. "It's Napier family tradition to get drunk at the folly."

"It's Napier family tradition to get into *trouble* at the folly. Please, mayn't we go somewhere else?"

Roland pushed the doors open and whirled. "You may join us or not, as you like."

Another huff and Celia crumbled to a seat beside me on the stairs. Roland and Freddie instructed where they wanted the rugs and wine to be placed. The footmen made quick work, setting the doors open, pulling corks, and polishing glasses before retreating to the house.

However, the glasses were unnecessary.

"Who's for white?" Roland plucked a bottle from the crate.

Celia took it, having a rather unladylike swig from the lip. "Oh, that's divine," she said, and handed it to Freddie.

He had a gulp. "Gorgeous. Bertie?"

I was laughing already, feeling old compared to the three of them. They'd all lived this way, they'd all been spoiled for a lifetime. No wonder Freddie found it to be his paradise. And none of them knew it would all be gone soon enough.

I accepted the bottle and drank. It *was* divine.

The afternoon unfolded thusly. Someone plucked a bottle and passed it round. We'd taste and taste, and drink and drink more. Without glasses, there was no way to know how much went down. Celia was the first to collapse in a fit of laughter, rolling on the rug. It caught to Freddie; of course, he and Roland had already been legless when they'd arrived. I drank more, faster. I wanted to be like them. I wanted my inhibitions to evaporate, wanted to feel young and as if I didn't know the truth, and as though I wasn't worried that Julian didn't love me.

My brain went from the warm tingle of tipsy to the slow, wavering, and wild place beyond. My companions were accomplished drinkers. They knew when it was time to stand up and move, to indulge in sausage rolls, cheese, and lemon tart until what had been drunk previously was absorbed and there was room for more.

At one point I began to dance with Celia. She leaned her head on my shoulder as we swayed. Her full lips were stained by a fine red, her breath sour as a white. "Don't you have a suitor, Bertie?"

"I don't. I'm a spinster."

"No!" Celia brought her head up, nose scrunched. "A spinster? No! Not you. You're too beautiful to be a spinster. Is she not, Roland?"

Roland had been kissing Freddie. He put his fingers over Freddie's lip as he turned to his name. "What's that, Cece?"

"Is Bertie not too beautiful to be a spinster?"

"Bertie is the most beautiful woman I've ever seen." He put his mouth back on Freddie's.

I laughed and shook my head. "Roland is quite drunk."

"I'm quite drunk," said Celia. "Though I should like some more wine."

She found a bottle to her liking and slumped onto the floor like a porcelain doll, glass eyes and rouged cheeks. Her curls tightened with August dampness at neck and temples.

It was warm, but with all four doors open, a cross breeze kept the building mild. The sky was turning orange in the distance, cows dotting the meadow became pink in the new light. How long had it been since we'd started? It would be night soon, and none of them seemed anxious to go anywhere.

Celia tipped her bottle down with a slosh, and handed it to me. I was finding that after so much, wine lost its flavor. It was sweet, thick, coating tongue and throat.

"I shall be a spinster with you, Bertie." She blanched, swilling more wine. "I didn't have a coming-out ball, you see, I wasn't *presented* . . ."

Roland pulled apart from Freddie and groaned. "There was a war on, you know."

Celia ignored him. "Nobody much takes interest in me, anyhow. We're a bad family to marry into." She pushed her fringe off her forehead. "All so *Julian* could have his thrilling affair."

"Cece!"

The wine bottle slipped from my lips as I set it down hard beside me. She knew, of course, that Julian and I had been spending time together. But I had hoped to keep the details a secret.

Roland was up now, and Freddie appeared over me, wiggling his fingers for the bottle. "Julian's having an affair, is he? I wonder, does she shinny up the drainpipe? Or slip down the chimney?"

"Nobody is having an affair," Roland said, sitting beside Celia.

She glanced sideways. "*You're* having an affair."

Freddie laughed with his mouth full. "Has Julian ever been interested in women? I've always imagined him as a sort of sexless being, like an angel of the Lord, or a daffodil."

"But he *did* have an affair," Celia said.

Roland looked ready to burst from his skin. "Will you ever learn to keep your mouth shut?"

She reached dramatically for a new bottle of wine.

So they weren't talking about me, at least. I relaxed a little. "Are you speaking of the girl he knew before the war?"

Roland's eyebrow turned up. "He told you about Lily?"

Lily. The name had an unexpected weight. "Only that he'd been in love."

Celia slurred, "I expect he wouldn't have told you she was our maid?"

I looked at Roland, but he only skulked with guilt. He stood and lifted Celia by the arm. She squealed and wriggled, but was too drunk to prevent him from sweeping her away to distribute her in the threshold of the far door.

"Enough of this," he said.

"She ought to *know*, Roland! He was rid of Lily, and he's likely to do the same to her!"

My breath stopped in my throat. I pulled my knees into my chest, the wine suddenly making me nauseated. I wanted to be far away from the folly, but couldn't move. All I could do was sit and wonder how my own skin still smelled so strongly of Julian.

"Bertie?" Roland. I picked up my head to look at him. "They were young. It isn't how it seems."

A sob rattled Celia's body, tearstained cheeks sparkling in golden twilight. "Why must you always defend him? Am I the only one in this family with any *bloody* sense?" She crumpled into Roland's open arms, voice muffled against his shirt. "It's his fault she's gone!"

Roland patted her head. "I should think we had best go in for dinner."

"Hear, hear," Freddie added, popping to his feet, apparently eager to leave the scene behind.

I didn't need an invitation. My head spun from the wine and the conversation. Insects chirped in the wood as I lumbered down the hill ahead of the others, turning over the pieces in my mind. Julian had had an affair with a maid. *Lily.* Before the war. He'd loved her, so he told me. And he'd been rid of her, whatever that meant. And the whole mess put Celia in tears. Like as not the reason she hadn't spoken to him since.

Perhaps he was not the man I thought he was.

I didn't wish to go back into the house just yet. Even in a building with more than a hundred rooms, I'd be too aware of Julian's closeness. In a giddy haze of wine, I folded my arms against the cool evening air and stumbled in circles until I came across the walled courtyard, which hid away the comings and goings of staff. Some wicked part of me wanted to push through the gate—to walk the steps of the woman who had generated so much controversy.

The gate was left unlocked, so I slipped in. The tradesmen's entrance was propped open, exuding diffuse smells from the kitchen and bashing sounds of copper pans and stove doors. Laundry still hung from a long wire stretched the length of the courtyard.

It struck me as terribly sad that I could recognize the sobs. Celia was hidden somewhere, her soft voice echoing between the thick stone walls. Then I noticed her leather T-strap shoes under a string of hanging linens, and took a deep breath before pushing one aside.

She sat with her knees hugged tightly to her chest, cheek pressed into her skirt, which was wet with tears. I didn't think she'd noticed me—thought for half a second I ought to retreat before making matters worse. But then she turned her big charcoal eyes, and hiccupped in my direction.

"I must be the last person you want to see," I said.

Celia sniffed, swiped her wrist across her nose inelegantly, showing her youth. I could only imagine if she'd had the upbringing she'd been promised—a feather in her hair, a presentation at court, a ball to follow with a dance from every bachelor in London with a title greater than or equal to her father's. Now she looked so small, so girlish. Not at all ready for that world, or any world outside of Braemore.

"You may sit," she said.

Perhaps it was the *Lady* in her name, but I obeyed, lowering myself down beside her where moss and weeds grew between cold setts.

"Quite the garrison you've found," I said, straightening my skirt over my folded legs. "Is this where you come when Roland and Freddie become insufferable?"

Celia saw no humor in my remark. "I used to come here with Lily."

Of course. "You were close, were you?"

Celia pushed her hair behind her ear. Her face was swollen, purple smears beneath her eyes, a mite green around the gills everywhere else.

"Until Julian wanted her for himself," she said. Blushing, I moved my attention to a dandelion, which I plucked and turned over in my lap, staining my fingers green. "He wouldn't speak to girls of our set—they intimidated him. I ought to have known sooner. He wasn't terribly good at lying."

That gave me an odd sense of comfort. "When did you find out about them?"

"Too late." I opened my mouth to ask how, but she turned to me abruptly, shifting her legs to one side. "They went behind my back for years. Julian was always running off in summers, not allowing me to join him, and Lily was always too busy, she said. She wasn't too busy when he was away!"

I didn't know what to say. Instead, I tried taking her hand, hot and clammy, and she allowed me to hold it.

"It was all pretend," she said, and the tears came again. "He only indulged me so I'd tell him what Lily had been up to while he was at school, and she only spoke with me to hear what he'd written in his letters home. Julian must have thought I was so *stupid*." Celia's voice broke, and she snatched her hand away to cover her face.

Now I felt the go-between, with the urge to defend Julian. I knew their distance hurt him so deeply he could hardly talk about it—hardly listen when I spoke of his bright little sister. He loved all of them dearly, as his own. But I had to be sensitive to Celia's side of the story, especially if I expected her to ever speak to me again. And I wanted her to. I feared losing Julian, because it meant losing all of them.

"You were only a child," I said carefully. There was still one piece of the story I was missing. "If he cared so much for her, why did Julian send her away?"

"He couldn't risk a scandal. But that wouldn't have mattered to the Julian I knew. He would have married the woman he loved, no matter where she was from—and Lily might have been my *sister*."

Her words chilled me. Like her, I wouldn't have thought Julian capable of such apathy. Would I be so easily discharged from his life?

"Julian was away for years," Celia continued. "By the time he returned from the war, so many of my memories of him were already faded. He was nothing like he was—nothing. And the shouting . . ."

She moved away from me again. I wondered if there were things she might tell me, as an outsider, that she'd be afraid might offend her family.

"You aren't frightened of him?" I asked. "His mask? Or his scars?"

Celia's lip quivered. I'd struck a nerve there. Her breaths stalled, tightening her shoulders as she tried to keep another sob at bay. "He isn't my brother any longer."

"Cece—"

"He isn't. And he wasn't the brother I thought he was before, so I hardly know who he is now. How am I meant to apologize to a stranger for something that still hurts?"

I wrapped my arms around her, feeling a knife in my ribs. I couldn't be sure if it was Celia's pain I was feeling, or Julian's. I only wished there was some way to put them in the same room, so all of this would be laid out where they could both see it—good and bad. Perhaps it would do nothing at all. But what if it made all the difference?

That was all I could get out of her, and by then it was nearing dark. When a maid came through the door to collect the laundry, we both stood at once and made our exit. Inside the saloon, we parted ways silently and I sulked off to my room.

I didn't wish to have company for dinner that night. A tray was brought to my door as I was getting ready to settle into bed. What I really wanted was a cigarette and something strong, but I managed with more wine that came with my meal.

As I tossed and turned that night, bedclothes in a tangled, sweaty mess, all I could think of were Mother's words when she'd first seen a letter come through the post from Lord Wakeford:

I've always been of the mind that a man of such few words has something to hide.

20

The next morning, I had a letter from my mother.

Bertie,

I've had word from Mrs. Lemm that you missed her invitation to tea. We all agree this is out of character. Please respond so we know you are well.

And that was it.

I responded, somewhat begrudgingly, with a short answer:

Mother, I could not spare the time to attend the engagement. I have sent Mrs. Lemm my regrets. I am well indeed, thank you.

It was the first time during my stay at Braemore that those words were given as a lie. Still, it was reassuring to know Mother was concerned. Perhaps I'd yet to fall entirely out of her favor.

Adding to my distress, I had misplaced my sketchbook. I couldn't for my life remember the last time I'd seen it, or even the last thing I'd drawn. The bloody wine had done me in. I spent the morning slave to my stomach. Everything had to go, no exceptions. But by the end of retching, I felt a new woman, and was able to eat breakfast, though the maid brought only toast and broth. I apologized over and over for the mess in the washbasin bowl, and she smiled sweetly as she carried it away. How humiliating.

With my stomach settled, I went looking for my sketchbook through the rest of the house. I recruited Freddie and Roland's help, and we searched behind furniture, underneath carpets, on top of the wardrobe—a place it had no reason to be, yet I felt the need to be sure.

In the end, I gave in. *Start fresh, Bertie*, my father had said to me the last time I'd misplaced a sketchbook. This time was just as devastating.

So I did start fresh, for at week's end came Castle Braemore's annual staff picnic. I had been looking forward to capturing the family mingling with their servants at what would be their final celebration. None of them knew this, so I made it my duty to document the moment.

The afternoon was cool, clouds threatening rain but staying at bay. How quickly the heat had given in to the promise of autumn. Summer had ended while nobody was looking, and I felt a deep sense of dread.

Extinguishing negative thoughts, I sat well back from the party to see it from the outside. A great white marquee had been erected on the lawn, and inside was a table stacked with lemonade, tea, and beer, pies, sandwiches, and cakes. There was a croquet court, though nobody seemed interested when cricket was on. The men had a match going, with Freddie and Roland on opposing teams.

I sketched the marquee, draped with colorful bunting and a banner with the words THANK YOU! stitched onto it. It was a lovely thing, this picnic, though I couldn't help thinking that with all Braemore's staff put up with, my sick included, it ought to have come more than once a year.

I looked up at Julian's window, wondering how he felt to be missing this. But no shadow moved behind the glass.

A little hand closed over my arm, nearly pulling the sketchbook from my lap. Anna stood before me in white lace, her straw hat falling to one side. She toted her brother in hand, who wore a sailor suit and had one finger in his nose.

"Hello there," I said. "Have you just arrived?"

Anna nodded, out of breath. "Mama went upstairs to see Uncle Earl and I'm not allowed to let go of Richie's hand. Is there cake?"

"There is . . ." I looked for Celia, but could not spot her. We hadn't exchanged many words since that evening at the folly. I couldn't tell if she was embarrassed by her hysterics or cross at me. In any case, she would not be happy to see Anna and me together, but I could hardly leave them to their own. "Let's go and have a look, shall we?"

I wasn't opposed to the idea at that moment either. With all the stress over my lost sketchbook and sorting my thoughts about Julian, I needed that slice of Battenberg for distraction.

We lost Richie to Freddie and Roland in the game, and Anna tugged on my hand to find a seat. In between bites of cake and watching Anna go to and from the tea tent until a toffee apple occupied her, I drew the match, and then I drew Anna and her apple, and then I drew the window where I wanted Julian to peer out of, for I worried over the reason why he yet hadn't.

I'd been thinking of little else besides his affair with the maid. But it was only part of the reason I hadn't seen him since that last evening. The distance had just as much to do with the imminent end to our summer, and his hesitancy to speak plainly about the future. I'd begun to plan for mine not to include him. It hurt. But I supposed that was love.

Anna popped up suddenly, running to collect a runaway ball and toss it, with a grunting effort, in the direction of the men. She smiled when she flopped back down beside me, proud of her efforts. A bit of string had appeared from under the collar of her pinafore, and when she shifted, a sparkle of gold tumbled out to hang round her neck. She didn't seem to notice the change.

"That's very pretty," I said, leaning closer to point.

Anna looked down, chewing like a cow, and made a little gasp, covering the ring with her hand. "Don't tell, please, Bertie!"

I chuckled. "Tell whom?"

She bowed her chin guiltily and removed her hand. My mouth came open. The ring was familiar, though more elaborate than the depiction I'd seen carefully painted. But the symbol was the same on Julian's stationery; I'd remember it anywhere. It being far too big for Anna's wormy fingers, she'd tied it round her neck with string that might have come from one of her shoes.

"I'm not meant to be wearing it," Anna said.

Far too precious, I'd wager, to be trusted in the hands of a child. But hadn't Julian said he'd lost it in the war? "Where did you get it from?" I asked her.

Anna lifted the ring and slipped it beneath her collar, where it was hidden. "My mama."

It was then that the cricket dispersed for another interval, and Freddie and Roland came jogging over with Richie, who wore a white mustache of cream. Roland held Richie's hand towards me. "I've been summoned to see Gwen in the study. I don't suppose you could look after him?"

I watched Richie lean into Roland's leg. "I'm sure he would rather be with Freddie."

Freddie ruffled the boy's hair. "I'm back to the game."

Roland smiled. "He means the beer."

Anna stood, still waving her half-eaten, sticky apple. "May I play cricket?"

"I'm afraid not, sapling," said Freddie. "You must be at least this tall." He held his hand out flat and she hopped to reach her head to it, but alas. Stuck with me.

Richie was drooping, so I scooped him up, and with Anna at my heel, found a patch of shade where rugs were laid out for the women to watch the games. He went immediately to sleep with his head leaning on my arm. Anna was just behind him, though she chose to recline against my folded legs, finding comfort I couldn't imagine. In no time she was asleep with her heavy head against my chest.

There was no hope of sketching now I'd become a human nursery. Instead I watched the party as it quietened. Things would be winding down soon, the staff returning downstairs to prepare for a light dinner, never to be seen again in one place. Although I was only a guest at Braemore, I was chilled by the notion.

The war had taken what precious little remained of Castle Braemore when Julian inherited his father's debts, debts he had taken no great pains to repay. The money, which once paid for lavish parties, was dwindling. The friends who had attended them had moved on. The land was now mostly owned by former tenants. The Dowager Countess of Wakeford herself was no more, withered away in her gilded prison. And her son had been crippled by an unthinkable war, to suffer for years to come.

I wondered how things might have been different if Lady Wakeford had lived. I would surely never have come. Freddie, neither. Roland would be a shell of himself if treated for a false illness. I looked down at the sleeping girl in my arms. Gwen might not have Anna. And where would she have gone instead?

Castle Braemore was breaking apart, but the most important things remained: the family's enduring love and loyalty.

Gwen caught my attention then, striding towards us in elegant cream silk chiffon.

"Ah, here are my children." At the sound of her voice, Richie perked up and took her hand without being told. Anna, however, slept on. "Celia told me you've been playing nanny all afternoon—bless you. I hardly meant to leave you with them."

"It was no trouble," I said.

"My many thanks, all the same." Gwen smiled down at Anna sleeping against me. "We've very clearly missed our naps." She released Richie to bend down, wriggling her hands under Anna's arms. With all the impossible strength of a mother, she lifted the girl, settling her on one hip while taking Richie's hand again.

"Goodbye, then, Miss Preston."

She began to go, and I scrambled to my feet. "Lady Stanfield?"

"Oh, dear. Not that again."

"Gwen." She nodded with a smile. "I wanted to tell you how wonderful it is you adopted Anna, giving her such a life—picnics and toffee apples and lace—risking the gossip."

I'd never seen Gwen blush, but now she went a bit pink at the neck. "That's very kind. She was a blessing, truly." She nestled her cheek against Anna's curls.

It was all too tempting. Here she was before me, nobody else about. My curiosity got the best of me. "I hope you don't mind my asking—and do tell me off if I've been too bold—"

"What is it, dear?"

I'd already asked Celia once, but I had an inkling one of us had been lied to. "Anna's parents. Did you know them, or—?"

Gwen formed the polite bend of the lip she constantly wore, whether cross, elated, or aloof. "It mattered little to me who they were, or what they'd done. Only that she needed me."

In the empty moment between Gwen's words and my response, Anna stirred. She looked up, unsurprised to be in her mother's arms. "Mama?"

"Yes, my love?"

"May I bring Uncle Earl his cake?"

Gwen gave her daughter a kiss on the head, and hiked her further up on her hip. "I'm afraid we must be going now, darling. Though, perhaps Miss Preston might be so kind?"

She flicked a pointed look at me. I was caught off my guard, yet again, as Gwen smiled. It seemed she was not yet through with me.

IT WAS A slice of Madeira for Julian. Everything besides had been gobbled up, leaving naught but crumbs and a sad hunk of sponge that nobody fancied. That was all right; he wouldn't eat it.

I carried it upstairs on a china plate and knocked on his door. I waited for his footfalls, but heard none. "Julian? It's Bertie . . ."

Nothing. No movement at all, not even the sound of the sofa cushions under his shifting weight. I knocked again, louder. "Julian—?"

I heard panic in my voice. Even in the reluctant early days of our friendship, he'd never taken this long to answer. My pulse lurched as I hurried to the bedroom door. I knocked there, calling his name again. I pounded my fist against the door like a madwoman. "Julian? Please, answer. You needn't let me in, only say you're—"

The key turned and the door opened. Julian stood before me in only trousers, his curls untamed by comb or oil, dirty and twirling out from the side of his head like an overgrown boxwood. His eyelid was pink and swollen.

I leaned to glimpse behind him. His bed was unmade. "Did I wake you?"

He nodded and scratched his brow.

"I'm sorry . . ." I tapped my fingers on the plate. I'd seen him in various states of disarray, but he was adamant about his routine. Waking, drilling, dressing. This wasn't like him. "Is it not a trifle early to be sleeping?"

He nodded again. Something about the wet stillness of his eye gave me pause. He didn't look himself. He looked empty.

"Well, I'll not keep you, only . . ." I raised the plate, the Madeira looking sadder than ever. "Anna wanted to be sure you had cake."

Julian regarded the plate, seeming like he mightn't take it until his hand came up lazily and plucked it from mine. His mouth opened to talk, the words taking a few ticks to make their way out. "Would you like to come in?"

I was torn between wanting to let him sleep, and the old nag that told me he ought not to be alone. So I accepted. He dressed and rang for tea while I paced the sitting room. Alarmingly, his desk was cleared and tidied. I should have been glad he'd finally replied to the letters, but had a suspicion this was not the reason they had gone.

I sat on the settee, chilled to the bone. My job had come to an end, but Julian and I were back where we'd started. Tea in his sitting room. Wondering if I should have knocked at all.

While I poured, a sheet of rain drummed on the roof. Julian watched the windows streak as I set a cup in his hand. "Everything all right?"

He tried a smile, slow and listless. "You must be keeping busy."

I stirred a lump of sugar into my tea and held it close, wanting the warmth for comfort. "Yes, I—I've been rather caught up in painting and . . . wine."

"I had planned on selling Braemore's collection," he said, "but according to Huxley there doesn't seem to be much left of it."

I felt I'd stuck a knife in him, and checked my lap for blood spatter. Julian lit a cigarette, far less bothered by his comment than I was.

"I'm to meet with an appraiser end of next week," he said. "I shall have to give Roland and Celia the truth . . . I'm uncertain how to begin."

I set down my tea to hold his hand. Little wonder why he was in such a state. All those unanswered letters, all that time he'd put things off for his siblings had at last caught him up.

"They'll understand," I said. "You have no choice."

Julian studied the burning end of his cigarette. "I've let it crumble. Everything my father—his father—everything they built."

"It isn't your fault."

Julian took a long drag. Smoke curled through his nose and floated to the ceiling. Outside, the wind angered. A rumble of thunder began as a hum, amplifying to a growl that shook the windowpanes. Julian tossed his cigarette in the tray.

He stood in a flourish, darting to close the curtains. I took his lead and released the others, confining us to dusky gloom. Julian stood paralyzed and I wrapped my arms around him. He leaned his weight into me, our hearts thrashing to meet.

"I've finished here, Julian," I said. "There's nothing left for me to paint."

His arms drew around me, clutching fabric to hang on.

"I haven't any reason to stay. Unless . . ." I wanted to beg. Plead. *Give me one. One measly reason.*

Julian dipped to kiss me. I started to push him away, but slipped under, intoxicated so easily by the taste of his lips. When I paused for a breath, it stuck in my throat. My tears gleamed on his cheek. He had begun to shake. I was overcome with the urge to hold on—to lock my arms around him so he could not slip away.

"Julian—?"

The pain he wore was so plain it broke my heart. "Why have you come?"

I held his cheek so he would look at me. Gwen had sent me here with purpose. She had given me the final chance I'd refused to give myself. The chance to tell Julian how I felt. To ask him if he would follow me when I left.

"Because I'm in love with you."

Julian pressed my face to his neck, cradling me as we shivered. I could not dam the flood of tears. For once, I was not the stronger of us.

"I know I'm a dreadful match, and I have nothing to offer, but . . ." I looked up, blinking my vision clear. "Ask me to marry you."

Julian closed his eye, setting his chin against my head. His silence was confirming. My breath left me again and I felt bodiless, fit to leak through the cracks between floorboards.

"This is not the life for you, Bertie," he said.

"Nor you. We'll make a new one together."

"I will not be responsible for pinning you down."

I jerked away, wanting space between us. "You don't need to be trapped. It's only been a few years since the war. You're still healing."

"I'm sorry I am not who you thought I was."

I shook my head. I didn't care what he apologized for; I wouldn't accept it. "You cannot simply give in. You cannot resolve to be alone this way forever."

His gaze went down. "It's what I want."

"I don't believe you. So if it's something else, please say. Even if it hurts me, Julian, I must know. Because what I'm feeling for you—it hurts already."

Thunder jolted us both. Julian's body went rigid. He was trying so hard to remain where he was, to stow away the memories of bombardment. It was all I could do not to comfort him. He had to understand that he could not carry on facing them alone.

"Don't you ever wish for more?" I asked. "Don't you wish for a family of your own? To pass on your title, to be a father?"

Julian balked. "I'm not fit to be a father."

"Of course you are. You practically raised Roland and Celia, and the way you are with Anna—"

At the sound of her name, he turned briskly away.

I looked over at the untouched slice of Madeira—a present from Anna. Anna, with her love of art, her midnight eyes, her mess of curls. Anna, adopted from a maternity home by a desperate viscountess. It all came together so rapidly, I nearly laughed at myself for being so blind.

Anna had Julian's ring because he'd given it away to the one girl he'd ever loved. A pregnant maid would never be kept on staff, especially if the father was her employer.

Julian sat down by the hearth. I knelt before the chair, one hand on either of his knees, watching the orange flames flicker over his eye. Many would overlook it. Things such as these were overlooked all the time. Denial is powerful. It takes a keen eye to see closer, beyond the ordinary, beyond the obvious. It takes an artist.

"Anna is yours, isn't she?"

Julian turned from the hearth, glare so severe I nearly recoiled. "What?"

"You and Lily—" He grimaced at the sound of a name he wasn't aware I knew. "Is it not true? That Gwen adopted your child to keep her close to you?"

After a pause, Julian stood, pushing past me with none of his usual mindfulness. I thought he might stride into his bedroom—shut the door and bar me from speaking to him further—but he stopped just a few paces away to look down at me with a reddening face.

"I invited you to be a guest in my home," he said, so suddenly loud it was alarming. "I trusted you with my family, with ruinous secrets, and you"—he pointed at me with contempt—"you had the insolence to go rooting about for grounds to condemn me?"

"No—no!" I was fully shaking now, petrified by Julian's words and how they were spoken. Neither was he steady, and I feared he might lose control. I didn't want to be in the room if he began his shouting. "Julian . . . I would never have gone to your bed if I didn't know you to be anything but good."

He scoffed with a bitter smile that looked nothing like it should. "Then why is it that you've come to accuse me?"

"Accuse you? *No*." I put my hand against my heart, beating rapidly. "My only hope was for you to finally tell me why you bear so much guilt. So I may help you carry the burden."

He went somewhere far away. The change in his eye was familiar to me, a sudden shift of light, like curtains being drawn over a window. The things behind them—Lily, Anna, the war, his mother—he wished no one else to see. It was what made him shake in the night, what made him shout when darkness fell. I hated that he was in there all on his own, but I knew there was no way inside unless he opened the door.

When Julian finally spoke, his tone was languid, quiet enough that he might have been speaking only to himself. "I wasn't a man, then, during the war. I was an animal, a creature. How could I think of the future—a wife, a child—whilst buried in shite and mud?"

I flinched, forcing myself to hold his eye when it came to me.

"How could I be a father? Knowing I had slaughtered dozens of sons with these hands? Led countless others to their deaths?"

I shook my head. This was only one of many injustices of war and, like the others, could not be explained. Tears soaked the collar of my dress. I gave up trying to blot them as they came.

Julian's face twisted in pain. "You say you want to help me carry this burden," he said, "but I would not wish this upon my worst enemy, let alone—"

The words died in his throat as his head fell, hand rising to meet it. I wanted to go to him, but I was rooted to the carpet, bone weary and guarded. It wasn't until he sank to a seat on the floor that I found the courage to move, to push his hair from his face and see the first hot tears.

"I love her," he said thickly. "From the first I held her, I knew. Anna is the best of her mother and the man I once was, but she cannot be mine. She's better off with my sister."

I put an arm around his back. Tried to gently smooth the tremors away. "What's happened to Lily?"

What tears he'd allowed were cleared. Some of his old lessons returned to him, and he found an evenness, if false. "When she began to show, Gwen ensured her place at a maternity home. My mother would have dismissed her directly and I was away; I couldn't have done a thing to prevent it." He struggled to draw a full breath. "Gwen wanted a child always and Lily wanted a life beyond Braemore . . . I would never have asked it of her, to bring on the child. But I was glad—when she told me Lily hadn't survived the birth—that some piece of her could return home."

"Why didn't you tell me?"

"I feared what you would think of me," he said. "I knew if I married Lily, it would have ruined us, and in a time when the estate needed rescuing by a dowry. But I ought to've done it anyhow. I wanted to. It was my fault she was in that home. If I'd married her, if she'd been here, perhaps . . ."

I didn't know whether to be cross or heartbroken, so I drew his hand to my lips and kissed his knuckles. If there was anything I knew that could cure one's own grief, it was helping another. That was how we all had made it through the war.

"I asked you here to paint Anna's history," Julian said. "For surely when I'm gone, she'll tumble to the truth and wish to see where she was begun. I'd prefer she not remember me as a beast who abandoned her."

"You did all you could do," I said. "Anna wants for nothing—"

Julian sighed my name: "Bertie . . ."

"It is not your fault Lily is dead."

"It is all my fault," he rumbled. "Every single thing which has gone wrong in this family is owing to my own bloody negligence."

"You're wrong."

"And you presume to know far too much of matters you cannot possibly understand."

The sudden snap was jarring. My arm fell away, and I searched my mind for anything I could say to mend the situation, but thought, for once, it was better to stay silent.

Then Julian was on his feet. He seized my elbow, hauling me up as I stumbled, twisted in my skirt. His voice took on a foreign note, firm and flat: "It's time you went home."

I wriggled uselessly, his fingers digging hard into my arm. "I want to talk about this. Let go—"

"There's nothing more to be said between us."

The words crushed me, a boulder passing through from throat to stomach, knocking everything else out of its way. I wiped my damp face. "Because I know too much, is that it? Do you think so little of me that you believe I'd tell anyone?"

"I think you've come looking to solve a mystery," he said, "nosing about where you don't belong. But as you've said, there is nothing left to paint and certainly no clues left for you to uncover."

Rather than continue to writhe, I thrust my elbow at him, but he was too solid to be put off balance. "Don't you care about me at all?"

His face was vacant as the one painted on his mask. "I have acted dishonorably."

"Julian—"

I was driven from the fire as the thunder became more violent. I let myself be towed along, useless with heartbreak, with astonishment, for how suddenly things had smashed. Was this how carelessly he'd turned Lily out? Was his heart incapable of more?

"I thank you for your work." Julian opened the door, hinges whining with age.

"Don't you dare," I choked. "Don't do this; I have done nothing but love you."

He winced as if the words had cut him, and pressed his hand against the doorjamb. "There's nothing for you here."

"You bloody bastard! Do you know what I've sacrificed for you? What I was willing to set aside for *you*? Not least of all my dignity."

"I am sorry if I've misled you—"

"You are not sorry!" Julian dropped his chin and I shoved him so he'd look at me. "You prove Celia right; don't you see? You prove you're just an unfeeling beast in a tower."

I was suddenly dizzy. The room spun and disappeared behind fog. Julian caught my waist, and I leaned into him while the floor swayed under my feet. When my vision cleared again, I wrenched away from his touch.

"You'll be alone again," I said.

Every strained crease on his face weakened and smoothed as if I'd dosed him with morphia. "That's all I want."

I waited. Hoping for him to change his mind. Pleading with my eyes for him to remember what we had. But there was nothing for it.

I had to walk away.

The Folly

SEPTEMBER 1915

Celia couldn't imagine where Julian had got to. He was meant to meet her in the hall fifteen minutes ago—he'd been so anxious she be ready on time. Everyone was waiting to wave the Earl of Wakeford off to war. Yet Lord Wakeford was nowhere to be found.

He ought to have been readying himself to go. But Julian was not in his apartments or his study or even the bathroom, which Celia had entered without even knocking first. She looked in every other room, even the empty bedrooms. He was not indoors.

It wasn't fair. Julian hadn't even told her how long he'd be away, like when he'd gone to Oxford. This time, his leave was mysterious and open-ended. If Julian was going to be away for so terribly long, Celia wanted to spend as much time with him as she could before he was gone.

Oh, but where could he be? If he didn't turn up soon, they'd miss their train to London. Celia trudged out to the drive, her new shoes crunching gravel. The air was crisp and cold—not at all a day for a stroll. And if he'd gone for a bathe in the lake, he'd lost his mind. It mattered little how much he enjoyed swimming laps all summer; he'd have to be mad to do it now. So she went beyond the gardens, calling his name.

Then she saw it. At the top of the hill, a light flickering within the folly.

Celia groaned for nobody to hear, and started up the hill. What on earth was he doing up there? Hiding, most likely. He did that often. Though he normally invited her.

It was an oil lamp. The doors were shut to keep out the wind that was biting Celia's ears. She pulled her hat down, approached slowly. Julian deserved a good spooking for running off without her, and she always prided her light steps. Crouching low, she crept up the stairs, glancing warily at the statues that made her skin crawl. Then she scurried to one side so as not to be seen through the glass doors.

All was quiet except for the wind, roaring to scare her off. But Julian was just inside. There was no reason to be frightened.

Celia peeked through the glass, cupping her hand around her eyes.

Julian had brought a rug, like the ones they put out by the lake to lounge in the sun. His new khaki uniform was in a pile in front of the door. Celia wrinkled her brow. Gwen would be cross when she saw him in London all rumpled. Soldiers were meant to be tidy. All straight. All solid. All alike.

Why had he undressed? she wondered. For he was cold, clearly; he'd brought along a blanket, too. He was moving beneath it so all Celia could see was the top of his oiled head.

Then Julian rose and threw the blanket off like a magician's cape. Celia gasped and closed her eyes. He was naked.

And he wasn't alone.

Though her knees trembled and her stomach went to stone, Celia couldn't help but look again. When she opened her eyes, she saw that Julian was lying on top of someone, a girl with long blond hair. She was naked, too.

He was hurting her. Celia nearly screamed, but bit down on her mitten. The girl was gasping, writhing beneath him. Julian took her face in his hand and turned her to look at him. She couldn't breathe! The girl's hands gripped Julian's bare shoulders, but he flattened her against the rug with his own body, thrusting and rocking until she cried out.

Celia's eyes spilled tears. Julian had never hurt anybody, not even a spider he'd caught in her room. He wouldn't kill it, not even as she shouted from where she stood on the mattress. He'd put it in a jar and carried it to the garden.

Julian was good. What had the army done to him?

Celia watched him move off the girl, rolling onto his back. She sat up, long hair swaying over her shoulder. She was crying. He rose to kiss her, wiping her cheeks with the back of his hand. She wrapped her arms around his neck, looked over his shoulder, and caught Celia's eye.

Lily.

Celia fled. Her shoes slipped on the slick grass, sending her sliding on her bottom until she could get her footing again. Tears blurred her vision, sobs making it difficult to breathe the harsh air. She felt sick. Not only had she found out her brother was an awful brute, but she had been too frightened to help Lily. Lily—whom she'd sworn to love and protect.

By the time Celia reached the house, she was desperate for air. She sat just inside the door, pulling off her hat, heaving and hugging herself. What could she do? Whom could she tell? Surely Julian would be in heaps of trouble if someone found out he was hurting Lily. But should he not be? She wished Gwen was there. Her sister would know what to do.

The door opened behind her, admitting a shock of cold air. Celia scrambled to her feet, backing away as Julian entered, dressed again in his uniform. When he saw her, he collapsed to his knees like he did when he had something of importance to tell her. So they could be eye to eye.

"Cece . . . ," he said. "I know you saw us."

Celia drew her sleeve across her face to dry it, though the tears wouldn't stop. She thought to run; she didn't want to be anywhere near Julian. Though a fire was burning in her belly, and the guilt of not helping Lily was like a great bellows, feeding it.

Without warning, it burst into wildfire. Celia flew at Julian, throwing her fists on his chest. "You brute!" she bawled, thumping and thumping him. "You lout! How could you?"

He didn't try to stop her. He took each strike like he knew he was deserving, allowing himself to be thrashed and jabbed. When she slapped his face hard, he only closed his eyes and waited for another. But the shrill sound of skin on skin and the sting in Celia's palm made her pause. Panting, she backed away.

Julian turned his chin. He'd never looked so forlorn. "I think you've misunderstood—"

Celia gasped. "You were hurting her!"

"I wasn't hurting her, pal. I would never hurt Lily."

"She was shouting! She was pushing you away! What have you done with her?"

He shook his head. "I'm sorry you saw that . . . It would be confusing."

Celia wouldn't back down easily. "I know what I saw. You went to the army and they made you a beast. I told you not to go. I told you!"

She had. When the war was announced, she'd gone right to him for comfort. It was all very frightening and sudden, and Gwen was not there. Her mother had cried, and refused to see Celia. So she clung to Julian until he took her in his arms and promised it would be all right. And when he said he must go to fight in the war, she'd begged him not to leave her alone.

Julian reached out, but she backed away. "Please, Cece, don't do this. Not today."

Something crumbled inside her, and her bones went with it. She wanted to throw her arms around Julian, to keep him there, to forget what she'd seen. But the thought of closing the space between them made her stomach churn.

"You can go now," she said, voice breaking. "I don't care anymore."

Julian sank. "Don't say that."

"Go to France and never come back." Celia crossed her arms and looked away.

Julian was silent for a moment. Then sat back on his heels. "You love Lily, don't you? I love her as well. And she loves me. She makes daisy chains for me. She tells me folktales. She pulls on my hair . . ." He smiled shyly.

Celia closed her eyes. Lily did these things for her, out of love. If she did those things for Julian, she must care for him, too. "Then why was she shouting?"

Julian exhaled slowly. "We ought to have Gwen talk with you."

"Gwen isn't here; she's left us."

"I know." Julian rubbed his palms on the tops of his legs, looking as he would before his speeches. "Celia, when two people love each other, they're overcome with the need to be one. It's impossible, of course, but they try. They get as close as they can to feel that they're no longer separate."

"I don't understand."

"No. No, I'm not explaining it very well." Julian raked a hand through his hair, glancing about the room for help that wouldn't come. "Lily and I wanted to be closer; closer than an embrace. And so we went to the folly where nobody would find us, because . . . because it isn't something two people should be doing unless they're married. That's why married people share a bed. To be close."

Celia thought of Gwen and Uncle Richard, wondering if they did this thing Julian spoke of. "But you aren't married."

"No."

"So you oughtn't have done it."

Julian sighed but said nothing.

"If you love Lily, why aren't you married?"

"I should think you know the answer."

She did. Julian was the Earl of Wakeford and Lily was a maid. Maids were not meant to speak freely to the master, let alone kiss him. They were meant to be like nuns. If they found a beau, they couldn't stay. Even the housekeeper, Mrs. Burns, was not married. And if she did marry, she'd have to wed someone of her set, like the butler.

Julian would marry a lady. That was the done thing.

It all made sense now. Perhaps Julian had wanted to do this thing at the folly, but Lily had not. Lily knew the rules. Lily must have resisted, Julian ignoring her pleas. He'd forced his weight on her and she might have been crushed. Celia's breathing grew unsteady again.

"That's why she was shouting. Why didn't you stop? Why didn't you listen to her?"

"Cece, please—"

"No! Lily will be in trouble now, and it's your fault!" Celia began to leave. Julian jumped to his feet and caught her by the arm. She pushed at his grip uselessly. "Let me go! Julian—stop it!"

"You stop!" He tugged so she had to look at him. "You haven't a father, so you must heed me."

"No—!"

"You're too old to behave this way!"

But she wailed, her face hot, her heart pounding so fast she thought it might get tired and stop altogether. This was not Celia's brother; Julian was calm and gentle, and this man before her was harsh and panicked, eyes wild.

"Hear me, pray," he said. "If Mrs. Burns learns of this, Lily will be dismissed. We must keep it our secret, do you understand? To protect Lily. Because we both love her so dearly and wish for her to stay."

Celia struggled. "You don't love her! You don't even care!"

"I do! Come, now—" Julian took hold of her other arm and then she could fight no longer; she was exhausted, tears making it difficult to see.

"She was *my* friend first! You stole her and you lied. Let me go!" she shouted. "I hate you!"

"You don't mean that."

"I do! I hate you!"

The grandfather clock bonged on the hour, making them both start. They were very late now.

Julian let go of her, walking away with his face in his hands. Celia saw her escape and headed for the door. She stopped when she heard Julian roar. That's how it sounded to her—a bear in a cage. Carved in the bright windows, his silhouette was bent and unfamiliar. She trembled.

"You may hate me, Celia," he said, turning to face her. "You may think the worst of me, but please—*please* come and see me off today."

Celia shook her head. She couldn't bear the train journey sitting beside him, nor a kiss on the platform. She wanted nothing to do with him.

"Please?"

She shook her head.

"Celia—" Julian's voice strained like someone had their thumbs pressed against his throat. "I would never wish to frighten you, but you must understand that from where I'm going I may not return."

Celia's hand flew to her mouth to hush a sob. It was the truth in all the whispers she heard from grown-ups, the truth they didn't wish for her to hear. Julian was not just marching about in his uniform, guarding an invisible line from bad people. War meant guns and death, like Roland told her, like Gwen scorned him for.

Her hand fell away. "I'll go. But I shall never speak to you again."

21

A mind often forces a state of bliss when there is simply too much for it to handle at once. During the war, I'd come to embrace this state, rather than fear what might follow. So I didn't leave Braemore straightaway. I would go on the day that was planned.

There was one thing left to paint: the folly. It stood proud and solitary on its hill, like a lighthouse watching over Castle Braemore and the surrounding estate. It was empty nearly all the time, unless someone needed a moment apart. There was nothing inside to make it suitable to live in, the room small and bare, the doors allowing drafts from every angle. At the same time, it was a sanctuary.

I set up my easel on the lawn, well back so I had the image of the hill itself and the folly on top. As I began, I wondered why indeed the folly was left alone. Who had ordered the structure? And for what purpose? Was it once enjoyed by many, or was it always just the slightest bit impractical? The earls of Wakeford did have an eye for frivolous pieces of architecture. But its placement must have been more calculated than the simple need to impress houseguests. Whoever had asked for it had a vision, had looked off the peak down to the heath and was moved to mark the place. Perhaps they only wanted an escape.

If I hadn't known better, I would think Julian had ordered the building of the folly. But it was much, much older than he was.

Because he'd asked me not to paint it, I wouldn't sell this piece; I wouldn't show it to anyone. It was just for me. To remember them by.

I painted with thoughts of Julian. I reread all the signs that warned things would end this way. His story of the girl he'd lost, which had no ending. His unwillingness to heal for the sake of his family or me. Celia's refusal to speak to him. I'd denied to myself that there was anything to see in them. Had it been my own fault?

Though I did love him. For better or for worse. I owed it to him to tell him that, and owed it to myself to make peace with it. I did wonder if he felt the same, but would never know.

A breeze blew the canvas, nearly taking it off the easel. I held tight until the burst faded again. It was an autumn gust. Early, but undeniable.

In the distance, a small voice, carried away on the breeze. I turned, surprised to see Anna hopping down the steps and across the pristine lawn, hair blowing out of her face. Now that I knew the truth, I better noticed the curve of her jaw, the slight hook of her nose, the roundness of her ears—all traces of Julian.

"Hullo, Bertie!" she called, red-faced. "I'm coming there!"

I cupped my hand over my eyes. "I didn't see you arrive."

Anna waited until she was at my side to answer, panting. "You were in the Music Room, and Mama said don't bother you, but I got new crayons I want to show you."

I looked up at the sky, threatening rain. I supposed there was nothing wrong with taking a break whilst the storm cleared. Anna helped me fold my easel, and followed me in to abandon it and the canvas in the Great Hall.

"My crayons are in here." Anna took my hand, pulling me towards the drawing room. "I already drew three of our dogs, Spencer and Phoebus and Mortimer . . ."

Gwen's voice spilled out through the cracked doors: "There is nothing to be done about it now. One of the men of this house must meet with the appraiser on Friday. End of."

Roland's strained voice came next. "I only learned we were selling *yesterday*. What good can I possibly do?"

"You can stand firmly beside the estate manager and nod along as the other man speaks."

I stopped in the threshold, cheeks burning. We were about to walk in on a very private conversation. The Napiers stood in a triangle, Roland with hands on hips, Gwen with hands full of papers, and Celia flushed and fluttering. Freddie sat, looking wary as I was to be audience.

"No! No—" Roland shook his head. "Julian must come down."

"And how do you expect we'll manage that, hm?" Gwen perked her brow. "You at his head and Celia and me at either foot?"

Anna tucked herself behind me, startled by the unusually stern tones of voice.

"I'm certain he'll see sense," said Roland. "I'll have a word with him myself."

"Oh, you will? A change of heart, is it? After how many years?"

"I tried—"

"You gave *in*. Everyone gave in to him apart from me. However, I am not responsible for Castle Braemore any more than I am responsible for Lord Wakeford."

"I handled things when he was away."

"Yes, and you were made to grow up much too quickly, and I do apologize. But you've had your fun with your motors and your wine, and now you must be of use."

Roland, who'd been standing still and rigid, came undone. "It isn't mine, Guinevere! It was never meant to be mine!"

Celia had her free hand waving, fighting for an open second to throw her word in. She was holding something at her side, something flat and covered in black leather . . .

"You really ought to have a look at this, Gwen," she said. "*Please*."

"Quiet, Cece." Gwen put up a silencing finger. "I'm not ready for you yet."

"But it's important, so long as Bertie is here. You must speak with him—"

Gwen pinched the bridge of her nose. "Cece, not this instant. Do sit down . . ."

Roland stepped between them, having grown a few inches. "I'll go and speak to Julian now, all right? We have a few days to sort things."

"You'll not bother him today," Gwen said. "He was poorly last afternoon and needs time to—" Her gaze came up and she spotted me in the doorway. I expected to be scorned, but she dropped her hands and sighed. "I told you to stay in the nursery! Where is Richie?"

Anna cowered behind me, but Gwen managed to reach around and fish her into the open without asking me to move.

"I only want to show Bertie my new crayons," Anna said.

"Now is not the time, my love." Gwen glanced quickly at me and back at her daughter. "Off you go upstairs to mind your brother. I'll bring your crayons in a moment."

Once Anna had gone, Celia folded her arms. "Should Bertie not be a part of this discussion?"

Roland scowled. "I hardly think it's Bertie's concern—"

"I've been looking all over for that." I stepped further into the room, pointed at the book in Celia's hand. She had her thumb between the pages, marking her place.

Gwen appeared at my shoulder, touching my arm. "Celia, why have you got Bertie's sketchbook?"

"Cece's been snooping."

"*Roland.*" Celia rolled her eyes. "I haven't been *snooping.* I found it at the folly and looked inside to see what it was." She took the book in both hands and opened it wide. All eyes moved to the page—the drawing of Julian, naked in his bed.

When I looked up, I saw the first tears spill down Celia's cheeks. They landed on the drawing, tiny, growing pools that spread the pencil markings and washed the lines into a blur. I found my anger dissolving and was unable to speak.

"He's led you as he led her," Celia said to me.

Beside her, Gwen shifted closer. "Celia, not here."

"It's all right," I said. "I know about Lily."

Gwen looked to Roland, but his head was down. Celia closed the space between us as if we were the only two in the room, gaze surer than I'd ever seen it. "She loved him back, but that hardly matters, does it? Lily has died and Julian has lost all he ever was except the part of him that was too selfish to marry her."

I shivered, unable to formulate a response. Celia had been looking after me all along.

Gwen was moving in again, putting herself between me and her sister. "Your brother has survived a war, Cece. I'm not certain you understand the gravity of that."

Celia closed the sketchbook with a thump. "The war is over."

"Not for him."

"You've only ever seen his side."

Gwen softened, reaching out, but Celia jerked away. "Julian explained things to you when you were a little girl. Now you've grown—you're a woman. Can you not understand?"

Her breath shook as she pushed her words through a sob. "I can understand Julian seduced Lily only to dismiss her, and banished her to that wretched place to *die*."

"Perhaps if you'd been the one to speak with Lily when she left," Gwen said sternly, "perhaps if you'd been the one to write to her while she was *in* that wretched place—perhaps you'd defend him, too."

"Oh, please!" Celia's voice tightened and surged. "Julian ruined her!"

I felt unmoored, stomach churning, the room rocking over a raging sea. No longer was I just a bystander; no longer was I a painter searching for a muse. If I was, Gwen would not continue, but she did, filling in the spaces of the story she wasn't aware that I knew. She wanted me to hear.

"He loved her," Gwen said.

"But he led her all those years; he brought her to the folly. If he was a respectable man, he would have ended things or married her long before the war. She might still be alive!"

Gwen's hand went to her head. "Heavens, you're so young."

"You disagree? You don't believe he was at fault? You believe it was entirely Lily to blame?"

"Yes!" Gwen's arms dropped to her sides. "Women who hope to keep their positions on the staffs of great houses do not open their legs to their employers."

Celia's eyes widened, struck by Gwen's crudity. I was taken aback myself, feeling a newfound wash of shame crawl across my skin.

"How can you speak of her that way?" Celia asked.

"Julian did not force himself on Lily," Gwen replied. "Lily disobeyed the terms of her employment, and because she could not have a baby under this roof, he—" She paused, checking her tone. "Julian took *my* advice and sent her away to give birth elsewhere, so if you'd like to place blame on someone, for God's sake, do blame me."

Celia did not waver. "It isn't fair that the woman should be punished."

"No! It isn't. But that's our lot, Cece!" Gwen took a long breath. "They oughtn't have acted on their infatuation, that much is true. But in her place, can you say certainly that you would not do the same? For love? I can't."

A tear slipped down my cheek and I brushed it away.

Celia had no answer. Gwen was right—she was too young. She had been so sheltered, never so much as courting with a boy her age. Gwen's admission was strong and sure, and I stood with her. For love, even as new a feeling as it was to me, I might have done all Lily did and more.

"I'm so sorry you've lost your dear friend, my girl," said Gwen, "and I wish you had not had to endure so many years here on your own without the love you deserve. But the one other person who still mourns Lily so fervently is the one you refuse to see."

Celia's body suddenly shook in a sob. In two strides, Gwen was there, wrapping herself around her baby sister. Roland sat heavily beside Freddie, and they leaned into one another.

Gwen spoke with her chin resting against Celia's temple. "You were always so much alike, you and Julian. It is of no great surprise to me that you were her two favorite people on this earth." Celia buried her face deeper into Gwen's neck. "You say Julian has lost all he was, but you forget this includes being your brother. *That* you may return to him."

Celia sniffed. "He took her from me."

"Lily was a woman, not an object to be passed about," Gwen replied. "In the end, if she had lived, neither you nor Julian could have held her forever. But you still have one another."

Celia wept as my sketchbook fell from her hands, pages down on the floor.

The room went upside down again, and I nearly lost my footing, holding a nearby chair to steady myself. Perhaps Julian had learned from his past after all. Then, he had not been strong enough to let Lily go before it was too late. But last night, he had asked me to leave him.

"Julian has no intentions of repeating his mistake." My voice roused the room, turning heads. Celia did not look up, but held her breath momentarily. Gwen's gaze widened. "He has asked me to go, and so I leave tomorrow."

Roland stirred. "He has? What's happened?"

Celia turned her head to see that my face was pale and drawn. I could not tell what she was thinking, but wasn't sure I wanted to know. "He's done it all again," she said. "He's had you to stay and be our friend only to turn you out again."

Oh, the poor girl. I might have done more damage, trying to help her. Her loneliness was so great, so immense, it affected every thought in her head, rational or not.

"Cece . . . I was always going to leave at the end of summer."

"I know," she said, "but you might have been asked to return."

Her words did their best to tug at my heart. She wasn't thinking clearly, and neither was I, even as I let myself cry at the thought of leaving. The truth pained me, but we both needed to accept it.

"I've come here to paint only," I said. "I'm sorry I have overstepped and have forgot my place, but I'm finished, so I must go h—"

A reverberating crack shook the still air.

My own wind left me, as if I'd been dealt a physical blow. As my heart thumped in my ears, I looked about for a cause. Celia broke away from Gwen, whose eyes went to the ceiling. The boys were on their feet. Freddie wobbled, and gripped Roland's shoulder for support.

"Dear God," he whispered. "That was . . ."

Gwen was off first, I at her heels.

I don't remember crossing the Great Hall, climbing the stairs, turning the corner, or racing down the corridor. But I arrived somehow at Julian's sitting room door, just in time to see Gwen dash to the next. I tried the knob. Locked.

Gwen didn't look up when I appeared at her elbow in front of the bedroom door. She worked the knob—locked, too. She threw her shoulder into the solid wood, letting out a growl of frustration followed closely by a sob.

"Huxley—" she said breathlessly. "He'll have a key. Run—Bertie, please!"

I nearly did, then pushed back on her arm. I could hardly speak through chattering teeth: "Your mother's room."

We ran at equal pace to the next door, holding up skirts. It opened easily to the dark and foreboding space. I kept my eyes front as we dashed through stale air to Julian's bathroom, where I was hit with the stench of gunpowder. Gwen barreled past me, head whipping side to side to survey the room. In the threshold, I shuddered, swallowing back sick at the thought of what we might find.

I drew a shaking breath, then stepped through.

Gwen had climbed up on the bed beside Julian. He sat propped against the headboard, but his body was wrong, torso slumped to one side, head tipped to shoulder, jaw open. His face was violet pale, eyelid loosely shut. There was blood. A thin line running down his left temple, dewdrops on the pillows. His hand lay crumpled in his lap, slick with swollen burns.

I hadn't the time to consider what had caused the bleeding, only that there was not enough of it. We had no doubt heard a gunshot, but an open skull would have drenched the bed entirely. Something had gone wrong.

"Julian!" Gwen cried, lifting him upright. She touched his cheek, smearing blood across his face. "*Julian?* Open your eyes! Look at me! *Julian!*"

Once the initial shock had been defused, the dormant half of me came awake.

I fumbled with the buttons of my cardigan, throwing it off. Kneeling on the bed, I cradled Julian's head in my hand, the dead weight making me shudder. I pressed the wool to his wound. Blood came away, but still, not enough. The laceration was not terribly deep—he'd need to be stitched, but the skull wasn't fractured. I pressed two fingers to Julian's throat, feeling the carotid for a heartbeat. Slow, faint. But there. He'd merely fainted.

Having moved away for me to work, Gwen crumpled beside her brother, head in hands. Red smeared over her forehead and silk dress. I had never seen her undone, and it frightened me until I realized she thought he was dead.

"He's breathing," I said.

Gwen looked up, bleary-eyed. I took her hand, Julian's blood sticky between our palms, and laid her fingers over his pulse. More tears spilled over her cheeks, streaking through red, and she covered her mouth to stifle a gasp.

I wiped a bead of sweat from my forehead with the back of my hand, and heard myself whimper. With triage complete, I could remember myself. The nurse stepped back and the woman returned, the woman who loved Julian. Her breath shook as she realized the blood on her hands was his. That he had woken alone, had walked his room all morning alone. Had picked up a gun and set it to his own head. She shivered and hugged herself.

I tried to keep busy, searching for the weapon. It was fallen to pieces in the mess of linens: the German revolver. Something must have been wrong with the ammunition, for the cylinder was mangled, the frame bent upwards. Shards of metal and wood from the grip had come away. Julian had been hit by a mere shred of wayward debris.

With a pang of horror, I remembered the Veronal in the bathroom, and stood to check the bottle. But as I whirled, Gwen shouted: "Julian—!"

He had come round, blinking and whey faced, trembling bodily from the shock. Gwen bent to cradle her brother's head in her lap, brushing his hair.

This was a strange man I didn't recognize, small and curled in on himself. Stunned by the brightness of a life he'd expected to leave. I might've been invisible, though I wasn't certain Julian was conscious of his sister, either, by the way he stared so blankly.

Why hadn't I fought for him? Why had I let him push me away so easily?

I didn't realize there was anyone else in the room until Celia screamed. She buried her head in Roland's shoulder; he was paralyzed himself, pale and gasping.

"Telephone the doctor," I said.

"Keep the children in the nursery," Gwen put in, "and the staff downstairs."

Freddie took the lead, moving Roland and Celia by their shoulders and out of the room. No stranger was he to such a scene.

Beside me, Gwen rocked Julian, dabbing his wound with her skirt, muttering: "*What have you done, my boy? Hm? What have you done . . . ?*" Julian's eye fluttered shut. "Bloody fool! I was here, damn you! I was right—"

Gwen allowed a harrowing wail that she might have been holding in for years.

BEFORE THE DOCTOR arrived, Gwen and I got to work stripping the bed. The bloodied sheets were hidden in the Countess Suite to be disposed of later on. The staff would never need know the truth of what had occured. Instead, we spun a story: Julian had slipped and hit his head in the bathroom. We could only hope the gunshot would not prompt any further questions.

It was nearly dark when I met the doctor as he was leaving Julian's apartments. Something kept me on a bench in the corridor, unable to return to my bedroom, where everything was normal. He smiled kindly when I stood.

"Did he wake?" I asked.

"Only momentarily," he said. "Frightfully muddled. I've given his lordship something to help him sleep through the night. Best thing for him now, I daresay."

I nodded, gave a polite goodbye, and went inside.

The room was too warm, fire blazing, windows shut. Gwen sat on a chair at the bedside, hand clasped around Julian's. He'd been undressed, and bandaged around the head, lying under a quilt brought from another room. The hand which had held the gun was thickly wrapped. Despite it all, he slept soundly, lips parted. His mask sat on the table beside him, staring listlessly at the ceiling.

"May I join you?" I asked, shutting the door.

Gwen offered a faint smile. "Come."

I brought a chair and sat beside her. She held my hand in her other, making us into a short chain of arms.

My throat closed as I saw the man I loved resting in the place he had hoped to find an end. How unfair that it took this horrific day to make me realize he meant more to me than romance. Than marriage. Than a certain, bright future. Now I could imagine my life carrying on without him in it, and saw only grey. He was more to me than anything—he was my muse. My whole heart.

"I cannot decide if he has all the luck or none of it," Gwen said.

I watched Julian's chest rise and fall. I wanted to climb in beside him, to warm him with my body's heat, to beg him to forgive me for my harsh words. To beg him to please, please never have such dark thoughts again.

"I knew," Gwen went on, "that he didn't wish to live, truly. But I never thought him capable of—" I squeezed her hand. "He told me once that he felt he shouldn't have survived the blast, shouldn't have come through it. I told him he was being ridiculous." Gwen ran out of breath, and released my hand to press her fingers against her brow. "I don't know what to do, my dear. I don't know what to do."

I wasn't sure if she was talking to me or to Julian, so I remained silent.

"What a bloody fool I was, to think I could repair him with chocolates and tea and . . . *you*." My cheeks flamed. When Gwen put her other hand over mine, I knew it was not an accusation. "I wasn't trying to use you, Bertie. I like you very much—I do. I think you were right for him . . ." A pause. She closed her eyes for a moment, then opened them. "Julian came to me years ago, and without explaining, begged me not to allow Roland to make his mistakes. It took me ages to realize the mistake he spoke of was not Lily's pregnancy. The mistake was taking my advice.

"He loved Lily for nearly a decade, and for all that time I told him endlessly to discontinue their friendship, that it was impossible for them to be together. I advised a marriage would ruin him, and the only thing was to sweep her pregnancy cleanly away . . . It was my fault he couldn't allow himself to be happy. By the end of the war it was all so trivial—class and rank and duty. It meant nothing to me, when I'd lost so much, and nearly lost him." Gwen took a nourishing breath and let it out sharply. "And here we are, ruined all the same."

I was ready with a reply. For I had spent nearly the entire summer convincing myself otherwise. "You are not ruined. You have Anna and Richie, Roland has Freddie, and Celia has all of you looking after her. You have love."

Gwen's shoulders shrank as a notion brightened her eyes. "Do you still love him?"

This time the answer came easily. "I do."

"He'll make it right. I know he will—"

Right how? I wondered. Change his mind, ask me to stay? Propose marriage? No—it was not the time for such things, not any longer. He had to come back from where he'd gone; he'd have to decide to. I had been able to treat the physical wounds, but now I had to step away.

Julian did not believe in his ability to be husband or father, and though I thought he'd learn in time, he would not learn from me. He would learn from his family, the only ones who knew the boy in the postcard, and could remind him that boy was still alive.

I had my own life to live now. I had to choose myself this time.

I wiped a tear and told Gwen, "I must go home."

A gentle knock put an end to our discussion. To my surprise it was not Roland, but Celia who came through. Gwen stood, as though to shield her sister from what she might see. But Celia came in, eyes red from crying.

"Will I wake him if I sit down?" she asked.

Gwen could only shake her head, astounded as I was. She stood and gestured to her empty chair. I watched Celia's face as she took in the state of her brother, for the first time since before the war. There were many changes besides the scars on face and shoulder, the new wounds, the bandages. There were whiskers, long hair, years of aging.

Celia's stoicism collapsed, and she cried in a way one does when completely alone. She clutched Julian's hand against her cheek, glazing his knuckles with tears. I wished he was awake to feel it.

"Is he going to die?" Celia asked.

Gwen answered, "No, my dear."

"But he wanted to?"

Gwen's eyes shifted to mine. I'm not sure what she was looking for, but she must've found it. "Yes, he did. Your brother is unwell, but we are going to help him get better."

Celia weaved her fingers into the spaces between Julian's, grasping for some part of him to realize her. I was rapt, for a moment, at the image of brother and sister together at last. What a lovely portrait it might've been. Then I stood to leave, wanting to give them time alone.

Gwen caught my elbow. "Won't you stay?"

"I want to be gone when he wakes."

"He'll blame himself . . ."

My stomach was heavy and solid. My heart broken. My knees weak. I might have slept for a week, or never again. "There's nothing more I can do for him."

After a long pause, Gwen gave a forfeiting nod and dropped my arm.

Before I went, I admired the sight of Julian one last time, remembering the smell of his hair, the taste of his shoulder, the roughness of his bare legs on my thighs. I remembered his words: *Compassion and empathy.*

Perhaps he was right. Perhaps they were my greatest gift.

22

When Mother came to the door, I wept.

The tears had sat dormant for the whole of the train journey. One does not weep in public, not even when one's life has fallen to shambles. Instead I'd kept my chin high, my throat choking me with every passing station, and thought of home.

I decided along the way that I would call at my parents' house. I would stand proudly before them and say I'd failed; I had nowhere else to go. And I'd be out with it.

For the first few weeks, I'd denied my late monthly was of any true concern, blaming the wine for my nausea and dizziness. But there was no denying it now. I had heard of girls hiding pregnancies almost until the end, even given birth without their parents ever knowing. I did not possess the nerve. My sisters had been forthcoming about their experiences with childbirth, and I was not, under any circumstances, going it alone.

When I arrived, I expected Mother to look down her nose at me and close the door firmly in my face. Instead, she saw the tears staining my cheeks and said, "Dear Lord, Alberta, what can have happened?"

"It's difficult to be wholly certain," I answered, "though I can expect with some confidence that I'm going to have a baby."

She hadn't anything to say at first. I waited, again, for the door to be shut. Instead, she brought me in. Took me to the parlor. Sat me on the sofa and fed me tea. My father wasn't at home, but would be soon, and as Mother paced back and forth, collecting her thoughts on the matter, I wondered where I would go. A mother and baby home, like Lily had, surely. My mother would wish to avoid the disgrace of an unwed pregnant daughter. I made a mental list of all the positives this scenario offered—I could draw nurses, I could draw babies, I could draw young girls with the glow of motherhood. And then I could draw this baby. *My* baby. Julian's baby. I did hope it would have his eyes.

A great, sudden wash of emotion consumed me. I set down my tea and put my head between my legs. Mother rubbed my back, saying something I couldn't hear. I think she expected me to be sick on the Turkey rug. But I didn't have to be sick—I'd been sick earlier behind the station, having got off the train without my land legs. Now, I was in a simple and easy-to-identify panic, because I'd realized with full and utter conviction that whatever was growing inside me was to be mine. Mine. Not had and given away. I wanted to be a mother.

My father arrived just in time, carrying one of his sailboats. He nearly dropped it when he saw the state of me, came rushing over to take a knee.

"Bertie! How? Where—?" He looked to my mother for assurance. "What the devil is the matter?"

I expected any number of reactions from *I told you not to allow her to go to that place!* to *Well, darling, our Bertie is a slut.* Instead, Mother rose calmly, took her husband's hand, and smiled. "Alberta is in the family way. Tea?"

And so more tea was had. I explained to them tearfully that I'd fallen in love with the Earl of Wakeford, who was young and handsome but stuck, emotionally, in the war. I told them about Celia and Roland and little Anna, the dinners, the teas, and the paintings—my very best work. I did not tell them about the gun.

Then, before they could ask, I told them there was no chance of a proposal of marriage, and they would not be meeting the father. This was no shock to them, which made me sad, though I took it gladly over a lashing. Instead, I received love—unconditional love. The very love I'd been taking for granted for as long as I could remember.

"I don't expect you to forgive me," I said, looking only at Mother. "I should never have left. I ought to have listened to you. But I've spoiled it all now—everything I've hoped for. And I cannot do this alone. I promise I'll give up painting, if only you'll allow me to come home."

My parents exchanged a look. Then my mother took my hand—hers were eternally polished, the color of cream and smelling of lavender.

"We don't want you to give up your art, dear," she said. "We were only ever trying to look after you. You needn't be so ashamed to live here with us until you get on your feet."

I was astounded and confused. I began crying again. "What'll I do, then?"

"You're going to stay here with us," Mother said, "and you're going to be a mother."

I wasn't sure if they'd discussed the prospect of an unexpected pregnancy before, or they had been married long enough to be completely of one mind. But my father seemed to be in unanimous agreement that the only place for this child was here, with its family, and he even smiled at me and pinched my chin. "My little girl, all grown up."

I hardly felt grown-up, though I supposed the time had come at last. My twenty-ninth birthday was only weeks away, and I'd be sharing it this time. The prospect made me smile, though all the while I couldn't stop imagining Julian tucked up in his bed, broken open yet again.

I could only hope he would make the best of his second chance at life.

IN THE COMING months I found I rather enjoyed being pregnant. For one, it was an excuse to eat whatever I wanted, and however much of it I could manage. My mother was of the mind that I had to be eating at all hours of the day to keep my strength up, to ensure baby was growing at the proper rate. She certainly liked me better now that I was carrying a grandchild.

And so I became accustomed to Jane entering my room, the parlor, the study, at any and all hours of the day to deliver a tray of something—Eccles cake, buns with butter, salmon sandwiches, egg tart, pork pie, and potato soup. Cream tea became as common an occurrence for us as was toast with breakfast. It didn't take long for the weight to show in my cheeks, but I quite liked how I looked.

I also liked the belly itself, so firm, so odd. I took to staring at myself in the mirror and became so vain that when my sisters came to visit, I questioned how big their own bellies were at this stage, and found mine was far superior. Heather, the oldest of us, wasn't as supportive as our parents, but Violet, being pregnant herself, was overjoyed. We knitted socks together and I felt her baby kick, waiting anxiously for mine to do the same. We hadn't got on so well since childhood.

I took myself on walks up and down our street. I'd been expecting the stares and disapproving glances, the inquiries as to whom I'd married so suddenly. It might've been fun to say, *Oh, I'm not married, though baby's father is the Earl of Wakeford.*

But I couldn't do that to Julian. I never spoke of him, not even to Mother. I drew him from memory only, every day, putting his face together like a puzzle.

Mother decided I ought to wear a ring. I'd been away, so why shouldn't I have got married during that time? And why shouldn't my fake husband be abroad for a few months on an important business venture? Some of our neighbors believed it. Mrs. Lemm, being one of them, frequently asked, "How is Mr. Neil? Have you had a letter this week?"

Freddie wouldn't mind.

I wondered about Julian, though. If his wounds were healing. If he'd mended things with Celia. If he'd explained to Gwen why he'd done what he did. If he'd met with the appraiser and sold Castle Braemore the way he'd planned.

I kept my eyes on the society pages, looking for a scandal. Had it come out? And what would people say if it had? I expected it wouldn't be words of concern, for him or any of the veterans who suffered equally enough to put an end to their lives. I was sure it would be only callous judgment.

At night, I tossed and turned to find comfort. Pregnancy gave vivacity to my nightmares, fine details in smells and colors, and often placed me back in the war, back in my apron, leaning over a cot where Julian bled, my hands stiff and slow, unable to stop it until he died. I'd wake in tears.

I wondered if the reason Julian had pointed a gun at his head and pulled the trigger was because he couldn't manage to leave his room—his prison of grief. Or if our final conversation had pushed him.

Painting was my only escape. Despite my condition, I had several commissions from neighbors keen for a Bertie Neil original. Not because they'd heard that I'd been painting for a lord, but because Mrs. Lemm's terrier was the talk of the village. And so I was kept busy indeed with portraits of dogs, children, and various other things—the new vicar wanted his parish church above his mantel, and the couple who ran the inn wanted something pretty to hang over the bar.

I had commissions sometimes from elsewhere—London even. Each of the letters mentioned *a dazzling recommendation from my friend Mr. Fredrick Neil.* I seemed to owe Freddie rather a lot.

At the end of several months I'd an account building up. I had enough money, in fact, that I could dream of renting a place of my own. Not a London flat—no, not with a child. I wanted somewhere with flowers, with room to run, with clear skies, with endlessly changing landscapes for me to paint, for my child to remember. I had grown too used to the quiet of Braemore, to the birdsong and long dinners and sunbathing afternoons. I could not keep up with the Freddies and Rolands, and I'd never fit in amongst the bright young people. Dancing and dresses and bachelors were so far from my mind, I felt it hard to believe they once meant everything to me.

I wanted my son or daughter to know me, to know they were loved. I was still haunted by Celia's loneliness, by how her life might have been different had her mother cared.

So now I dreamt of my own little house, with net curtains and overstuffed chairs, and a room for baby. I dreamt of wallpaper patterns and cutlery and sweeping dirty floors in my slippers. Another year of painting, and I'd be there. Somewhere in the country. Somewhere people would pass without noticing.

Then Mr. Beaton called.

Beaton was Julian's solicitor. When he explained who he was, my heart nearly stopped. I hadn't spoken the name aloud since returning home—*Lord Wakeford*. And he'd used it so easily, so plainly, as though it mattered little.

I was five months gone, my belly at the point of no question whether it was a big meal or a baby. Jane let Mr. Beaton in and offered refreshment, though the squat man was not interested. I told my father I would speak to Mr. Beaton alone.

In the parlor, I sat opposite him, hands poised proudly on my belly. "What can I do for you, sir?"

"It isn't what you can do for me, Miss Preston," he said, fishing in his breast pocket to remove an envelope, "rather what I can do for you." His eyes caught on the belly, the ring. "Forgive me, have I got your name incorrectly . . . ?"

"Oh . . . yes, I'm—" I lifted my hand to see the humble silver band.

Mr. Beaton blinked at me, waiting for an answer. But I shook my head. I couldn't have Julian thinking me so flighty. "No. Still *Mizz* Preston."

Beaton nodded and coughed into his fist, managing to be discomforted by the thought. "In any event, I've come at the instruction of the Earl of Wakeford to deliver this personally."

I eyed the envelope as he held it up, making no motion to take it. "What is it?"

"Remuneration, miss."

There were moments I wondered about this. My paintings, ten of them total, were left behind at Castle Braemore. I thought at first I might have a letter from Roland, asking me what I'd like done with them. But no such letter had come. I couldn't blame them, of course, they'd enough on their minds with Julian's troubles.

So I was surprised to be handed payment, of all things.

"His lordship has agreed to negotiate," said Mr. Beaton. "He's given me permission to amend the amount according to your wishes."

I was devilishly curious what Julian thought my paintings were worth. I can't deny that I knew he'd pay whatever I asked, and I could indeed ask a price that would make my life comfortable for years to come. Though I could only think of the pile of unanswered letters on Julian's desk, the sound of his shouting, his blood on my hands. I could not take his money.

"No, thank you, Mr. Beaton. You may tell his lordship the paintings are a gift."

This stumped him. A lawyer had surely never seen someone turn down a check, and by the look on his face, he knew the amount written on it, and it was very, very significant.

"Miss Preston," he said, adjusting his spectacles, "I have been instructed not to leave with this envelope."

"Fine. Give it here; I'll put it in the fire."

"I beg you to reconsider—"

"And what does it matter to you?" I asked calmly. "You will be paid all the same, I expect, and if you leave it with me, you'll have done your duty."

"I know Lord Wakeford well," said Beaton, "and I can say with complete assurance that he wishes you to have this payment, as he feels your work is deserving. He's instructed me to ensure you want for nothing." He handed me the envelope, and put his other hand on top. "Take it, Miss Preston. Please."

I stared, thinking. Julian must have been getting well. He must have settled his debts, or was in the midst of doing so. But why hadn't he come himself, if it was so important? Why hadn't he written?

In the end, I took the envelope. For my child.

A quick peek told me there was enough to rent that little house with the net curtains, and more besides. As Mr. Beaton stood to leave, I thought of another conversation Julian and I had had at the beginning of our friendship, and gestured for him to wait.

"I have something for his lordship," I said. "Only I shall need your help with it."

My prizewinner, *Something for the Pain*, still hung in my bedroom where I could see it each morning. Mr. Beaton kindly took it down for me, holding it carefully as we went back downstairs to the foyer. I knew Julian loved the painting. I knew having it would make the amount of money he'd given me worthwhile. That gave me peace of mind.

As Mr. Beaton left, I stood at the front door to watch him go. In my belly, baby leapt and tumbled. I was so shocked I squeaked.

Mr. Beaton turned around. "Everything all right, miss?"

"Yes, I—" I looked briefly at my stomach. "How does he do? Lord Wakeford?"

Beaton's face melted into a kind smile. "Well, miss. The family have left Braemore for a house nearer to his sister's."

I tried to imagine Lord Wakeford anywhere but Braemore and failed. The house had been a living being, with Julian its heart. Without its heart, the body would surely perish.

"How sad . . . ," I said.

"Indeed. Shame to see the estate change hands."

"What of the house? It's not to be demolished?"

"The house was sold. It's to be a boarding school for girls."

Mr. Beaton began to leave again, but I stepped out of the doorway. "Wait—Will you tell his lordship that I don't regret our contract?"

I could tell he took the true meaning. "Yes, miss."

"And tell him . . . tell him I say thank you. For everything."

Laurel Gate

APRIL 1923

Julian woke with a groan and turned over to push his good ear into the pillow. Perhaps if he ignored her knocking, she'd let him be. Sleep would come again.

But Gwen was nothing if not persistent. She got in by some other means and peeled off his quilt. "Good morning!" she cheered. "Beautiful day."

Julian curled in on himself, knowing how childish it looked and not caring. Even with the medicine, he hadn't slept well, restless with anxious dreams.

Gwen threw open the curtains, allowing in the sun to burn his eye. "I should think you've slept long enough. Celia said you missed dinner last evening—you must *eat*, Julian. You're a living, breathing thing, mind, and we like the world better with you in it."

Julian didn't move. Not until Gwen sat on the edge of the bed and tickled the top of his ear. "I know you can hear me, darling brother mine."

He shoved her hand away. "I'm tired."

"Clearly." Gwen tilted her head, peering down at him as his eye came open. "But you cannot behave thusly or you shall become your mother."

Julian sat up dizzily. He held the side of his head where things had healed on the surface, but still ached within. His left hand was beginning to move when he wanted it to, though the burnt skin was oddly thick and didn't stretch.

"How did you get in?" he asked.

"The door doesn't quite lock. Looks to've been hung sideways."

He'd have to engage someone to repair that, along with the drafty windows, the plumbing in the kitchen, the leaking roof. Though it was a lovely Tudor house, Laurel Gate—plenty of rooms, with oak walls, low cornice ceilings, and ivy crawling up the brick. The property was nestled in a quiet piece of country with wildflowers and a lake. Julian had liked it instantly, and was so desperate to be out of Braemore, he'd taken it the day he'd seen it.

That was the first day he'd left Braemore. His bones had smarted, jostled by the deep tremble coursing through his body. Despite having Gwen at his elbow for support, he'd had to pause outside the front door to get his bearings, doddery as an old man. She had waited patiently whilst he breathed, counted to ten, counted to ten again, and opened his eye, waiting for the tunnel to open up and allow him to see the world more fully.

When it did, there was the fountain, the hedges, the lawn, the gravel, and Anna and Richie chasing each other round the motor. On weak knees, Julian had stepped down, one stair at a time until his shoes touched the earth—hard and cold and solid. He had stopped again.

"There's nothing to fear," Gwen had said, nose rosy from the wind. "Apart from a chest cold."

He'd looked over at her, and though he couldn't bring himself to smile, he felt warm. It was by this warmth he got into the car that took them to Laurel Gate.

When he'd stood before Castle Braemore for the last time, he'd had no remorse. He had only felt free.

"Come," Gwen said now, "we must get you up and about. Jolly big day, this."

As she scurried to his wardrobe, Julian took his mask from the bedside table. He passed his fingers over his scars as he did each morning, to ensure they were still there and he was truly home, that war was over and he'd returned alive. The copper mask was always cold in the mornings, and as he pressed it against his cheek and eye, he shivered.

Gwen returned with a grey suit, a crisp white shirt, and the silk tie she'd given him for Christmas 1913. He remembered because it was the last Christmas they exchanged frivolous presents.

"Routine," said Gwen, laying the clothing on the bed. "I still believe in it, you know."

Julian scratched at his whiskers. "I'm not sure of this."

"Something darker, perhaps?"

"Not the suit."

Gwen sat with a sigh and rubbed circles over his back. "Change is healthy, my boy."

They looked about at his new bedroom. The walls were pale yellow, the furnishings taken from Braemore not in keeping with a place so humble. Julian hadn't taken his father's bed, nor anything from the apartments. He'd wanted never to see any of it again.

Thinking of that room now, he bowed his head, holding the place where the gun had burst beside his ear. He was glad he had gone unconscious, and not lain aware of himself as he'd been in the blast. There were moments while he recovered during the war when he was disoriented, unsure of where he was or what was happening to him. But nothing had been so confusing as waking in bed following the gunshot to see Celia smiling at his side.

He'd thought their voices were nurses', and that he'd been thrust back in time to a field hospital in Amiens. Then he had seen Celia and thought her Gwen. Too old to be little Cece. But she'd taken his hand and smiled and said, *Did the starlings talk?* and he knew it was her. They'd discussed Lily for a time, and it had been good to speak of her with someone who had loved her. Then they had discussed everything else—all the lost years—until they knew each other again.

Julian had wanted an end. He had lost his home, his money, his pride. He had lost his sister's trust and good society's respect. He had lost Bertie. He had lost any hope that life could be more than the days he spent alone inside his apartments, for he could not bring himself to leave. He didn't resemble himself, nor feel himself, and he had wanted the stranger that occupied his space in the world to be gone.

His hand had shaken when he'd brought the gun to his temple, but it had been easy to pull the trigger. He'd come close to death before and it wasn't frightening. It was peaceful.

In the end, he was glad to be alive. Mr. Beaton said Bertie was having a baby. Julian had not been ready to go to her, though it pained him to stay away. Leaving Braemore had been difficult, and he'd yet to travel on his own. If he was going to see Bertie again, he would stand strongly before her, or not at all.

"Julian?" He brought his head up and tried to focus on Gwen. "You're all right, you know." She set her hand against his heart. "Tick, tick, tick. That's all it takes."

Julian put his hand over hers. "Thank you."

"No need for that."

He tightened his fingers around hers. "I ought to have thanked you every day since I learned to speak. It is you alone who has prevented this family from falling apart."

WHILE JULIAN CHANGED, Gwen joined Celia downstairs. Her sister stood at the dining table, fluffing a bouquet of crocus and daffodils whilst humming to herself.

Gwen wrapped her arms around Celia's shoulders. "Those are lovely."

Celia leaned back into the embrace. "The garden is bursting. If I don't pick enough of them, I fear Julian and I may be eaten up."

Gwen chuckled and kissed Celia's cheek. "Is all ready?"

"Yes—come and see." She took Gwen's hand to lead her into the parlor.

It was a relief to find Celia had taken to Laurel Gate much as Julian had. Gwen wasn't sure how she'd feel about staying in the country, when Roland was off to the London flat Julian had taken for him. But Celia was content enough to run this house for her brother, and was close enough to Stanfield to help Gwen with her charity work—with luck, her reputation could be salvaged. By any means necessary, Gwen would see to it that her little sister found a place of her own in the world.

The house suited Julian's personality—stately, yet snug and characterful. And though Huxley and Mrs. Burns had retired from service, he kept on Cook and a few of the maids. Things were not so different. Yes, Laurel Gate had done splendidly.

The large leaded window in the parlor was left open, primrose sweetening the inside of the house. Richie and Anna played with marbles on the worn floorboards, where Celia had rolled up the rug and pushed it to one side. She'd set an armchair near the window, with a stool alongside holding a basin of water and a new shaving kit.

"He's no excuse now, has he?" said Gwen.

"How does he seem?" Celia asked. "He slept later than he'd promised."

Gwen touched the surface of the water absently, watching the ripples. It had been a long eight months, from the weeks Julian spent recovering from the shock of being alive, to the agonizing months that followed, when Gwen had to force him out of bed, make him eat, lead him out of his room a bit further each day so that eventually he could leave Braemore entirely. He'd done it, at last, and now he appeared lighter. The wounds healed, and though it still took much to make him smile, he left his room to listen to the gramophone in the parlor, and swam in the lake, and took meals with Celia. Things were far better than they'd been.

"He's ready," said Gwen. "I feel sure of it."

From the hall came the creaking of worn treads. Celia made a gasp so that the children would look up. "Who's coming?"

Anna jumped to her feet. "Uncle Earl!"

They went to the hall to wait while Julian dragged his heavy feet downstairs. He looked well in a fine suit, and was smiling by the time Richie and Anna reached him. He ruffled Richie's hair and hugged Anna to his side. There was a new way in which he looked at her that transformed his face, and each time, Gwen felt the sting of tears.

"Right—Anna?" she said. "Have you something to give to your uncle?"

Julian eyed her skeptically, but she ignored him, instead watching as her daughter reached into the pocket of her coat and pulled out an ancient gold ring. It was one of the few possessions Lily had left behind, and he'd refused it the last time Gwen offered it to him. Now it looked massive in Anna's little hand.

Julian crouched to her level and held his palm out for her to drop it in.

"I've looked after it really well," Anna said.

He smiled, and brushed his thumb over her cheek. "You've done a fine job of it. But wouldn't you like to keep it?"

Anna glanced over her shoulder at Gwen, who merely raised a brow. "Mama said to give it back. That you need the ring for permission."

"*Tradition*, Anna." Gwen chuckled.

"Oh—I meant *tradition*. It's got your coat of arms on, not ours."

Julian took up her hand to press the ring into her fist. "Dash tradition. I want it to be yours." Anna threw her arms around his neck, elated.

"All right, all right," Gwen said, ending the scene before she broke down completely. "Outdoors with the both of you before the weather turns."

The children were more than happy to oblige. With heaps of overgrown garden to explore, they could hardly miss Castle Braemore.

Celia took Julian's elbow as he rose to a stand, and swept her hand theatrically towards the parlor. "Right this way, my lord. You've reserved the finest seat in the house."

Julian looked warily at Gwen and she chuckled, giving him a shove. He stumbled over and lowered himself into the chair with a groan, rubbing his burnt hand in the other. Gwen's memory of their father was fading fast, but the way Julian looked just then, in the dusty fog of the parlor, with his beard and his straight shoulders, she thought he resembled the late earl.

Julian said, "I'll need to see credentials before I turn my life over."

"Worry not, pal." Celia collected a folded towel from the stool. "Roland gave me a lesson."

She shook out the towel and draped it over Julian's front, fastening it behind his neck with a safety pin. When she moved round to face him, he smiled at her and she returned it. It had taken Celia nearly eight years to move past her grudge, and less than a minute for Julian to forgive her. That was what big brothers were for, Gwen supposed, taking a few on the chin for their little sisters' sake. Julian had survived quite a thrashing.

Gwen stood by the window, one eye on the proceedings and the other watching her children in the garden. While Julian removed his mask, Celia dipped the soap into the basin to wet it, and worked the brush over for a thick lather. Then, with her brow pinched in concentration, she painted the soap over Julian's whiskers. The ones on the right were thick now, though there were only patches on the left. That would be the tricky bit—where the scars made things rough and uneven.

When Celia took up the razor, Julian lifted an eyebrow.

"Just relax," she said. "And remember, it grows back."

Julian's beard fell into his lap in dark curled tufts. As Celia shaved him, he closed his eye, allowing his chin to be turned and tipped. Once it was smooth, Celia cleaned him off with a wet towel, and Gwen went to stand next to her, putting an arm round her shoulders.

Her breath shook until she held it. It had been ever so long since she'd seen the precise lines of his short chin and round jaw, the hollows of his flat cheeks, the youthful bow of his lip. There was an oddness to seeing clean face and overgrown hair, but he was certainly much closer to looking like the brother she knew.

"Well done, you," Gwen said to Celia. "He's five years younger, at that."

Julian's eye opened. "Have I still got my head?"

"For now. But it's next to go."

Celia took up the scissors. This was the task Gwen was not so confident her younger sister could master. She stood close beside Celia, supervising as she snipped and snipped, and walked around Julian's chair to see his head at all angles. All the while, Julian might've been asleep, sitting so calmly with nothing but trust for them.

In the end, Julian's hair was trimmed closely at his nape and round his ears. They'd left enough length on top that the curls remained, the way Roland wore his. Celia stuck a finger in his pot of brilliantine and rubbed it between her palms before combing it through Julian's hair. When she and Gwen stepped back to see him fully, Gwen's eyes filled with tears.

"Oh, do stop," said Celia. "It's only Julian."

And it *was* only Julian. The way he was meant to look. The way he'd looked for so long before the war. This was not the man who was consumed by melancholy, but the one who had risen above it, had come through, who'd struggled every day to heal.

Gwen waved her off. "I'm allowed to cry; I've been through a lot."

Julian felt his cheek with his good hand and looked around him at the fallen hair at his feet. There was quite a lot of it. He reached behind his neck to feel where it had all gone, and turned pink. "Better or worse?" he asked.

To which the women replied in unison, "Better!"

Then the front door was thrown open—Gwen really had to rid Anna of that habit—and her daughter came darting towards them. She stopped dead in the threshold, mouth falling open.

Julian's chin dropped to his chest, his hand covering his scars, shoulders shuddering with uneven breaths. Gwen touched his back to comfort him. Anna had never seen him without his mask.

"Darling," she said, "you cannot leave your brother outdoors—"

"Uncle Earl!" Anna ran right into Julian's knees, looking up at him so there was nowhere to hide. "Where has your beard gone?"

Gwen held her breath, exchanging a glance with Celia.

Julian said, "To the floor, mainly."

Anna kicked a bit of it with the toe of her shoe. Julian tucked his hands under her arms and lifted her onto his lap with an exaggerated grunt. He held still while she prodded his chin and cheeks, paying no mind to his scars, if she noticed them at all.

"Can you get it back?" she asked.

"In a week or so."

"Oh, good."

Gwen let out a long breath, lovingly pinching Julian's shoulder.

Anna settled in with her legs spilling over his lap and looked up at Celia. "What's that for?"

Celia wiggled her brows. She'd retrieved a silver hand mirror from the stool and was holding the glass against her chest. "This is for your uncle to have a look at himself."

Julian's gaze slid to Gwen. She wanted to laugh at the pale terror on his face, for the notion was ridiculous to her. When she looked at him, she felt nothing but adoration for what she saw. Why should he be so frightened? But she remained steady for his sake and nodded her encouragement.

"I suppose," said Julian, "it's as good a time as any."

Gwen stood behind Celia with her hands on her shoulders and gave them a rub. Anna propped herself up so her face would be in the reflection, too.

"I know it's been a long while," said Celia carefully. "But remember that how you see yourself in this mirror is how *we* see you, and we love you so very much."

She smiled, and turned the glass.

23

By April, I understood the meaning of *confinement*. My back and hips ached so badly I hardly wanted to move out of bed. I did, though, if only to reach my easel. The project was taking far longer than I should have liked. Each time I stepped away to have a rest, I ended up falling asleep and then returning to a mess of paints that were tacky and no longer willing to blend. I'd huff; baby would kick. Then I'd undress again and start over.

The project was my first self-portrait. I had the idea in my seventh month, keeping it secret. If Mother knew what I was doing, she'd surely lose her mind. The idea that I had sexual organs and used them to produce a child was fine with her, but creating evidence of this for anyone else to see would be appalling.

Nobody else would see it, of course. I merely wanted a souvenir to remember my pregnancy by, like Julian had wanted a painting of Castle Braemore for Anna.

Now I undressed—slowly, as pregnancy made this a chore—and stood in front of my mirror, bare skin prickling from the chill. My belly was really coming along, navel poking out. I felt my bones were out of place, loose and dangling in a way I never knew bones could. If I were to strip myself of my skin, I was sure the skeleton would fall to the floor, a pile of twigs with no notion of their purpose. My breasts were sore, nipples stuck straight, well aware of their use.

I touched my belly to feel for baby's heartbeat. Strong as ever.

The thumping of the little heart kept me painting that afternoon, despite the cold, despite my aching back and feet, despite my useless bones and never-ending need to relieve myself.

I rang for Jane then, my stomach grumbling, and got into my dressing gown. I'd finished painting my body for the most part, and could do my face happily wrapped in warmth.

When a swift knock came, I said, "Just a moment!" and drew my folding screen in front of the painting. No use scaring her off.

But it was not Jane. Mother stood before me, face flush. I expected she might be cross to see me undressed at such an hour, but she only looked frightened, lips parted like a codfish.

"What's the matter? Is it Violet?" Violet's baby had arrived two months before, and I often got reports on her varying states of recovery.

"You've a caller," said Mother, worrying her hands.

"Oh?" Briefly, I wondered if it might be Mr. Beaton. I wasn't sure I'd had any callers since he brought the check.

"You'll want to dress," she added.

"Who is it?"

Mother's eyelids fluttered and she pressed a hand to her own heart, as though she could possibly be as anxious as I, still in the dark. "Darling, it's Lord Wakeford."

I wasn't the sort to swoon, but at that moment, my vision closed to a point, and I felt myself moving—down, I think—until my mother took my arms and pulled me back up. She held me in an embrace for a moment before I could see once more that up was up and down was not a very good idea.

Julian was here. In my parents' home. Which meant he'd not only recovered but had left his house and got in a motor, in a train, and traveled all the way here. To see me.

"He isn't for small talk," said Mother.

"No."

"I've got him in the parlor. We haven't anything in, I'm afraid; only a few measly digestives on the good china."

"That's all right," I said. "He doesn't eat much."

The moment of practical conversation was somewhat calming. But poor Mother; you'd think the king had come for tea. For years after, she made a hard rule that there should always be a proper Victoria sponge at the ready for surprise callers.

I was finding myself rather calm, following my spell. I dressed slowly in a simple day dress, and wore my slippers down to the parlor. My hand shook on the railing as I took the stairs one at a time. Baby kicked and thumped in time with my steps.

All stood as I entered. With their eyes on me, I felt regal, though they were wide with a mixture of confusion and caution. Julian had been sat on the sofa alone, neither of my parents daring enough to sit beside him. He'd been holding a cup of tea, and set it down to button his jacket.

My hand went to my mouth. Not only was it terribly odd to see Julian anywhere but his apartments, but he was shaved—rather shocking how much face he had under there. His lips, which I had studied frequently, appeared more prominent than they'd been, pinkish grey and set perfectly in a half oval to match his mask, where no evidence of my paint remained. His cheeks were flat and shiny, with a dimple just beneath the bone that I hadn't noticed before. His hair was cropped above his ears, with perfect waves arranged on top.

He looked absolutely good as new.

I approached, impressed by how Julian held my eyes rather than looking at my enormous belly. He'd known, surely? Mr. Beaton would have told him.

He cleared his throat, bleached and stiff. "I hope you will forgive how rudely I've pushed in unannounced. Are you well, Bertie?"

Mother shifted at the sound of my Christian name on the earl's lips.

I, however, smiled, and touched my belly to feel baby pushing a hand towards his voice.

"I'm well, Julian."

His face relaxed, and then his eyelashes trembled downward. As Julian took in the rest of me, his shoulders rose and paused momentarily in a held breath. He was pleased, I thought. Not burdened.

"To what do I owe this honor?" I asked.

Julian's chin inclined and he looked frightened again. "I was hoping you might spare a moment to have a word with me. That is, if you haven't any prior engagements."

"I haven't."

Father shifted on his feet, no less spooked than my mother. "We'll give you the parlor, then, shall we?"

"No," I said. "We'll go upstairs."

The proposal left my parents gaping. Though I didn't see why it should matter that a man be in my bedroom, considering I was already pregnant, and this one had induced it.

I took Julian's hand and he followed wordlessly, even as I climbed the stairs at the rate of a tortoise. When I paused for a moment on the landing, he put a hand on the small of my back, and with his silent support, I made it to the top. In my bedroom, I closed the door behind us.

Turning, I said, "You look different."

Julian colored as his hand went to the back of his head, smoothing his exposed nape. The long face he gave me roused a chuckle.

"Like the postcard," I added. That eased him.

Holding his burnt hand in the other, Julian looked about at the striped wallpaper, the white furniture painted with roses, the frills of bedding chosen for a young girl. His attention lit on the table that held my palette and brushes.

"Still painting?" he asked.

I spread my hands over my belly. "You didn't suppose I'd let this darling creature stop me? We've been making quite a name for ourselves, as it happens. I've even submitted a piece to the Royal Academy Summer Exhibition—still waiting to hear."

Julian's lips quirked, and he tried to scratch a beard that was no longer there. "That is splendid news, well done. And what are you working on now?"

"A self-portrait." Perhaps it was the sheer need for the artist's work to be acknowledged, but I wanted to show him. "Well, you've seen it all, haven't you?"

He didn't take my meaning until I moved the screen aside to reveal what rested on the easel. There I was; exposed, naked and round.

Julian approached the canvas cautiously, lips pressed together. Closer now, I smelled on him the sting of too much aftershave and the cigarettes he'd smoked in the train. He studied the painting for a long time, and then looked at me—eyes, not belly.

"It's stunning, Bertie."

A familiar rush of pride burned my temples. "You must think it frightfully vulgar."

Julian shook his head. "You're beautiful."

I chafed my goosefleshed arms, waiting for him to speak again.

His eye drifted to the empty nail left in the wall where *Something for the Pain* had hung. "Thank you for the painting. It hangs in my study."

"I thought it should belong to someone who appreciates it."

Julian bowed his head. "I ought to have called by sooner, to have written—"

"I'd hoped you would."

"—but I couldn't. I wasn't well enough."

We fell into a tense silence. I knew he would need time to formulate what he wanted to say, that I was probably making him nervous, and perhaps he'd never been in a girl's bedroom before. The notion tickled me, and as Julian observed the view from my window, I sat on the bed.

There were many things I wished to speak of. Mainly, I wanted to know if he was well. Physically, I could see he had recovered, but what he'd done meant there were deeper, more painful wounds underneath, and those were the ones I meant to inquire about. I didn't want to upset him; he appeared wary enough to be there at all. But I needed to know he was not still the man who had wrenched me out the door.

"What does that mean? You weren't well enough?" I asked. "Your solicitor came in January; he said you'd already left Braemore."

He couldn't look at me. Instead he plucked a clean paintbrush from my desk and rolled it between his palms. "It was November when I left," he said, "and once I was settled in the new house, the days following were—difficult." When he met my eyes, I saw the apology in them. "I did not have the words then, not after all I'd done. I wanted to be certain I was worthy of speaking to you, and I couldn't be certain until I'd stepped onto the train this morning."

He had answered my question thoroughly, and at once, for perhaps the first time since I'd met him. That was enough for the moment. "Tell me about your new home, then."

Julian set the brush down gently on the desk, as if it was made of glass. "The house is called Laurel Gate; named for the hedges lining the front fence."

I closed my eyes to picture it, crisp, bright green leaves of laurel dotted with cream buds. Certainly a simpler welcome than the gatehouse of Braemore. "How'd you come across it?"

"Gwen did, in fact." Julian took a tentative step towards the bed, rubbing his hand. "There was little time to find a house, so she volunteered to look for me whilst I—" He shook his head. "I asked for something with plenty of rooms and good swimming."

"It sounds charming."

Another smile, careful and practiced. "I'm rather fond."

The conversation paused again. Julian was left nervously idling in a room with no good options for sitting. So I patted the space beside me. He came slowly, unbuttoning his jacket. The mattress buckled under his weight, and our arms brushed.

Now that he was close, I could get a long look at him. There was more color to his cheeks and nose—he'd been outdoors. He looked healthier, too; still lean, but no longer gaunt.

"Do Celia and Roland approve?" I asked.

"Cece does, rather. Roland's in London now, with Freddie."

"All is in the rights with Celia, then?"

"Yes. All is well."

My heart warmed.

"I've been, er"—Julian reached into his breast pocket to produce a folded bit of paper—"sketching some, here and there."

I smiled as he put it in my hands. I opened it slowly, one fold and then the other. The drawing was done in pencil, and with the same quick, rough strokes he'd used to draw me. This portrait was of Celia, one arm resting on a surface in front of her, the other bent at the elbow so her chin could rest in her hand. I chuckled. It was clear from her twisted lip and lifted brow that she had been coaxed into modeling. I could imagine Julian smirking across from her as she tapped her feet impatiently under the table.

"They wanted to write to you," he said. "Cece and Roland. I asked them not to . . . lest it upset you further."

"Why would that upset me?"

I gave him the drawing and he took his time replacing it to his pocket. He'd drifted from me again, too bashful even to meet my eyes. In the interval, my attention was stolen by his hand. I took a chance, pulling it into my lap. He turned his palm over, exposing the slick and shiny scars where sparks had burned his knuckles. Seeing them sent me back to the moment we'd found him, my hands covered in his blood, Gwen crying, the gruesome smell of gunpowder. My stomach lurched, but I fought it.

It must not have been easy to heal from such a trauma. A long, long eight months.

Julian pinched my ring between his fingers. "What's this?"

"Oh—my dignity, I suppose. Mother's idea." I looked at him, but his eye was still on my hand. "How are you feeling, Julian?"

"I'm sorry that you had to—" A sharp inhale. "Gwen told me that you . . . helped her."

"I was glad to. But are you well?"

A nod.

"Julian—?"

I blanched as baby's foot found my ribs. *A blessing*, Mother had said the first time I'd complained of this, *means baby is the right way round*.

Julian kneaded my lower back, somehow knowing an ache was there. But I wasn't finished with him. I would not accept nods. Not for what he'd done, not for what took the courage of hopelessness and had come just after we'd quarreled. I'd been left with eight months of silence, and I wouldn't accept a minute more.

"I need you to speak," I said. "I need you to say what happened—that it won't happen again, that you're better, that you're healing."

Julian's hand dropped to the mattress behind me. He looked over his shoulder, and I caught his masked cheek to keep his face with mine.

"It's difficult for me to explain," he said.

"I know it is. But silence is your greatest enemy. It's why you didn't ask for help, is it not?" Again, no answer. "Just tell me—I don't know—tell me what was missing. Tell me it wasn't something I've said."

"It had naught to do with you, Bertie."

"Then why did you send me away?" He tried to move, but I had him now by the lapel and wasn't letting go. "When I left you, you were cruel and resentful. You were so blinded by your grief you couldn't see sense. You couldn't accept my feelings for you, so you turned me out. How can I be certain you are different?"

"Perhaps I should not have come—"

I started to pull away his mask. He helped, and when it was off, I didn't see the new scars or the old; I simply saw Julian and instantly felt better. No wall. No barrier.

"Why do you say that?" I asked. "'I should not have come.' Why?"

"Because I wish not to burden you."

I gripped his arm hard so he'd know I meant it. "You are not a burden, Julian."

His hand fell again to his lap, and he held it out, palm up—for me to choose. I chose hand-holding, and baby agreed it was the right decision, somehow feeling the spark between us.

"Why did you step onto the train this morning?" I asked. "Why did you come here, stand before my parents, who already bear the shame of my indiscretion, and ask to speak to me?"

"You deserve an apology," Julian said.

"That's right. So pray give it before you think of dashing off again, because I haven't much time."

I didn't realize I was crying until a tear fell onto the top of my hand. Julian brushed it away.

"There is no excuse for my behavior," he said. "I was dishonest with you. I led you without intention, for I knew a simple end would come." I turned my face from the truth, but he brought it back with the tips of his fingers. "I knew an end would come, and so I cared little for the consequences, not the least of which was falling in love with you."

Tossing my arms around his neck, I pulled him as close to me as the belly would allow. They were words I'd been so desperate to hear for so very long, I thought they'd never come. To my relief, Julian sank into the embrace, pressing his lips to my neck, warm breath sending electricity down my spine. I kissed his scarred cheek, my tears left behind like dewdrops.

"You knew all along?" I asked. "Had you known when you hired me? When we were lying in bed together?"

"Not in that particular moment." Julian's mouth twitched, but neither of us felt the humor. "I was so tired, Bertie. I was so overwhelmed. Nothing could have changed my mind."

"But if you'd have let me stay—maybe, I might've—"

He jerked suddenly, shaking his head. "Don't do that—don't go backwards. It's done, is it not?" With a sigh, he thumbed my tears. "You asked me if I'm well—I'm uncertain. But I see now what I nearly lost, and this helps me carry on. You were always light, Bertie. I would have you know that. You were a light, but God forgive me, I couldn't see past the dark."

I pulled him close again, tightly, as though he might slip away, vanish like smoke, break apart like a memory. His solidness was reassuring. His presence, a comfort.

"You say you had no intention then," I said. "What is your intention today?"

Julian drew away slowly. "To beg your forgiveness. To assure you that when I turned you away, I only ached to have you closer. To tell you that I have longed for you all these months, but did not feel I was worthy of you—worthy of being this child's father."

"And now?"

"Now I wake most mornings without dread," he said. "I wake grateful, instead, that I've lived to see Celia at the breakfast table again. That Roland has found a life of joy. That if I ask her, Gwen will bring the children round to play in the gardens. That I might see you again, and you might yet take me as I am."

With his cheeks bare, I could see the muscles in them straining. Julian glanced away from me, and I saw more clearly the scar over his brow where the debris had cut him. What agony he must have felt, to realize he was unsuccessful and had done nothing but strip more of himself away. More wounds to heal, more bandages, more medicine, more scars to hide. My God—how strong he was. To get out of bed, to leave his home, to start over. To come here.

I admired him so much, but hadn't the words to tell him.

"I love you, Julian," I said. "It isn't easy because you fight it so ardently, don't you? You don't feel worthy, but you are. You're not alone; you never were. And you won't be again if you allow me to adore you."

Julian wiped at a glistening eye. He lifted my wrist and, tentatively and delicately, set his closed lips against the inside, resting them there until a full tear escaped.

"I wish for you to live," he said, "to see the world, to paint, above all.

And so I shall never pin you down, darling girl." Julian reached into his jacket to produce a small red box and set it tenderly on the shelf of my belly. I was still looking at it when he pressed his cheek to mine and whispered, "But I promise to love you for as long as I live."

When he kissed me, I was crying, our tears mixing between our lips. The baby threw limbs, desperate to get out, desperate to meet their father. Desperate to be called Lord or Lady.

My smile broke our kiss. I took Julian's hands and pressed them to my belly so he could feel the life he'd helped create within me. That life, whoever it was, would keep us together, and keep us whole. Be his reason for another day.

"Good Lord," he muttered, making me laugh. "Hello, pal."

I tapped his chin to get his attention. "I should like to see Laurel Gate. May we go?"

Julian smiled—a true smile, and not at all dampened by his scars—and pinched the fake ring on my left hand. "Only if you wear mine."

LAUREL GATE WAS hardly visible from the lane, so overgrown with trees and plants that were happy to embrace the brick as their own. The gate itself sat under an arch of vines so thick I had to duck and push them from getting caught on my hat. I placed my hand on the weathered wood, admiring how new my left finger was with a diamond atop it, and pushed.

The hinges whined. In I went, heels on paving stones that had sunk into thick grass. I heard Julian shut the gate behind me, but didn't turn back, for I was already rapt by the look of the place.

It couldn't have been more different to Castle Braemore. There were no griffins, no obelisks, no gilded domes or Roman pillars. There were simply brick and wide windows and dormers across the top floor, covered in ivy.

"There's a sizable attic," said Julian as I cupped my hand over my eyes to look up. "It's bright—fit for a studio, I should think, once the roof is repaired."

That tickled me. "The Earl of Wakeford has a leaking roof?"

The walk to the house was not long or winding, nor lined with topiary. It was not grand, nor ostentatious. Whoever had built this house long ago had not done it to impress, but to shelter. And the front door was simply that—a door—hidden beneath a cloud of fragrant wisteria.

When I turned the knob, it opened easily.

No great hall welcomed me. Instead, I entered a humble reception room with a low ceiling. The windows were open, allowing in the dusty smell of country in spring. The hearth was tall and wide and fit for standing round after a long night's ride. Yes; it was rather a house for plotting and tankards of mead.

"It suits you." I turned to give Julian a smile. "I'm reminded of your bed. Have you got Anne Boleyn in the pantry?"

He chuckled. "Go and have a look at the parlor."

I followed his pointing finger under an arched doorway. Here was some of the furniture I recognized from Braemore. Despite Celia's presence, there didn't seem to be much of a feminine touch to the place, besides flowers. They were everywhere. I was sure Celia spent half the day in the garden picking and filling vases. Dozens of them—on the mantel, the sideboard, the desk, the windowsill.

Life, I thought. Yes, well done. Fill Julian's house with the promise of life.

It had taken me a moment, but my eyes eventually trailed to the oak-paneled walls, where old frames held new canvases. My paintings.

I spun and found they were everywhere, all about me. Castle Braemore behind the lake, the egg-shaped hedge with Roland on the bench, Celia in her turban, Julian at his piano, the cricket game on the lawn, the towering fountain, and the castle ruin surrounded by daisies.

The Napiers may not have had a gallery any longer, but they had this snug little room, lit with the colors of their last summer at home.

"Here only for safekeeping, of course," Julian said, "until Anna has a home of her own." He came up behind, wrapping his arms around me. "Do you reckon by then you'll have something to replace them with?"

I put my hand on his smooth cheek, unable to take my eyes from the walls. "I certainly do."

Author's Note

Though I strove to ensure this story accurately reflects the history of the period, there are no doubt a few errors made by mistake. Here, I would like to acknowledge the places where I knowingly bent the truth.

Firstly, the Earl of Wakeford and Viscountess Stanfield are entirely of my creation, as is the estate of Castle Braemore. I drew my inspiration from a number of English country houses, the dominant (and my favorite) being Castle Howard in North Yorkshire, which appears on the cover of this book.

The catalyst for Bertie's story, the art contest put on by the Royal British Legion, is a fabrication. The British Legion is a real foundation that has been helping military veterans and their families since 1921. Because I wanted Bertie's prize painting to be related to the war, I chose to include this charity, which was quite new at the time.

Mutism was a common symptom of shell shock, and was one of many conditions that doctors of the time were unsure how to cure. Gwen mentions that Julian's mutism was treated with electric shocks. These types of treatments were given by Lewis Yealland, a Canadian doctor in London who was considered at the time to be the expert on treating functional sensory-motor symptoms. However, these sometimes cruel treatments were mainly given to enlisted men—records I have seen show only one officer among Yealland's patients—so while plausible, it is perhaps unlikely that a man of Julian's rank would have been in his care.

It would have been very unlikely that Julian and Richard would have had leave to go home the night before embarkation. I took this creative license so I could compile the family's emotional goodbyes into a single moment.

Finally, I want to acknowledge my choice to include Anna Coleman Ladd as the sculptor who created Julian's mask. It is estimated that over sixty thousand British soldiers suffered head and eye injuries, and London sculptor Francis Derwent Wood is credited with having raised the need for portrait masks. In 1917, he began to create masks at 3rd London General Hospital, which then became known as the "Tin Nose Shop." When Ladd heard of Wood, she contacted him and they worked together to improve their techniques until she received permission to work in France. While it may have been easier for Julian to travel to London rather than Paris for his mask, I wanted to take the opportunity to highlight one of the many incredible women who contributed to the war effort. I felt Ladd's story would resonate more strongly with Bertie, as it had done with me.

Acknowledgments

Throughout my journey as a writer, I have been fortunate to have an incredible group of people who have supported me. Happily, that group has only expanded in the years I have been working on this book—years that were difficult for all of us. I am eternally grateful for the time and effort that so many people have put into this book despite the tumultuous nature of 2020.

First and foremost, I need to thank my incredibly brilliant agent, Abby Saul. Abby, you unknowingly plucked me from the depths of despair when you called me to talk about this book. From comforting emails to tweets and GIFs, you are always there when I (and my work!) need you the most. You are genuinely one of the loveliest, most generous people I know, and I could not have imagined a better partner and champion for my work.

My team at Berkley is made up of so many kind and talented people, whose excitement always reminded *me* to be excited when things were stressful:

Kerry Donovan, from the moment I first spoke to you on the phone, you showed such an immense understanding of the story I was trying to tell. I cannot thank you enough for trusting me to elevate the book to where it is today, and helping me every step of the way. I am so grateful for all the thought and passion you have invested in my work.

Mary Geren, along with your encouragement and guidance, you provided such incredibly wise insight during the revision process. You seemed to understand my characters even better than I did, and your notes truly shaped this book into something beautiful.

Many thanks to Brittanie Black for your work on publicity, and to Bridget O'Toole for your savvy marketing. Thank you both for ensuring this little book is seen!

A few years ago, through the magic of the internet, I found three of the most incredible critique partners who have become my lifelong friends:

Casey Reindhart, your friendship has meant the world to me. I have learned so much from you, both as a writer and a woman, and your presence in my life has elevated my craft in so many ways. You listen to me groan, challenge me, and help me celebrate every success. I never know what my books are about until you tell me. From the bottom of my heart: thank you, thank you, thank you.

Rick Danforth, thank you for being a friend and a first reader and for ensuring my characters sound properly English. I owe you a debt of gratitude for driving me all over Yorkshire and showing me Castle Howard—that visit became the first spark for this novel. Next beer is on me!

Sarah Yeack, apart from being an incredible friend, you are a powerhouse critique partner. Your frequent internet hugs have got me through some of my lowest lows, and our brainstorming sessions have rescued more than one of my books. I'm so grateful you are always just a Discord message away.

From the first moment I put pen to paper, my family have provided unwavering support of my ambitions. Christopher, thank you for being my biggest cheerleader. I don't think there's anyone else in the world who believes in me like you do. Mom and Dad, thank you for paving the road for me to follow my dreams, and for approving of my decision to go to art school to study fiction writing. (It paid off!) Mom, thank you for being a brave first reader and assuring me this one was my best yet.

This book is dedicated to my late grandfather, Sam Hughes, who always provided my brother and me with unyielding generosity. Pops was an avid reader and told me countless stories of his time as a Marine on the Pacific front of World War II. I have him to thank for sparking my interest in history and storytelling at a young age.

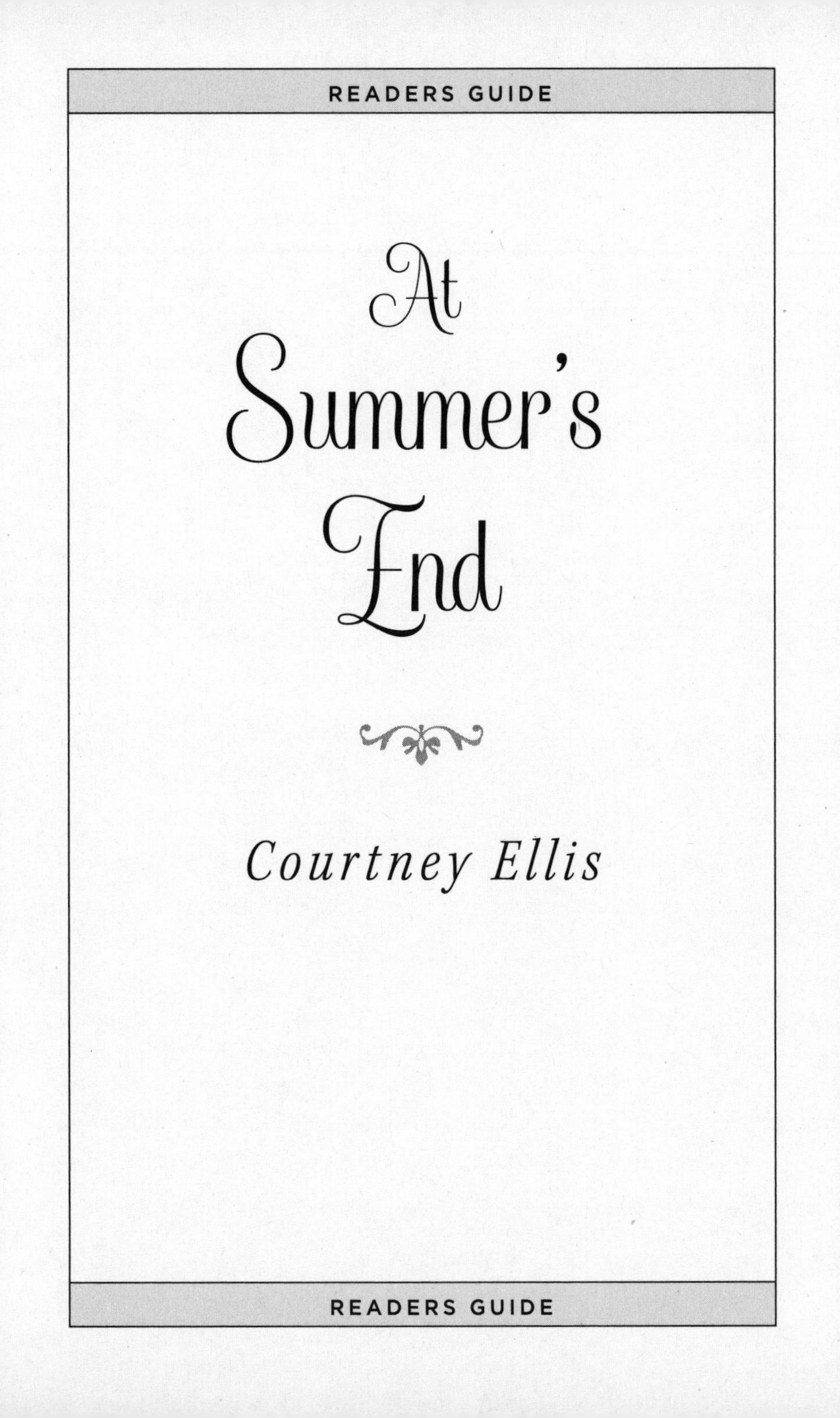
READERS GUIDE
At Summer's End
Courtney Ellis
READERS GUIDE

Questions for Discussion

1. Bertie's painting resonated with Julian enough that he invited her to his home after years of isolation. What aspects of the painting do you think appealed to him most? Have you ever been affected by a work of art in this way?

2. Bertie becomes the first person other than Gwen that Julian has seen in nearly two years. What do you think made him open his door to her that first day? Why do you think he invited her back?

3. While this is mainly Bertie's story, the author chose to include three other points of view in chapters that take place in years past. Why do you think these particular scenes were included? How do you feel they affected your understanding of the story? Did glimpsing the world through the Napiers' lens influence, or even change, how you viewed their characters?

4. The Great War did a lot to further the fight for female equality, but the battle was far from won in the 1920s. Bertie, Celia, Gwen, Lily, and even the Dowager Lady Wakeford experienced misog-

yny and prejudice toward women. Did you notice any issues explored in this book that women are still experiencing today? Were there any specific moments that reflected your own life experience?

5. Despite being so young, Anna plays an important role in the book. How do you see her presence at Castle Braemore influence Bertie's experience and feelings about the Napiers? How does Anna's presence in the lives of her family affect their relationship to the world and to one another?

6. There are many types of women in this story, each of them having a unique experience of the war. In what ways do these women display their strengths—both traditional and nontraditional? Do you relate to any of them more than others? Why?

7. After spending years trying to keep Julian and Lily apart, Gwen was quick to support a romance between her brother and Bertie. What do you think influenced her decision? What might she and Julian have discussed that afternoon?

8. Apart from Bertie, Freddie is the only other character at Castle Braemore who is not a Napier. What does his inclusion bring to the story? How do his thoughts and opinions—which sometimes contrast with the Napiers'—influence Bertie?

9. When Julian confides in Bertie about his father scorning him for his nerves, she says, "It's a dreadful shame that masculinity must mean hardness." What ways do you see this idea affecting each of the men in this story, specifically Julian's relationship with Roland? How do you think it might have influenced the young men

who enlisted during the Great War? Do you think this concept is still prevalent today?

10. At the beginning of the book, Bertie is at odds with her mother, but when she returns home, they begin to see eye to eye. What did Bertie experience or learn at Castle Braemore that might have changed her mind about her family? What growth might Bertie's family have noticed in her?

11. Celia went seven years without speaking to Julian, only able to see his side once she realized how unwell he had been. What do you think were the most significant driving factors behind her bitterness? How do you think the war further influenced those factors and her relationship with Julian?

12. At the start of the book, Bertie believes to marry would mean losing her independence, and asks, "Was there not more in life to be excited by than babies?" By the end, she is engaged to Julian and eagerly awaiting her own baby. How do you think the events of the book influence her change of heart? How has she retained her independence and freedom? Do you believe she made the right decision?

13. Take another look at the quote at the front of the book. Why do you think the author chose to include this particular quote? In what ways does art "repair the damages" that have been inflicted in the lives of these people? Has art (whether that be books, films, paintings, etc.) ever done this in your life? Provide examples.

Be on the lookout for
Courtney Ellis's next novel,
coming in 2022 from Berkley.

ENGLAND, 2019. When Audrey Collins inherits a house from her adored grandmother, she flies to North Yorkshire, expecting to find a grand country estate—the perfect place to escape her own problems. After all, Gran shared nothing of her past in England except one thing: her father had been a lord. But upon arriving in the village, Audrey learns from the locals that there is no grand estate, only a small farmhouse, and there was never nobility living at the now abandoned property, only a single mother and a shell-shocked man who kept to themselves.

Confused, Audrey enters the charming stone cottage and is surprised to find it is perfectly preserved to the day in 1941 when Gran left it, down to coats hung and wellies waiting near the door, and a ration book carefully laid in a drawer. It is only when she uncovers Gran's birth certificate that Audrey is sure her grandmother *was* telling the truth about who her parents were. But if Gran's mother was truly the highborn Lady Emilie Dawes, how had she ended up milking cows on a small holding? Who was the mysterious man she ended up there with? And why had Gran abruptly left England and never returned?

FRANCE, 1915. English VAD Emilie Dawes arrives at a tented military hospital on the Western Front. Having escaped the restraints of her tumultuous home life, she believes she has achieved the independence she has always dreamed of—so long as nobody ever finds out what she's done to be here. But before long, the claws of war begin to grasp at the three most important men in Emilie's life, and when a familiar face winds up in one of her hospital beds, she realizes she cannot escape her past until she faces it.

ONE HUNDRED YEARS APART, Audrey and Emilie each see their worlds turned upside down, and must fight to find purpose, love, and a place to call home. Courtney Ellis's next historical fiction novel is a harrowing family saga celebrating the courage and tenacity of underestimated women—and the power a secret can hold across generations.

Photo by Kelly Gleason

COURTNEY ELLIS began writing at a young age and developed an interest in history from her grandfather's stories of World War II. After obtaining her BA in English and creative writing, she went on to pursue a career in publishing. She lives in New York.

CONNECT ONLINE

Courtney-Ellis.com

CEllisWriter

CourtneyEllisAuthor

CourtneyEllisAuthor